The King of Sunday Morning

By

Jay B McCauley

For Kylie

If you think you're in this book, you're wrong.

If you are in this book, hand yourself in to the nearest police station.

To admit that you are in it is a crime all its own.

The King of Sunday Morning

CHAPTER ONE

How To Make A Geezer

Geezer (noun) is a British slang term, in its simplest form meaning a man.

Derived from the differently pronounced 'guiser', a name for an actor in a mime. Possibly related to disguise.

It can refer to a man whose name you do not know. It is also used to refer to a man who is overtly manly, masculine, or heterosexual, also someone noticeably capable, reliable, plainspeaking or down-to-earth. Although essentially a masculine quality it is not synonymous with macho however, and its usage may be thought of as very similar to that of the US English word *dude*. Example: Joe Cole referred to Prince William as a "nice, relaxed geezer." In the British 1971 pop song by the Piglets, Johnny Reggae was described as being "a real tasty geezer".

In Australia, the term *geezer* is often used to refer to someone from England, due to the belief that the English say *geezer* a lot; however, it is not as popular as the term *POMMY*.

The Mile End Mambo

1990

He held him in his arms and looked into the glassy eyes. Yellow flecks dotted the cornea. This boy was dead a long time before Roger had run him through. He knew the look. Too much top shelf and not enough down time.

The body from which life dramatically seeped away began to convulse. It would not be a Hollywood death. It would be a harsh demise for this gangster. Unexpected but unavoidable. He had stepped on the wrong toes and nobody touched Roger's patch.

The big screen had always glamorised death but there was nothing glamorous about having a gaping 12-inch gash where your stomach had once been. Roger's white shirt was splattered with blood and sputum. He noted to himself with an air of cold detachment that he would have to dispose of it later. The boy soldier's back arched in agony. A gurgling noise rushed from his throat and then he was gone.

Roger put his arm underneath the boy's knees and slowly lifted him from the red morass that had filled the doorway. He cradled him in his arms and walked slowly along the pavement. A young couple averted their gaze as he struggled with the limp body. They knew not to look. This was after all the witching hour in the East End. What you don't see, you can't tell. He turned the corner and moved into another shop doorway. It was a Dixon's electrical shop exalting the latest stereos and TV's.

Roger placed the body carefully on the ground. He took one final look at what 10 minutes ago had been the epitome of arrogance, bravery and youth, then left. He walked quickly to the edge of Walters Street, turned into Burden and darted through a now deserted car park and onto Rially. He saw a red telephone box just up from Dunston Road. He opened the door and tried to ignore the stench of piss and shit. He dialled the number and waited patiently for the connection.

"Rudi?"

His rich baritone West-Indian voice caressed the receiver.

"Yeah, he's in Dixon's shopfront on Walters Street." He paused, digesting the question on the other end of the line.

"Yeah he's dead. Dead as a door nail. See you at home."

With that, he hung up the phone and disappeared into the night. His red Rasta beanie swaying as he loped through the shadows. The victim wouldn't be missed. Roger had nothing to fear. The status quo had been maintained and an example had been made.

Most of all, Rudi would be pleased.

Steak Au Cheval

1992

"How the fuck did he do that?"

"With a fucking big ladder guv!"

Ron lent back in his chair well pleased with himself. The information was priceless insomuch as the kid had shown some fucking ingenuity that even Ron was impressed with.

"I mean he's got fuck all bollocks Ron! His ring must have been going nineteen to the dozen. I don't fucking believe it!"

"Desperation can breed inspiration boss. He has been doing it tough lately. Word is he has been eating horse steak every day. Fucking disgusting if you ask me."

"It's fucking as common as a Big Mac over there Ron. He told me once. Reckons it's right tasty. No different from beef and he won't eat the shit we do. Jellied eels frightened the fucking life out of him I can tell you."

Jimmy McCarthy paused and stuck his hand inside his shirt a la Napoleon Bonaparte.

"Who'd he flog 'em to?"

"Who'd you think Guv? We couldn't let him deal with those camel jockeys in Marseille. They'd have cut him for sure. The Doc knew what was going on and stepped in. He says its all square now."

"Like fuck it is!" Jimmy bellowed across the kitchen table empty save for a lonely plate of kippers.

"The fucking monkey can kiss my fucking bare lily-white arse! His wife's extras were all tidied up with her being none the wiser right?"

"Right!" Ron flinched.

"And those pills got top dollar, right?"

Ron nodded.

"Okay, well tell that overpaid excuse for a chemist, he can keep doing what he's fucking doing and if anything else happens to Tray to let you know. I tell you, if that boy gets damaged in any way, you can tell The Doc I will rip his arm off, shove it up his clacker and he can pogo up the Champs E-fucking-Leezay!"

"Yes Guv."

"Now let me eat me kippers!"

"Yes Guv."

Ron turned smartly and left Jimmy McCarthy hunched over the plate of pan-fried fish. He heard him mutter incredulously under his breath.

"The cheeky fucking cunt. The whole fucking lot!"

Ron smiled even though the whole affair worried him. They had told him to lie low. If this was Tray's best effort at staying in the shadows he would like to see what standing out in a crowd meant. This was indeed 'well fucking cheeky'. The boy had stolen the entire speaker system for the finishing area of the men's Olympic downhill at Val D'Isere. Some twenty speakers in all and two days before racing was due to start! Un-fucking-believable! The kid might make something of himself yet.

Between A Rock and
A Sand Cliff

1977

He knew, as young as he was at seven years of age, that this was wrong. He had been up here for a long, long time with Samuel. They had sneaked off from the beach without their parents knowing. The two brothers had climbed the cliffs together. They were enormous, daunting cliffs to the boys but they were in all essence just large sand hills. Samuel had followed Tray on his great adventure. Tray had seen the older boys venturing up the perilous slope and then jumping out into thin air, landing in the soft forgiving sand.

Samuel had tagged along, which had initially annoyed Tray but he soon started to brighten up when his younger brother began to whoop with joy. He didn't know why Samuel made him cranky. He didn't know it was natural sibling stuff. He was seven and a quarter, Samuel was only four. Samuel couldn't do the same things he could do. He was too small. Too stupid. Not strong enough.

They had been calling for ages. Samuel wouldn't jump and he wouldn't climb down. They were stuck. They had been calling out for their Mum in the way that only children can. Turning it from a one-syllable word into two. 'Muuu-uuuum!!!' rained out from the top of the dune but their parents could not hear them. Samuel began to sob uncontrollably. He tried to console him but to no avail. Samuel was getting worse. Eventually he could do no more and Tray began to cry himself. One of the older boys who had also climbed the hill spotted the two small kids weeping. He looked down at them, winked and then jumped out into the sky.

He could see the teenager run over to his parents and point back up the hill. His heart sank as his Dad loped over to the dune. He knew he was going to be in big trouble. They were always telling him to look after his little brother and he was always forgetting him or leaving him behind. Now he had led him straight into danger.

Their Dad huffed and puffed like a big bad wolf as he scaled the slope. As he got closer, the fear rose in his chest and suddenly he could feel the pee running down his legs. He had wet himself and that made him more upset than he already was. He began to really sob. His shoulders shook and the snot ran freely from his nose. Finally his Dad stood towering above them. He bent down and picked up Samuel. The young boy flung his arms around his saviour and wept into his huge hairy chest. His father glared down at him.

"What's the matter with you son!" It wasn't a question. It was a statement. Within it contained the clear implication that there was something very, very wrong with him. His father turned and walked down the slope with his brother in his arms. He was to follow; there was no doubting that.

As he followed the great brute in front of him, he became aware that people were laughing. Then he realised that they were laughing at him. The older boys pointed at the wet patch in his groin. He bowed his head in shame as the boys called out names like 'baby', 'pissy pants' and other words he had never heard of before.

He knew then, in whatever infantile terms he could express them, that he, Tray McCarthy, would never, ever again fail to be his brother's keeper

Missing In Action

1997

Barry Flint was dying. He was drifting in and out of consciousness. Killed by the cancer and chemotherapy, his body was giving up the fight. He knew his daughter was by his side. He knew he was in the prison hospital. Thank God it would be over for her.

Jo had followed him wherever he had gone. After embezzling five hundred large out of the wine store, they had needed to scarper quick like. He had thought about Spain but found The Algarve far more anonymous. From Essex to Portugal and back again. All up four years on the run and for what? To die a creeping death in a cage of fools.

She had followed him to Wandsworth Prison when Interpol had finally caught up with them. Away from the romance of her life. Away from the one man who would love her in spite of her father. He had made a deal with the people that mattered. Jo would be safe but she would never feel that blinding love that she had found on those sun-kissed shores with Tray. Barry had never forgiven himself for that and the guilt had wracked him ever since. Perhaps that was why the cancer had manifested itself. A display of the guilt he felt towards his daughter.

He surrendered to the morphine. He was so dosed up he couldn't open his eyes but he could feel her presence.

"Dad?" His eyes flickered but remained firmly shut. "There's someone here to see you."

Again his eyes rolled behind the lids. Jo made way for a man that she recognised but did not know. Once, when her Mum and Dad were counting out fifty-pound notes on the lounge room floor, he had come round and taken away plastic bags full of cash. He had mentioned something about cleaning and left. She had never seen him again until this moment.

The suited, burly man bent down and spoke softly into the ear of the emaciated body. Barry recognised the smell of his aftershave first and then the deep voice of yesteryear unfurled like wisps of smoke in his ramshackle mind.

"He says 'thank-you' Barry", the man gently touched Barry's shoulder. "You have nothing to worry about. A promise is a promise. Jo will be sweet."

Barry smiled. Jo saw it. She gasped. The darkness swirled around him as she felt for his hand. He remembered what he had done and why and suddenly he was there. Amongst those dunes.

The wind stung his face as it blew off the Atlantic. The muzzle flashed. He left the body where it lay, face down in the sand. 'Scum', he thought to himself. He put the gun inside his jacket and turned his back on the boiling ocean. Now his journey home could begin.

The tears started to flow. He didn't want to stay anymore. He felt her squeeze his hand. The darkness descended, never again releasing its hold on Barry Flint. Jo Flint slowly let go her father's hand and inevitably, her father with it.

*

1993

"Who did what?"

'Déjà vu' thought Ron as his boss thudded the table. Ron took a deep breath.

"Twice Jimmy. He threatened Tray with a gun. Then threatened Sam in the main square. Don't ask me where Tray got the courage. This guy is one mean motherfucker. Got form. Runs guns for the Micks. A real fucking tough guy."

Jimmy looked up and fixed Ron with a chilling stare. Ron had been brought in by the chiefs after the Rudi Stone affair. Just to make sure Jimmy didn't do anything stupid. Well this was pretty fucking stupid if you asked Ron but family was family after all. It was a mantra that flowed through the East End. Ron knew what was coming next. You didn't have to be Einstein to figure that out. Ron would have to comply. Ron was there for Jimmy. Like he always would be.

"Will the Micks miss 'im?"

"Hardly, he's fucked up plenty. He's not only on the run from the English, the Proddies want him for something in Omagh and the Paddies have just about had enough".

"Wipe him then!" thundered Jimmy.

"Jimmy you sure? That's a big call. Do you think the chiefs will authorise it?"

Ron knew the answer without hearing it. Now was not a time to question the boss.

"Ron, who am I? Am I not Jimmy McCarthy? Friend to all those chiefs you 'ark on about. I kid you not, this Irish cunt is gone! Tell them we will deal with it. Barry wants back in right?"

Ron nodded.

"Well get him the fuck on it!"

"He'll have to do bird if he comes back. There's no other way."

"Well that's his price. He knows what will happen. He's run out of coin and his missus is shagging some Portugeezer. I'd want come back if I was in the same boat. He'll want us to make sure Jo is okay so this is how he helps us to help him. This is the perfect opportunity. No messing Ron. If Barry wants our help, then this is the debt paid".

Ron shuffled his feet slightly. He was uncomfortable with this particular order. It was something completely alien to Barry Flint. He was an embezzler and a con man and that's where his criminal expertise started and finished.

"Jimmy, he's not a killer."

"No but this Irish cunt is and he went too far. Next time the boys might not be able to handle him!"

Ron knew that Jimmy was right. Tray had stopped the prick twice but who knew how long he could fend him off. This fucking Irish whore was messing with the wrong people and Ron suspected that he had no idea who the boys were.

Nobody knew where they were and they liked it like that. None of Tray's crew had a clue and they were forbidden to look for the brothers. No phone calls from the boys, no letters. Apart from a brief sojourn in Val D'Isere which Jimmy had not approved, the boys had remained completely anonymous. They had disappeared just as Jimmy had wanted and now they were at risk. Frank was supposed to be watching out for them but he couldn't be everywhere. He had contacted Ron as soon as he had found out.

Fuck it! This Macguigan was a memory already.

"I'll call The Pope. Explain the situation. I'm sure they'll be grateful," said Ron.

"Tell him that doesn't mean that we are getting in to bed with them. I don't want nothing to do with those murdering Irish terrorists!"

'Ironic', thought Ron.

The Irish knew not to question Jimmy. They had tried to lean on him once before. That had led to a message being delivered that had left everyone clear about where Jimmy McCarthy's loyalties lay. It certainly wasn't with the IRA or any of their supporters. Now he had ordered the killing of one of their men. It didn't matter to Jimmy. He was protected. Much more than this gunrunner was at the moment. Ron wondered how Barry was going to do it. Poor Barry. This would be hard for him but not as hard as it was going to be for Macguigan.

*

Larry Macguigan was sweating bullets. The hot Portuguese evening air was stifling but not as stifling as the situation he currently found himself in. Bound and gagged, trussed up like a turkey. He was the next offering on the dinner table minus the trimmings. So therefore he sweated.

He knew it was over. He had no idea who had snatched him. London? Maybe. He had been getting pissed. Arsehole drunk. He had tipped himself out of the *Avenida Bar* and was taking a leak in the street when the cold muzzle touched his neck.

"Hold very still or you're dead right here!"

They didn't even give him a chance to zip up. They had covered his mouth with masking tape and stuck a hood over his head. They then tugged his arms behind his back and lashed them together with what he assumed were cable ties. He heard a vehicle approach and the grinding of a sliding door as it was dragged open.

He heard someone say 'Obrigado José, I will take it from here', and then at least two sets of footsteps faded into the night. He was roughly turned around and shoved into the vehicle. His head slammed into what he could only figure was the opposite side of a van. He was aware of his flaccid member resting on cold metal. He flinched away from it but found himself pressed hard against the floor as something heavy pinned him down.

Brilliant stars pierced the darkness as he was belted across the back of his head. He heard the same voice again.

"Don't you fucking move!" growled his captor.

He couldn't move anyway. What with the weight on his back and the hood on his head, he was finding it difficult to breath. He heard the door slam shut and the engine fire up. The Beatles' 'You Can't Buy Me Love' swirled eerily around his head and then it all went black.

*

He awoke to the feeling of wetness. His clothes were soaked through but he soon realised that he was still in the back of the van. The hood had been removed. He opened his eyes and recognised the muzzle of a silencer cocked about six inches from his face. The figure holding the gun remained blurred, framed in darkness. He had been turned onto his back with his hands still tied behind him. The interior light of the van was bare with no cover. It bathed him in harsh direct white light. There was no comfort here. No salvation. He knew the score. This was not a return trip. You didn't waste comfort on a hit.

His legs hung out of the open sliding door. He could not feel his hands. No circulation he thought to himself. A myriad of explanations raced through his mind. He had been careful. He hadn't let anyone know he was here. Paris and Amsterdam had let him go. He had paid them good coin to make it that way. The Africans were pissed for sure but not enough for this. That left his controllers in Dublin. But this didn't smell of them. This was different.

The figure reached forward and grabbed him by the hair. He tugged at his black locks and drew him to his feet. The masking tape was ripped from his mouth. He yelled in pain.

"What the fuck!" he shouted. He was immediately thumped with the butt of the gun. Once again, all he could see was stars. He slumped against the side of the van. He started to shake. The fear rose in his throat along with the bile. He was grabbed by the upper arm and pulled away from the van.

He shook his head and tried to force the concussion from his mind. His training took over. He looked around him. He couldn't see more than ten to fifteen feet. He could smell and hear the sea. Salt. Everywhere. He could taste it on the stiff Atlantic breeze. They were standing at the edge of some tall sand dunes. Tufts of grass permeated the ridges of the shifting sands. It was isolated. Storm clouds scudded across the moonlit sky. He sweated a river despite the biting wind blowing in his face. He could feel the sweat running through his scalp, dripping into his eyes. Sand stuck to the sweat. His lips were encrusted with the stuff.

He took a glance at his captor, trying not to look him in the eye. He had to try and stall him. Eye contact would only escalate the situation. All in black. Head covered by a balaclava. Nothing left to chance. The gunman had run to fat but his weapon dictated that he currently had the upper hand. Maybe he could get the better of him. Hope rose faintly in his chest. It was a big maybe.

"Move!"

The voice was calm but menacing. The gunman gesticulated towards the dunes. His legs wouldn't work. They had turned to jelly. He was pushed in the back and it gave him the impetus he needed to stumble forward. They were heading for a gap between two dunes.

He kept his head down as the gunman continually poked and prodded him forward. He zigzagged towards his fate. He lurched along a narrow path until suddenly a huge beach and the thundering Atlantic Ocean was revealed to them. Powerful surf pounded the lonely, desolate beach. Fingers of white water curled its way towards them. It tried to snatch the duo from the shoreline before collapsing in on itself and then retreating back from whence it came. The moonlight trickled through the cloud cover and gave the beach an alpine feel. Instead of sand, the ground looked like it had received a fresh dusting of snow, waiting for some intrepid snow bunny to make their unique carvings in the virgin powder.

The gunman kicked him in the back of his legs and he fell to his knees. He desperately tried to twist his body so he could face his captor but he felt the gun at the base of his skull. He stopped struggling and attempted to stay stock-still.

"At least tell me why?" he pleaded.

"IRA?" he yelled against the breeze.

Silence.

"Proddies, Libya?"

No answer.

"Well who then?"

The only reason he knew that the gunman was still there was because he could still feel the gun against his skin. The sand shifted beneath his knees as his executioner bent forward.

"Tray and Sam"

He scanned his memory. Two names he wasn't expecting.

"Who?" he heard himself stammer.

"Tray and Sam, you Irish cunt!"

Then it came to him. The two English brothers from town. But they were fucking nobodies. Two bar workers! He had a run in with both of them last week.

He repeated his thoughts.

"But they are nobodies!"

"Really?" replied the voice, "You have no idea who they are?"

"A DJ and a doorman! I roughed the elder one up for having a big mouth but it wasn't him! It was someone else. Someone who looked like him!"

He heard himself pleading. Begging for his life like so many had done to himself. But he didn't understand! They were just travellers.

"You really don't know do you?" The gunman was mocking him.

He shook his head and focused on the ocean before them. Who were they? He had never seen them before. When he drifted anonymously into town, he had picked them for a couple of pingers. Living in the nightlife and sleeping all day. Taking advantage of the cheep hash and funnelling a decent amount of trips and e's down from Amsterdam or London.

But they weren't just some ordinary backpackers, were they?

"No!" he finally answered, exasperated.

This could not be how it would end. Some silly mistake. No glory. No freedom fighter's death. No heaving throng mourning his passing on the Falls Road. No memorials to his life.

"Tray and Sam *McCarthy*?"

The gunman stressed the surname. The names still meant nothing to him.

"Jimmy *'London'* McCarthy?"

"Oh fuck! Fuck! Fuck! Fuck!" Fear, piss and shit. They all let go. All at once. He had sent Sean's head back in a bag when they had tried to lean on him. The London crew had been told to back off and unbelievably they had. People with more power than they wielded had stuck two fingers up at the IRA and the terrorist organization had backed down. No one messed with Jimmy McCarthy. He was off limits.

The Irishman hobbled from knee to knee. He tried to scamper away but a reaching hand grabbed him on the shoulder and the gunman pressed the weapon firmly against his neck.

'London Mac', the name screamed at him. He gulped but his mouth was dry and all he could taste was salt and sand.

'Fuck! London Mac!'

*

The headline for The Sun newspaper for 14/4/93 read 'Terrorist Found Dead In Holiday Paradise'. Discreetly hidden on page nine amongst the irreverent fluff stories could be found the following two-inch piece, 'Essex Embezzler Deported'.

Keeping Mum

1990

"Friends, comrades and fellow South Africans. I greet you all in the name of peace, democracy and freedom for all".

His hero Nelson Mandela stood before him in the safety of his own living room. Tears welled in his eyes. Finally the pleadings of Jerry Dammers' with his song 'Free Nelson Mandela' had come to fruition. Mandela, the African lion, the man who had come to symbolise the struggle against apartheid, was addressing his people. Free from his house arrest in Pollsmour Prison and his incarceration on Robben Island, Nelson Mandela stood on the precipice of gaining not only freedom for himself but freedom for an entire people.

"Change the channel Trystan."

His Mum came sauntering into the room with her habitual cup of tea in hand. Dressed impeccably in summer florals, his Mum was oblivious to the history being made in their living room.

"To what Mum?"

He turned his head from his position on the floor. He loved to watch TV whilst spread-eagled like a sniper on the living room floor. He cuddled a pillow to his chest. He found it comforting and for this epic moment in history, he wanted full comfort and no interruptions.

"To BBC 1 Trystan. My favourite program's on."

She smiled at her eldest son. A bit lazy but a loving boy. She only called him Trystan when he was in trouble or she wanted him to do something for her. To everyone else he was known as Tray, basically because his younger brother Samuel had not been able to pronounce 'Trystan' when he was learning to speak.

Trystan McCarthy had far outgrown his parent's education by the time he had turned seven. They had sent him to private school. It had made him a little arrogant and superior when he spoke to her sometimes but she knew he would indulge her this small Sunday afternoon pleasure.

"We're on BBC 1 Mum. They have cancelled all programs today for Mandela."

"Man who?"

"Nelson Mandela Mum".

"Never heard of him. Is he important?"

Tray couldn't believe his Mum sometimes. One of the most influential figures of modern times, a living legend and she had no idea who he was.

"Mum, he's been in prison for nearly 30 years for trying to free his people!"

"I don't care Trystan. 'Antiques' Roadshow' is supposed to be on. Where's my program?"

His Mum was addicted to the program. That and Ski Sunday and incredulously any prime time boxing match.

"I don't want to watch this rubbish. Turn it off!"

"Mum! This is history!"

Tray was missing it. He had been alive nearly as long as this man had been in jail. He had never heard him speak and now he was missing it.

"Turn it off Trystan and get on the phone".

"Mum!" protested Tray.

"Ring up the Beeb and ask them when they are going to put the program on. Come on! Do this for your Mum."

He knew there was no point arguing. She would make his life hell if he didn't comply. So while the world stopped and listened to the voice that had remained mute to an entire generation, he was speaking to an equally surprised public servant who could not believe that someone was complaining about the Mandela broadcast.

Tray had not turned the TV off because his Mum had left the room muttering. He could see Mandela raise his fist. He heard the Zulu cry of 'Amandla'. A tear trickled down his cheek.

"Why are you crying Trystan?"

"Because Mum, when Neil Armstrong walked on the moon. You can tell them where you were. When JFK was shot, you can tell people what you were doing".

"Yes I remember them. Wasn't it Louis Armstrong? I remember someone walking on the moon."

She smiled her mother's smile oblivious to Tray's despair. He threw his arms up in exasperation.

"No it was **NEIL**! He paused and then continued without thinking, "Look Mum, when my kids ask me what I was doing when Mandela, probably one of the most significant men in the twentieth century, was released from prison, I can tell them that I was calling the fucking BBC and asking them why Antiques Roadshow had been fucking cancelled!"

She slapped him across the face.

"Language Trystan!"

Luxury

1988

He didn't talk about the old days much, so he sat like an acolyte at the feet of his master.

"You know why I hate the fucking Germans son?"

He shook his head.

"Cos they bombed the fish and chip shop in Francis Street. We had no fish and chips for two years. But what's more is they were fuckin sneaky about it too. We fucking really hated them after that".

"What do you mean sneaky Dad?"

Jimmy McCarthy stroked his arthritic knuckles and stretched them in front of the gas heater.

"Wasn't a bombing raid like in the Blitz. It was one of those bastard doodlebugs. You know, them rockets they sent over. Nearly took me and your Uncle Tommy out at the same time." He paused. "Make us a cuppa son."

Tray moved to the ramshackle school desk which substituted for a tea station.

"Me and Tommy were playing on the oval opposite Nan's place. Then we heard it. It was like a low groan in the sky. We looked up and saw this dark shape. Then the noise stopped and we were shitting our pants."

Tray closed his eyes and tried to imagine the scene. He knew the street his Dad was talking about. Rows and rows of pebble-dashed terraced houses. All identical. All hiding the misery of war, death, rationing and poverty. His family had been poor. Nothing new in that part of the world. No one owned their own house. Everyone had someone who had died in the war. It was a cold, drab place where love was a stranger that rarely visited.

"We hit the deck. Rule was, if the engine cut out, you hit the deck. That meant it was on the way down. There were no sirens and you got to understand we missed a

25

lot of The Blitz so we weren't casual about it like the older kids. I was fucking scared. I hadn't been bombed. They sent me to a farm in Cornwall run by a pair of dyke schoolteachers when war broke out. I loved it! They taught me to read and write. I had a horse. I didn't want to come back I can tell you."

The father and son were surrounded by piles of disused scrap metal and junk. It was a scrapyard version of Stonehenge. In the centre sat a mahogany altar dedicated to the haphazard nature of its owner's life. It was a huge desk. Strewn with unpaid invoices and a bank of telephones. Wedged in the far corner was a TV continually on silent running. It showed midday re-runs of old cowboy movies. It was silent just in case Jimmy's wife called. If she rang and she could hear the TV in the background, it would lead to a certain visit from her. And he NEVER wanted her down the shop. There were certain things that his family could not know about. Even having Tray there was a liability of sorts.

"Anyway, this thing started fucking gliding. I kid you not. Me and Tommy could see the fucking serial number on it's belly. It kept fucking falling. We watched it clear the oval and it flew just over the top of Hacking Street. Then there was this low thud. We felt it before we could hear it or see it. The ground shook. Then we saw the smoke and then we heard the noise of this massive explosion. We stayed on the ground for a long time."

Jimmy paused and thought back to that frightful time. No kid should live their younger days in fear. He hated the Germans for that. It was June 1944. D-day was under way. The Krauts were on the run but they were still causing damage on the home front. They took away so much innocence. All in the pursuit of the master race. Fucking bastards!

"We stayed on the ground cos they were like buses. You didn't see one for ages then a couple would come along at the same time. One after another. Nan came running out of the house and then Rodney and Sid came screaming up the road. Arse hanging out of their trousers and grime down their chops."

"They were calling 'Mum! Mum!' Me and Tommy sprang to our feet. Didn't want our brothers seeing we was scared. Mum gathered all four of us up, checking that we were all okay."

"Rodney was still shouting 'Mum!' He could never wait to tell Mum something. Always had to be first. He was gulping in huge gobs of air. Sucking eggs he was. Eventually he got it out. He told us they had bombed the fish and chip shop in Francis Street!"

"You know what that meant?"

Tray shook his head.

"No fish and chips for two fuckin years. Those Germans have a lot to answer for".

"I know Dad. You already said."

The hate was clearly evident on Jimmy's face.

"You know I was pretty fucking angry with you when you started to learn German at school. They killed so many of us during the war and I can't forgive them for that. But you know what?"

"What's that then Dad?"

"I realised you could call them 'cunts' in their own language!"

*

1938

He remembered his Dad walking him down Wood Street. The sun was shining. He would have been about four. It was before the war. Men in suits would nod to his Dad. Occasionally he would hear an 'Alright Mac'. His Dad strode purposely towards the White Swan.

They crossed the road not looking for the unusual sight of a motorised vehicle. Cars were still a rare commodity back then. They stopped beside the fence at the back of the pub. He recalled that the fence was faded. It hadn't seen creosote for a long time. From behind the fence he could hear the roar of a crowd. Mainly men accompanied by the occasional shriek of a woman. His Dad sat him down. He looked up at the red-haired giant. Knuckles covered with scabs. Face bedecked with scars and digs. His Dad oozed toughness.

"Sit down Jimmy and wait here."

It was an order. He sat on the kerb resting his feet on the cobblestones. His Dad let go his hand and made his way over to the corner shop. He soon came back walking stiffly with an ice cream cone in his hand. Jimmy smiled broadly. This was a rare treat.

"Here have this."

"Thanks Dad."

He took the ice cream and sunk his face into its richness.

"Now I'm going to go in there for a while."

His Dad pointed at the fence.

"You wait right here. I'll be a while and then we'll go home".

He heard his father but didn't look up. The ice cream was just pure luxury. His Dad disappeared through a gate behind him. He heard the roar of the crowd. He felt but didn't understand their passion. He heard a voice rise above the rest but couldn't make it out clearly.

He had no idea how long he had waited there. He had picked at the scabs on his knees after he had finished the ice cream. He watched the cars dodge between the horse and carts. Then there was a thunderous roar from behind the fence and suddenly his father was standing before him.

His shirt was open and blood streaked down his face. His son gasped at the picture.

"Its alright son. Your Dad's not hurt and look what I've got for dinner."

He looked down and saw the biggest bird he had ever seen hanging limply from his Dad's right hand. Blood oozed from his knuckles.

He didn't realise until many years later that his Dad used to go down to the White Swan every Sunday for their dinner. He would fight bare knuckle against all comers. He very rarely lost.

"We'll eat like kings tonight son!"

His Dad **was** a king. Well respected in the rough and tumble streets of East London. His Dad was his hero. He wanted to be like him. One day he would be.

*

1958

"Fuckin cop this!" He smashed the shovel into his brother's face.

"Jimmy stop it!"

Rodney grabbed his arm mid swing.

"Enough Jimmy!"

"You know what the cunt did?"

"Yes I know Jimmy, but don't kill him. He's your brother."

"First person in our family to own a suit and the cunt takes it down the hock shop."

"I know Jimmy! He was shitting himself he was!"

"Yeah! Didn't stop him taking the dosh down the track and putting it on a dog. He lost the whole fucking lot Rod!"

His brother lay moaning at his feet. His face stained with blood. Unrecognisable as his brother Daniel.

"I should fuckin kill him Rod! Fuckin cunt doesn't respect me!"

"He will now Jimmy! Please don't kill him. I'm begging you!"

Jimmy looked at his eldest brother. He could see the sadness and panic in his eyes. He shrugged Rodney's arm away and threw the shovel down at Dan. He spat at him. The hate swept through him. So close to ripping the heart from his brother's chest.

"Fuck off Dan! Fuck off out of town!"

He took aim at his brother's groin. He delivered a huge kick to his nuts. Dan shrieked. Rodney looked on and didn't intervene. Jimmy turned and marched out of the coal yard. He didn't look back. Rodney followed his youngest brother. Jimmy was in charge now. No doubt.

Top of The Pops

1989

How long ago did he take it? He knew it depended on weight and metabolism but he didn't know for sure. It wasn't an exact science. He had always banged the scotch down and smoked a lot of hash but this was different. This was the real deal. He'd heard it on the grapevine. These new pills from New York and Amsterdam were changing the social fabric of London. It used to be beer and punch-ups and now it was pills and loved-up. Arrests for unsocial behaviour were down and more importantly, the establishment was scared. It had been justly challenged with punk and then the gay abandonment and sexual ambiguity of Boy George et al nearly tore the nation asunder. But ironically Boy George then turned into every grandmothers' favourite bingo partner and the urban landscape returned to its safe, apathetic roots and bland normality.

Then the people of the night tipped the world on its end. Space cadet record execs were bringing these pills back from New York. These little portents of love were apparently amazing. They took you elsewhere, gave you love in abundance and made the girls love you back. The summer of love, Woodstock itself, was being re-invented right in front of everyone's eyes. The Sun and The Daily Mirror revealed the shocking threat to the nation and he believed the propaganda until his cousin told him to stop being daft.

He was nineteen and it was about time that he jumped onto the hedonistic bandwagon. He had missed out on punk and ska. There was hardly any rebellion in the 80's. It was make-up and silly love songs. What had started out with the Sex Pistols and The Clash dived headlong into the rapture of Spandau Ballet and Duran Duran. There was no class struggle. Greed was good according to Margaret Thatcher and Reaganomics ruled the roost. Live now pay later. Ostentatious displays of wealth, cocktails and the word 'yuppie' were the order of the day. And guess what? The young had just about had enough.

The corporatisation of the weekend. The theme pub. The Saturday night super club. Big burly bouncers telling you, 'Wrong shoes mate', or 'Wrong shirt', even, 'Sorry mate, just don't fit the image'. Enough was enough!

Free parties were on the rise. Dance music was exploding. Warehouses were being taken over by huge sound systems and the kids and the drugs were everywhere. It was 1989 and the great British party massive had started.

They were in Slough, West of London. Slough was one of those peculiar afterthoughts of British planning. Pronounced 'slau', its name sounded ugly and its streets were much the same. A post Second World War new town. Pebble-dashed terraced houses built cheaply, without imagination and without soul. The only reason you went to Slough was because it was on the way to somewhere else. The English equivalent of Belgium.

It was one of the biggest holes he had ever been to but tonight it was his paradise. It was his conversion on the road to Damascus. For tonight he would experience the roller coaster ride that was MDMA and witness the world's best on the wheels of steel. A warehouse. A laser. A bass bin. Tonight he would turn away from the beer soaked ravages of a football bender and become enveloped in the rush and the beautiful shiver of the white dove. Tonight he would be Top of The Pops.

Hong Kong Fui

<u>1990</u>

"So, who's the coolest guy you know Tray?"

The question hung in the air in the deeply middle class backwater of Chigwell. They were sitting in his oldest friend's parents' kitchen. Brinn had asked him the question. They had been out partying all weekend and their eyes were rolling around in the back of their heads. Sunglasses provided the protection they needed to avoid detection from Aunty D.

Doris or Aunty D was in turn Tray's Mum's oldest friend. She had married a villain in every sense of the word. Not a hard man, just a man shy of hard work. 'Uncle' Del as he liked to be called, had amassed a small fortune without managing to do an honest day's work in the last thirty years. Doris knew that their lifestyle was made possible by her husband's shady dealings but she didn't ask any searching questions. Her motto was 'let sleeping dogs lie'. Anyway she loved the fur coats, expensive holidays and flashy cars. If Del didn't tell her that the money was hot then it must be honest money then. 'Little white lies' she called them.

Terry Wogan was babbling away in the background on Radio 2 and Aunty Doris was fussing around them. They were trying very hard to chow down on some marmalade and toast but weren't really making much of an impression.

"Easy. James Barker" replied Tray.

"Who?"

"James Barker" repeated Tray.

"Never heard of him"

"No but you know him Brinn"

"I'm pretty sure I don't" replied the gangly teenager.

Tray and Brinn were like chalk and cheese. Tray was broad and bulky with blondish hair in a style akin to Albert Einstein. Brinn was tall and lanky, around 6' 4", with limp, dark brown hair. He was all sinew and tissue. The thing that both of them had in common though was pills, music and intelligence.

"Well, why's he so cool then?"

"Well besides him being the first person I know to get a TV satellite, he also pulled off one of the biggest blags I know"

"And you reckon I know him?"

"Yep" Tray nodded.

Brinn was confused. He tried to shake the cobwebs from his mind.

"Well, what did he do?" he asked.

"Well you know I work for Lloyds Bank," replied Tray.

"Yes"

"Well I am on this fast track program for foreign exchange dealing see. This bloke James had already gone through it and was a high flyer. We got on really well and he became my mentor. That was until about a year ago when he got sent to Hong Kong to take over the options desk."

"This was a real coup for him 'cos he was in his early twenties and managing a massive portfolio. Anyway this form of trading is big, big money and if you get it right you can just earn fucking millions for the bank".

"Language!" Aunty Doris did not like swearing in her house.

"Sorry Aunty D".

Tray tried his best sheepish look. Doris liked him the best out all Brinn's buddies so he could always get away with it. Brinn was right into the story. He loved listening to his mate spin a yarn, especially when he was pinging. He could hardly contain himself.

"Yeah well what 'appened next?" Brinn fair chugged at his tea.

Tray smiled.

"Well he had been raking in the money for the bank. James was the blue-eyed boy. The *wunderkind*. Anyway he comes back earlier this year for a heads of department conference"

"Yeah."

"And on his first morning back a couple of auditors pull him into their office".

Tray took a nibble on the toast and despite it being covered in easily edible marmalade, the bread made it feel like he was gargling sand. He had to wash it down with a couple of gulps of tea. This annoyed Brinn because it interrupted the flow but he waited.

"They start laying down some print-outs in front of him and proceeded to tell him that someone is sucking some extremely large amounts of *moolah* from the branch. They were pretty sure who it was but they needed James' help just to confirm some details and nail the guy. James said it was pretty disturbing and would let the chairman know over their impending lunch. He told them they would be back that afternoon to see what they could do. If they knew who was doing it, then they need not panic," he paused again and looked down at his hands. "James then leaves the building, goes to Dover gets on a boat and is never heard of again"

"But why?" begs Brinn.

"Well turns out that the member of staff sucking the money out of Hong Kong was a phantom. James had created him out of thin air. It was James who had been stealing the money"

"Get Fucked!" shouted Brinn.

"Language Brinn!" shouted Doris.

"Sorry Mum. How much did he get away with?" asked Brinn.

"Well they're admitting to twenty but I reckon if they're willing to admit to twenty, I reckon it's more like forty," answered Tray.

"Forty thousand?" Brinn was surprised.

"No Brinn, *million!*"

"Fuck me!" thought Aunty D.

"Fuck me!" shouted Brinn.

Tray sat back and smiled.

"I reckon any man who can casually talk down his possible captors, walk out of the building and disappear with the money intact, is dead set the coolest man in the world."

"Too right" replied Brinn, "but you reckon I know him?"

"You do Brinn."

35

"I honestly don't know anyone named James Barker Tray.

"No but you know The Dish!"

"Fuck me! That knob end!"

That was it. Aunty D rapped Brinn across the knuckles with a wooden spoon.

"Ow!" shouted Brinn rubbing his hands together in pain.

'Fuck me', thought Uncle Del, 'Forty fucking million. I could do with some of that action'. He had been listening the whole time behind the lounge room door.

Fishing For Krays

<u>1989</u>

Its not every day you find out something naughty about your prim and proper mother. Where he came from your parents didn't have sex. They sort of met in the middle of the bedroom one night with the lights out. They had both fallen over drunk and your Mum had somehow and completely by accident gotten pregnant. To think about them doing it was just something that did not bear thinking about. It was strictly taboo. Sex was something you just didn't talk about. Babies were God's miracle and nothing more.

The naked human body was also conspicuous by it's absence in their part of suburbia because basically his Mum was a prude. She had completely burnt his entire porn collection which he had so carefully smuggled back from France. She had caught his brother having a wank on the toilet whilst he perused those sacred pages which contained equal amounts of armpit and pussy hair. His Mum had thrown an absolute fit. It was as if Satan himself had entered the house. She had wailed like a screaming banshee and tossed the whole lot on the bonfire.

So his Mum was always the rock in their house. Fierce morals that should never be tainted. A set of rules that were set in stone that had served her so well over all these years. She never spoke of sex or boyfriends previous to their Dad except one Sunday morning when her cousin Johnny came round for tea.

London's most infamous gangsters, the Kray twins, had been in the news all week. Some do-gooders were trying to get them out of jail as they were no longer a threat to society. Some old photos of the pair flashed onto the TV screen as they all sat down to tea and chocolate hob nobs.

His Mum tutted at the screen as she made herself comfortable in her favourite armchair.

"What you tutting at Betty?" asked Johnny.

She blushed as she gazed across the collection of Dalton china cups at her wayward cousin. She gave him one of those looks that only Betty could give. It was a look of, 'Shut up! Do not continue this line of conversation'. But Johnny did not fear Betty like her sons did and anyway Jimmy was not here so he could have some fun.

"What's up Betty? Don't the boys know?"

"Know what Mum?" the boys intoned.

They loved it when Johnny came round. He always had some way of stirring Mum up.

"Sshh Johnny. The boys don't want to know about such stuff!"

Betty was squirming uncomfortably in the chair. Johnny raked his hand through his silvery hair. He leant forward and began to pour their tea. The boys were positively salivating. Almost in unison they shouted, "Yes we do!"

"Come on Betty. Its such a good story, I can't believe you've never told them".

The boys were so intrigued they were nearly falling off the couch. Exasperated, Betty threw her arms in the air.

"Ok then, but no tall stories Johnny. Just the short and the sweet."

Johnny sat back in his chair and sipped on his tea.

"Well boys, your Mum here. Straight-laced Betty McCarthy. She was Reggie Kray's girlfriend."

"What!"

Both boys turned incredulously towards their mother. She couldn't meet their gaze.

"Yep. Your Mum dated Reggie Kray for a while. She came over to me Mum's place one weekend to pick up some tea. Tea was still rationed you see. Couldn't get it for love nor money and I had procured some on the black market."

"Piled to the ceiling it was", interjected their Mum. " He gave me so much I was pretty sure I was going to get nabbed on the bus."

"Anyway", continued Johnny, "Betty was going on about this bloke called Reggie and telling me how he was taking her to all these great clubs and buying her shit and stuff. I asked her his name and sure enough she came up with Reggie Kray from Bethnal Green."

"I went 'Betty, you sure can pick 'em' and proceeded to tell her what a villain he was. She nearly died on the spot. She's pretty naive your Mum."

He gave Betty a warm smile. She smiled back but didn't know how she would ever live this down.

"And you know what? She stood him up outside the Tottenham Royal and never spoke to him again. The cheek of her! Reggie Kray! The Colonel's brother. The most feared villain in London."

Johnny shook his head.

"And he didn't come after you Mum?" asked Tray.

"No he did not!" She exclaimed, finishing the story by stuffing a hob nob in her mouth.

But it wasn't the end of the story. They didn't tell the boys that it was through the twins that Mum had met Dad. That Reg didn't come after Betty because Jimmy had 'knocked him the fuck out' in a bar room brawl. From that day on The Twins respected Jimmy. He was untouchable at least until they went to jail. After that he had to prove himself again and prove it he did. Betty was just thankful Johnny had not told them that part.

Family Business

1990

"So, what happened then?"

"I shouldn't really be talking Tray. This is your Dad's business."

"It's not like it doesn't concern me. I was the one who was threatened."

"Tray this is family business. You should be asking him."

"Micky you know he will never tell me. I just want to know what happened."

"Okay, but you didn't hear it from me Tray."

"So what happened then?"

Micky held on to his whisky and looked Tray full in the face.

"Well after Del left your place, your Dad called your Aunty D telling her not to worry. It was just a misunderstanding."

Tray thought back to last Sunday. He had been chilling in his lounge room. His one-bedroom maisonette was small but it was good enough for him. He had just sat down to watch 'The Great Escape' on video when there was a knock at the door.

Del stood in his doorway, larger than life. He had his cashmere overcoat on and wore the massive Fedora on his head. Jammed between his lips was his customary eight-inch Cuban cigar. He filled the whole doorframe. He stood at six foot six in his silk socks and was a big broad man. Del thought he was a modern day Al Capone but he was more of an Arthur Daly.

"Hello Tray."

"Hello Uncle Del. What are you doing up here?"

Del had never been to Tray's place before. In fact Tray was surprised he knew where he lived at all.

"I was just visiting a mate in the area and thought I'd drop in."

Tray made way for this giant and allowed him inside his sanctuary. He was glad he hadn't been toking on a joint or had some speed lined up on the coffee table. Del didn't approve of that sort of thing and Tray didn't want him to be telling any stories to his Mum.

"Fancy a cuppa Del?"

"Yeah. Would be nice son."

Tray nipped into the small kitchen while Del sank himself into a sumptuous armchair. He took off his Fedora and placed it on the arm. Del looked around him. It was a nice little pad stuck around the back of North Weald in Essex. Not bad he thought. It was comfortable and out of the way. Had its own little garden and a covered parking spot.

"So what you been up to Tray?"

"Not much. Had a quiet weekend for once. Got a big week next week. The Kuwaitis have got some forwards maturing and I've got to try and reprice them. Last thing we want is for them to mature them and take the business elsewhere."

Del had no idea what he was talking about. The kid was involved in some big city trading desk and the amounts of money involved were insane. Del now needed in on that action though. He had lost all his dough in the stock market crash.

'Try and go legit', his accountant had said. And so he had washed most of his money through his favourite casino and invested heavily in the market. For a while it was all looking good until the market had plummeted. Del had bought lots of get rich quick companies. The dot com boom was running along showing no signs of abating.

When that fateful week in October had ended and the margins called, Del was penniless. More than that he owed and he owed big. He was scared to think about how much was on the table. Two possibly two and a half million quid. His house was living on borrowed time and his wife had no idea that they were bankrupt. A lot of people had been calling loans in and Del had nothing to give them. That's why he was here. Tray was his last resort.

"And I have a huge gig on Saturday night. The boys from Sunrise are putting on a rave somewhere around Southend. Should be massive. Brinn's coming."

Tray waltzed in from the kitchen with two steaming mugs of tea in his hand.

"Is that so?"

Del leaned forward as Tray placed the mugs down on a small mahogany coffee table. He sat down on the two-seater lounge. Another item that had somehow found its way off the back of a truck. Del laid the cigar down in a glass ashtray recently purloined from The Kings Head and picked up his mug.

"Two sugars right?"

"Yeah, that's right Tray. Nice one."

Del sank back in his armchair and cradled the mug. He blew on the tea as Tray gazed across the room at his uncle. God there had been some stories about this man. He had saved Tray's life once. When he was three, he had fallen off the back of a houseboat on the Norfolk Broads. Del had dragged him out as he was sinking. He should have died that day but Del had brought him back.

He had also won eighty grand on one hand of poker. Tray had nearly died when Del had told him that but Del had shrugged his shoulders and said it just paid off his gambling debts. That was cool.

Tray had imagined the scene a thousand times. The games took place in a boxing gym off the Leyton High Road. Classic East End bravado. A round table in the shadow of a boxing ring attended by veterans of the game of high stakes poker. Tray could just imagine Del stubbing out his cigar as he flipped the cards one by one to reveal four kings and claim the pot.

Forever the showman, Del would have said something smart and raked the money in. There was certainly ice in his veins or maybe just rank stupidity. Either way it made Del fearless. A dangerous commodity for a man with very few, if any, morals.

He had been to court more times than any man had a right to. Mostly for winding up companies illegally and selling the stock for cash before any of his creditors could get any money back. He had never done any bird but it had been touch and go last time.

Del had opened a plumbing supply business and wound it up. He had got rid of most of the stock and declared himself bankrupt. This time though the cops were on to him and he was charged with fraud. When they had gone to court Tray's Dad had trumped the money up for bail. That had been a big risk for Jimmy because they all reckoned that Del was going to do a runner.

However Del had surprisingly kept his word and stayed. On the day the verdict was read out, Del had fallen asleep in the dock. Absolutely cool as fuck! The bailiff had to wake him and drag him to his feet as the foreman read out the statement.

To everyone's amazement, not least of all the judge and the police prosecutor, the verdict was 'not guilty'. The rumour was that the jury had been nobbled but no one could prove it and Del Connor was free to walk the streets of London once more.

You would have thought he would have stopped there, but no, not Del. He started a furniture warehouse just outside of Walthamstow importing cheap knock-offs from India. Once again he started running low on cash, most probably because of his incessant gambling on the nags. So to make up the shortfall in his cash flow crisis, he torched the place.

Only problem was, Del's mum was working at the place as a machinist and receptionist. She had popped by to pick up some swatches for cushions. The warehouse had gone up with her inside it. Grandma Connor had nearly perished in that fire from toxic smoke asphyxiation. Mainly due to the illegal foam used in the production of the shoddy gear. She had managed to get to the front door when the firemen had pulled her out.

The fire investigators couldn't prove a thing and the fact that his mother had very nearly died in the 'accident' just increased Del's semblance of innocence. The family believed differently but Del denied everything. The insurance paid out and Del was solvent again. He showed absolutely no remorse and that was what scared people the most about Del Connor. He didn't care about anyone else but himself and if anyone was hurt along the way, that was their fault.

Now that money had run out as well and it had all gone to shit. Del didn't want to do this but what else was there to do? What he was about to ask Tray was not on. This was a betrayal of trust. But what the hell? The boy had to grow up some time and if he knew him like he thought he did, he would do exactly as he was told. He fixed Tray with his hardest stare.

"Tray, you're going to do something for me and you're not going to like it"

Tray just stared at the floral curtains that hung from the bay window. Inside his stomach was jumping like a pill-head on two grams of whiz. What was up now?

43

"I heard you talking with Brinn about your mate from Hong Kong."

"Uh huh."

What was actually going through Tray's mind was a more apprehensive, 'Oh-O'. He nodded slowly.

"Well there are a couple of people I know who would be very interested in you doing the same thing for them".

Del paused waiting for the reaction.

Tray exploded.

"You fucking what Del?"

"You heard. I told some people exactly what you do and they want you to skim some cash from the bank."

Del calmly sipped his tea, placed it back on the coffee table and rested his elbows on top of his knees. He grasped his hands together as if he were praying.

"You know what Tray? You talk too much. I've heard you tell Brinn plenty of times how you reckon you could get money out of the bank. Well now you're gonna have to."

"Fuck off Del. There's no fucking way I'm going to do that for you."

"I thought you'd say that, so we added an incentive."

Tray was starting to sweat. His eyes were wide with shock. What was Del doing? He had come to Tray's house and was now threatening him. This was fucking bollocks!

"If you tell anyone what is going on, your Dad will cop it."

Del sat back satisfied that Tray would be shitting himself enough not to call his bluff.

"You're fucking kidding right? Dad kept your arse out of fucking jail."

"Yeah I know Tray. Fucking sucks doesn't it?"

Tray couldn't quite believe what was going on. Del pulled a mobile phone out of his pocket. They were all the rage at the moment. Relatively new, all the yuppies at work had them. Tray hadn't quite made the switch. It was wrapped in paper and bound with an elastic band.

"Tomorrow you will get a call on that phone explaining what you are to do exactly. There is a name on that paper. That is who will be calling you. Don't deviate from their instructions."

Del reached for his cigar. He put it to his lips and sucked on its soggy end. He rolled the cigar between his thumb and fingers and then blew the smoke back at Tray's face.

"You understand what's going on here Tray?"

"Yeah you're fucking with me right?"

"No Tray. I'm not fucking with you. I'm fucking you full stop. You are going to do this for me and do it right. Otherwise you are going to find out what suffering really is."

"Del, you're fucking nuts!"

"No Tray. Desperate. And the people who want you to do this don't care if I am fucking nuts or who the fuck you are. Either you do this and you'll be sweet or you don't and you'll be begging to be killed because the alternative will be far more painful."

"Del, you can't ask me to do this!"

"I am not asking Tray, I am telling you. So stop whining and just cope with it".

"How am I going to do this?"

"Just wait for the phone call Tray. Everything will work out. You'll see."

He tapped Tray on the knee and stood up. He reached for the Fedora and carefully placed it on his head.

"I'll let myself out."

He turned, walked to the door, opened it and strode out into the afternoon sunshine. Tray would do it. He had no balls. He could almost smell the money.

Tray sat in the lounge room. He was in shock. He stared at Del's unfinished mug of tea as wisps of cigar smoke still floated around the room. What was he to going do? This was fucking harsh. He couldn't do this. He picked up the phone.

*

The first thing Tray did was the one thing that Del hadn't expected. He called Aunty D. Doris hadn't believed him. She called him a liar and became angry. So angry in fact that she slammed the phone down and called Betty.

Betty in turn had told Jimmy. Within two hours Tray's angry Dad was sitting in the same chair that Del had been sitting in with the phone sitting conspicuously in the middle of the coffee table. Jimmy hadn't believed Betty when she had told him. He thought that his son was exaggerating. When he saw the fear on his son's face and the phone on the table, he knew that he was not.

Tray was scared. Scared for his Dad and scared for himself. Jimmy told Tray not to worry. That it would all be sorted. He took the phone and told Tray to come home for dinner. This would be dealt with.

That was six days ago. Tray had not heard anything more about it from his Dad. His Mum had gone round to Del's house and apparently physically assaulted him with a stiletto shoe. The balloon had gone up big time but Del and Jimmy had not talked about it since. The subject became mute. Unsaid. Tray was so worried that when his engine blew a piston that week, he thought someone had tried to kill him.

His Dad once again told him not to be daft and that Del was not going to do anything. Even his Mum, normally a source of so much gossip, said nothing. Brinn came over on the Wednesday but he didn't know anything either.

That was why he had contacted Micky and invited him out for a drink. If anyone would know, it would be Micky.

"You know nothing about your Dad do you Tray?"

"Not really. He just works and sleeps. When he's not working, Mum has him doing some project around the place. He never fucking stops."

"Has he ever spoke about when he was growing up?"

"No not really. Mum doesn't like his old mates so he never says anything."

Tray stirred his drink.

"Why, what'd he do?" asked Tray.

"It's not what he did do, its what he didn't do."

Tray absently scratched his head. His Dad was his Dad. He had sent him and Sam to private school and as far as he knew, was just a man that had risen out of abject poverty to become a semi-successful local businessman. He was tough but fair at home and had sacrificed a lot for his sons. Or so he had thought.

"What do you mean?"

"Jimmy could have been anything when he was young. He was a phenomenal boxer. Middleweight. He was perfect. Word was that he could have beaten anybody and I mean anybody. He got beat once fighting for the ABA championship at Wembley. Apparently he froze. Big occasion and all that. He was so embarrassed that when he met the same guy in an interclub competition, he pulverised him. He put the guy in hospital. They said he was so quick, slick and powerful. Most guys were knocked out before he even got in the ring. He was fearsome."

Tray knew his Dad had been a handy boxer but how good he had never known. He didn't mix with Dad's side of the family much. Betty didn't encourage it. There was something there she didn't quite like.

"Well Jimmy grew up with the tough guys on the manor. He knew 'em all. The guys who eventually went on to run things. But your Dad met your Mum and his world changed. No more dodgy mates. No more dodgy dealings. He went straight and had you two. But he never left his friends behind. You want to know why he hates Betty coming down the shop?"

"Why?"

"Because that's where he gets to see the old firm. That endless procession of middle-aged men that pop in just to have a cuppa? Well they run East London, the whole shebang. These guys are your Dad's mates and if he ever needs a favour, they are more than happy to oblige. Nothing goes on in this neck of the woods without them knowing".

"What're you saying? That Dad's connected?"

"He is much more than connected. Your Dad knows more about these guys than their own mothers. He did National Service with some of them. Went to school with others. Dated their sisters. Jimmy could so easily have run the whole lot if he'd wanted to but his love for your Mum won out."

"Wow!"

Suddenly it clicked. When Tray had been down the shop, blokes would come in and sit down with his Dad over the trusty cuppa. They laughed and nodded slyly at one another without saying much. Not in front of Tray and Sam anyway. They always joked with Tray but gave him a certain amount of respect which Tray had always found strange because he had never done anything to be afforded it. Whenever they came in, Jimmy would find some errand that Tray had to perform urgently. By the time he got back Charlie, Frank, Dave or whoever would be gone. Tray had never thought anything of it.

"So what the fuck happened Micky? I've been shitting meself all week!"

"There's been no need Tray. It's been done."

"Yeah but how?"

"Well I'm not going into details or names okay?"

"Okay."

"Well Del was grabbed on Monday morning and told in no uncertain terms to leave you alone."

"Who did that?"

"Like I said Tray, No names. Suffice to say Del understood the message."

"What about the phone?" asked Tray.

"Oh yeah don't worry about those fuckers. They are dead in the water. Jimmy's mates paid them a visit too. Apparently this is all over money that Del owes them. They managed to work out a deal. Del's partners have been paid. Del now owes Jimmy's mates and has been given considerably longer to pay the debt. If he hadn't been married to your Mum's best friend, the fucker would be dead."

"And they did all that for free?"

"Not exactly Tray. Cos your Dad is way off the radar for the pigs, he's decided to let the barns out the back of your place be used as a storehouse for some items of interest."

"What items?"

"Pills, millions of them!"

"Fucking hell!"

"Yeah and he's done all this for you Tray."

Tray was momentarily speechless. A state of affairs that was just about unknown to him.

"I thought he didn't care about me. That I was just an embarrassment like."

"No Tray. That man loves you. Now you know just how much. He just never tells you."

Micky gulped his whisky down.

"Is that enough Tray?"

"Yeah mate more than enough."

They both sat there in silence for a while as Tray digested the revelations.

"Thing I don't understand Micky," started Tray,"Del would know that Dad is heavy. Why on earth would he try something like this?"

"Beats me", said Micky, "Just fucking dumb I guess."

"I guess," replied Tray.

Fucking hell! Pills, thrills and villains. His old man was a sly dog! He wondered if his pals would miss a couple of pills here and there. Most probably but hey, his dad was connected, who were they gonna complain to?

Cocaine Diplomacy

1994

"You want me to do fucking what?"

Pedro had asked him to do some stupid things in his time but this took the fucking biscuit. He had once asked him to be a mercenary in the Angolan civil war. Tray had told him in no uncertain terms what he had thought of that particular suggestion. For a start Tray was colour blind. How the hell was he going to see anybody in the jungle once they were in camouflage? Secondly he was white and large. He would stick out like a sore thumb. Thirdly, he didn't know one end of a gun from another. Possible survival rate: Nil.

This was worse. Tumbles, so called because he looked like he'd just fallen out of a tumble-dryer, sat next to Tray. Creased, bedraggled and with the facial expression of a stunned mullet, he was not quite sure if he had heard him right either.

"I have a contact in foreign service. He can get you a diplomatic passport and diplomatic seals. We can travel anywhere in world with a sealed bag. No one can touch it. We can put whatever we like in it. You can go anywhere. No one will ever stop you. Its, how you say? What's the word?" He ummed and aahed until he got his light bulb moment.

"That's it. It is *foda* (fucking) fool proof Tray".

"Well why don't you do it then Pedro?"

"Because I am known criminal fucking Tray. You my friend are clean fucking".

Pedro's English was good but he hadn't mastered the intricate art of swearing. Laced with his heavy Brazilian accent he sounded more like Manuel from Fawlty Towers but looked like an out and out mobster.

"You're a fucking moron buddy! My Portuguese ain't that good pal."

"It doesn't have to be Tray. You would be going to countries where they don't speak pork and cheese. You'd be picking it up in South America. You would only have to say 'Bom Dia'. They are not allowed to question you, detain you. Nothing. It fucking is so sweet".

"Do you really think I am going to go all the way to Colombia, Bolivia or some other fucking tin pot fucking hole, pick up a ton of coke and bring it back here?"

Tray couldn't believe what Pedro was asking him.

"You wouldn't be bringing it back here. You would be taking it somewhere else. You are just a courier. Even if you do get arrested, you have diplomatic immunity fucking. Its perfect."

"Pedro you really are fucking nuts!"

Tray rose from the table. Tumbles couldn't believe what he had heard either. He shook his head at Pedro but didn't leave. After all he hadn't finished his beer and it was free.

Putting The Boot In

1990

"They're out then."

"Who're you talking about?"

"The Mickelson brothers, you know full well who."

"It don't bother me Micky, you know that."

"Jimmy, you know people been saying you going soft."

Jimmy turned towards the big, red-headed Irishman.

"Soft for what? I don't care what they been saying. Anyone wants to have a pop, I'll cane 'em."

"I know Jimmy, but still, you got to do something."

Tray was sitting in the corner with a couple of his mates. Jimmy looked around him. The Gardeners Arms Pub, so named because it didn't have a garden. Nor a downstairs for that matter. Bloody ironic, if that was the word. Tray would know. He gazed down into his pale ale as he pondered Micky Flynn's words.

Micky was a giant of a man and no doubt would crush most men's heads in his right hand. He was just a good friend and worker to Jimmy but most people thought he was his bodyguard. He swayed at the bar after consuming what had to be his eighth double scotch in an hour. His blood-shot eyes gave off that thousand-yard star that shellshock victims have when they came back from the war.

"Jimmy McCarthy!"

The voice rang out like a shot across the smoke-filled bar.

Jimmy and Micky turned from the bar to see a crew cut, muscle-bound monster, redolent in a full-length leather raincoat, standing at the top of the barroom stairs. He had a scar running from his right eye to the top of his lip. A result of a long ago argument with a pint of Harp. It gave him a perma-sneer. It also made his face lop-sided.

His right hand held tightly on to a leash which held in check a massive Alsatian. It's lips curled quietly as both it and its owner scanned the bar. The laughing stopped at Tray's table. Everyone turned to the newcomer.

"And what can I do for you Tony?"

"A chat if you don't mind Jimmy."

"Well actually I do Tony, seeing as how you've disturbed my afternoon drink. But I suppose you've forgotten how to behave since you been in stir so long. So what have you got for me?"

"I ain't got nothing for you Jimmy. It's what you are gonna give to me!"

Tony Mickelson, The Cutter as some called him, swaggered towards the bar. Tray and his mates began to rise from their seats but Micky gave them a gesture and they slowly sat down. Two other 'geezers' appeared at the top of the stairs clad in leather bomber jackets. Their hands were stuffed in their pockets, intimating that they had something far more sinister within. Ballsy, that's for sure.

Jake, resplendent in a white frilly dress shirt, stood stoically behind the bar. He seemed oblivious to the scene unfolding before him. A huge mirror extolling the virtues of some long forgotten gin hung behind him. He leant on the bar. Both hands gripped the rose-coloured wood. Jake had been the landlord at The Arms for as long as the grotty carpet had been covering the floor. He was the institution. No one touched the pub and no one touched him. His pub was off limits and everyone knew it. His face was impassive. Not a word of emotion was etched on it. His short black hair formed a widow's peak at the top of his pasty forehead.

A bead of sweat developed in the furrows of his brow. He felt it trickle down to his eyebrow, felt it hang momentarily defying gravity. As if in slow motion he watched it drop to the varnished bar top. It created a perfect crown as it rebounded against the bar's hard surface, then collapsed in on itself as the laws of Newton did their work.

Jake reached below the counter for a rag. Tony strode with menace towards Jimmy. Then the world turned upside down. Violence begat violence and Tray's world would never be the same.

The Dish would never forget that day. He had always known that Tray's Dad was hard. He never knew how hard and from that day on, he would never look at Tray in the same light either. They had been sitting in their usual corner in The Arms waiting for the evening's festivities to begin. Tray was carping on about some bird he wanted to shag but would get nowhere with as usual, when this monster of a man came to the top of the stairs.

The leather-clad heavy looked over at Tray's Dad and shouted something that he didn't quite catch. His face looked lop-sided on account of some huge scar. He glanced at Tray. A look spread across his face that Dish had never seen before. This was not jovial Tray. This was something different. Something mean. He switched back to the bar.

The monster strode towards Jimmy. Two more men in bomber jackets appeared at the top of the stairs, hands in pockets.

The monster spoke.

"You know what's going on here Jimmy?"

"No Tony, why don't you enlighten me?"

Tray began to rise from his vinyl-covered chair. Dish followed suit as did Jay and Brew. A quick signal from Micky Flynn stopped their brief show of force. They slowly regained their seats. Burt Bacharat sang in the background through a shitty speaker system. He competed with the fruit machine and their annoying melody of electronic banality.

Jimmy smiled at this 'Tony'. Dish picked up his bottle of Corona, saw it shake in his hand and put it back down. He felt Tray shift his weight on the bench seat.

"Well Jimmy, word is you're past it. Me and Dave, we reckon you're overdue. 'Bout time you paid your dues to people like us."

"Is that so Tony?" replied Jimmy.

Jimmy didn't move a muscle as Tony got within a gnat's chuff of the middle-aged man. All Dish knew about Jimmy was that he was an ex-boxer. That he ran a successful business down the High Road and that people respected him. Tray didn't say much about him and Dish hadn't been that interested in him. The most he had seen of Jimmy was when he funnelled Micky Flynn down the stairs of The Arms every Friday afternoon after his usual shed-full of alcohol. This was something he hadn't seen before. It was like gunfight at the OK Corral. He was shitting himself.

"And where is that bucket of shit Dave, Tony? Still sucking on your mum's titty? Or is she changing his nappy?"

Tony sneered.

"Actually Jimmy, he's driving round Chingford looking to do some damage."

"You fuckin cunt Tony!"

Jimmy went to move. The dog snarled. Micky placed his hand on Jimmy's shoulder.

"Easy Jimmy."

Jimmy shrugged off the hand.

Dish felt Tray tense up.

"You threatening me Mickelson?"

"You betcha Jimmy. You're gonna drop me a thousand a week or Chingford ain't gonna be the suburban dream you think it is."

"Go fuck yourself Tony!"

"No, fuck yourself Jimmy!"

Mickelson let go of the leash.

"Attack Scar!"

The dog lunged.

*

Charlie Fenton heard every word of the conversation from the stairwell. He pulled out the two pistols from their shoulder holster and took off the safety. He heard Mickelson order the dog to attack. He reached the top of the stairs in one bound.

He shoved both pistols into the ribs of the goons standing guard at the top of the stairs. He drew back the hammers. The goons heard the click.

"Don't be silly boys. You don't want to die for this prick."

The goons' hands moved slowly from their pockets. Their hands rose to the ceiling. Charlie saw the dog lunge.

*

Dish saw the dog lunge too. The seemingly sozzled Micky Flynn punched the dog on the muzzle. It dropped like a stone. Unconscious or maybe even dead.

Jake raised a sawn off shot gun from behind the bar and pointed it at the goons opposite the bar. They raised their hands in slow acceptance of their plight. Jimmy moved but Dish didn't really see it.

A right hand snaked out like a whiplash and cracked Tony Mickelson full in the face. It was followed by a left uppercut that stood the wannabe stand over man on his tiptoes and then a crushing right smashed into his right temple. Mickelson was out before he hit the floor. His leg shook uncontrollably as he sank to the ground.

*

Jimmy looked down at the two bodies sprawled on the carpet in front of him. Jake held on tightly to his beloved shooter. Jimmy looked over at Charlie. The two goons looked as though they were about to let go of their lunch.

"Girls, is there somewhere you would rather be?"

Jimmy directed the question at the two men.

"Yes Mr McCarthy."

The two bomber jackets were not looking too hopeful that they were going to get out of there alive.

"What you doing with this pile of shit anyway?" asked Jimmy, kicking the unconscious Mickleson in the process.

"We didn't know we were coming after you Mac. Honest!"

Charlie Fenton, head enforcer for the East London Chiefs looked on in amusement.

"Let 'em go Jimmy. They're next to useless anyway. They'll never work round here again. Getting rolled by two old men and a piss-head ain't too good for your job prospects."

The guns had mysteriously disappeared from Charlie's grasp as he 'advised' Jimmy what to do. Jimmy nodded his agreement and Charlie led them to the stairs.

Jimmy called out.

"And Dave Mickelson?"

"Dentist," replied Charlie.

*

Tray walked over to the unconscious piece of shit. He had known what the quip about Chingford had meant. They were after his mum. He swung his leg back and let fly. He kicked Mickelson square in the balls. He groaned. No mercy for this cunt, that's for sure.

Dish and the others followed over, not sure what was going to happen next. This was not their world. They hadn't seen anything like this before. Tray hadn't spoken a word to them. He looked at his Dad.

"Bring this fucker round Jake. He is gonna remember today!" instructed Jimmy.

Jake came round from behind the bar and threw a jug of water over Mickelson. The once mighty tough man now cowered on the floor as he looked up at Jimmy McCarthy and his boy.

"Throw this cunt out Tray!"

Micky and Tray bent down and dragged Mickelson across the ash-strewn carpet. Micky sank an elbow into his face. More bone crunched inside the already broken nose. Mickelson howled.

Micky and Tray threw him down the stairs. Tray was full of anger. Pumped. A state of being that was new to him. Mickleson fell down about five steps and became lodged. Tray kicked him down the rest of the way until he tumbled out of the pub door and onto the drab pavement of Wood Street. Onlookers averted their gaze. They didn't want to know. The unwritten law.

There was a black BMW waiting outside in the street. Charlie sat behind the wheel awaiting instructions. Jimmy and Tray's mates followed Mickelson out onto the street. Micky stuck his knee in Mickelson's back.

"Grab his hands Tray!" barked Jimmy.

Tray obliged, grabbing the battered man's wrists.

"Pop the boot Charlie!"

Charlie popped the boot.

"Now shove his hands inside the boot!"

Tray looked at his Dad but didn't question.

"Dish, help us out here. This cunt weighs a ton!"

Mickelson started to struggle but he was spent. He started to beg for clemency but none would be given. With Micky's help they managed to get Mickelson to the rear of the car. Mickelson started to sob.

"Not so fucking funny now is it Tony?" asked Jimmy.

Jimmy was going to really hurt this guy. Micky knew what was coming next. He was surprised how Tray and his boys were stepping up. This was way out of their league.

Mickelson managed to get to his knees before Jimmy snapped his next order.

"Shut the fucking lid!"

In one sudden movement Micky Flynn let go of Tony Mickelson and slammed the boot lid down on his hands. Mickelson shrieked in agony. He threw up, getting vomit all over the back of the BMW.

"Now drive Charlie!"

Charlie put his foot down on the accelerator and pulled away from the kerb. Mickelson didn't even get a chance to get to his feet as he was dragged behind the car. You could hear his shrieks all down Wood Street.

Tray looked on in disbelief. Slack-jawed. Stunned. The Dish couldn't believe that they had done this in broad daylight and no one had said a word. Who were these people?

"Tray?"

"Yes Dad."

"Not a word to your Mum."

"Yes Dad. Dad?" Tray absent-mindedly scratched his head.

"Yes Son."

"I didn't know Uncle Charlie had guns."

"There's a lot you don't know about your Uncle Charlie."

"Like what Dad?"

"Like he's the toughest cunt I know."

Jeez thought Tray, after all the shit that Micky had told him, he must be one tough fucker.

The Game of Can't

1993

This winter had been particularly miserable for their buddy. He was heartbroken. Business was pretty bad in the Algarve and the club was only open on the weekends. That meant they had five days to fill. All the girls had gone back to their respective countries to see their families. Freddy and Ricky's had gone back to South Africa. Tumbles' had gone to Brazil and wouldn't be back for another couple of months. Adrian never pulled women and Tray wasn't interested in them at the moment. Combine the loneliness with some extremely damp and shit weather and you got a good idea of what winter was like in Lagos.

Tray was still working on the radio station and was a little bit of a local celebrity but his heart wasn't really in it. The boys were really concerned about him. Tray was getting a little too depressed for their liking.

To alleviate this depression, Freddy and Adrian had invented the game of 'Can't'. It was a board game that was much like snakes and ladders with incentives. The buy in was 20 pills, 10 grams of speed and an ounce of hash. LSD and coke were optional depending on availability. If drugs were ever legalised Tumbles reckoned it would make them millions.

Much like Monopoly, it had 'chance' cards that entertained the construction of various drug implements like bongs, joints, snorting utensils etc. and the active consumption of a full range of narcotics. Cards like 'everyone skin up' would be turned. Then you might get a 'you must smoke all prepared joints before next person's throw - do not share – failure to do so go back to start'. There was also 'drop a pill'. 'rack up', 'snort', 'do some base' etc.

The game was very often played over a number of days and was almost impossible to finish. The final 5 spaces all resulted with your stash being stolen by all the other players and going back to the beginning. Only one seemingly impossible combination of consecutive double throws and a six could land you on the finishing square which was called the 'Legalised Square'. This meant that you had finally managed to buy your 'Superclub' and play your dream tunes.

Tray was thrilled when the boys presented him with the game. He had been curious about the name when they gave it to him but Adrian soon explained it to him. That it was pronounced 'Cunt'. How that had made him laugh.

The first time they played it, the game had not finished after five days and they were so mangled that they nearly didn't open the real club. That led the boys to introduce the 'Soft Cock' card which was much like a 'Get Out Of Jail' card. This could be won by any player during the game and could be introduced at any time to end the game without determining a winner. It was called 'Going To Rehab'.

Tray never took the card and so never ended a game. The others, not being in the same consumption league, very often took advantage of the card as a trip to the funny farm beckoned if the game continued. Tray never backed down even when his stash was stolen more times than seemed fair. He always took the chance, slamming the dice down and shouting, 'Let's play this fucking game boys!'

In one of their more lucid moments, Freddy asked what his superclub would be like.

"Private rooms, a laser light show to die for. House music made by angels. So many beautiful women that it would hurt the eyes. On the beach with access to the sea. A swimming pool, a pool bar. Open-air terrace, music under the stars. Man it would be paradise."

Tray's eyes glazed over. He folded his arms, sat back in his chair and dreamt of his perfect club.

"Hey Tray?"

"Yeah Adrian?"

"You've landed on a chance card."

"What's it say?"

"You're stash gets stolen, share with other players. Go back to start."

"Not again. This game's a right cunt!" he reached forward and gave his stash to Adrian.

"Right boys. Let's play this fucking game!"

All of them looked at Tray. It was going to be a long, long winter if Tray carried on like this and they all doubted if they would be able to remember any of it by the time the girls got back.

Away

1991

"They've just crucified a copper on the railings!"

Brummie was scared. *'Hide him for a couple of months'* they said. *'Just until the heat dies down'* they said. He never thought in his wildest dreams that his pub would be surrounded by a baying mob intent on dragging out Tray McCarthy. But Brummie was nothing if not staunch. If they dragged Tray out, they would have to drag him out too. This was Tray after all. Not some fuckwit patsy that Jimmy had asked him to hide. This was Jimmy's son.

"Fuck me dead! We gotta get outta here!" shouted Tray.

"You fucking reckon Tray?"

"Where we gonna go Brummie?"

"A-fucking-way! That's where!"

'Far, far away' thought Tray as the copper's screams were drowned out by another window being smashed by an incoming brick.

*

1993

He kissed her deeply. He looked into her eyes. He drowned in her love. He held her face in his hands. He loved her more deeply than it was possible for a man to love a woman. From a world where love lived precariously alongside the shadow of violence, they had briefly shone like a brilliant star on a distant horizon.

He knew that the pain would never go away. That it would nestle deep within his soul and no matter how far he travelled, no matter how glorious the world could be, he would never find her again. He would never feel that surge of emotion when she touched his hand. He would never look into the eyes of another human and feel so totally enveloped in their spell. So lost in their heart and so safe in their love.

A tear snaked down his cheek. He tasted it on his lips. She shivered as he wrapped her in his arms. He could not bear the loss. His heart ached at the very thought of her gone. Tray smelt her golden tresses as he sank his face into her neck.

Their fate was sealed. Life proved greater than love. How can a man who wanted no more than the thunderbolt of love, be denied it by the life he led? She sobbed uncontrollably in his arms. She knew she would never be loved by another man with so much depth, so much fervour, so much strength. She asked herself whether it was better to have loved than to have never loved at all? Or was it better **never** to have known the ecstasy of perfect love and then lose it? She didn't know. All she did know was that her man, Tray McCarthy, was going to be ripped from her because of the crimes of her father and not his. Unexpected as well as unwanted.

Jo felt her heart break as the realisation came to her that this would be the last time that they would meet. She was his love. He was her soul. Now that bond had been taken away from both of them. Forever lost in the crimes of their families. Just like a modern day Romeo and Juliet. If it wasn't so painful, they could have made a film about it.

CHAPTER TWO

'Once In A Lifetime'

How Did I Get Here?

She rolled in to him and let his ample arm cradle her head. He was warm, like a mini furnace and she liked to live off that heat. She was in love with him, completely, unquestionably. He was like no other man she had ever met. For a start he was English but not like the ground-out whingeing poms that she had met in the sweaty bars of Kings Cross or Bondi.

He had already lived a life. He had been to places she couldn't even find on a map. He spoke so many languages, she wasn't sure what he was even saying to here half the time. He was an unfathomable man. A man of mystery and yet a man so open that she couldn't decide whether he even did have something to hide. But despite his gentleness, despite the sheer love he expressed in his eyes, there was pain there too. She had never seen him argue. Never seen him so much as raise a finger to another man and yet and yet.....

The question nagged at her. Like most women she couldn't just let things be. She just couldn't accept things for what they were. She had to search for that which she knew nothing about. She just couldn't let it go. She knew that everyone loved her man. Men and women alike were drawn to him. But she had also seen people be scared by him. Not because of what he said or how he had threatened someone. Tray didn't roll like that. It would be a look. Something that sat behind his eyes. It was something unsaid but which said it all.

Although he was no fighter, he feared no man. He tried to convince her he was tough but she always laughed it off as some macho bravado. She was sure he was talking it up just to impress her but now and again, she saw the change in him. She had heard it called 'doing the London'. If she hadn't seen it herself she would have said people were lying.

They were walking down Oxford Street once at some ungodly hour. There was a group of some no good Lebanese spread across the sidewalk, just looking to cause trouble. They threatened people just by their presence. She had been out with many men who had been confronted by the same situation. They usually steered her across the pavement and crossed to the other side of the street or bowed their heads and strode through the group. There was no eye contact, just a headlong rush to avoid trouble at any cost.

Tray reacted like no other man she had known. His normal shambling shuffle transformed into a purposeful gait. He puffed his chest out and held his head high. He looked hard into the eyes of those infront of him and confronted them in his deep Cockney accent.

"Evening boys. Alright?"

And yet it wasn't even close to being a question. It was a statement. It was suggesting to the young men that if they left him alone, **they** would be alright. To react any other way would mean certain trouble for them and they understood that.

She had seen him go amongst a group of guys at a club and strike up a friendship with men that many Australians wouldn't even chat to. One night in particular, she remembered him asking the leader of one particular group of gangster wannabes 'Do you all get a group discount for tracksuits at Rebel Sports considering you all look the same?'

For any other person this would have resulted in a mass beating but instinctively he smiled at the guy and told him to chill out. The gang leader either couldn't believe the balls on this English guy or thought he was a bit tapped. The result was always the same. Tray just got away with shit.

But she couldn't quite understand how this London manboy, the class clown to all intense and purposes, commanded this undercurrent of respect without being an overt tough guy. Geoff tried to explain it to her once.

"He's just not scared Lizzy. Guys know that. He doesn't have to be tough. He doesn't have to be handy with his fists. Fellers just know that you don't want to upset him is all. He has a very, very long fuse. The worst thing he said to me once was that I had disappointed him. I was absolutely devastated. Its just something you don't normally hear from blokes. He just has a way about him. You could have a go at him all day long and he wouldn't arc up. But pick on someone he loves and I reckon he wouldn't stop until the person was in a world of pain."

"He's subtle with it too. I have seen someone badger him for an hour. Most men would've fronted after five minutes. But Tray just sat there and told the guy that he wouldn't fight him because he didn't want to. It was never a question that Tray couldn't fight him, just that he wouldn't. Eventually when Tray got off his barstool something in his eyes finished the stand-off. The guy backed down. It wasn't Tray's size. It wasn't anything he said. Like I said Liz, it was in Tray's eyes. They said 'this could be the worst mistake you will ever make'. And he backed down. It was a great example of how silence can frighten a man".

"Lizzy, there's just something special about him. Whatever he was before he came here means that he just doesn't give a fuck. I don't know what it is. I'm one of his best mate and I know nothing about him from before Oz. His family don't talk. None of his mates ever come over. It's like he just appeared here with no history. He'll tell you stories but nothing that really explains why he does what he does. Something rough must have happpened that made him that way. But you know what? I really don't care. The upside is he will do anything for anyone and we love him for it".

But she did care. Geoff's comments had troubled her. She wasn't happy to just let it go. She wanted to know what or who had shaped her man. As she listened to the heavings of his gargantuan chest, she decided that tonight she would ask him.

For the first time in her life, she shared a bed with a man who she did not fear. What did frighten here was where the question might take them. Oh why couldn't she just be satisfied with what she had?

*

He had fallen hard for her. Mind you, he always fell hard. He was perpetually in love with someone but to be helplessly and completely in love was something different. It had happened before. Twice to be exact. But those loves had been ripped from him. Forces out of his control had nearly destroyed him. He had been so close to completely giving up on life but he had come back from the brink to rekindle the passion in his heart.

He thought back to his first great love. Back to the Algarve and those glorious summer days on beaches kissed by a burning sun. He could never have imagined a life without her and after all that had happened, all he could think about was what his life could have been. The Algarve loomed large as his mind wandered back to that time.

It had been a normal night. He had closed the club around 5am. Smashed as usual. He had visited the fisherman's café on the way home. He was a creature of habit after all. Every morning after a night of bachannal pleasure at the club, he would visit this rundown café with a couple of his mates and either drink on, take drugs or eat; whichever his body was capable of doing.

The café itself was Lagos's best kept secret from the tourists. Tucked away on the main road, it was essentially there to service those brave souls who would depart before dawn to pull in their daily catch. Crusty old men with gnarly hands. Knuckles, grazed and swollen from pulling a lifetime of nets. Flat caps, brown craggy faces perpetually covered in stubble, these were the men who worked harder than anyone in the ancient seaport.

They would wear brown or grey thick suits tucked into wellington boots. They came into the bar, whose walls were bedecked in traditional blue and white tiles depicting scenes of days of yore, to warm up their aching bones. The proprietor, a grumpy middle-aged man called 'José' hated strangers or *'estrangeiros'* as they were called in his native tongue. He barely tolerated Tray and his group of smashed hangers-on. It was only because it meant increased revenue that he allowed them in. He was greedy for money but strangely enough wouldn't accept any other group of party time *estrangeiros* in his *Adega* at that time of the morning except Tray's.

Tray would either be pouring whiskies down his neck or having a flat white coffee depending on what his weapon of choice had been at the club. Pills or acid would mean coffee. Hash would mean coffee and his favourite snack *Bifanas.* Whisky would mean more whisky until the weather outside got too hot to tolerate. He would then go home and spend some time with Jo before descending into a complete and all consuming slumber. Then it would be up at three-ish and down the beach.

He never mixed his weapons. Alcohol and hash didn't agree with him and alcohol and pills just numbed the effect of either. What it did mean however was that any one weapon made driving home a bit of an issue. Therefore spending time at the *adega* was a necessary evil, The police knocked off at 8am so if he stayed at the adega til that time, he would never get caught under the influence of anything unless he crashed. Even then he could bribe his way out of it.

José barked his normal command of "Diga!" as Tray stumbled in with Fernando, Adam and Tumbles. Tray wasn't too sure of the exact translation but assumed it was something like 'Order!' The early morning sun's rays followed them in as the sunrise peaked above the horizon. The sweat tumbled down their faces as they took their seats. Tray especially sweated like a Trojan when he was on the pills. He couldn't help it. It just came in rivers.

José looked at him as always with suspicion. He rubbed his hands on his apron and peered through the piles of plates stacked high on the serving counter. Party drugs were still uncommon in the Algarve except where Tray was concerned. He had the contacts and they were cheap for him so it was party time 24/7. José knew the boys were on something. He knew it wasn't the life-taking heroin that his nephew had succumbed to. This was a happy drug. It was more euphoric. The Englishman came in nearly every morning in this state. Normally he hated these types of people. His customers certainly didn't like foreigners but this man spoke passable Portuguese, respected his establishment and never caused trouble like the normal tourists. They also spent a lot of money and that made up for some of their peculiar behaviour.

The four 'gurners' took their positions at the rickety table and chairs that looked like they had been there forever. Tray ordered beer for the boys, a water and a coffee with milk for him and a load of *'bifanas'*. These were the local snacks that Tray was hooked on. Lean cuts of veal, shallow fried in an old skillet with tons of garlic and served on the freshest of crusty rolls. The *'bifanas'* would most probably remain uneaten but because the boys would be there for another two hours, they ought to spend a decent amount of money. It was a kind of mantra for Tray. He would never go into someone else's establishment and order a glass of tap water. He would always pay and expected people to do the same when they came to his.

Various fishermen walked in, coughing up a lung and ordering their expresso coffees and shots of 'madrona'. A combination either to jump-start their day or to keep them going. A traditional high-velocity speed in a shot glass. Tray marvelled at how these tough men of the sea could go on day after day without the need for modern narcotics. Their constitution was amazing.

Tray passed a dime bag under the table full of pills.

"Get in the bog and get one of those down your neck!"

Tumbles took the bag and wandered very conspicuously over to the toilet. In moments he was back and the process was repeated four fold. After about thirty minutes the four were a set of giggling Girties, lampooning and guffawing like muppets on laughing gas. The early morning rush of fisherman had dissipated and the four were careening around the bar like whirly tops. José's demeanour improved with the rising sun and as the drinks turned from beers to spirits, thereby becomng increasingly more expensive.

Eventually the witching hour came and Tray had to bounce off into the side streets to avoid bumping into normal people. He had to search for his van. As normal, one of his mates had borrowed it and left it parked on one of several possible cobbled lanes. His van was a VW campervan. It was brilliant sky blue and had seen much better days. The sliding door had been replaced due to excessive rust with a door from a breakers yard that just fitted the hole. It was dark maroon and because it was not an exact fit, remained permanently shut. The front and back axle were not fixed firmly to the chassis and to prevent them from falling off, were tied to each other with thick towrope.

Despite its shortcomings, it had made it from Portugal to the French Alps and back again and had gone over the Pyrenees twice. Not bad for two hundred quid. It had no right to be on the road. It would fail any mechanic's inspection even in deepest darkest India. It still had its English plates on it despite residing in Portugal for two years which made it approximately 21 months overdue for its Portuguese registration. A state of affairs that was allowed to continue because of his ongoing friendship with a couple of the members of the local constabulary. One of whom was engaged to his flat mate. A very very handy connection.

He climbed in, grabbed a screwdriver, stuck it in the ignition and started up the multi-coloured beast. It coughed like an old man in his death throws and rattled in much the same manner. A big plume of blue smoke exploded from the rusty exhaust. He stomped on the clutch, threw it into first and trundled off up the hill.

Before too long he was on the dual carriageway on his way to Praia da Luz and the warm embrace of his love. A dry, brown, depressing landscape rushed by his driver's side window unnoticed. The flora of the Algarve was perpetually starved of rain. It was not the most captivating of scenes and Tray never really took in how the earth just begged for some nourishment. It was just a world he was passing through on the way to somewhere far more rewarding.

Turning left off the highway and down into the small fishing village, he soon became surrounded by blazing white villas that were the holiday homes for so many German and English tourists. He rounded the corner and slipped into the complex that held Jo's parents house.

As he turned into the street where 'DunRoamin' sat, a mess of police cars, dark blue and white confronted him, all with lights flashing. He looked over at Jo's house. Barry, her father, was being led away in handcuffs by two uniformed policemen. His wife Mary and Jo were standing in the doorway surrounded by other officers. They were in floods of tears. Barry caught Tray's eye. He shook his head slowly so as not to catch the attention of the officers beside him. Tray understood. He drove on by, taking care not to look at the scene.

*

Jo heard his van before she saw it. She was crying uncontrollably. What had just happened? The police had rushed in mob-handed. Four cars sat outside as her Dad stood there looking out of the sliding window.

As a member of Interpol read the charges out, he turned away from Jo, resigned to his fate. Her Mum had shrieked in despair as they placed the cuffs on him. Her father looked at her embarrassed, forlorn. She had trusted him her entire life to protect her. Now that protection was being taken away.

She knew her Dad was less than honest but he wasn't a bad man. He was like the man she loved or rather he was like her Dad. As she watched her mother descend into hysteria, she grabbed her arm and followed her Dad out of the front door.

The van spluttered round the corner. She saw Tray look. She saw him look away. She watched him drive away. And she knew at the moment, in that chaos that was tearing her world apart, that the little paradise that she had found in this peculiar part of the world was gone.

*

As he lay there reminiscing about a world that was some 10 years old, she felt him sigh. It was a huge sigh. It exuded sadness. It cut through a veil of memories she was not privy to. She knew that he was somewhere else. Somewhere where she didn't live. She wanted to know that world.

She lifted her head from his arm. She looked at his face framed in a shock of tumble down hair. The sadness was etched deep on his lips.

"Tray?"

"Yes baby?"

"How did you get here?"

*

He heard the question and knew he didn't want to answer it. He knew it had been coming. One day he knew she would ask it. How could she share so much and he so little? It wasn't a question of sharing his love. That was unquestionable. It was sharing his past.

He knew everything about her. The childhood scar on her arm was a badge of honour bestowed upon her as she tried to climb out of her bedroom window in a ridiculous attempt to have a sneaky cigarette. At the age of thirteen, her ears had been stapled to her head to prevent her looking like the FA Cup. She had drunk two bottles of very expensive Grange on her 21st birthday. Her father had been livid. She hadn't cared.

She only knew of his life in Australia. Of his broken marriage. Of his descent into a depression that he had barely recovered from. She only knew snippets of his life in Europe. His dysfunctional family barely communicated with him. Out of sight, out of mind.

He had met her only three months after the marriage had broken down. She had been very wary of this. Concerned that she was the rebound. But he had assured her that the marriage had been over for some time. The only thing that had kept them together was his proud devotion to his morals and the promises he had made in the sight of God.

He went on the rampage after she walked out. Free from the humdrum marriage that had caged him, he had reverted to type and partied the house down. He was a huge flirt, had an engaging smile and a sense of humour to die for but what had excited her was that all he cared about was having a good time. Life was a party and he was a veteran of both.

She knew he had lived in Portugal and France. She knew he had been on the road to deejaying stardom. That he ran a nightclub. That his club had been on the lips of everyone on the backpacker circuit. She had heard that from others. Apparently his club was the one that you just had to experience. No luxuries. No fancy stuff. It was what it was. The place where you could listen and dance to the latest tunes from London with absolutely no interference from security or anyone else. Drugs were consumed openly and no behaviour was considered taboo.

He was the first English DJ to play house music in Paris. He had worked in Val D'Isere during the French Winter Olympics but beyond that, nothing. He didn't want her to know. His life was his to know and it was better that way.

She looked at him again. She raised herself onto her elbow and gazed onto his face. His eyes were closed and his lips pursed. She saw a tear form in his duct and snake down the right side of his face towards his ear.

He raised an arm to his face and wiped away the tear. He turned his head towards her and opened his eyes.

"Lizzy, do you really want to know?"

"Yes honey"

"Why?"

"Because if I am going to spend the rest of my life with you, I need to know".

Tray flinched at this. He had known she loved him but this was new. The rest of his life in exchange for the history of it. She put her left hand on his chest. She smiled at him. Moved her hand to his face, held it softly then bent down and kissed him.

She pulled back.

"Its not how I got here baby. It's why I stayed away".

"Well then, why did you stay away?"

He looked at her. She said nothing. Waiting for an answer. He closed his eyes. Swallowed. He opened them again.

"Cos I can't go back!"

*

"Cos I can't go back!"

She heard those words echo inside her head. Her world. Her life. Her heart. It had all come tumbling down like the walls of Jericho. He looked at her. His heart was crumbling in front of her. The fragments of hers were scattered like the pebbles on the

75

beach upon which they stood. He held her in his arms. She could smell his cologne. Sweet. Inviting. She shook with the deep wretching sobs that took hold of her.

She knew he couldn't go back. She knew she couldn't stay. Her Dad being pinched had put paid to that. If she stayed, people would be watching her. If she left, he couldn't follow.

She knew all about him. She had grown up with him and loved him forever. This much she knew. From when she had first tied his shoelaces at primary school to when he had come back from France speaking fluent French at the age of sixteen. They had never kissed then. Both were too scared. Too close. Like brother and sister. And then they had drifted apart. He had started to DJ and she had stuck to her studies.

Jo watched from a distance as he lived two separate lives. He became a foreign exchange dealer by day and a DJ by night. Acid house was on the rise and he moved in the circles where pills, coke and beats were the three kings. She couldn't stand the champagne swillers from the city and the club life just wasn't her thing. She started a career in marketing until that fateful night when her mum and dad had run around the house and bundled everything into the car.

They had given her an option. Stay in Essex and never see them again or come with them overseas and live a life in relative comfort. Her Dad had embezzled a small fortune from the off licence on Epping High Street but the game was up. They were onto him and they had to go now. Tonight. What option was there?

They had jumped into a battered old Ford Cortina and headed for Calais. The car wasn't theirs. They journeyed through France and dumped the car in Spain. Eventually they had arrived in Portugal after about three months of travelling. Her Mum and Dad had never been happier. They found a perfect anonymous little villa and began to live their other life. Her Dad had worked for a bloke from the old manor doing a little bit of handyman stuff to keep the cash rolling in. Her mum wrote for the local tourist magazine and did some house cleaning. Jo worked in a local bar.

They settled into the Algarve life, creating a small coterie of friends who were none the wiser to their past. She had a string of holiday romances but begged for something more substantial. She dreamed of what Tray was doing. Where he would be. Who he was seeing.

Then one day she spotted his brother in town. He had never wanted into the family business and was an awesome skier. He had jumped ship ages ago and had become the proverbial ski bunny. Instead of doing a season in New Zealand, he had come down to check out Lagos with one of his fellow ski instructors.

She had watched him strolling through the main square. His long blond locks reflecting the spring sunshine. He had developed into a strong man. His shoulders had filled out. He was not as tall as Tray but he walked like him. Shuffling slowly from side to side. Looking at nothing but taking in everything. She had waited until he had sat down at one of the cafes and ordered a beer.

She sat down opposite him. His jaw dropped. He was genuinely happy to see her. They had spent the entire afternoon together. He filled her in on what he had been doing. She told him why she was there. Sam had known why they had taken off. It had been all over the local news but their secret was safe with him. He knew the ways of the manor and anyway Jo was almost family. She didn't bring up the subject of Tray until late in the day.

First thing that made her heart leap was that he was on his way to Lagos. Something had happened. Tray had left the bank and something had happened. She didn't know what exactly but it was enough to make Tray leave the home he loved. He was also single. Sam said he been getting a bit fucked up and that's also why he was coming but it was nothing that the good life couldn't sort out.

And then two weeks later he was there. Tray had no idea that she was there either. He had cried when he saw her. She had too. And then their love affair began. This was no innocent childhood love. It became the blinding light that everyone searches for and few ever find. They had found in each other that which was missing in themselves. Tray no longer had to duck and dive. She no longer worried about the future. Their love could remain anonymous and hidden from the prying eyes of London. They could share their love in the quiet of the Algarve. She knew they were safe here.

That was until three weeks ago. The police had changed everything. This was the first time she had seen Tray since then. The reporters were snooping around her and she had heard that they wanted to talk to her boyfriend. Tray had let Tumbles look

77

after the club and headed for the hills. The whole town had clammed up on the subject of all things Tray. All the bar workers knew better than to talk. Word had gone out from a couple of respected geezers in that part of the world. Jimmy McCarthy had silenced that particular outlet. Frank had made sure of that.

Tray's head bouncer, who was also head of the local gypsy mafia, had also made it clear to all and sundry that the shutters were to come down. And they had. It was only a small story anyway and once Barry was whisked back to London, the press would fly with him.

Now they stood on Burgau Beach. Cradled by limestone cliffs and fanned by a gentle Atlantic breeze. They remained in the shadows as the sun disappeared behind them. She knew this would be the last time she would see him.

She saw that this was killing him. The man that she loved more than herself. The man who loved her more than any woman had a right to be loved. To protect the ones they loved they had to deny their own joy. She didn't know if Tray would ever survive this. She doubted whether she would either.

She kissed him one last time. She could not look him in the eyes. She turned to walk away. Tray sank to his knee as he grabbed her hand. She turned back to him and sank to her knees. They kissed each other passionately like they were giving life to one another. They snatched at each other like they were trying to contain water. Every touch, every caress conveying the gift of love. They stayed like that for a long time.

Tumbles looked on from the foot of the cliffs. This was too much even for him to bear. People should not have to endure this. People should not outlive their love. Tray would not be a happy man.

*

"Cos I can't go back bitch!"

His wedding day had been one of the happiest days of his life but this was turning out to be one of the worst. His wife, not exactly his paramour, had just told him that she was on her toes. That she was out the door. With the man who walked their dogs no less! This was a fucking joke! He had travelled to the other side of the globe for her. To Australia. Away from everything he had ever known or loved. So far away from Jo that he would never see or hear from her again.

Now he was really alone. His mum was dying from cancer and the family were too busy to concern themselves with his petty marriage break up. They were dealing with life and death, literally. He had told his Dad in one of their typically short two-minute phone calls of the events that had happened over the past couple of days.

Felicity, ironic concerning the circumstances, had decided she had an epiphany and was leaving the roost. They had been unhappy for some time but it was something he thought they could work out. But he wasn't too sure if he wanted to. He had left Portugal with her because it seemed like a reasonable solution to his problem. He wanted to get out of there and he did love her but not completely.

Her parents made it worse. Her Dad hated him and her Mum was indifferent. The lack of support for him over this whole sordid affair was more than enough proof for him. He had vowed his love for her but even at the altar knew he was betraying the promises he made before God and his friends. It wasn't that he would cheat on her. Far from it. He took his vows of fidelity very seriously but he loved another.

After several years she knew it. She felt guilty too. He had left all that he had loved behind for her or so she thought. He had supposedly given up his music and his club life for her. She thought he resented her for that but he never mentioned it. All he wanted now was the quiet life. The once exciting club owner/DJ had now become boring and staid. He knew it. She knew it.

The tepid passion that once existed had evaporated into the ether. She had not turned him on for years. But he was old school. He didn't think they should give up so easily. Mind you he didn't know she was pregnant to the guy from down the road.

She had suggested that he go back to London and this is what had elicited the angry response. He had never been so angry. In the space of five years so many things had been taken from him. Jo, his Mum and now Felicity. Ordinarily both her and her secret lover would be flying off some bridge somewhere with nothing but a scream on their lips to save them. That's why she was being so reasonable about things. She knew how dangerous the ground was on which she was treading. If Jimmy hadn't been so preoccupied with his own wife then she could well have disappeared by now. Anyway he was most probably glad the relationship was over.

They had never liked Felicity. They didn't forgive her for taking him away from the ones who loved him. She didn't understand that. He wasn't even living in the same country when they had left for Australia but it wasn't their decision and she reckoned that was what rankled with them.

He had tried to make it work but he knew deep down that she would never be enough. He went through the routine but his heart wasn't in it. But still he wasn't going to give up. He was a man's man after all. Stubborn. Unmoveable. Like a block of granite.

She had to be so careful now. If she was not frightened for herself, she was certainly frightened for her new love. He didn't understand the situation and she sure as hell couldn't tell him what was on the cards. Its why she didn't want a child with Tray. She didn't want them in her life. She didn't want a child of theirs having anything to do with the life he had known. She realised early on the control they had over him. She wanted no part of it and that was final.

Despite the anger he felt, he also felt a little relieved. He knew deep down she had met someone else. Someone who would maybe make her happy. He had been trapped. Inextricably contained in a marriage of lies. This was his way out. His path to adventure.

*

She stood beside his graveside. There were many mourners there who she did not know. Men in bulky misshapen suits. Women in sturdy peroxide beehives and garish makeup. Her mother was conspicuous by her absence. She had not returned from Portugal with them. Not tough enough to face the music. *'Traitor!'* She had betrayed her father's memory. Jo forced to live in misery in cold distant lonely London.

The cancer had materialised during the trial. Eighteen months they had taken to sentence him. Once the cancer had been diagnosed, they had given him bail. At least she got that time to spend with him. She had watched him go through the chemo. She had watched the ordeal crush him. They sentenced him to three years. He would never feel freedom again. He had managed to stay alive in that wretched place for almost another two years.

She had gone back to University and taken a masters in sociology. She had passed with flying colours and found she was in hot demand from a lot of overseas aid donors and NGO's. She turned them all down and resumed a career in marketing. She couldn't leave her poor Dad. He was all alone in that place and she couldn't bear that guilt. She'd already lost one man in her life and now she was going to lose number two. One was inextricably linked to the other but what other choice had there been? Her Dad had needed someone and her mother had bolted, leaving a hole that only she could fill.

As they lowered the coffin, Jimmy wheeled Sam to her side. He was a paraplegic now, the result of a skiing accident somewhere in Europe. Nobody said too much. People were watching. People were always watching. They were targets. Targeted by whom she did not know. She did not want to know.

"I am so sorry Jo".

"So am I Jimmy. He loved you, you know".

"I know Jo. But everything he did, he did for you"

She looked at Jimmy. She could see no trace of Tray in his father's face.

"Where is he Jimmy?"

"Who?"

"You know full well who Jimmy. There is nothing left to hold me here anymore. Where is he?"

"I can't tell you Jo. You know that",

"Jimmy. You'd better tell me. You owe me that much".

81

Sam looked embarrassed. Like a little boy once again seated next to his giant of a Dad.

"Jo, he's in Australia and you need to know something else", he paused not knowing how to deal with this.

"He's married".

"Liar!" The word ripped into the old man. He recoiled like he had been slapped in the face. She threw the single rose that she had been holding at his chest.

"Liar!" She bent forward as she yelled at him. Jimmy reached forward and grabbed her to his chest. He held her to him like his son had done so many times before. Tightly. Tenderly. Today she had finally lost all the men she had ever loved and Jimmy had been largely responsible for it. The mourners looked away. Embarrassed at her grief. Everyone let them have their moment of privacy. All except one.

A beady pair of eyes looked out from behind the chapel of rest.

'At last', he thought to himself. 'A connection'.

CHAPTER THREE

A Message To You Rudi

Snitch

He watched the barge slide gracefully through the turgid Thames. From his vantage point he could just catch sight of Tower Bridge and the Tower of London. He had paid big time for this place but he could afford it. Canary Wharf was filled full of white yuppies. Accountants, traders, lawyers, doctors. All the upper echelons of the white community were represented here. There were not many brothers. A few Pakis but not much colour at all.

Chante had suggested he move here. Make himsell look a little more respectable and a little less gangster. He liked it here but he missed the rough and tumble of the streets. He loved the hustle but it had been a long time since he'd hustled anything. He was big time now, or almost. He still didn't wield real power like the old school still did but he would one day. He just had to bide his time. He turned from the picture postcard tourist scene and sat at the modern glass desk.

It was smoked black, had a bank of telephones on top of it and a computer to the right. In front of him sat Don, the only white boy he had ever trusted. He slouched in his chair. He wore baggy stonewash jeans, an ice hockey top with the number 69 on it and white flat cap. His grandad would have called him a wigga. One of those white guys who wanted to be a nigger.

"If you want to come here Don, you need to blend in a little. Canary Wharf is a long way from Harlem".

"What's wrong with what I wear Rudi. I am truly fly".

"Don you are a yid from Chigwell. You are whiter than Celine Dion. Get off this black shit and act like the businessman you are".

"I thought it would make you feel more comfortable. Anyway it scares people and I'm all over that". Don shifted his weight in the chair. "Besides, it makes up for the fact that you've gone all Barry Manilow on me. Take a look at you. You look like you come out of an Argos catalogue. There's nothing ghetto about you at all".

Don was right. Rudi had left the neighbourhood far behind. Dressed in Armani slacks and a black v necked sweater from David, he was the epitome of new money. Classy yet understated. There was no indication of the business he was in. That he had learned from the movies. All the ostentatious displays of wealth had always landed the niggers in jail. If you tried to be white then people left you alone. No chains. No BMW with the UV underlights. In fact he didn't even own a car. He did everything by taxi. It meant he couldn't be bugged and was a lot harder to follow. Don said he was paranoid and Rudi said that was correct. Paranoid was good. Paranoid meant that nothing was gonna sneak up on you.

"Well what's the news Don. Any leads?"

"No Rudi. Nothing. No one knows. Its just like he vanished. Whoever he knows has gone through a lot of trouble to keep it quiet".

Rudi picked up a pen and tapped the table top with it. Then stopped abruptly. Chante would be well pissed off with him if he scratched it. He carefully placed it back in its holder.

"Don't worry Rudi. Something will come up. He can't hide forever."

"Well he's laid low for a bloody long time now. Wherever he is, he'd better not come back. He's a dead man. I don't care who his Dad knows. When Roger got killed, it all fucking changed".

Don wasn't too sure if Rudi's change of heart had been a wise one. It wasn't anyone's fault that Roger had been killed. It was an argument that had got out of control inside. His Dad knew people. They had nearly got the boy in Coventry but the police had finally got control of the area.

"I'm gonna get that bastard Don. No matter how long it takes. He's responsible for putting him there. If he had kept quiet, Roger would be sitting next to me right now".

Don nodded in agreement but deep down he knew Rudi was wrong. Roger would have been killed by some mug somewhere. He was too much of a hothead. Eventually he would have run into the wrong person. The fact that he had met his end in prison was just an unfortunate circumstance. He had been too obvious and Tray McCarthy had taken advantage of an opportunity presented to him. But revenge was a powerful emotion. Rudi had built a small empire on the back of it and he didn't see why he should change the habit.

Don had asked him once what he would do if he ever nailed him. Rudi had replied, 'I don't know. Haven't even thought about it'. Don thought then as he did now, what would happen to him if Rudi got nailed first.

Who Let The Cat Out?

"Well baby, you most probably wouldn't have had a bar of me when I was younger. I was an arrogant fucker. Thought I could do anything. Invincible I was".

"Not much has changed there baby".

"Oi", he flicked a random pillow in her direction. "I'm trying to share here. Don't have a go!".

Lizzy wasn't too sure if he was serious. She never was. He was so hard to read. She looked over at him and saw a smile spread across his face. Tray put his hands behind his head and interlocked his fingers. He was staring at a fixed point on the ceiling. He didn't turn to look at Lizzy. If he had, he may have stopped sharing.

One of her huge milky breasts had escaped the confines of her neglige and hung like a mini torpedo. Tray loved breasts and anytime Lizzy had them out meant that he had to worship them like they were the last pair he was to ever see. She casually pulled her neglige up to cover herself. Not because she was embarrased by them. Far from it. She loved showing herself off for him but now was not the time. Maybe once he had finished his story.

"I ran with some right cowboys back then baby. We were on the verge of making some big waves in the area. Me Dad had started storing pills for some very heavy guys from the old days. I had pinched a couple of thousand and had built up enough of a float to start my own business. I organised my own supply lines and made sure Dad never found out".

Lizzy had been surprised by this. Tray had always been a massive consumer but he had always been on the other side of the ledger when it came to drugs. He may have stockpiled a couple for his mates and passed them on at zero profit but he had never dealt in the true sense of the word.

"I was becoming a 'playa' as they say these days. And I was beoming greedy too. We were having to sell the pills out of the back of a van at raves. Things were getting too risky. We could have been caught so many times but we were lucky".

He slipped out from under the sheets.

"Where are you going baby?"

"Just for a piss honey".

She hoped he wasn't going for a smoke. She hated him smoking and had nearly not gone out with him because of it. But as she watched his bare white arse giggle out of the bedroom she remembered why she did. He may have been fat but she didn't see it. She found him incredibly sexy. It was just something about the way he moved. He was happy with the skin he was in and if you didn't like it, stiff shit. Tray was Tray. Unique, one of a kind. A true original

She heard him as he pissed in the pan. He never closed the door except if he was having a number two. She constantly complained about the open door policy and the fact that he always left the toilet seat up. She hated always having to put the seat down. He countered it by saying why couldn't she leave the seat up. It wasn't a hard thing and she guessed he sort of had a point if you thought about it. But she wanted to see if he would change for her. Up until now he hadn't. He had already admitted he was arrogant and pigheaded more than once, so what was she really expecting?

He ran back into the bedroom and dove under the sheets. It was April and it was getting a bit nippy around the cockles. Tray's house was in a narrow valley in the Sutherland Shire. God's house they called it. Everyone else in Sydney called it the insula peninsula and Woronora was known amongst the Shire residents as the arse crack of the Shire. To Tray, it was the slice of paradise that he had been looking for.

He had a quaint three bedroom, fifties style cottage one street back from the Woronora River. The entire village was its own cul de sac. One way in and one way out. Most of all it was a community. Tray needed to feel that sense of belonging. It was something he had searched for when he had left Portugal. He had found that same quaint spirit in Woronora and it felt like home for him. He had sold up all his assets back home to buy it with his ex-wife, so there was nothing left back for him in the UK except family. So his piece of paradise had cost him more than money. It was the knife that severed his ties to his homeland. It was his future and his past. A huge millstone since his wife had left but one he stubbornly wore around his neck. It was the price he had to pay for the deeds of his past and he wasn't about to let it go.

Paradise came at a price though. It suffered from negative temperature inversion. It meant that in the summer it trapped heat in and was 'bastard fucking hot' as he liked to put it. In the Winter, the valley was so narrow that it got the sun late and it left early. That meant it was 'brass monkey weather'. The entire phrase, like so much of what Tray said, was cut short. A typical Cockney morph of something more substantial. Freezing was what it really meant.

Australian houses never seemed to be built for the cold. It always appeared to come as a surprise when Winter brought down its hammer. No one ever had enough warm clothes and the houses just let the chill in. Most houses felt like you were living in an igloo. Oil fired heaters were the order of the day but just like the houses let the cold in, the heat just escaped to the outside world, leaving the occupants to constantly rug up against the cold. Sometimes in the Winter Tray had said that he had had to scrape the ice off his windscreen in the morning, Now that was cold in anybody's language.

He pulled the duvet up to his chin and let the electric blanket do its work. He went 'brrrr' as the heat took hold. She always laughed at this as it would only be five minutes before he started to feel too warm and would have to dangle a leg out of the bed. She could never understand that.

"So you were a bad ass", she purred as she swung a leg over him. Resting her pussy against his thigh. He went to turn towards her. She felt him go hard but she pushed him back down.

"Not yet honey. Tonight I'm going to learn about you and you might get a naughty if you tell me everything".

"What about a naughty first?"

"What and have you fall asleep? No way".

"Now you know that's your bag baby. Ain't no doubt about that!"

He pinched her. She squrimed. He was right though. They had a complete role reversal from the normal relationship. When he made her cum, the release was so all encompassing that the energy just drained from her body. Many a time she had fallen into a deep slumber without him gettiing to the vinegar strokes. She hated herself for doing it and she knew he secretly resented her for it. But what could she do? He shouldn't be such a good lover.

"Now spill the beans big boy or you're getting no action at all tonight".

He laid back calmly and once again put his hands behind his head. He closed his eyes and transported himself back to that time.

"Sam wasn't around. He was off pioneering this new sport called snowboarding. I stayed behind, bought my own place, worked in the bank and played tunes at the weekend. When we started dealing pills, the money started rolling in but it wasn't enough and like I said, [t was getting too risky. The real money-earner was in the clubs. If you could control a club then you could make a fortune. You had a captive consumer 'cos they couldn't go anywhere else and you could charge what you liked".

He rubbed his nose with his right hand.

"Anyway there was this club in London where this coloured crew used to run the drugs. The owner had no choice. If he didn't let them do it, they would shoot the place up and he would be out of business. The drug dealers would always find an outlet for their pills".

"So I was there one night when I popped outside for some air. As I went outside, I saw the guy who controlled the drug trade murder another black guy".

"Jesus!" She stared at Tray. He was stock still. Only his lips were moving.

"He was a really tall Rastafarian. He had just run this black kid through with a machete. I saw him wipe the blade on his cheeks and then as he died, pick him up and carry him off down the street".

Lizzy said nothing.

"I saw an opportunity right then and there. If I suddenly became an upstanding citizen, I could grass this bloke up and free the club of this element. Then I could muscle in on their business and even give the owner a slice of the pie".

"So I snitched. I gave this guy up not knowing who or what he was. I went to the police and as cool as mustard, I grassed him up. Once the process had started, it couldn't be stopped. Once the pigs had identified him, the race was on to get him inside. I hadn't told my Dad until it was well on its way. And believe me he was well pissed".

"This guys name was Roger Stone. He was the brother of a high up Yardie called Rudi. Rudi had power. Not absolute but power nonetheless. He could pull strings but not that many. My Dad however is very well connected. I never knew how much but now I know".

"Rudi wanted me gone, especially when Roger got fifteen years. But the real headbangers, the ones who really control what goes on, they worked out a deal. They pointed out that Roger had shit on his own doorstep and they weren't happy about it. But they were also not happpy that I had turned into a grass".

"They never found out about me availing myself of some of their pills but they found out I had been trading without paying a tribute and that pissed them off even more. The only thing that saved me from a knock was the fact that I was Jimmy's son. The big boys wielded enough power to warn Rudi off. They said Roger would be looked after in prison and that Rudi would receive a large number of pills gratis. My attempted foray into club dealership was nipped in the bud and I was ordered to stay low".

"That was the second favour that Dad had to call in to save my arse and it would be the last. I was told to keep my nose clean and stop causing problems for the big guys. I thought Dad was gonna kill me but he didn't mention it again and never told Mum. She was just proud that I had put a murderer away".

Lizzy hadn't expected any of this. Her head swam with what he was saying.

"It didn't stop there. Everything was sweet. I sort of dropped out of the scene and concentrated on working in the bank. But then something went wrong. The guys who were looking out for Roger inside had fucked up and somehow Roger was killed. I don't know the details. All I know is Rudi went insane with rage. He blamed me personally. He held me responsible. He thought we'd pulled his brother's protection."

"We hadn't. Honestly. He had upset the wrong person and he paid the price. We couldn't be everywhere all the time. So word got out that he had put a hit on me".

"No baby. You're kidding!"

"No I am not. Please baby don't interrupt. I got to do this in one go or I am not gonna get it out at all".

"Okay honey". She tried to touch his face but he pushed the hand away.

"I laid really, really low. Took some stress leave from work. Wasn't unusual considering the type of work I did and hid up in Coventry. Two of my mates owned a pub in a government housing area and I starrted to spin some tunes down there under a different name. But I should've known".

"I was starting to get known as a fucking good DJ and someone must have blabbed. Coventry is a really black area and this pub was on the middle of an estate. The police called it a riot but they were after me. About that there was no doubt. For four days they surrounded that pub before the police got it under control".

"They threw Molotov cocktails, fence palings. At one point they even fired shots into the place. But Tom and Brummie stood firm. Staunch friends baby. They could have easily given me up and saved themselves a world of heartache. But they didn't. They saved me from a fate worse than death. These guys who were trying to take the pub even crucified a copper on a building opposite. It was fucking unbeleivable. All we could do was barricade the doors and windows and pray that the police would eventually put it to bed".

"That they did and I was whisked back to London in the back of a van and dropped off at Mum and Dad's place. I had had enough. It was becoming very scarey. I really wanted out. I had become a liability to everyone I knew".

"Finally Rudi told those that mattered that all bets were off. If he found me, I was dead. The same went for my brother and Sam had done nothing. Dad was untouchable. Rudi wouldn't dare take that bear on but I was a different matter. Apparently Dad offered Rudi the world to back down but he was mad for me. There was nothing but mine or Sam's death that would satisfy him. He wanted a good old fashioned eye for any eye. My Dad, for the first time in his life, was powerless and that really pissed him off. He was forbidden to take Rudi down. No one wanted a war".

Lizzy got out of bed and walked to the door.

"What're you doing baby? There's more".

"I'm going for a cuppa. I need one".

"Scared baby?"

"You know honey. Before I was scared because I didn't know who you were. Now I'm scared cos I know who you are!"

"Baby, you wanted to know".

"You could've fucking lied!"

"Yeah I suppose I could have. But you need to know who you're sleeping with and I needed to tell you. No secrets remember?"

She nodded. Holy shit, she was fucking Al Capone's son!

East Side Story

They had gotten pretty close in Coventry. It had only been a couple of months after Roger had been killed. They had holed McCarthy up in some pub on a council estate. The brothers down there just couldn't get inside. The police had known what was going on but the rest of the estate hadn't. So near to getting that bastard and yet he had squirmed away. The fucking blood clot. They had wanted him so bad.

Roger had been a good general. A little too ready to go for the dramatic but he was his brother and he was given a bit of leeway. He had stepped over the mark in Mile End but there was no need for McCarthy to send him down the river.

Like Don had told him before. He saw an opportunity but he had picked the wrong horse. That had cost McCarthy's Dad plenty of buckshish and Rudi hadn't wanted to take the offer but Charlie had insisted. They would be able to get him out earlier than the fifteen years he got sentenced to and Charlie had offered protection inside.

Charlie was old school. A little ferret of a man. He had run with the Krays and when they got sent down he had taken over the reins. They had run protection rackets, clubs, illegal gambling dens and dabbled in the drug trade. Then as the seventies grew into the eighties, the drug trade grew. Unlike in Manchester, there were no ice wars. The territory had been carved up years ago.

The legacy of the Krays was that they didn't like drugs. The big boys stayed out of the direct trade as much as possible. They would be the go-between guys. They would make sure that the stuff got in through their contacts in the docks and the airport. They had it all sewn up. The Essex boys looked after the coastline drop offs. Most of the drugs came through from Amsterdam. Fast boats would rush the North Sea when weather permitted and drop the gear off at some deserted cove. Like smugglers of old, the North Sea was a buzz with illegal traffic.

Either that, or it would come through Tilbury in containers. Customs wouldn't even check it. The gear would be off loaded before anyone had a chance to see it and it made its way out of the facility in a variety of dockers' bags and cars.

Holland was full of chemists, MDMA and pill presses. There was a constant supply of manufacturers willing to take the big risks. The hash also made it in through Amsterdam via the Middle East. Either that or through Sicily, Portugal or Marseille. Truckers were also now making a fortune ferrying smack through the old Eastern Bloc countries.

The ex-communist countries weighed in with endless supplies of amphetamines and steroids. The systematic doping of elite athletes during the cold war had led to a professional network of qualified chemists who were capable of making a plethora of synthetic drugs. The headlong rush for money after the Berlin Wall collapsed led to a massive influx of this sort of drug. Pharmacologists, who now couldn't afford to buy bread, became chemists for hire. What happened to the people who became addicted to their drugs was irrelevant. The chemists were just looking to survive. The nurturing hand of the State had gone and they quickly learned how to adapt to private enterprise.

The Hong Kong Chinese and the Triads controlled smack. This was something that the white boys stayed away from. Smack turned the neighbourhoods to shit. No one likes to see skanky, drawn-out junkies on their back door. But the demand was there and the Chinese made it freely available. Rudi thought sometimes that it was why coke was so cheap in London. The general public seemed to tolerate people on coke rather than low lifes on smack or ice. Coke just seemed to be a little more exotic and exciting. The drug of the glamorous rather than the drug of the gutter.

He wondered if the players made it that way so that they kept the junk out of their own back yard. No need to shit in your own garden. If you can keep coke cheap then everyone was happy. Rudi was on heavy notice about how to cut his coke and how much to charge. Charlie's crew were very specific about that.

However it came in, Charlie controlled it. His organization then passed it down the line to distributors like Rudi who in turn farmed it out to the dealers' dealers. Then it would make its way onto the streets to Joe Public.

Pills were the mainstay of suburbia and coke was the habit of the social elite. Coke in particular had become a huge deal. London was awash with it at prices that were phenomenaly low. That was dealt direct through South America and Europe. It then came in through similar routes as everything else.

The Colombian cartels were no figment of the Miami Vice imagination. They were very real. They were also very frightening. They had no fear or respect for the extended family. They earned more money than some small countries and they had the influence to destroy many an organization. They even had their own banks. The collapse of BCCI had highlighted that particular penchant for high finance.

They frightened many they dealt with. If you crossed them, your entire family would disappear and they would suffer immeasurable pain before they departed this earth. They fronted all the transport costs. It was like DHL for coke. All you had to do was pay them the money. If the drugs got busted en route, you didn't have to pay. You only took responsibility for them once you took delivery. But the amounts of money that was involved were mind-boggling.

Rudi was glad he wasn't at the pointy end of things. Being a distributor suited him just fine. He bought from Charlie and tried to keep him at arm's length. He was thinking about switching supplies from some upstarts who had muscled in from up North. They had lasted about a month. The Northerners had ended up being hung from London Bridge with their guts hanging out. Word is that they were left to die like that and strung up only after they had watched their guts slip out onto the floor in front of them, much like their own lives. They were found on a Sunday morning by a Korean tourist and the news made the front pages all over the world.

That was enough of a warning to let everyone know where their loyalties lay. Rudi was glad he hadn't got in to bed with them. Charlie was just a necessary evil that had to be tolerated. He didn't want to have a shot at the title. He was busy just keeping his own territory under wraps. That was what Roger's incident had been about.

Rudi had told Roger that it was all about location, location, location. Just like the real estate industry. The better the location, the better the profits. He remembered telling him, 'Protect your real estate. Its your kingdom. Never let anyone undermine your territory. If people detect that you are weak, they will take it from you'.

Roger had taken that literally. When a young buck from a rival gang took a shot at taking over the drug trade at 'Dukes', Roger had killed him. Right at the entrance. He hadn't been subtle about it. Everyone knew who had done it. It was a display of arrogance and it was sloppy. It went against everything Rudi had told Roger.

McCarthy had seen it. Wrong place at the wrong time. He had also seen an opening. With Roger out of the way, he saw his chance to get some real estate of his own. So he did something that people from his world never did. He grassed. He told who had executed the kid and made plans for the future.

Roger had been picked up almost immediately. It was hardly like he was unknown to the local community. He had been ruthless in his enforcement of Yardie law and there were many who would be glad to see him gone. With Roger inside, the owner was happy to spill the beans on the drugs that were flooding through the club. Roger's fate was sealed.

Initially no one knew who had grassed up Roger. The police had suppressed McCarthy's identity to protect him from revenge attacks. Apparently this had been a prerequisite for McCarthy coming in. But Rudi was resourceful. He made use of his contacts. It had cost him a ridiculous amount of money but he eventually got a name. Tray McCarthy.

He had gone to Charlie with the name. It was rare that Charlie and Rudi met face to face. Both were careful not to be seen together. Charlie had baulked at the name. He told Rudi a hit wasn't possible. Rudi wanted to know why. The little weasel refused to tell him. Rudi couldn't understand what the problem was. He had never heard of this McCarthy or anyone associated with him. He told Don to investigate the matter. When he got back Rudi was so shocked, Don reckoned he went a whiter shade of pale.

This McCarthy was the son of Jimmy McCarthy, a name that was also unknown to Rudi. Don pointed out to him that Rudi did not mix in white circles and that he was first generation West Indian/English.

"You weren't here in the old days Rudi. When the Krays ran things. When the East End was run as tight as a drum. This McCarthy grew up on those streets. Rumour has it that old man McCarthy knocked one of the Krays out over a bird. He is respected Rudi. He's not in the game but he knows the game like no other".

"Because of his surname, the IRA thought he might be sympathetic to the cause. Apparently he or someone close to him sent the messengers head back in a box. They were warned off and they stayed away. Its not every day that the IRA back down from something like that. But they did. He is untouchable Rudi and so is his family".

"But why Rudi? What makes this Tray McCarthy so special? Charlie fair shit himself when I showed him the name"

"Because Rudi, he is Charlie's Godson".

"Fuck me! Are you sure?"

"As sure as I am that you are black. Despite what he's done, you can't touch him. But you can use it. Tell Charlie there's a price to pay. McCarthy is living on past glories anyway. You'll be able to make something out of this. A lot of money at the very least".

That was ten years ago and the fucker still wasn't dead. They had been close to finding him once but the trail had gone cold. They missed him by a couple of weeks in Portugal but now he had disappeared for a long, long time. He had almost given up but he was determined and tenacious.

He had made a promise at his brother's burial. Tray McCarthy would pay for his mistake. Jimmy McCarthy couldn't protect him now and Charlie, well for Charlie it was just business.

One Foot In The Grave

As she pottered around in the kitchen, Tray remembered what had gone on that Easter ten years ago. He had been spirited back from Coventry in an anonymous Toyota panel van. They had gone straight to the family home.

Jimmy had moved up in the world. He had bought a six hundred year-old cottage in Essex. In a small hamlet of six, the cottage was surrounded by fields on three sides and the old manor house on the other. It had a hundred metre driveway and sat on a five-acre patch of dirt that was worth a million plus. This had been Betty's dream and Jimmy had been happy to oblige. It had a massive courtyard surrounded by barns on three sides. It had another huge double garage out the back that Betty had converted into a summerhouse. Next to it were some more barns in which Jimmy used to store the better items of scrap he collected.

The view from the back of the summerhouse was uninterrupted for some three miles. Rolling farmland which was either bereft of crops for six months of the year or covered with wheat or rapeseed for the rest of the year. It was idyllic. Betty's friends now belonged to flower arranging groups or the local wilderness protection society. Her world was perfect but today it was all falling apart. Her boys. Her loving boys. What was going to happen to them?

*

As Tray stepped out of the van he spotted the bodyguards immediately. Big men with short haircuts. The customary ray-bans covering their eyes even though the weather was cold and dreary. Next to Jimmy's Rolls was a huge Bentley. It oozed luxury. It also belonged to his Uncle Charlie. His Mum ran out to greet him along the gravel driveway as the van did a u-turn and pulled back out on to the road.

"Tray!"

She cuddled him and held him close as Jimmy came out from a concealed doorway in the summerhouse.

"Tray!"

"Dad"

"You alright son?"

"Yes Dad. Not bad".

"Well come 'ere you bloody idiot. There's someone here who wants to see you".

"Jimmy! Let him come inside and rest a little. He looks exhausted". Betty gave her husband a pleading look.

"Betty. We haven't got much time. I'll send him in when its done. Come on Tray. Let's get this over".

Jimmy never showed much emotion. A by-product of his childhood. He put his arm around his son's shoulders and steered him towards the summerhouse.

*

Charlie stood up to greet his Godson. He hadn't seen him for some time and the boy had turned into a man. Not strikingly handsome but big and broad with a shock of blonde hair. He had his mother's smile and her heart. His body though was McCarthy through and through. He would have made an awesome prop forward if he hadn't smashed his shoulder.

"Alo Tray".

"Alo Uncle Charlie"

Tray nervously took Charlies outstretched hand. Charlie was small and diminutive. Tray, not an overly tall guy, towered over him. Tray had known this man his whole life. He was an import/exporter and was the only man that Mum tolerated from the old days. Charlie's wife and Mum had been good friends way back when until she had died in a car accident at Whipps Cross. Tray had never known her but Charlie and Dad had remained close all their lives.

Jimmy had asked Charlie to be Tray's Godfather. A responsibility Charlie took seriously. Without Tray knowing it, he had benefited from the covering protection of London's most lethal gangster. Charlie had remained in relative obscurity his whole life. He managed an organization like a blue chip company. His life was more than comfortable and he was at the top of the tree. Of course all of this was unknown to Tray. To him Charlie was just his Godfather who had bounced him on his knee when he was a kid and given him a five star holiday to the South of France for his eighteenth birthday.

"Sit down Tray".

All three took an armchair as Betty magically appeared with a tray of tea and biscuits.

"I'll leave you boys with it then. You play nice now"

"Course Betty. Its all good. Don't you worry".

Betty walked out knowing everything was far from good. Oh why did Tray have to go and do that? He had fucked everything. Oh now she was swearing in her own head. She secretly cursed Tray for doing that.

"Tray?"

"Yes Charlie".

"I'm going to tell you a story. You are going to listen and then you are going to do what I say".

"Yes Uncle Charlie".

"I am going to tell you a story about your Dad. Something very few people know and something you are never going to repeat. Got it?"

"Yes Uncle Charlie".

Charlie leant forward, performed the niceties of pouring the tea and sat back in the armchair. He looked at his Godson. He was lost now. At least to his family here. But Charlie had a solution. Not ideal but at least he would be alive.

"I met your Dad during National Service. Us Cockneys stuck together. Your Dad worked in the laundry in Egypt. He had a top racket going. He would steam press all the soldiers' uniforms when they were going on leave and charge for it. He made a small fortune from it. He had more money when he came out than when he went in".

Tray looked across at his Dad. Jimmy would not meet his son's gaze. He was afraid of what Charlie was going to reveal but it was about time. Little did he know that Micky had already spilt the beans to a certain extent.

"Anyways, me and your Dad picked up some work in the East End working for the Krays once we were demobbed. All a bit hooky. Stand over men mainly. We were making plenty of cash. We would get out on the piss and hook up with the birds. We got plenty of action I can tell you".

Charlie smiled at Jimmy. Jimmy just looked meekly back.

"One night we were drinking in the Greene Man in Bethnal Green when Reggie Kray walked in with this absolute bombshell on his arm. She was blonde with a pair of legs that Rita Hayworth would have been proud of".

Tray looked puzzled. He had no idea where this story was going and who the fuck was Rita Hayworth?

"Look Tray, concentrate! We haven't got much time!"

Tray snapped back to attention.

"Reg is a bit sideways and starts slagging this girl off at the bar 'cos she ain't putting out. Anyway your Dad takes exception to this and tells Reg to behave. That 'It ain't no way to treat a lady' or something like that. Reg didn't take this too well and he took a swing at your Dad".

Charlie paused and sipped his tea.

"Your Dad is very useful with his fists. He can really throw 'em. Reg didn't fair too well. He copped a couple of rights and lefts and was knocked the fuck out in about thirty seconds. He just lay there on the floor. Jimmy apologised to the girl, offered her his arm and took her home. He had to step over Reg to walk out of the place".

"The next day Ron paid me a visit. He asked me what had happened. I told him. I said Reg had it coming. That he had disrespected the girl. Ron said fair enough and they let Jimmy go. He never worked for them again. But you know who that girl was?"

Tray shook his head.

"Your Mum, Betty".

"What? You told me you met her at the Queen Elizabeth?"

"That was our first date Tray. But that's how we met!"

"You knocked out Reggie Kray and lived to tell the tale!"

"Yes son, mostly thanks to your Uncle Charlie here".

Charlie picked up the story once again.

"So your Dad was out but I stayed in. I worked my way up through the ranks until I became their right-hand man. I did some nasty shit for those two poofters but I did it 'cos I knew they would eventually fuck up. That they did. They knocked one too many people and 'Slipper of The Yard' finally got enough on them to put 'em away for life".

"That left a gaping hole in the organization. A hole that I filled".

Charlie let the news sink in. Tray understood. His Uncle Charlie was the man.

"I run it all Tray. I know where all the bodies are buried. I have it all. I took the business back underground. I didn't run it like the twins. I kept things very quiet. That it is until now".

"Your little act of betrayal cost me plenty and meant that I had to drag your Dad back in. We kept those black bastards at bay when that Roger went down. I promised them we could look after him but some hothead didn't listen and that Roger got necked. His brother runs the yardies as you know. Well, he has gone fucking nuts. He holds me personally responsible and now you are a target".

"You don't fucking say Charlie. Do you know what happened in Coventry?"

"Course I do. It was all over the news. And that's the point Tray. You are too hot. Always will be. Someone will always recognise you somewhere. You got a little too famous didn't you? Fucking DJ! Why couldn't you just have stayed in banking and become a grey man".

"Cos I ain't no grey man Charlie. You know that!"

"Yes, can't help good genes I s'pose," he paused. "I can't keep you safe here. Rudi has vowed revenge. Your Dad is safe. No one will ever touch him. They know that they would be wiped out if they ever did that. But you and your brother are at risk. I can't look after you here. Not after what you did. So you've got to go away".

"What?"

"If Rudi gets taken down for what you did, there will be all out fucking war. No one wants that. There are literally fucking hundreds of millions of pounds at stake and your relationship to me can't stand in the way of that. The knock-on effect to the drug economy would be nothing like that stock market crash you were involved in. It would be bigger and far-reaching. Everything would be affected. You would be starting something that the Triads, the Colombians, the Russians, you name it, would all be pissed off about with me being slap bang in the middle. Your life is just a drop in the ocean compared to that. I can't protect you if that goes down. And if you or Sam got knocked, I would never be able to live with myself or look Jimmy in the face".

Tray never had a clue about any of this. Charlie had played everything so close to his chest. He clicked his knuckles and looked at his Dad. He was about to say something when Jimmy interrupted.

"Listen to your Uncle, Tray!" Jimmy couldn't look at his son. His heart was literally breaking.

"So what gives Charlie? Can't Dad pay him off like before?"

"Not this time Tray. I have offered him more money than I have offered any man before. He staunchly refuses to take anything. He sees you as taking a son away from his mother and you are going to have to pay the blood debt".

Tray shivered. He knew the Yardie reputation. They would not stop until you were fucking down in the ground. What the fuck was he going to do?

"So Charlie, what are my options?"

"You only got one son. I'm sending you to a little village in the Algarve".

"Fuckin Portugal! What am I going to do down there?"

"Fucking live Tray. That's what. I've got friends down there. You will be safe as long as you keep your head down. My mate's got a club down there that you can help run but don't let it get out of control. Keep it cool Tray. Sam is already down that way. You're gonna have to calm him down because he ain't happy about it and its all your fault".

"Its quiet. Its out of the way and most importantly the jigaboos don't go there for their holidays. No one will get wind of you unless you kick up a fuss"

104

"When am I going?"

"You're booked on a plane for first thing in the morning. Tomorrow you will be on a beach in the Algarve".

Charlie sat back.

"Fuckin what about Mum and Dad? What about me mates?"

"No contact Tray. Nothing. Now and again your Dad will get word to you. But besides that, no contact with the manor or your past life. I mean it Tray. Nothing!"

"I may as well be dead," said Tray

"Here you go Tray. Nice cup of Tetley's"

Lizzy's voice shook him from his memories.

"So do want to hear the rest baby? It doesn't get much better.

"How could it get any worse?"

Fuck me, he thought, she didn't know the half of it.

Crazy

She put her tea down on the bedside table and snuck into bed. She couldn't wait to tell her sister this. She couldn't believe what he had told her. It scared her and excited her at the same time. Her man was connected. It made her feel very horny indeed.

"You know baby, you can't tell anyone about this. No one. Not even Tracey".

"You're kidding Tray. I've got to tell someone".

"No baby. No one. Not a living soul. If you do, I'm out of here and gone. Out of the country to somewhere else. Do you want that?"

"No Tray. Course not. I promise. My lips are sealed".

"Not too sealed baby. I want to stick something in there later on".

"Oh you dirty bastard!"

She kicked him under the covers.

"Ow!"

"Now let's continue life according to Tray".

*

"So no one wanted a war and it was arranged that I would disappear". He saw no need to mention Charlie. He didn't need to tell her everything.

"I was sent to Portugal. Out of the way and off the reservation. Sam was down there with me. He was none too happy. He couldn't go home and he was well pissed off. But he soon brightened up when he found out how easy the pussy was. He had a different bird every week. He was in pussy heaven. But he started to skitz out when the summer finished. He managed to do a repeat season in Andorra without anyone finding out. He worked for John Major's brother in a club, so he was heavily protected".

"Who's John Major?"

"The English Prime Minister dummy".

"What? The ridgy didge English Prime Minister?"

"Yes baby. The one and only. So they had secret service sort of shit going on there. They didn't need anyone taking down the Prime Minister's brother, so he was surrounded by protection. That made Sam feel a lot better about things and Dad was happy that it was a very quiet resort".

"Anyway, he came back to Portugal and played up with me but by the end of the Summer he really wanted to go home. So we came up with a plan. We reckoned if Sam had a serious accident and came back a paraplegic then no one would touch him. I mean who would kill a cripple? It was a risk but we hoped it would work".

"So we called home and made out that Sam had a ski accident in Europe somewhere and couldn't walk anymore. My Uncle Bert came over to pick him up. They drove over to Greece in a campervan and then took a flight back from Athens to Gatwick. They were met by a private ambulance and taken straight to a private hospital. Everyone made sure that news got out that Sam was an invalid and would never walk again."

"But he's alright now babe, right?"

"He was always alright baby. We just had to convince Rudi that he was disabled and it seemed to work. No one is going to take out someone who is stuck in a wheelchair. That would be pretty low. That's Colombian sort of shit. Anyway Rudi had sort of mellowed on the idea of taking out Sam. He was in no way connected to what I had done and Dad's connections had made a deal over that. Sam still had to keep up the pretence whilst still in public but at least he wouldn't get knocked. At least Mum had one of their sons back."

"That all seems a bit too easy Tray. You sure you're not missing something out?"

"Believe me Liz, it was far from easy. Someone had to give up some territory and a lot of money changed hands. That was twice Dad had to pay this black cunt off. There wasn't going to be a third time. And all that it meant was that Rudi became more powerful and I was becoming increasingly paranoid. Combined with Jo leaving, I got really lonely. Contemplated some really stupid stuff a number of times."

Her antennae were up.

"Who's this Jo?" She had never heard this name before. Who was she?

"No one special. Just a girl I'd hooked up with".

She knew he was lying. His lips pursed when he was telling a whopper. It was the only facial impression she could read. It was a good one but that was about all she wrote on that subject. She knew when he was lying but she couldn't get him to tell the truth if her life depended on it.

"Yeah so what happened then?"

"I met Felicity, that's what happened and the rest they say is history".

"Well I thought you said it got worse".

"Well if you call making your brother pretend he was a cripple. Make him spend six months in a rehab clinic. Run to the other side of the world with someone you don't really love. Lie to her, lie to everyone back home and then to top it all, not even be able to go home when Mum was sick. Not even be able to go home for the funeral. How bad a son and a brother could I possibly be? I made one mistake and everyone I have ever known has paid the price for it".

"Oh Tray, its not your fault"

"Bullshit Liz. I am the only one to blame".

She could taste the guilt in his heart. How wrong could this be? He was guilty over everything that had happened to everyone else. He had let the world down and he had been carrying that around for the past 10 years. That and the fear that he would be killed. How can a man live like that? Everyone makes choices. The people around Tray had made theirs. Tray couldn't see that. He felt he hadn't given them a choice. She held him to her as he cried. He sobbed like a baby. His heart was so broken. So incredibly battered. This was not fair.

He had been living half a life for more than a decade. Afraid to live the life he should be leading. Afraid to take a chance. Afraid to be all that he could be. No wonder he was sad. This would have been killing him. How could she fix this for him? How could she bring him out of the wilderness? She couldn't imagine how he had survived this long. She would put him back together but first she was gonna fuck him into happiness. Tonight he would go to sleep first.

CHAPTER FOUR

Leaving On A Jet Plane

Dusty

She sat under the shade of a very old tree. Its branches stretched out overhead like a network of broken fingers. She let the strange music wash over her. The tree stood to the left of the dry, dusty square. To the side of her sat trestle tables decked with exotic fruits and pastries. A goat kid was being roasted on a spit, the carcass continually turned by a boy enveloped in a traditional white gown. He had a small white hat atop his head and was obviously concentrating on his task as the smoke stung his eyes.

On the other side of the square, a group of boys, also in traditional dress, were running around after a half deflated football. The square was surrounded on all sides by dilapidated mud brick dwellings. They were crumbling at the edges but were the homes for large extended families. As she looked up on to the surrounding hills, she could see herds of goats being cared for by more small children. She knew if the music hadn't been there, that she would be able to hear their distant bells as the animals searched for their sporadic feed.

Fatima was with Ali. In traditional bridal wear, face covered to protect the men from her beauty, she danced with joy. The women warbled their joyous cries and the men slapped each other on the back as the great day began to turn into night. She watched her friend. She didn't really quite understand how she could go from an educated woman to this subservient bride but she was happy for her. Ali was a good man and most of all, they loved each other.

She had always intended to come here, even though she knew that at some point she would become melancholic. This was her friends' day after all. But things like this were a constant reminder of what she had lost.

Her mind wandered as the dancers moved in faster and faster circles, whirling around at fever pitch. She was hiding here. She knew it. Hiding from the world that had caused her so much pain. There was danger here for sure but that gave her a thrill. She felt alive here.

After the funeral, she had gone home completely devastated. Jimmy had told her that Tray was married. How could he? She had always assumed that Tray would wait for her. But in reality, how could he?

She had been away from him for three years. He wasn't able to talk to her. It was too dangerous for him, her and her Dad. She had always believed that one day they would be together but Tray had read the situation different.

She knew that Sam had come back a supposed cripple. Word was that he would never walk again. Poor Betty. Her family had been decimated because of Tray's mistake and he knew it would haunt her until her dying days.

Jo had not got in contact with the family. She couldn't put Tray in that sort of danger. They couldn't have anyone make the connection. That had hurt her but they had their own problems. Apparently it had taken a good couple of years for Sam to come good. In that time he had met a nurse who had cared for him. He worked in the family business so that Jimmy could keep an eye on him.

She never heard anything much about him. He didn't go out. He didn't mix in any of the old circles. She had driven past the shop a couple of times and saw him seated next to the washing machines and ovens outside. How she wished she had the guts to rush out of the car and ask him what had happened to Tray.

But she kept her word. She hadn't seen Jimmy and Sam again until that day at the cemetery. Sam had looked embarrassed when he saw her. There was genuine grief in both the men's hearts and there was something else. She didn't see it then but after, in the confines of her little flat, she recognised it as guilt.

That evening, as she had sat all alone with just a bottle of merlot for company, she went through the old job offers she had received. She poured over them, concentrating on the ones that were furthest away. The next day she would see if they had anything for her. It was time that Jo Flint took control of her life.

But she hadn't really. Everywhere she went, every man she met, reminded her of him. She just hadn't found anyone who matched his heart. It was causing her some concern. She hoped she wasn't going to end up an old maid. She wondered what he was doing now. If he had kids. What kind of man he had become? Was he still the best man she had ever known?

She sipped the grape juice in her hand and closed her eyes. A stiff evening breeze coming down from the mountains was replacing the dwindling sun. She shivered a little and began to doze off.

She woke with a start as a hand grabbed her shoulder. It was Fatima. Her eyes the only visible part of her face that Jo could see.

"So Jo Flint! You like Afghanistan now?"

Its My Birthday

He sent out the text message.

'Bro. Its 106km to Pennant Hills. Billy Whiz is running for the door and I have 72 hours to carve up my birthday. No stopping til 2125. Did you get the tickets for Bolivia?'

Daz laughed out loud. Only his mate could do this. The message translated as; 'I have 106 pills for my birthday, heaps of speed. Did you pick up any coke?' Well of course he did. It was his best mate's birthday after all. Fucking Peanut!

Tray was an underground legend round here. Older to know better, his capacity to consume was more than unbelievable. It surpassed all normal human conditioning. This weekend would be massive. Daz was just hoping they would all be alive come Monday.

The bar owners would be notified that Tray was on a mission. People would turn a blind eye. After all Tray was never any trouble. He didn't drink. He didn't get violent. All that people were really concerned with was that the pigs didn't pick him up for his eyes rolling around in the back of his head. A constant worry where Tray was concerned.

Tray had just appeared out of nowhere or so it had seemed. Recently divorced, the geezer had just rolled up to the bar one night pinging his tits off. Like a lot of Londoners, he knew about dance music but it wasn't until a lot later that Daz really knew how much.

Tray had been there at the beginning when raves had started and when it was all about the music. Daz was a DJ and spun tunes around the local bars. He was on the beginning of the journey, Tray had written the road map. Tray saw in Daz the vibe that had always existed in him. He told stories of the old days. How the music had developed. How he had played with some of the greats and how the pills had been so much better back then.

Tray didn't look like a DJ but he sure could play. He was no poseur. He let his tunes speak for themselves. He had an innate ability to pick a tune that no one had heard before and predict how huge it was going to be. Daz learnt from Tray without even knowing it. Tray had subtly helped a lot of people out over the years. He didn't tell people what to do, just guided them along without them even knowing it. He was always on the cusp of doing something huge in the local scene but then something always held him back. He always seemed to want someone else take the limelight. Daz always found it strange because he had the ability, he just didn't seem to want to wear the mantle of greatness.

He was Daz's biggest fan. Always encouraging him. Always telling him to go for his dreams. He would go to gigs where big international DJ's would be playing. Daz knew that Tray knew them but his friend never went backstage. In fact, he made a fervent effort to keep away from them. Some people said Tray was full of shit but Daz knew better. He did know these guys. Intimately. He knew who had built the scene. He knew who stood head and shoulders above the rest. He knew where the talent was. There was just too much knowledge for him not to know these guys.

It didn't matter to Daz what his detractors said. Tray was a solid citizen. He didn't surround himself with idiots. His friends were of the same cloth. A lot of people thought he was rude or standoff-ish but Daz knew better. It was either due to the fact that he was off his head and couldn't talk, or because he trusted very few people. Either way, he didn't talk to many people unless they were female and had big tits. He was human after all.

So Daz had collected the necessary and for the next three days, they were going to get so smashed that they would not be able to remember their names.

He sent back a text message.

'Tickets for Bolivia confirmed!'

*

"You ready Lizzy?"

"Nearly baby!"

Tray had been ready for over an hour. He hated waiting and Lizzy made him wait the whole time. He had his weekend planned. They were going to Cronulla first. Smash as many drugs down their necks as possible and then into the Cross. He had booked a double suite for everyone in a hotel up there. They would party hard there until the pigs had stopped doing the random breath tests. Then they would go back to the Shire, party hard and do it all again until Monday came around.

He loved his birthday. Another year of raging against the machine. Another year above ground. Given his history, it was a celebration worth having. No one understood why his birthday was so big for him. Maybe because he never spoke about Rudi and Roger, Charlie or anyone else for that matter. His past life was his to know and for no one to find out about but the fact that he had survived another 365 days was for him a cause celebre.

"Baby! Come on! We got things to do!"

"Two minutes baby!"

He scuffed the carpet with his shoes. He just wanted to be on his way. Then she walked into the room. He caught his breath as she sauntered towards him. She was wearing thigh high stiletto boots laced to the top. She wore a tight black top that showed off her mammoth tits. She looked demurely at him, batted her eyelids.

"You like?"

"I like!" He went to grab her. Fuck the party. He wanted her now.

"Uh Uh Tray!" She struggled away from his lecherous grasp.

"Stop it! There'll be plenty of time for that. I'm telling you right now to get some of that Cialis 'cos I am going to fuck you in some dark alleyway in Kings Cross. My birthday present to you is that you can fuck me anywhere, anytime over the next 3 days. You call it, I'll do it"

Fucking hell! What a present. He went hard in his pants right there and then.

"What about now then?"

"No baby. Not until we are partying"

"Shit"

"Oh don't feel so hard done by. Now let's get going. We've got to pick up Tracey and Vic"

He grabbed the keys and skipped out the door. As he got into the car, he whispered to himself. 'Fuckin hell, anywhere I want. I am going to wear my cock off'.

*

Tracey was all dolled up too. She had a figure much like her sister but two kids had taken their toll. Her tits had dropped and she had that pot roast just above her fanny. She was starting to get 'bye-bye arms' but she hadn't developed into a boiler as Tray so quaintly put it.

She had been jealous of Lizzy when she first met Tray. He was a good man. Had a government job working for Border Security and also loved to party. Lizzy needed that. Most men her age had become mired with kids, exes and all sorts of baggage. He loved Lizzy, she was sure of that. She wasn't too sure how deep that love went but it was love nonetheless. She wanted something like that but with two kids and the wrong side of thirty, she was afraid lately that she was going to be left on the shelf.

And then she had met Vic again. Victor Vukovic had been an ex-boyfriend from many years ago. They had been good together but he had been done for assault too many times when they had been going out. The last time had been enough. She dropped him and got on with her life. Two broken marriages later she ran into Vic once again.

He had a successful plastics business down in Caringbah and seemed to have changed his ways. He had never married and was loaded. For six weeks it was like they had never been apart. He had a Maserati and let Lizzy and Tracey drive around in it whilst he conducted business.

The sex was great and the drugs even better. Tray wasn't too keen on him though. Tracey had thought it was just male ego and a cock-measuring contest. Lizzy

117

assured her it was all cool but Tray didn't hang out with Vic even though Lizzy encouraged it. Perhaps tonight they would hit it off. She hoped so. She wanted both the sisters to be happy for once.

*

They pulled up outside the bar in Vic's Maserati. Heads turned as the four of them got out of the high-class vehicle and walked inside. The bar owner greeted Tray with a smile. He didn't really know this guy but he had always given Vince a smile and was good friends with his DJ and his chef. He left the group at the bar and told the barmaid to set up a tab for them. They would be spending large tonight. It was Tray's birthday.

Tray left the three at the bar and bounded over to the DJ booth. Daz was just setting up, making ready for the night's festivities. CD's and vinyl everywhere. He hugged his mate, nearly knocking the baseball cap off his head.

"All good mate?" asked Tray.

"All good!" replied Daz.

"What's doing?"

"The kitchens all closed up, so stick it in the deep freeze".

Tray was pretty nonchalant about carrying his drugs on him but tonight he had enough on him to put the local chemist to shame so he had to stash them somewhere.

He slid through the doors to the side of the booth and found himself in the kitchen. A melange of strip lighting, white tiles and stainless steel. At the back of the long narrow kitchen was a deep freeze. Tray opened the lid and moved a couple of frozen steaks. He dove in his pocket and pulled out a fist-sized bag. He placed it in the freezer and covered it with the steaks. He then realised he had forgotten something and removed the bag.

He untied the top and pulled out ten pills. He replaced the bag in the freezer once again and walked out the door back into the bar. He climbed into the booth and handed Daz two pills.

"Double dumping bro?" inquired Daz.

"What do you reckon geezer?" replied Tray.

They both put the pills in their mouths and washed them down with Daz's rum and coke. Daz hugged his mate and whispered in his ear.

"Happy birthday bro".

"Oh mate, you just don't know how happy its gonna get".

*

This was going to surprise the fuck out of him that was for sure. Sixteen hours on a fucking plane! He would never get used to this. It had just been a happy coincidence. He had been in regular contact through Graham in the States. He had to. He wouldn't have been able to run the business otherwise. Tray had done everything in his own head. Not much paperwork and he couldn't work it out. Everyone had thought him incapable of doing it.

Tray had planned it well. A chance meeting with an old school friend had allowed him to get in contact with Graham. Tray couldn't have anyone connected with his mates back home getting involved. Loose lips cost lives and it would only have been a matter of time before someone back in the UK let slip. Rudi was still offering serious money for Tray's whereabouts.

Graham had proved a valuable connection. Tray's lifestyle couldn't be supported by his job in Australia, so he had to supplement it somehow. So in return for Tray's generosity, he had shovelled Graham regular amounts of money by international wire and Graham would then in turn get it to Tray in Australia. He didn't know how. It was unimportant to him. He was just happy that Tray had provided him with some additional cover. He was happy to oblige. Things were going on swimmingly and the club was becoming a real money earner. Then one Xmas he received a postcard at the club.

It had a picture of the Rydges Hotel in some place called Cronulla. On the back was one line.

'Tumbles. My Birthday. C U There. T'

So here he was. Sydney airport. Tumbles had told Graham he wasn't coming. Wrong time of the year, too busy etc. But there was no way he was missing the call.

He passed his passport over to immigration.

"Welcome to Australia Senor Gomez"

He didn't react.

"Mr Gomez?"

"Oh Sim. Obrigado". *(Oh Yes. Thank You)*

He would never get used to that name.

*

Something was wrong. He could smell it. He had a nose for it. There were people here he didn't recognise. Despite being so buckled he could barely talk, something was very wrong. He gave Daz a knowing look and rose from his chair.

He casually walked into the kitchen and went straight for the freezer. Daz had since deposited his coke in there as well. Tray took both bags and ducked out of the fire exit into the rear car park. He quickly darted over to the other side of the car park and stuck the bags in an abandoned cardboard box. He lent it against the side of long since closed restaurant and then turned and went back across the car park and back into the bar. His instincts had always served him well. If the bags went missing he could always replace the drugs. It wasn't a fortune.

As he went back inside the kitchen, he looked through the service hatch. All hell had broken loose. There were police everywhere. They had made a beeline for

Lizzy and Tracey and were dragging them out of the door. Vic was nowhere to be seen. Fuck, he would have to let her go for the minute. Deal with it later.

He made for the back door once again. As he got outside, a figure stepped out of the shadows.

"Tray McCarthy?"

A hand was placed on his shoulder, stopping him in his tracks. The figure spoke again.

"DJ T?"

"Tumbles?"

"You bet you fucking arsehole!"

"Fuck! Let's get out of here fuckhead! You got a car?"

"Yeah over there!"

He pointed to a white Corolla.

"Well come on then!"

They both sprinted for the car but not before Tray went over to the box and recovered his bags.

"Throw that away Tray. Wait 'til you see what I got!"

"There's some good cash there!"

"Don't worry geezer. I got plenty". He paused as he fired up the Toyota.

"Tray, why is it every time I'm around you life just gets a lot more interesting?"

"Dunno. Just bad luck I guess".

"You kidding? Life's been too quiet without you".

Still Dusty

"I'm ordering you to leave Jo".

"And I'm telling you that I'm not going!"

Boy this woman was stubborn. The Taliban had just released her and she was still not going anywhere.

"What am I going to do Ryan? Go back and sit in a flat in East London and stare at the walls?"

"No, you could join another organization and go elsewhere".

"Same shit different day Ryan. I'm not going to do a desk job. So where am I to go?"

"Jo you could write your own ticket after the work you've done here".

"I don't care Ryan. Believe it or not, I feel safe here. Where would I go? Rwanda, Sudan, Nigeria. It would all be the same".

"Jo, what are you running from? No one would blame you if you left".

"Ryan, I don't fit in the real world. Don't ask me any questions about it. I am begging you to let me stay. Just do me this favour. You owe me after what I've been through".

She was right; She had been snatched from a wedding in the Peshawar valley. No one had heard from her for about a month and then, from nowhere, she had been dropped off outside the charity's headquarters in Kabul. Everyone had thought she had been executed but here she stood in front of him. Beautiful as ever and as angry as a cut snake.

Rumour was that the women of the region had been in uproar. Despite what the outside world thought, the women in Afghanistan wielded power in the homestead. What happened in public was very different to what happened at home. He could just imagine the Taliban fighters being nagged to death by their women.

"Please Ryan. Don't send me back".

Ryan sighed. He knew she wouldn't stop until he agreed.

"Okay, but for fucksake take some time off".

"Yeah right, don't you know there's a war going on?"

CHAPTER FIVE

Should I Stay or Should I Go?

Boom or Bust

"What the fuck are you doing here?"

"You asked me to come you muppet."

"Yeah I know. But you said you were too busy. Left here mate. Then left at the lights".

Tray pointed out the window. As Tumbles looked to the right for oncoming traffic, he saw a swag of police cars all with lights blazing. Tray looked too. He went pale. Tumbles looked back at his old boss and mate.

"What's up T, you look like you've seen a ghost".

"They were Feds Tumbles. Not your normal coppers. They are fucking serious. They picked up Liz and Trace. I don't know if they are after me. I've been clean geezer I can tell you. You know how careful I've gotta be. Under the radar. I don't know why they pulled the girls. Do a blocky. Turn left here"

Tumbles did as he was told. They turned left into Bourke and then left into Croydon.

"Now turn left again but slowly. Let me slide down in my seat."

He slid down as Tumbles turned onto the Kingsway. He looked to the left. Tracey and Lizzy were standing next to two female coppers. Vic was standing facing the wall. Hands cuffed behind his back.

The police were pouring over his Maserati. A couple of cars past it they were pulling out length after length of plastic pipes from a white van. Next to the van there were two blokes of what the police would call 'Middle Eastern appearance'

"That's a good sign".

"What's that then?" Tumbles said without looking.

"The girls aren't cuffed".

"Tray what you into now?"

"Nothing geezer. I swear".

"It don't look like that to me. Fucking hell! There are cops everywhere".

"Yeah I know. Go down to the lights again and turn left. We'll go down the beach".

"Ooh lovely and romantic"

"Fuck off Tumbles"

"Oh welcome to Australia. There's never a dull moment with you T".

*

They had pulled up in North Cronulla facing the beach. Some dunes hid the sand itself but Tumbles could make out the surf pounding the beach.

"Looks like Portugal"

"Yeah. Does, doesn't it? You should go further South on the Great Ocean Road. You wouldn't know the difference?"

"So what gives T? I come here to see you and the fuzz is raiding the place. I saw you nip out the back before they walked in. So I left and headed you off at the pass".

"Well I'm fucking glad **you** saw me and not the pigs".

"Yeah well I'm pretty sure they weren't after you otherwise they would have sealed off the back as well. Looks like they were targeting the bloke your bird was with".

"Mmm you could be right there".

As he was musing over what Tumbles had said, his other phone sent off a text alert. Only three people had this number. Sam, Graham and Liz. It was only to be used in the case of dire emergencies. It wasn't so bad. It was one of those prepaid phones and was registered in someone else's name. He would have to ditch it now though. That would cause a lot of problems but right now he needed to know what was going on.

It was from Liz.

'where are you?'

He sent back

'**Safe-you?**'

'**Okay - V has been pinched**'

'**what for?**'

'**Pennant Hills**' came back.

He typed in '**They were Feds**' and sent the message.

'**He was a million miles from Pennant Hills**'.

"Fucking hell!" blurted Tray.

"What?"

Tumbles had said nothing whilst Tray had been using the phone.

"Lizzy's sister's boyfriend has been pinched for possession of pills".

"Mate if they were Feds he had more than a couple on him. How many did he have?"

"A fucking million apparently"

"A fucking million?"

"A fucking million!" repeated Tray.

"I knew I didn't like him but that was because I thought he was a flashy cunt. Didn't think he was involved in anything like this".

The phone went off again.

'**we are ok - they haven't asked about you**'

He sent back. '**Don't give 'em nothing about me - NOTHING**'

Tray breathed a sigh of relief.

Another message came in.

'**Understood babe - Trace wants 2 go station. I'm going with her**'.

Tray sent back.

'**K.**'

'**where are you going?**' replied Liz.

'**Hotel - ring me landline from payphone 1 hour**'

"What we doing?" Tumbles interrupted his train of thought. Tray was still very fucking bent but the adrenaline had taken over and masked a lot of the symptoms.

Now that he knew his girl was safe, the pills kicked back in. His eyes started their customary rolling.

"Fucking hell, how bent are you geezer?"

"Buckled!"

"Here get some of this into ya!" Tumbles reached forward and pulled out a huge plastic bag of white powder.

"What's this?"

"Top shelf, moron! You know how I roll"

"Fucking hell, how much is here?"

"An ounce fuckwhit. Go easy as well. It's nearly pure".

"That's about five grand over here and that's without it being cut. You've got about twenty grand street here".

"Happy Birthday mother fucker".

'Fuck, what a night' he thought to himself. He dipped his finger in the bag and sucked the powder off it. Aah the sweet taste of Colombia. There was no denying it. This stuff was the top of the top shelf.

"Where we going birthday boy?"

"The city. Let's get the fuck out of here".

"You said it. Which way?"

"Well it ain't fucking forward is it?" Tray pointed past the windscreen and out to sea.

"Fuckin smart arse".

"Yeah the fucking smartest".

Lock Up

"Tracey!" She screamed her sister's name as the coppers bundled them out of the bar. They had been standing at the bar doing shots and sipping champagne. Tray had been up the DJ booth with Daz. She didn't mind. It was his birthday after all. Now and again he would wander over, pass her a bag or a pill and subtly stick his hand up her skirt. Every time he did it she got sopping wet. She loved this.

Then it all went haywire. Two men had approached Vic and held him by the arms. Another man brushed infront of Liz and pulled out a warrant card.

"Victor Vukovic?"

"Yes" Vic stammered the reply.

"We have a warrant here for your arrest"

She heard her sister yell, "What For?"

"For the importation and distribution of a controlled substance"

The coppers dragged Vic through the packed bar. A female copper came up to Lizzy.

"I think you should come outside madam".

"But I haven't done anything"

Liz looked for Tray but couldn't see him. The whole world seemed to be piling out the door.

"We know that madam but I think you should come outside with us. We may have a couple of questions for you".

Once outside, there were coppers and blue flashing lights everywhere. Seemed the whole world wanted a peek. Vic was face forward against the wall, hands behind his back. He stayed staring against the wall. He looked neither left nor right. He didn't look at the girls as they were guided away from him.

"Just stand here madam. We'll be with you in a moment".

Her and Tracey were left to stand about 10 metres from Vic. The police had cordoned the bar off and were trying to control the crowd.

"What the fuck's going on Liz?"

"How should I know Trace? He's your boyfriend"

She twisted her head towards Trace. She whispered to her sister.

"Trace?"

"Yeah?"

"Do me a favour. Don't mention Tray. Not a fucking word".

"Why?"

"Don't ask. Just don't say a thing. Please".

Tracey looked at her sister. She could see the desperation in her eyes.

"What am I going to tell them if they ask?"

"Just tell them he was a random. Someone I just hooked up with".

"But why Lizzy?"

"Cos I just asked you to".

"But why?"

"Because there's more at stake here than your boyfriend".

Tracey nodded as a policewoman approached them. She pulled out her diary. Liz knew the type. Hard-nosed bitch. Possibly lesbian. Nothing feminine about her. Had to be one of the boys to get along.

"Now ladies. Have you got any idea what is going on here?"

The sisters shook their heads.

"Yeah we thought as much. Can we get some confirmation of details please?"

She turned towards Tracey.

"Tracey Rogers right?"

"Yes that's right. How'd you know?"

"Because we've had this prick under surveillance for the last six months".

'Fuck' thought Tracey.

The copper turned towards Liz.

"Liz Rogers right?"

'Fuck' thought Liz.

*

She'd never been so relieved when the copper turned to her and uttered those immortal words.

"Okay then. That's it. You're free to go".

"Excuse me?"

"That's right. Free to go Ms Rogers. We know you're not involved. You should tell your sister she should be more careful about who she dates".

The copper went to leave. Tracey had also been informed that she was being released. She smiled at her sister. Tracey looked as though she had pissed her pants. In fact Lizzy was pretty sure she had.

"Excuse me officer?"

"Yes madam?"

"Can you tell me why he's being arrested?"

"I suppose you've earned that right," the copper nodded over towards the white van that was still being unloaded.

"MDMA. Kilos of it".

"What?"

"You heard Ms. Rogers. Pills and powder, millions of pills. Maybe one of the biggest busts we've ever had".

"Shit!" said Liz.

"You said it Ms. Rogers".

Lizzy turned to face her sister. She walked over to her and put an arm around her.

"C'mon sis, let's get you out of those clothes".

Tracey shouted out to the coppers as Lizzy guided her back inside the bar.

"Where are you taking him?"

"City Central."

Tracey didn't thank them. Lizzy took her to the rear of the bar and the DJ booth. Daz was still there.

"What the fuck was that all about Lizzy?" asked Daz.

"Vic just got pinched".

"You're kidding?"

He glanced at Tracey. One look told him she was not.

"What for?" he asked.

"Pills. Millions of 'em".

"Fuck me dead. What are you gonna do?"

"Is our bag still upstairs?" asked Lizzy.

"Yes," replied Daz.

"We need to get changed Daz. Did you see where Tray went?"

"I think he ducked out the back. Not sure though. I was too busy turning up the lights and turning off the music.

"Where's Vince?" she asked.

"He's arguing with one of the coppers. Asking them who's gonna compensate him for loss of earnings".

"He's a cheeky fucker!"

"You got that right Lizzy. Just get changed upstairs. I'll make sure no one goes up".

"Thanks Daz. You're a star".

"No problem darling. Just make sure Tray is alright".

"I will."

Lizzy took Tracey into the kitchen and up the stairs into the storeroom. She found the bag and pulled some clothes out and handed them to Tracey. She had started to shiver and Liz presumed she was suffering from shock.

She pulled out her phone and typed a text message. She sent it to the emergency phone number. In five minutes she was much happier than she'd been ten minutes ago. Tray was safe.

Tracey said she wanted to go to the police station to check on Vic. Lizzy didn't think it was one of her best ideas but her sister had insisted. She was his girlfriend after all but Lizzy didn't know for how much longer. She would call Tray at the hotel once everything had settled down.

Tracey got changed and they both went back downstairs. Daz was waiting for them.

"Well did you get hold of him".

"Yes Daz. He's okay".

"Sweet. So what happens now?"

"We're going into the city to check that Vic is okay. I'll call Tray from there. He's on the way there now I think."

"Call me if you need me".

"Of Course I will".

"I think its all still on Daz. He's going to the hotel. Just stay by the phone. He'll call you when its okay. Don't call him, alright? Something weird is going on".

Daz found it all a bit strange.

"Don't worry Daz. Its still his birthday".

*

"Hello. This is Steve speaking".

"Um, who's this?"

"Ah Lizzy I presume."

She started to panic. What's going on? She had never heard this voice before.

"Yeah. Who are you?"

"I told you". The distant voice paused. "T is a little detained".

She didn't like this at all. The accent was definitely from London. Stronger than Tray's. What if he was after Tray? What if he was one of those people who were going to kill him? What if? What if? What If? The question tumbled through her mind like rolling thunder.

She screamed down the telephone.

"Where the fuck is he?"

The line went quiet.

Tracey squeezed into the phone booth.

"Liz what's wrong?"

She dropped the phone from her ear.

"Someone's got Tray".

"What?"

"Someone from London".

"What?"

"Liz! Liz! Lizeeeee!"

A voice was shouting down the line. Liz put the phone to her ear.

"Tray?"

"Yes baby". Tray's voice was calm.

"Are you okay? What do they want? What do I do?" The questions came in a rush. Running one into the other.

"'Course I'm okay. What does who want?"

"That other guy. That guy from London".

"Who? Steve?" Tray giggled. He was smashed she could tell.

"Oh have I got a surprise for you"

"Yeah well I could do without them at the moment," shouted Liz.

"I know honey. I'm sorry. I got the surprise of my life as well. I'll tell you all about it when you get here. What's going on with Vic?"

"Nothing. His lawyer's here. His family has been called. I don't think there is much we can do here".

"Well pull your arse out of that hole and get yourself over here".

"Tray, there's something you should know".

"What's that baby?"

"Vic has been under surveillance for six months".

"Fuck. Well I told you there was something wrong with him".

"Yeah baby. You're the king. I know".

"No baby. Its not about that at all. Now honey you're going to have to ditch your phones. Both of you".

"We'll do it tomorrow".

"No baby. Now! Leave them at the police station. They can bug themselves".

"Tracey will ask questions."

"Fuck Tracey. She got us into this mess in the first place".

Tracey heard the quip. She leaned into the booth some more.

"Fuck you Tray! My boyfriends in jail…."

She didn't have time to finish the statement. Lizzy slapped her full across the face. She glowered at her sister.

"Don't you give me that look. Don't you dare blame us!"

Her sister had no idea what was happening. Her world had just turned upside down. Now her sister had slapped her and was giving her attitude.

"Lizzy!"

"Tracey. He's right. Now stop your whining. We are out of here".

"Liz?" Tray was back on line.

"Yeah baby"

"Just get in a taxi. I'll tell you everything when you get here"

"Ok Tray"

"Lizzy?"

"Yes baby."

"Its still my birthday".

"Yes it is honey".

"You still gonna be my Martini girl?"

"Huh?"

"Any time, any place, any where!"

"Oh Tray. After tonight?"

"Baby after you get here, you just won't want to stop".

"Huh?"

"Don't you worry about it".

The Battle Of The Biscuit

She rapped on the door. It cracked open a little. All she could she was a thin nose and one solitary eye.

"Yes?"

"Its Lizzy"

"Well come on in then"

The door to the penthouse suite opened. In front of her stood a very thin man. Around thirty-five years old, brown straight shoulder length hair. He was wearing a crisp white shirt and some suit trousers. He was looking very smart.

"Lizzy" He stuck out a hand. "Steve Brown but everyone calls me Tumbles".

She shook the outstretched hand.

"Lizzy Rogers and this is my sister Tracey"

She half turned and let this Tumbles catch a glimpse of her sister.

"Nice one," he raised his hand. "Rough night hey?"

"You could say that," said Lizzy.

Tray's head popped over Tumbles' shoulder.

"Hey baby!"

"Don't baby me!" She barged into the room and started whacking Tray on his right shoulder. He turned his back to protect himself.

"Baby!"

She kept hitting him. Huge swinging blows.

"You scared the living daylights out of me!"

Tray turned towards her. He caught her arm.

"Baby I'm sorry."

"I thought he was a hit man!"

"What?" said Tracey.

Tray looked at the sister.

"I'll explain later Trace," said Tray.

He looked back at his girlfriend. She looked beautiful when she was angry. Her hair cascaded onto her shoulders. Her eyes were ablaze. He felt her anger. Jo had looked at him like that in Burgau. He melted. He tried his best smile.

"Come on baby. I've got something to show you," he slipped his hand down her arm and grabbed her hand.

"C'mon. You'll love this."

*

"So what's going down Tray?" Tumbles lay on the bed. On the bedside table next to him sat four huge lines of coke, a half-opened snap lock bag and a rolled up hundred dollar bill.

"Lizzy is telling Tracey all about my past".

"Is that wise?" asked Tumbles.

Tumbles brushed some wayward flakes of coke from his shirt. Ordinarily most people would have dabbed them and then sucked their finger but Tumbles had the marching powder in abundance. No need to round up skanky bin-ends. Tray considered the amount of coke he appeared to have but let it slide for the moment.

"Tracey needs to know what's going on. She needs to know why me and Lizzy freaked out tonight. Especially considering what her boyfriend's been up to."

"Fair enough. Can she be trusted though?" asked his friend.

"I'm going to have to. Fucking hell! What a fucking night!"

Although his face was as numb as fuck, his mind was on fire. Thoughts raced through his mind like the rat-a-tat of an automatic rifle. Twenty minutes ago he had pulled Lizzy into the suite and shoved the bag of coke under her nose. Then he had dragged her, head spinning, onto the balcony and told her all about Tumbles. The abbreviated version because the full version would just have taken too long.

"There were a couple of things I didn't tell you about my past, just because they weren't important"

"No shit shylock"

Her head was thumping, the coke had made her teeth tingle. This was good shit. Unlike anything she had before. It made her horny. Her pussy was once again expressing the need to be filled. The need consumed her. It would not be denied.

She held a blanket around her as she gazed over the Sydney nightline. The towering office blocks gave off a light show as good as any nightclub. The night air cracked with electricity. Everything seemed brighter, fuller. Colours bounced off the rooftops. She could see the Coca Cola sign in the Cross. She giggled, finding it ironic.

Her pussy yearned for him. She tried to concentrate on what he was saying but ended up grabbing his face and kissing his lips. She sucked on his top lip and then bit it. His tongue darted out and she sucked it, drawing it deep inside her mouth.

He grabbed her ass with his left hand and pulled her tight to him. She grabbed his groin with her right hand. He was excited. She felt like getting dirty. Then he stopped abruptly. He put his arms on her shoulders and moved back, holding her at arms length. He looked at her from top to toe, taking her all in.

"Baby, I must tell you about Tumbles, then you've gotta talk to Trace. And I can't take too long otherwise he will be fucking her for a month of Sundays".

"Just like I want to do to you now honey"

Lizzy sucked her finger demurely and batted her eyes at him. Tray resisted the urge to throw her onto the floor and fuck her right there and then.

"Stop it Liz. This is important"

She suddenly stopped her attempt at seduction.

"Lizzy, Tumbles works for me".

"What do you mean baby?"

"I never relinquished control of the club in Portugal."

"What? I thought you left everything behind."

"I did sort of. I couldn't rely on Dad for money and I had to make my own way in life without drawing too much attention to myself here. When I left with Felicity, I had enough money for airfares and some pocket money to set ourselves up with. We did that. She started her own company. I began working for Border Security keeping very low under the radar".

"Before I left, I set up a profit sharing scheme with Tumbles and Fernando. Fernando was head of the local gypsy family. That's sort of head of the local mafia. They ran pills and hash through the club and we would take a cut. The club itself was raking it in. I left that in the hands of Tumbles. He's not the best businessman in the world but that club is like a cash cow. You don't have to do much except open the doors"

"Anyways, every month, Tumbles sends me some moolah via a friend in New York. Its rather complicated but suffice to say that it can't be traced by anyone including the tax office. I get to live a full life, Tumbles gets to shag anything he likes and Fernando keeps his family business rolling along. Everyone's happy".

Lizzy frowned.

"I wondered how you managed to party so hard on your salary. You aren't that high up."

"That's why I mask it with the occasional DJ gig. Keeps my hand in and gives me some cash without having to explain too much to too many people."

"Oh you're so crafty baby. You are just like some international criminal. You make me feel so sexy."

"Baby concentrate. This is important. I have told you more than I have told anyone before. There's some shit even Tumbles doesn't know and I have kept all this buried for a fucking reason."

He reached forward and held her face in both hands. He searched her eyes. Her pupils were as wide as saucers. She was absolutely racked up to the max. He didn't know if she was taking this in or even if she could do what he needed her to do. Tumbles' presence. Vic's arrest. It all added up to one thing. Now Tracey had to be told. Tumbles and Tray hadn't discussed it. Tray knew he was taking a chance but what choice did he have? Tracey needed to understand and she wouldn't stop asking questions unless Lizzy made her aware of how serious this shit was.

So he had told her to take another bag into in the toilet and hold up in there until Tracey fully understood what was going on. Tumbles was to be explained away as just a friend from Portugal, nothing more. If Tumbles wanted to share, that was his prerogative. Tray and Tumbles had benefited from a relationship worked out on the beaches of the Algarve but what each other had done since then was unknown to both of them. They had a lot of catching up to do and speculation would only lead to shit that would have to be cleared up later.

As predicted, Tumbles was trying to work his considerable magic on Tracey when they came back in from the balcony. Tray had just about saved her from Tumbles' relentless advances.

So the girls were still in the toilet and the men had been chatting some more, snorting coke and had MTV playing in the background. The new age Aussie barbecue: Coke on the table, alcohol on tap and food... well food was optional. Tumbles had ordered some bubbly from room service. Tray had rung Daz and the crew were on their way. Daz had been advised that there were to be no questions asked and that the birthday celebrations were back in full swing.

The hotel they were staying at was in the heart of Kings Cross. It was undergoing major refurbishment and Tray had secured the penthouse suite for next to nothing. All the other rooms were vacant on their floor and the floor below so that Tray and his crew could party without interference. Now with Tumbles' assistance, the night was going to go off like a frog in a sock.

*

It was like an advert for a good time alco-pop. One after another his buddies traipsed in. All variously inebriated or high. A sensational effort considering it was now 4am and well into the night. Tray welcomed them all with a line of top shelf and introduced them to his long time associate. Tumbles' real name was never used and he was just introduced as a friend from the old country.

About fifteen people turned up. They were all there. The ones he loved and who loved him back. Tray was very particular about who he associated with. Everyone was given a chance but only one. No repeat offenders and no forgiveness. If a girlfriend got too loose or someone was considered a liability, they were chopped from the roster.

It was just that Tray had been used so many times that his circle of friends became smaller and smaller. Now and again there would be a small addition and occasionally they lasted. Geoff was one of them. A solid individual from outside the Sydney basin, he had been Tumbles' replacement in Oz.

They were like chalk and cheese. Geoff was skinny and lithe. Taller than Tray coming in at some 6' 4", he was like a gangly preying mantis on the dance floor. But the two were inseparable in the wake of Tray's break up. Their relationship had waned somewhat since he his affair with Lizzy had started but they were still close. Geoff called Tray his 'Maverick'. Tray called Geoff his 'Goose'. They still believed they were top guns.

Then there was Daz's girlfriend Rachel. Wise beyond her years and a capacity to do pills only surpassed by Tray, Daz, Lizzy and Geoff. Her arm was made of the proverbial rubber when it came to partying. Despite an undying commitment to have a 'weekend off', she invariably couldn't resist the allure of MDMA and would stand front and centre alongside the boys in their pursuit of unbridled hedonism. She was young and blond, vivacious, sassy and above all made of fun. She was the epitome of the three-letter word. She would bring light into the room when there was nothing but darkness. Her skill was seeing the best in everyone. No matter what someone had done, Rachel would try and find that one thing that made them better than they themselves thought they were. It was her finest quality.

There was also an overabundance of sexy women. That was the way Tray liked it. For some reason he always gravitated towards girls rather than boys. Even though there was no doubting his sexuality he just preferred their company. He liked the way they loved him. He liked their softness and the way they fussed over him. Not that he didn't deserve it. He would be there for them for the midnight phone call. When their latest beau had either slapped them or dumped them or just even plain ignored them. It mystified Tray why these beautiful, drop-dead gorgeous women would tolerate such treatment. Why they would select such inappropriate men and then complain about them.

Before Tray met Lizzy, he would sometimes bemoan the girls and tell them that being a friend of theirs was like going for a job interview. Here they had Tray, a perfectly good candidate, well qualified for the job of boyfriend. Absolutely perfect in every way. However there was another candidate, totally unsuitable with very little in the way of bona fide credentials. There was never going to be any chance that this candidate was going to be successful in the role. However the girls were going to give the inappropriate candidate the job. Not only that, did they mind if they rang Tray every other week and complain about the bloke they had chosen over him?

It left him completely perplexed. Why do girls chose that which causes them so much pain and when the bloke finally walks away, fall apart in a flood of tears and chase him like he was the only man on earth? In reality they were the only men they should never have a relationship with. Tray had put it down to his theory that nice guys always come last but then he met Lizzy and all that changed.

This coterie of sexual princesses was made up of six women. They were sexy beyond mere looks. It existed in the way they moved. The way they spoke. The way they held Tray close to them. The way they told him their secrets. But most of all, in the way they loved him. For they did love him. They cherished his friendship and he cherished them in return. He also revelled in the way that everyman looked at him when he walked into the room with one of them, although invariably it would be with three or four of them. He liked the way that men would puzzle at how he could attract so many beautiful women. How he could walk into a strip club with them at their behest. It made him smile and that was something that had been missing from his life.

At first Lizzy was jealous but then she realised that their presence was borne out of Tray's need to be loved by women. Not sexually, just pure unadulterated love from the opposite sex. She surmised that it was because he missed the uncomplicated love of his mother. He had missed her death. He had missed the last ten years of her life and for that he felt so much guilt. So unconsciously, she believed he transferred that love onto this small group of women. Women he could love on his own terms. Women that would dote on him without the complications of sex.

They would sometimes withdraw from the group in pursuit of some ill-fated lovers tryst but they would always come back and their love for Tray never diminished.

They were like a coven of witches but there was absolutely no evil in them. They were Tray's guardians. They had vetted Lizzy before their approval was given. Lizzy almost had to give references. It had nearly put her off going out with him before one of them pointed out that Tray had gone through so much heartache that they just wanted to protect him from himself. They really did love him.

There was Franky, Suzi, Vanessa the Undresser, Belle, Michelle and finally but by no means least Kylie. Lizzy considered them all to be stunning. They had perfect bodies, some with surgically enhanced tits. The million-dollar smile. Legs that Tray liked to say 'went all the way up to their armpits'.

Lizzy felt frumpish in comparison but Tray had said that it was much more important to look beyond that which stood infront of you. Beauty fades and when it does, all that you are left with is a heart and soul and the stuff between your ears. If you didn't have any of those three qualities, Tray would lose interest in that person very quickly.

Lizzy felt proud that Tray had chosen her over these girls. She was so happy that she was sleeping with him. Franky purred to Lizzy once how she could never have slept with Tray because he was like her brother. Lizzy couldn't understand that. It was those very qualities that they found cutesy and brotherly that stoked her furnace down below. The bottomless font of giving that showed no hint of running out. It was this quality amongst many of his others that had intrigued her the most and which spurred her on despite her reservations.

Other members of the quickly-convened party massive included Brick, Brendan and Saxby. Three men devoted to enjoying life to the max. They came as a package and spent nearly every weekend 'on it', 'off it' or 'amongst it'. Brick was basically the size of a brick shithouse whose daytime job was working on the docks as a crane driver. The height and breadth of a single storey dwelling, gargantuan in his appetite for drugs and food, he either didn't eat for three days or ate voraciously for four. He was loud, huge, outspoken and well versed in all aspects of offbeat trivia. His loyalty to Tray was unquestionable and he would defend him to the point of violence. Tray felt extremely comfortable when Brick was around.

Brendan was the quiet one. Deep and brooding with a shock of blonde hair, he said very little but what he did say was direct and cutting. He analysed situations. Calculated the outcome and delivered his verdict. Intelligent and well educated, he was the very antithesis of what a drug dealer should be but that was exactly what he Brick and Saxby were. They funnelled a stack of pills through the Shire but all low-key. In fact all of Tray's male friends dealt pills and powder to some degree. It bemused him sometimes that this was the case and if the police ever looked too closely at him or any of his friends, a tangled web of Cronulla's best drug suppliers would be swept away with a clinical sweeping brush.

Saxby was another abstract portrayal of a drug dealer. A father to his kids every other weekend, the middle-aged man would split his business between custody weekends and free weekends. An incurable romantic like Tray, he would fall hopelessly in love with a woman one week and then be heartbroken the next. Life was always colourful around Saxby and that was what rocked Tray's world.

So in this room of Bacchus at the Bayview Hotel sat, lay or danced fifteen of the closest of close friends. High on drugs and drink and with only one thing on their mind; to get more smashed than the person next to them.

A biscuit whistled past Kylies powdered nose.

"What the Fuck!"

Rachel had failed the biscuit challenge. Tray had set her the task of eating as many digestive biscuits as she could in five minutes. This was normal for Tray. He liked to spice up the festivities by challenging people to eat cheese, wafers, marshmallows, dry bread, whatever was the most difficult to swallow when your mouth was as dry as the Gobi Desert. Rachel had managed about a third of a biscuit and instead of gracefully accepting defeat, had launched an unrelenting barrage of McVitie's finest across the crowded hotel suite.

And so it began. Without retribution. No prisoners taken and no quarter given: The infamous Battle of The Biscuit.

No Picnic

The plan had changed. Considering what had happened at the bar they had all decided that it might be better if they stay out of the Shire for the time being. At least until the heat from last night's events had passed.

Before The Battle of The Biscuit had commenced and the rest of the crew had arrived, Tracey had exited rather ashen faced and completely perplexed from the bathroom. She looked at Tray. Her world had fallen apart tonight. All men were bastards, including Tray. Her boyfriend had put her entire family in jeopardy and Tray wasn't much better. He wasn't the man she thought he was. Connected and in effect on the run. He was just as bad as Vic. Lizzy had tried to convince her otherwise. As Lizzy continued her story, Tracey realised that Tray was trying to atone for his sins. Not adding to them like Vic had done.

Instead of being the hard man of London that his father had wanted him to be, he had turned into the soft man that his mother wanted. Life it appeared had dealt him some cruel hands in return for making the wrong decision and saving his own life. He had forsaken everything he had known and loved. No wonder he never talked about the old country. There was so much fear there. So much violent intent.

Then there was Vic. How could she not have seen what was going on? So much flash cash. So much gangster behaviour. She had fallen for his charm once again but instead of the long ago violence of his youth, Vic had turned into a major player on the drugs scene. Or so he had thought. Someone must have given him up. What a spastic!

Lizzy had made her talk to one of the detectives at the station. Tracey had made sure that she was in no way implicated in what was going on. The detective had led her into a small interview room at the station. Lizzy sat next to her in the sterile room. There was no comfort there. Bare walls painted in the drab government beige. Four chairs, a table and nothing else.

The detective was dressed in a navy blue suit with a faint pinstripe. His shirt was white and topped off with a pale blue tie with a fat Windsor knot. He was like a male model. He had brown straight hair in the classic short back and sides style and wore some severe glasses. Rectangular in shape, they didn't soften his features, rather they made him look stern and impassive. All part of the image Lizzy thought. *'Groomed for success'*, she thought to herself.

Tracey searched for Lizzy's hand on the table and held it tight. The detective noted the fear in the girls' eyes but was impressed with their courage. They had no idea what had been going on. Just plain stupidity on their behalf. Tracey Rogers had picked the wrong horse that was for sure. For the past six weeks they had heard her fuck and suck him and been impressed by her stamina. They had vision of them doing drugs and tapes of the girls driving around in his Maserati whilst off chops.

They had thought about turning them at one point and bugging Tracey's car but it had all seemed a bit pointless. It was patently obvious that she was just along for the ride and had no idea what Vukovic was up to. Anyway they had enough on him already and they were too close to the exchange to follow these two idiots around as well. The budget only extended so far.

So he had heard Tracy Rogers bleat how she had just met Vic six weeks ago and it had been a bit of a whirlwind of romance and sex. All this he had known. She was fearful for her kids. Worried that they were going to take them away. Detective Swanson thought about letting her sweat for a while but then thought of his own young family. It wasn't fair to trifle with someone's parental concerns, especially when they were innocent.

He took off his glasses. All part of softening his image and raised his hands, palms outwards, imploring Tracey to stop talking.

"Miss Rogers, its okay. You really have nothing to worry about. We know you're just an innocent player in all of this".

Tracey's shoulders relaxed. Her vice like grip on Lizzy's hand released a little.

"What you are guilty of is a completely inappropriate choice in boyfriend. However you were never to know. He's a bit of a chameleon is our Vic. We've been watching him for a considerable amount of time".

"So you've been listening to us in the car. In his house. Everything!"

"Yes Miss Rogers. All part of our job I'm afraid"

Tracey blushed. In the bedroom and everything. Oh how glad she was that her mother wasn't here.

"If I can add one thing and this is for both of you girls. Don't drive around whilst under the influence of pills. We wont let it go next time."

Both girls stared in disbelief.

"We could've picked you up any number of times but it would have tipped our hand so we let it slide. Next time you won't be so lucky. Take it from me, you've been warned and the locals will be on your case when you're out and about".

Lizzy took the lead.

"We'll take it on board Detective"

"Good. Your actions have been a bit reckless to say the least".

"Understood", said Lizzy.

"Good. Well I think we're all done here".

Detective Swanson went to rise. The girls remained seated, a bit confused by it all.

Lizzy rose and went to shake the detectives hand. Tracey did not move.

"What happens now detective?" asked Lizzy.

"Well Mr Vukovic will be remanded in custody and I don't think he will be seeing outside a cell for some time. The charges are very serious. This is one of the biggest hauls in Australian history".

"Yeah so we've been told".

"Well I don't think you will be seeing him tonight. He will be interviewed for some considerable time but not before his lawyer gets here. There will be some press snooping around soon too so I would make myself scarce if I were you".

Lizzy thanked him for the advice and turned to Tracey. They nodded to each other, understanding exactly what the policeman was saying. No point in getting their names up in lights. What would the kids think?

That had been some time ago. They had partied back at the hotel despite the shock of what had happened earlier. Tracey had been furnished with all the information that Lizzy thought she could handle and even that had nearly turned Tracey inside out. Now she lay on the green grass of the Botanical Gardens. Lush and soft, no matter what the drought conditions in Australia, the Botanical Gardens on Sydney Harbour were always like the original Garden of Eden.

The gardens themselves nestled snugly behind the Opera House and the Harbour Bridge. It seemed to have every native tree and shrub known to man. They had all set up camp under a sprawling tree on the edge of the gardens. The position afforded them a great view of the harbour and its myriad of craft jockeying for position on this crystal clear morning.

They watched an endless procession of rollerbladers and power-walkers storm past them ignoring the glorious display that nature was giving them. Tracey lay on her back watching the few wisps of cloud float by. She tried to make out shapes in the clouds when a sky writer began his incredible journey through the pale blue yonder. It took a while but eventually they all managed to grasp that he was trying to conjure up Sydney's mythical statement 'Eternity'.

It made them all smile. It was a statement that most Sydneysiders were proud of. Something that established them as different and unique from the rest of the world. As far as any of Tray's friends knew, it was just a piece of graffiti that some old looney had just written in chalk on the sidewalk in random areas of Sydney. Despite it being washed away by the rain, the statement left an indelible mark on Sydney's citizens. It seemed wholly appropriate that a skywriter, a person whose work would remain in the sky for the briefest of moments, was rekindling that old man's work.

Tracey rolled over and looked at Tray. Dark sunglasses masked the state of his eyes which would have been a dead giveaway for anyone involved in the enforcement of the law.

"Are we gonna be okay Tray?"

"I think so Trace. Just play it cool. We'll sort something out. But I think Vic is sunk".

"You were right about him Tray"

"I wish I hadn't been Trace. It brings me no pleasure I can tell you".

"You know I think I believe you".

"Why not Trace. I never wanted this to happen. I only want you to be happy babe".

Tracey tried to focus but the coke was blurring her vision. Tumbles came over and knelt down next to Tray.

"Hey T come and have a walk with me. Show me what these fucking flowers are".

"Sure"

Tray struggled to his feet and wobbled slightly once he had regained them. He put his arm across Tumbles' shoulder. Lizzy perked up and looked at the two men.

"Where are you two going then?" asked Lizzy.

"To have a look at the wildlife baby."

"You wouldn't know a koala from a kangaroo Tray!"

"Maybe but neither does Tumbles so I can't get anything wrong can I?" laughed Tray.

"True baby. True".

With that the duo wandered down to the water taking in their spectacular surroundings.

'Now I wonder what those two are up to?' thought Lizzy out loud.

*

The two men walked away from the small group and towards Lady Macquarie's Chair. Tumbles looked across the water. He could understand why Tray had settled here. It was a world away from the hustle and bustle of London despite being a major city itself. The Aussies certainly knew how to live their life. Laid back, laconic, they lived life to the full and let the minor things in life take care of themselves. They rounded the point and sat down on the grass.

They just looked like any two mates chewing the fat on a Sunday morning except they were still wearing their going-out clothes. Tumbles reached in his back pocket and handed Tray a small booklet. Tray immediately recognised it as a passport.

"What's this then?"

He turned it over in his hand and flicked through the well-used document. It had a myriad of stamps in it from all over the world. He flicked to the photo. Underneath the familiar picture of Tumbles read the unfamiliar name 'Fernando Gomez'.

"Well, what the fuck is it then?"

"Diplomat fuckin passport idiot. Didn't you read the fucking front?"

Tray closed the passport and studied the front. Sure enough it was a diplomatic passport. It appeared genuine.

"What's all this about then?"

"It's been my passport to heaven geezer. Life's been an absolute picnic with this baby"

"What do you mean Tumbles?"

"I got one word for you T"

"What's that then?"

As Tumbles went to speak, Brick came ambling over waving. They watched him stumble towards him, newspaper above his head.

"What's the word then?" asked Tray.

Tray's world turned ever more surreal as Tumbles uttered the word 'Pedro'. *What did Pedro have to do with all this?* He mulled the question over in his brain as Brick told them both that Vic had made the morning news.

What a fucking birthday!

*

"They've been pinched Mo"

The voice echoed down the phone. Bad connection.

"What do you mean?"

"The whole lot. And Sitch and Dave. It was a fucking disaster. I told you that Serb was a fucking risk!"

"Don't fucking worry about that. What about the cargo?"

"Gone"

"Fuck! What about the money?"

"Got no idea. You know what the deal was. It's gone. I didn't see any cash at the site. The Feds may have it."

Feds! This was beyond bad luck. This was a serious fuck up.

"Find it!"

"Fuck Mo, I got no idea where he hid it! He didn't trust us remember."

"I don't care about that. We can't drop that sort of bundle Tarry!"

"There's Feds everywhere Mo. They're all over his factory and his house. The van has been unloaded and his car's been impounded. As soon as the flashing lights turned up I legged it to the factory. There were about ten cars there. They were dragging out the pill press. Tarry lobbed straight over to the house. Same deal. They were carting out boxes of stuff including computers".

The line went dead for the moment.

"Get yourself back here. Someone's dropped him. Best we find out who it was."

"Okay Mo". He turned off the phone and threw it in the bin. No good to him now. He'll have to get a new one.

Fucking hell. The powder and the cash! This was not a good day. Thank God he'd kept some walls between him and that moron. Someone was going to have to pay for all of this. Starting with that fucking Serb.

CHAPTER SIX

The Walls Come Tumbling Down

The Kangaroo Cartel

Fuck! What had happened? They had been living it up. Tracey was loving it and Lizzy was enjoying herself. Tray was being his rude self but Vic had more important things on his mind. The van had pulled up. He had got the nod from the Leb who was working the door. Then what had happened?

He heard Tracey and Lizzy scream. He saw the warrant. He heard the words. He remembered being bundled out the door, his feet barely touching the ground. He was read his rights, cuffed and turned around to face the wall. He could hear the cops congratulating themselves but he ignored them and the droves of onlookers flooding out of the bar. They were busy taking pictures on their mobiles. No doubt they would sell them to the media later. No chance of sweeping this under the carpet.

They then threw him in the back of a paddy wagon and sped him to Central for processing. This detective Swanson was obviously heading the case. He had popped into the holding cell several times and now they had dragged him out to this interview room.

The Feds didn't mess about. They grilled him without a lawyer present. They asked about the drugs. They said they knew everything. They just wanted him to confirm it. They would go easy on him if he rolled over and named names. He kept quiet. He reiterated his request for his lawyer and then the questions stopped. There was too much at stake here for them to jeopardise everything by not following procedure.

Vic remembered the advice he had received so many years ago. Say nothing. Admit nothing. If they had anything, don't confirm it. Wait for a lawyer and work out a strategy. No matter what they had, it was never as bad as they made out. They wouldn't ask questions if they had an airtight case but it didn't look good for him. They had the powder and pills but it wasn't his van at least. They also had the pill press. Something he couldn't easily explain away.

His lawyer wouldn't be able to be contacted until the morning so he had at least another six hours of cooling his heels. He heard the regular slamming of cell doors. The incessant screaming of some junky who was so strung out that he was driving everyone mad. Whenever he had been pulled before he'd been put in a communal cell where everyone told him how smart they were. Vic hated to point out to them that if they had any smarts at all then they wouldn't be in the cell with him. Smarts meant not being caught.

This was different though. He was an important pinch. They wanted him alone. They wanted him scared. Fair enough, he was shitting himself. The consequences of tonight's actions were inevitable. He had been caught with his hands in the big leagues. He knew how much was in the van. More MDMA and pills to keep Sydney's insatiable appetite for recreational drugs churning over for some considerable time. Where had he gone wrong?

It had to be the Lebs or the chemist. There was no one else except the overseas connection but surely they wouldn't jeopardise their cargo. He thought back to that meeting in Amsterdam. He had gone back to the old country and bumped into some family friends who used to be in the paramilitary during the war. They had connections with the drugs trade in Europe. They had the muscle and the power to command the respect of those that funnelled the drugs around the continent and more importantly they could set Vic up with them.

He hadn't gone looking for it. It had just fallen into his lap. It had all been so easy. Pills in Europe had gone on the slide somewhat. Coke was the order of the day and it was so cheap that the demand for ecstasy had fallen through the floor. It was the capitalist system at work. Supply and demand. If you flood the market with a superior product then the prices for the inferior product drop like the proverbial stone. You'd be lucky to pay more than 4 Euros for a pill retail so wholesale was just ridiculously cheap.

For Vic it was like manna from heaven. Pills were the drug of choice for an entire generation in Australia. He knew the people who knew the people who could shift large amounts down under. Even if he couldn't get rid of them all in Sydney, there was still Brisbane, Melbourne and Perth. In Brisbane and Perth in particular, pills were selling from between thirty to fifty bucks sometimes as high as sixty. The tyranny of distance meant that top quality product commanded top prices.

A lot of pills in Australia were produced locally and that meant that quality was pretty low. If the MDMA content could be guaranteed then Vic knew they would be able to offload them like hot cakes. So he had made the quick trip to Holland. Europe's chemical plant.

He felt like someone out of a Hollywood blockbuster. He and his cousin had been picked up from the airport in a limo and driven out to a mansion on the outskirts of Amsterdam. There he had sat down with an ex-paramilitary leader from the conflict. They had discussed prices, delivery, and methodology. No money up front. Cash and maybe some bearer bonds on the back end. The Serbs would take responsibility for the shipment until it arrived on Vic's doorstep. Then he would pay for the goods and the rest would be up to him. This would be a one-time deal. Incredibly cheap but not to be repeated.

He was made aware of what would happen to him and his entire family if his credentials didn't check out or if he wasn't on the level. Even though he was a Serb, that didn't guarantee him a free run. His cousin Grab was known to the Colonel. They had fought alongside each other during the war. That still didn't give Vic any comfort.

Grab had told him what these men were like. They had massacred whole villages during the war. They didn't hold life sacred. They spilt blood like an old woman would spill a cup of tea. They were ruthless. They would kill anyone associated with him if he fucked up. They were the smiling assassins. Vic understood. This was no walk around the park. He tried to remain calm. Look like the big man on campus.

The Colonel knew he had an amateur in front of him but everyone had to start somewhere. Even he had joined the army as a lowly private but his single-mindedness and desire to rid the stench of his enemy from the face of the earth had seen him rise up the ranks. Everyone still called him Colonel even though he had long left the conflict. He was now an entrepreneur. He had chemists, soldiers, accountants, lawyers even police on his payroll. He was head of a company with no name and fought for his own flag. Not the flag of a country but for his own family crest. He had lost much during the conflict, now it was his turn to take it all back.

Vic was a whole new supply line for them. The pill trade was so bad that they had what in the European Economic Community was known as a pill mountain. He had just dropped in at the right place at the right time. Bold and ambitious, he was their answer. They would more than break even on their investment if Vic held true to his promises. They had a lot of cash tied up in the product and they wanted to get rid of it as soon as possible and try something new. Coke definitely was it and the Serbs had to change. It would mean getting involved with the Colombians but what choice did they have? The times they were a changing and they either went with customer demand or just stopped the business they were in. The business they were in was drugs and they would have to learn to diversify just like everyone else.

It seemed that Australia's isolation was going to serve the Colonel well. It lagged behind the rest of the world in current trends and drugs were no different. In a league table of world consumption Australia nearly led the world in all departments. A poll in Mixmag had declared that per capita of population, Australia consumed more pills than any other country. It was also in the top three for two others, namely speed and weed. However in terms of Cocaine it barely registered a mention.

It all seemed so simple to Vic. Cheap, high quality pills delivered to a nation of pill heads. It was a no-brainer but the money involved was way beyond what he was capable of. He would have to be the broker. The go-between. He could cream enough off the top to set himself up for the rest of his life.

So he had come back from Europe with a shopping list and a head of dreams. It wouldn't be easy. He would have to be very careful. He would only deal with the top dogs or deputies and wouldn't be able to tell a soul. Clearly though someone had talked.

The door opened and Swanson poked his head in the cell.

"C'mon then. We have your lawyer here. Someone dragged him out of bed".

"He'll be fucking happy about that then".

"Most probably. When we told him what it was about he seemed pretty excited".

"Yeah, excited about the money he's gonna earn".

*

Vic had been true to the promise he'd made to himself. He'd grown up in Greenacre, a hotpot of ethnic diversity. He had gone to school with Lebs, Chinks, Vietnamese, Turks, Greeks, Italians, Macedonians, and Croats. You name it; the ethic blanket of Australia was represented. One guy in particular was the cousin of Mohammad Aziz. He was rumoured to be the king of the Lebs, a title that went with a fair amount of respect when it came to the dark side of life. Affiliated to the guys who ran the Cross, he was big time.

Vic may have been an amateur but he was far from stupid. He had read many gangster novels and watched many movies. He reckoned he knew where many of them had gone wrong. Too much flash not enough brain and too many opportunities for the law to bug or record illegal activities.

From the outset Vic was careful. He had decided from the very beginning to meet Mo only the once. Everything else would be done by a USB drop. Mo and Vic were the only ones that would know the true details of the deal. The less people that knew the better as far as Vic was concerned.

He established the need for wheels within wheels. 'Chinese walls' the financial sector called them. He therefore took the extraordinary step of dispensing with phones. All communication between he and Mo would be done via notes. Except these days it didn't even have to be on paper. Vic would use USB flash drives.

It was a bit laborious and time consuming but both Vic and Mo were surprised about how well it worked. Vic had got the idea from the leader of the Sicilian mafia. When the authorities eventually caught up with the Godfather of all Godfathers they found that he had communicated all of his orders by handwritten notes. There was no phone line to tap. No conversations to record. Every single thing had been communicated through the written word rather than the spoken one and that meant the 'Cosa Nostra' was secure.

157

The USB idea was actually a stroke of genius. Even if people were under surveillance there was very little chance that any communiqué could be traced to anyone. Short notes could be typed and saved onto a USB flash drive and then passed between Mo and Vic at their leisure. The flash devices were so small they could be passed down the line amongst a bit of change, in a handshake, through the smallest of human contact. Even slipped into an empty coffee cup at a café. It was fantastic and as far as Vic knew, unique. It was a shame he couldn't patent it. He was sure he could make a fortune out of it too.

The only problem was getting the drives to each other without involving one another directly. Mo had come up with that solution. Another convenient act of genius that left them both feeling secure about their deal.

Every business needed cleaners and Mo had a finger in a lot of pies. As well as running the obligatory security company, he had invested a tidy sum in various other outlets to legitimise himself. He had bought a couple of premium car wash businesses. Bought some fast food enterprises and placed various members of his family in them. He had even invested money in a funeral home. Like his Dad had said to him 'everyone died'.

But the one business which had surprised even himself was the cleaning business. Everyone needed their offices and business premises cleaned. It was just one of those necessities in life. The overheads were low as well as the wages that he had to pay out. The jobs were mainly taken by recent immigrants who would work for a very low price. This meant minimum wage and a very compliant workforce. The return in the first year had been phenomenal and Mo wondered if he could quit the drug world all together and just live off a legitimate income. This deal with the Serb could absolutely secure that and mean that he would eventually be able to look his mother in the face without lying.

All Vic did was sign a contract with Mo's cleaning company. The cleaning company itself was owned by a holding company which in turn was owned by another company. As Vic said, 'wheels within wheels'. Mo designated a particular cleaner for Vic's offices. When Vic wanted to communicate anything he would leave a flash drive on his desk. The cleaner would then take the drive over to one of Mo's cafes. He would hand it over with the money to another of Mo's cousins when he ordered something. The cousin would ring Mo and tell him that the new pistachios were in or something equally banal and he would pick up the drive from his cousins house. To anyone looking on, Mo would just be visiting a family member and life would look as blandly normal as life could.

For Mo to contact Vic, the whole process would work in reverse. The cleaner would pick up a drive from the café and leave it on Vic's desk. The only thing that could possibly go wrong was that the cleaner did not turn up. Mo was careful who he chose. He picked a recent arrival from Vietnam who was on a student visa. He paid him under the table so that he could earn while he studied. His English was poor but improving but Vic also knew he was terrified of being found out and deported. The Vietnamese was more than grateful and did as he was told. There would never be any questions from him.

It had all been so simple. Simple, neat and as far as Vic was concerned, flawless. Their only meeting and Vic's first and only pitch to Mo had taken place nowhere near Sydney. The mutual acquaintance of Mo's cousin had let Vic know that Mo was taking his family for a holiday in Fiji. It had been hard to gather all the strands together but Vic had managed it. So on the white sands of a pacific beach they had nutted out exactly what each other had needed. They had sat in the shade of a resort bar and quietly discussed the situation. Mo had left all the details in Vic's hands. The rest was up to the Serbian. Mo continued his family sojourn and waited for Vic to contact him. There was no rush. As far as Mo was concerned the deal was going to be so sweet, it would be worth waiting for.

*

Vic had learned in business to trust no one. That first and only meeting with Mo had been the deal breaker. As the Colonel had promised this was an offer that blew all others out of the water. He had priced it up like a discount warehouse closing down sale which is exactly what it was. By the time Vic had established a buyer some two months had passed. His way of communicating with Europe was no less complicated than the flash drive drop-off.

He thought the best way to contact the Colonel was to use his cousin in the old country. He was the vital link between both men. Email seemed the way to go but he couldn't spell it out in plain English. He would use his native Serbian to confound the authorities and to make it even more complicated he would use a cipher. It would be easy. He would use a revolving word count. He would start off by using the tenth word in the first sentence. Then the ninth in the second, and the eighth in the third and so on until the count got down to the first word in the ninth sentence. Then the cipher would start all over again.

The first email to Grab read in the following way:

"Mum and Aunty Fatima went to Westfield to go shopping. I gave them money because they had a list. They did not find what they really wanted because the store doesn't stock Serbian spices. I had to buy Fatima heart tablets because her Serbian prescription had run out. We got all of her spices from a friend in the end. So she is nearly as happy as she is in the motherland. She is feeling well and heart isn't giving her any more problems. I will give you a call soon. Give me your new mobile number and I will let Aunty Fatima call you whenever she wants. Details of all her medical tests will be coming back soon.

Speak soon Vic"

The message received would read, 'Shopping list wanted tablets spices as well give me details'. That meant that Grab had to get a shopping list together for pills and powder and get the details back to Vic. The Colonel had been aware of the rough amounts involved and sent via airmail an itemised list of prices from Amsterdam.

Untraceable thought Vic. That was all he cared about. The anonymity that all this subterfuge afforded him. It would be well worth all the cloak and dagger stuff and anyway it gave him a bit of a thrill if he was to admit it to anyone. Which he couldn't but all the same, it spun his wheels.

Vic sent the email via hotmail from an internet café in Rockdale. Far from his factory in Taren Point and to anyone looking on, it would just appear to be a random act of family business. It was perfect and to anyone on his tail it would be a non-event amongst many other non-events.

*

It had taken about a month for the bill to come in. Vic saw no harm in the factory address being used. Grab had made another personal visit to the Colonel rather than rely on any other mode of communication. He had been treated well by his former army colleague and it didn't take too long for the Colonel to get everything in motion. He gave a copy of the invoice to Grab and dispatched the original to Vic.

First item on the agenda were the pills: Five million of them with an MDMA purity of 75% at a price of 50 cents per pill. Then there was the MDMA powder itself. Enough to make about 10 million pills at the same purity or more if you wanted to cut them. Anything above 25% was more than was currently available at market prices. All up the deal was going to cost 5 million Australian dollars.

Vic was going to take a cut of the retail price for setting up the deal. Conservatively they estimated that they would be able to offload the pills on the open market at ten dollars per pill if they were clever about it. Mo had the connections in all the major cities to allow that to happen. That meant a bumper payday of 150 million beautiful Australian dollars for the 'kangaroo cartel' as Vic liked to call it.

Vic's 'cartage' was 10 percent of the payday. Paid on delivery of the pills to Mo. Vic was also going to allow his factory to be used to process the powder into pills. Mo would supply the chemist and Vic would supply the pill press. This would be smuggled in from overseas via the Colonel in several shipments. Broken down it would just look like random pieces of metal and would be easily hidden amongst other items of machinery from overseas.

That had cost Vic a tidy sum of one hundred thousand dollars. He had gone overdrawn at the bank for it but the business had more than enough assets to pay for it. He figured it was just like any other investment. Once the deal had been done and the pills manufactured, he would be able to sell it to Mo and recoup his outlay.

The dollar signs just kept rolling around in Vic's head. On receipt of the cargo from Europe he would receive 1.5 million in cold hard cash. Then for the production of the pills themselves from the MDMA powder he would receive another 25 cents per pill. That would be on a pay-as-you-go basis but it would amount to another 2.5 million dollars in his pocket. That meant 4 million bucks for Vic for doing little more than being the broker.

Mo was equally happy about the arrangement. He had been a bit sceptical when the Serb had first walked into his life. His cousin vouched for Vic but Mo did his research anyway. The guy had form for some minor scuffles but besides that had been clean in every way.

Still, he kept him at arms length until he saw something concrete come in through the door. It had taken quite a while to set up. Primarily because Vic was being so careful. Vic gave nothing away to Mo. He didn't know who the supplier was and didn't know where the product was coming from. That was safer for Mo and he liked it that way. Until the goods arrived, he couldn't be connected with anything. No evidence of conspiracy to import, no connection with anything until they took possession. Hopefully within the next six months The Kangaroo Cartel would be in full swing and they would all be rolling in cash.

Now in the confines of the interview room, the Kangaroo Cartel didn't look to be in such good shape. Vic had listened to Detective Swanson crack on about how much trouble he was in but at no point did he bring up Mo's name. Perhaps in the grander scheme of things this Swanson had no fucking idea. Vic hoped so.

Dirty Gomez

He couldn't stop crying. Anything with just a hint of emotion made him well up with tears. It was the comedown of all comedowns. He had done so much cocaine over the past four days that he was going to have to pay for it eventually. He and Tumbles had been battering the marching powder until their whole bodies went numb. Everyone but Tumbles and Tray had dipped out by Monday morning. Tray was definitely 'The King Of Sunday Morning' and for that matter any other morning of the week if someone wanted to take a shot at the title.

Anything he watched on TV made him get all emotional. The sight of a dying child, the cries of a distraught mother, even the national anthem at a rugby match; they all had the combined effect of making him blubber like a lost child at the shopping mall. Tumbles sauntered in to the room. A towel draped around his waist. An emaciated body of twisted muscles that showed no chance of flowing into fat. Tumbles' party lifestyle had left him with the skeletal conditioning of a concentration camp victim.

"Are you fucking weeping again"?

Tray wiped his sleeve across his eyes. He didn't think the statement needed an answer.

"Geezer you need to toughen up!"

"Yeah well. Very easy for you to say. I miss things and the coke makes me a bit la-di-fucking-da".

"I know mate, I'm sorry," Tumbles lit up a fag. "Do you think Rudi will ever stop looking for you?" he continued.

"No I don't. If you held someone responsible for your brother's death, would you stop until he were dead if you had the means?"

"I don't have a brother," replied Tumbles.

"Don't be a silly arse Steve. You know what I mean".

"Mate, if someone did the same to you, I wouldn't quit until they were brown bread and we're not even blood".

163

"That makes me sound like a right cunt!"

"Hey it is what it is. You were young and you made a mistake. Your Godfather let you down. It was hardly your fault but some people don't see it that way. The one person who doesn't see it that way is the most important. He nearly got you in Portugal, you know that. He had people fishing around for months but you were gone. He couldn't be really sure it was you who ran the club. You were a changed man and no one really recognised you. Keeping a tight group of friends saved you. Living out of town definitely helped. I caught a bloke called Don snooping around asking the wrong questions. Our friend Fernando took care of him. Went back to London in traction. There were no more questions after that."

"How come you never got word to me?"

"Didn't seem to be much point. You had disappeared just the way we planned it. Sam was back in London pretending to be a cripple and no one could tell where you had gone. Applying for an Aussie visa through the embassy in Paris was a stroke of luck. If you had come back to London to do it someone would have spotted you for sure. Its not like you are not well known. You were one of London's up and coming DJ's and then you just dropped off the face of the earth. You were like the Mary Celeste or something. A ghost DJ who had held the dancefloor in his hand and then disappeared with London beckoning. Give it another couple of years and someone will do a 'where are they know' piece. Then you'll be up shit creek. To this day, I can't work out how some muppet didn't give you up in Portugal. Remember how long you had to hide when EMF came to town. They were sure it was you. They had seen you play in Nottingham. Lucky for you that they are as thick as all shit".

"You know what buddy?" started Tray. "I find it all a bit surreal. I have been away so long, its like it never happened. My life has been so quiet since, I sometimes think its worth going back and taking the risk".

Tray closed his eyes and stroked his chin. He leant back in his armchair.

"Tray perhaps you need to hear this then. A couple of years ago it was rumoured you were going to play a set at the Essex Country Club. There were no flyers out. Just a rumour circulating that the mighty DJ Tray was going to rock the joint".

"I never had any intention…" Tray trailed off as Tumbles continued the story.

"You know that. I know that. But Rudi didn't," said Tumbles.

"How come I never heard of this?" asked Tray.

"Because no one really knows what happened that night".

"What are you talking about? What night?"

"Don't you ever read the newspapers geezer?" asked Tumbles.

"Not if I can help it. I live in Australia remember. I try to avoid being one of those people who never let the old country go. Anyway the news from the UK is always so depressing".

"Well it was pretty depressing for four bouncers at the Country Club," Tumbles stubbed out his ciggie.

"I don't follow," said Tray.

"The night you were supposed to play, four bouncers were shot outside the club. The papers reported it as a turf war over drugs. That was the official version anyway. The reason that got about the county was that whoever did the shootings were after you. The bouncers had sworn blind that you weren't gonna play. But whoever did it wanted to make sure that the promoters got the message. They shot the bouncers and sped off on motorbikes. The bouncers survived but the club was shut down the next week. It hasn't been reopened since".

"Fuck me dead!"

Tray couldn't believe it. He hadn't heard a word about this.

"You didn't know?" asked Tumbles.

"Course I didn't know. What do you think I am? Fucking psychic?"

Tumbles could see that his friend didn't know any of this. Tray really had been out of the loop. When he had told him about Pedro last Sunday Tray had nearly flipped.

"Tray, the world has turned since you been away"

"I should fucking coco!"

"Yeah you fucking should," answered his friend.

Tray really hadn't even considered his celebrity or its demise since he had left the UK. To him it had just been a brief meteoric journey whose star had dimmed before it had really shone. But some people still spoke about him as the man who would have been king and how he had just disappeared. Conspiracy theories or downright concern continued unabated amongst a select few who remembered him.

He had since hidden his talent as a result. Buried it deep under the blanket of mediocre clubs and pubs. He hadn't spoken to a promoter in a long, long time. Not that he could. Unless he was willing to go under the knife and change his whole being, DJ Tray, the rhythm assassin, was just a blip on the musical landscape.

"So Pedro?" asked Tray.

"Yes"

"Tell me once again how you manage to ship kilos of cocaine undetected all over the world".

"The long or the short version," asked Tumbles.

"Your version Tumbles. The best version".

*

"Remember the day when Pedro offered you a chance to cart cocaine all over the world under the auspices of diplomatic immunity?"

"Of course I do," answered Tray.

"Well you left that day and I didn't. Pedro decided he needed somebody and that somebody was me"

When Tray had originally heard the story on the banks of Sydney Harbour he had very nearly clouted Tumbles. How could he be so stupid and put everything at risk? Tumbles had been expecting something like this, so he had been prepared. There was no connection to Tray and there never could be. It wasn't a big thing but it was big enough.

About four times a year, always in the European winter, Tumbles would travel to South America. It could be Brazil, Argentina or Peru. Pedro would arrange the details. He would attend the Portuguese embassy in that country. Usually he would

166

contact some undersecretary or just an administrative assistant. He would take charge of a suitcase.

A diplomatic seal would cover the bag. Under international law, the bag could not even by sniffed at by a dog let alone searched by customs. Tumbles had received a diplomatic passport from Pedro via a contact in Lisbon. It was just as easy as Pedro had said.

Tumbles had been travelling regularly from South America to Europe carrying at the very least 10 kilos of 100 percent pure cocaine since Tray had departed. For every trip, he received twenty five thousand US dollars. Not too excessive a cut considering he was carrying usually around one to two million dollars worth of coke.

He would drop the cocaine off at the Portuguese embassy in his destination country and receive his cut at the same time. He had earned a lot of money for doing this and he could easily explain away his trips as his end of season bonus during the Portuguese winter.

As a result, Tumbles had bought a villa at Sagres and also an interest in a Portuguese *adega* or Inn which gave him another source of income. His trip to Sydney was the first he had made to Australia under the auspices of cocaine diplomacy and it just happened to coincide with Tray's birthday.

"Mate, I wondered how you managed to stay in that shit hole without going mad. Now I fucking know," said Tray.

"And the best part about it Tray. I don't open the package, test the gear or anything. I am just a well safe mule. No one in the world can touch me when I have that passport and seals. I get paid and I keep everyone happy."

"You are one fucking lucky bastard," exclaimed Tray.

"Yes, but I have you to thank for that".

"Yes. You do"

There was a knock on the door. Tray stretched his head around the back of the armchair. It was Tracey and Lizzy.

"Tray baby?"

Tumbles always laughed to himself about the cute way Tray and his women spoke to each other. It never changed no matter the depth of the relationship. It would

167

always be honey, sweetie, love, darling; he used every pet name known to man. It was how Tumbles judged that Tray and Felicity would be doomed from the start. He used her full name most of the time and the pet stuff occasionally. It certainly didn't match the ardour that Jo and Tray shared. Tumbles turned to the two women as they entered the room. He was going to have to shag Tracey before he left. She was vulnerable after all.

"Yes honey," replied Tray.

"Tracey's got something to tell you".

Bugging Out

"Get your shit together. We're leaving!"

"What? When?"

She rubbed the sleep from her eyes and glanced at her bedside clock. It showed just after midnight. She had come back from the camp and crashed around 3pm. She was exhausted. A month in the field had almost destroyed her.

"Now!"

"Where are we going?"

"Anywhere but here. We've got transport waiting and there's a car running outside".

"How much time have we got?"

"Absolutely none!"

She grabbed her backpack and a can of coke. She pulled the laptop off the makeshift desk and her camera.

"C'mon girl. We've been ordered out!"

"Why? What's happened?"

"I'll tell you in the car. But everywhere is going mad".

They jumped into the banged up Toyota which was indeed running at the steps of the building. The gates slipped back and they exited the compound. Outside the gates the world reflected Dante's inferno. There were people everywhere. Shouting, letting off guns into the night sky, setting light to whatever vehicles remained in the neighbourhood .

"Lie down!"

The order came from their driver. He reached back and covered them in a blanket.

"Stay under there!" he barked.

She tried to take a peek at her colleague but he was hunkered down underneath the blanket as ordered. Ryan was petrified. He hated this sort of stuff.

"Where are we going Ryan?"

"Airstrip!" His voice was strained.

"Are you going to tell me what the hell is going on?"

"They've fucking bombed New York Jo".

"Who have?"

"Who do you fucking think?"

Oh fucking hell. They wouldn't have. They couldn't have. But here she was being bundled to a no name airstrip under a threadbare blanket. Proof that they had done exactly that. Fucking hell! Were they gonna make it this time?

"Ryan what are we going to do?"

"Pray that someone doesn't stop this car and blow our fucking heads off!"

"Ryan!" She was scared. More than when the Taliban had grabbed her.

"Jo just shut the fuck up! If we get out of this I swear I'm gonna kill you myself!"

Jo did just that and listened to the suspension creak and moan as it hit every single pothole on the road out of town.

The Money Go Round

"I said to keep an eye on that fucking money Tarry."

"I did but we lost it. We dropped the suitcase in the back of the car and waited. We were sitting there waiting for Vic to turn up when the cops arrived. They were just doing a routine sweep of the car park. There had been a lot of cars stolen there apparently and were keeping an eye on things. They didn't like two Lebs hanging around in a Cronulla car park and asked us to move on"

"The cops made you as well"

"No I don't think so but we couldn't hang around."

"You better not have! I can't afford to be involved!"

"Mo I think they were just beat cops. They weren't Feds. By the time we went back ten minutes later, the car was gone. We drove around for a bit to make sure we weren't tailed. When we got to the bar all hell had let loose. I swear there's something strange going on."

"Yes there is Tarry. I'm down six and a half million and you're sitting here like there is nothing gone wrong. Yous shit me!"

"Mo he can't be undercover or we'd be sitting next to him. They've got pills in a van that don't belong to us. I don't think they've got the cash. I don't know why but I think he's fooled them on that count. It just doesn't feel right."

"Find out what's going on Tarry. Get some information from somewhere. Some bastard's got our money and I want to know who it is."

"It might take a while Mo. This is the Feds."

"I don't care who it is. No one takes six and a half million from me and gets away with it!"

Thirty Minutes

He had been interviewed for three days but he hadn't given them a thing. He had learnt that he was the victim of an international investigation. The Colonel had been picked up along with his cousin and many others in the Serbian's organization but Vic had done well. They were fishing for local names but they had nothing. He would not budge. They had been watching The Colonel for many months when Grab visited him a number of times and they tracked him back to Serbia. He had not been careful like Vic. He had been lazy. He had used his home computer and his email account to communicate with Vic and it hadn't taken them long to break the cipher.

Fucking stupid peasant! He should have done it all himself. One weak link and he was stuck in here. They kept asking about where he had gone after he had been in Cronulla. They had tracked him via a GPS bugging device but he had changed cars. Despite what many think, the police don't usually tail people anymore especially when there is federal funding involved.

The police had obtained a warrant to put both a listening device in his phone and in his car. The Maserati already had a tracking device in it. They just simply hacked into the signal and hey presto, Vic was under constant surveillance.

But they had lost him in Cronulla. He had parked up in the car park of Cronulla mall. Left his mobile in the glove compartment and simply disappeared. By the time they had got to the car, he was gone. They were kicking themselves. They were desperate to find out what had happened in the thirty minutes he had disappeared. Vic could taste their desperation. It was like the local over thirties disco where to be unattached at the end of the night was like wearing the mantle of complete failure. It made you the lowest in the tribe. Vic could see that same desperation in Swanson's eyes.

The missing thirty minutes was behind the decision to move in on the cargo. If Vic could lose them that easily in Cronulla, they were certainly in danger of losing the entire cargo once it moved outside of the Shire. Swanson had made the decision

172

despite not knowing who the buyer was going to be. He was certain he could turn Vic anyway. The threat of a lifetime in jail usually gave people pause for thought.

But Vic was nothing if not stubborn. His lawyer had advised him well. No news was for him, good news. So he had been charged with conspiracy to import a controlled substance and sent to Long Bay Jail pending a trial date. That would take some time said his lawyer. Maybe a year or more and there would be no way that he would get bail. The pill press and the international connection ensured that.

Swanson was pulling his hair out. The DPP wanted more evidence against Vukovic and that missing thirty minutes nagged at him like an itch he couldn't scratch. What had he been doing? Where had he gone and with whom? The car had not moved from the location and that meant Vukovic had only fifteen minutes each way to do whatever he had to do. They had searched the cameras in the mall. Nothing. The cameras in the car park were down due to building work. They had lucked out there. Where the fuck had he gone?

He hadn't gone far. He had waited for the Lebs but they weren't there and he was on a tight schedule. The sun had just gone down and it would be safe at the moment. He jumped in the red Mazda and pulled away. He had borrowed it off Tracey whilst he said the Maserati was getting serviced. He switched on the ignition, reversed out of the space and then wound his way down the multi-storey facility. He kept an eye on his rear view all the time. Nothing, not a car to be seen. He turned left out of the car park and then took a quick right and then right again at the roundabout. He then turned right just before the Kingsway and snuck up a small alleyway. He smiled to himself. He was practically right behind Cronulla Police Station but he wasn't going there today.

He got out of the car and opened the boot. There was the suitcase as promised. He quickly unzipped it and looked inside. There, nestled neatly in bundles, were piles and piles of hundred dollar bills. There were also some US dollars in there as well. Unmarked thousand dollar bills. He didn't know how Mo had got them but it saved on space and made things a little easier.

He didn't have time to count it but he was sure that Mo wouldn't skim. He wasn't that cheap. He zipped up the suitcase, put a small padlock on it and then dragged it out of the boot. He walked quickly through the back of alleyway and through a gap in a chain link fence. Next to the gap was a shed. It was open. He walked inside, knowing the layout like the back of his hand. He hid the suitcase behind a large metal storage cabinet and then darted back out of the shed. All in the space of two minutes.

He jumped back in the Mazda and then retraced the route that had brought him there but instead of turning right into the multi-storey, he turned left and parked up in the dark and unlit car park of Cronulla Bowling Club. He knew the car park had no cameras on it and Tracey's membership ensured that the car wouldn't raise any eyebrows if it were left there overnight.

He ran across the road and up into the farthest stair well. He finally got onto the roof and jumped into the Maserati. All up he had been gone twenty-eight minutes. Excellent! He chuckled to himself as he retrieved his phone from the car and called Tracey. Six and a half million bucks was currently residing in the maintenance shed of the dour and dowdy Cronulla Bowling Club. It was no less than thirty metres from Cronulla Police Station and in his experience that had made it as safe as the Crown Jewels.

Tracey had been sitting in the bowling club the whole time waiting for Vic to return. She had been clock watching, tapping her foot. Impatiently waiting for the evening to begin. She answered the phone angrily because she didn't like to be kept waiting. Vic had placated her and asked her to meet him outside. She chugged the rest of her Lemon Russki and made for the front door.

For the early part of that evening he had worried how safe that money would be. Now he knew, by luck more than judgement, that Swanson had no idea what he had been doing in those thirty minutes. He therefore couldn't get his hands on the money and couldn't hang anything on Mo. That was the good news. The bad news was that Mo would want the money back!

CHAPTER SEVEN

RUMBLE SON, RUMBLE

In A Land Of Strangers

What had happened? Grab had travelled a long way to wind up in a prison cell. He wasn't an Australian and his English wasn't so good but he knew why he was here. They had been busted. He had kept the cargo company all the way from Amsterdam. Through the Mediterranean, the Suez, the Indian Ocean. He had been so fucking sea sick he swore that he had thrown up his stomach lining. Eight weeks of torture for him. And for what? The consulate had abandoned him. He had nothing to fight with. All he had was his cousin and he couldn't talk to him. He waited for his Aunty to get in touch.

Most of all though, he remembered his rights. He didn't understand this country. They had arrested him for a massive crime but they treated him like a god. He had good food. They hadn't tortured him. They just locked him in a cell for many hours and then dragged him out occasionally and asked him questions. His answer was always the same. 'No comment'. Eventually the Australians had provided him a Serbian speaking lawyer and his Aunty had come to see him.

They had laid it all out for him. He was looking at spending an extremely long time in jail if he didn't cooperate. He asked if Victor had been cooperating. He was told he had not. If his cousin were saying nothing, then he would do the same. He would say nothing until his lawyer authorised it and his lawyer would authorise nothing without Victor's say so.

Life wasn't so bad. He had lived in a lot rougher circumstances during the war. At one point he had eaten nothing but rats for a couple of weeks. It is surprising what a person will eat when there was nothing around and starvation is gnawing at you like a rabid dog. Here he had three meals a day and more than enough literature to read. He had seen his name in the paper along with Victor's and the mysterious Colonel. There was also the Serbian who had travelled with him from Amsterdam, Slobodan Bledovic. He was there to pick up the cash upon delivery to Victor and also to guarantee the security of the cargo. Once through the Australian border it became Grab's and Victor's responsibility and payment was to be paid immediately.

He had stood outside a bar in a strange land as the cops had pulled him aside. They had unloaded the Mitsubishi van. Tube after tube of plastics were pulled off. He glanced to his left and the cop beside him had turned his head to face the wall. There were so many noises. There were people everywhere. The police were trying to manage the crowd but they surged forward to take a look. Eventually a policeman pulled out a loud hailer. He urged the crowd to disperse. If they did not do as they were told, they would be hindering a federal investigation and would be arrested.

He didn't understand the exact words but he understood the sentiment. The crowd did as they were told. They removed themselves to the other side of the street. Still, he could hear them murmuring. They shouted obscenities at the police. Unbelievable! In his own country they would have been beaten for showing such disrespect. How soft these people were! He thought they needed to be shown what life was really all about. Perhaps a bomb under their safe Australian cars would show them. Or a shell from an anonymous mortar. Perhaps they should have their youngest child taken away by a sniper as they struggled to bring back water from the only working standpipe in the street. Perhaps they needed just a bit of misery in their lives just so they could learn how to value it.

He had heard Victor speak about these people. Their lives were so perfect, so safe, that they needed to abandon it on a regular basis. They drank like fishes. They consumed enormous amounts of recreational drugs. All in an effort to escape their perfect lives. *'It is an obsession'*, Victor had said. If the Australian government managed to stop the flow of drinks and drugs, Australians would go out into their garden and spin around as fast as they could until they fell down unable to get up. Such was their desire to get 'out of it' that nothing would stand in their way. This was the legacy of their bloody Anzac spirit.

Victor had said that they celebrated one horse race above all anniversaries. That it was a race that 'stopped a nation'. But it was not the race that stopped the nation. It was the drinking. Every year, Australians would dress up in their best clothes in order to gamble and drink themselves stupid. Victor said they barely noticed the proud animals elegantly entertaining the crowds. It was a celebration of a celebration, nothing more.

An officer walked in and ordered Grab to his feet. He led him from his cell towards the now familiar interview room. His new lawyer and his Aunty were waiting for him.

"Grab?"

"Yes Za Za."

"Sit down, Mr Smythe has some news here for you. Come on. Sit. Sit."

Heard It Through The Grapevine

Swanson sat at the head of the long table. To his left and his right sat his immediate subordinates and further down the line were other members of his team. At the other end of the table sat his superior Chief Superintendent John Fraser. They had been waiting for this call for over two days. Their entire case hinged on it. No one spoke a word. There were various coughs and splutters around the table as they waited for the call to come through.

The room itself was much like many non-descript government conference rooms. Bland decoration with a cheap oil print hanging on the only solid wall in the room. The other walls were floor to ceiling glass but were blocked out with Venetian blinds. The squawk box in the middle of the table broke into life.

"Detective Swanson?"

"Yes Maggie."

"He's on the line now. Just connecting you."

"Thank you Maggie."

The squawk box clicked and the air filled with static.

"Captain Hoogebund?" asked Swanson.

"David is that you?" The disembodied voice crackled from the speaker.

"It certainly is Captain. I also have Chief Superintendent Fraser here and the rest of our team"

"Good. How are you all?"

Various salutations and greetings were directed towards the squawk box. Swanson thought that Hoogebund would not have understood a thing.

"What have you got for us Captain?" asked Swanson.

"I think you are going to be pleased. The Colonel has told us everything in return for us not sending him back to Serbia. There are many people there who want to see him dead."

The Dutch policeman spoke his words softly. He almost whistled the phrases down the line. It reminded Swanson of the soft shwooshing of skis as they cut through soft winter powder.

The Dutchman continued.

"I do not think that we will be able to keep our promise but he does not know that. He gave us all the dirt on Vukovic. He confirmed that he had supplied the pill press for him. He confirmed the prices, the amounts everything. We have at least seven hours of videotapes to send you. That is only the preliminary details."

"Well done Albert. That is great news," beamed Swanson.

Swanson sat forward in his chair, resting his elbows on the table. He looked across at Fraser. The man was looking very satisfied with proceedings. Everybody in the room appeared pleased with themselves.

"Its not all good news David."

Swanson shifted his weight in his chair and nibbled on his pen. He once again looked at Fraser. The smile had gone.

"We can't find out who the cargo was meant for. I'm actually pretty sure that The Colonel doesn't actually know. Vukovic was very careful. We got most of his emails from Grab and there was never any mention in the ciphers. Maybe we are missing something but I am pretty sure they do not know the connection at this end."

'Shit!' thought Swanson. That was a bit of a problem to say the least. They definitely had Vukovic but they didn't know who the stuff was meant for. Vukovic was playing hardball. He hadn't budged one bit and neither had his cousin. It was very frustrating and Swanson didn't know if they could squeeze it out of him.

Swanson's team riddled Hoogebund with questions. Dropping names and urging him to use everything in his power. Swanson gazed at the cheap print hanging from the wall. He studied the faded petals of a sad lonely daffodil as its head hang bent from the lip of a water jug. Bent and beaten. Far from the image he had of Vukovic at the moment. Victor was being stubborn and proud. Like a lonely pine rebuffing the harsh advances of winter.

His daydreaming was broken by someone calling his name. It was Fraser. 'Oh shit', he thought to himself, 'here it comes.

High Jack

"What's up girls?"

Tumbles sat on the floor and picked up a mug of steaming hot tea. The girls traipsed into the room as the late afternoon sun filtered through the hanging vine that grew outside the lounge window. It left the lounge room bathed in dappled light.

Lizzy always loved this room. It oozed comfort. It was a home. He had made it his haven and an escape from the outside world. When the partying all got too much Tray made for this refuge and got away from it all. In the summer he would take a dip in the pool or go down the park and sit by the river. In the winter he would light up the big wood burner, sit in the warmth and play some big dub reggae beats on the huge sound system. It was his bliss.

Today though that bliss was broken by the worried face of Tracey and Liz. Tray saw it straight away. Tumbles knew something was up too. Lizzy gave Tray a long slow kiss and then moved around the coffee table and gave Tumbles a peck on the cheek. She hardly knew the man but a mate of Tray's had to be respected and a mate who had taken such a risk for him was a man she wanted on her side.

Tracey didn't kiss Tray or Tumbles. She plonked herself on the sofa and allowed herself to be swallowed by the sumptuous cushions. It provided her no comfort. The last five days had been a harrowing experience for her. It was etched on her face. She had become haggard and drawn. Vic's name had been all over the papers. She was so glad that she hadn't introduced him to her kids or her parents. They would have disowned her.

She had been forbidden to see him by Victor's family. They had battened down the hatches. Their house had been besieged by radio, print and TV reporters and they had ignored everyone, including Tracey. She felt betrayed. The woman spurned. At first she had been worried for him. Now that worry had turned to anger. Not one word from that bastard. He had lied to her. He had used her. He had made her fear for children. He would pay for that and pay big as Tray liked to put it.

*

Tray knew that Lizzy was busting to tell him something but he wasn't going to rush it. He had had enough over the past couple of days. Tracey was on the phone to Lizzy every five minutes and when Lizzy wasn't talking to her, she was relaying each painful blow back to Tray. Normally he would have indulged his girlfriend but Tumbles wasn't going to hang around for too long and they both wanted to catch up on things. As far as Tray was concerned, Vic was a chapter that had to be closed and closed quickly. He was frankly over the man. He had bitten off more than he could chew and nearly dropped them all in it in the process.

"Tracey whatever you've got to tell me just let it ride for the time being. Tumbles is looking to spend some quality time with us, so how about we open some champagne and play some Trivial Pursuit."

Tracey had just grunted. Lizzy thought it was a great idea and shuffled off to the fridge. Tumbles went and got a mirror and a straw but Tray thought they should leave it for the night. He'd had enough for the time being and wanted his body to have a bit of rest. Tumbles looked at him questioningly but didn't ask. He had never doubted Tray when his friend wanted to pull up stumps. He knew his body better than most and he knew when the engine needed cooling off.

So they had spent the afternoon playing Trivial Pursuit which Tray had won as usual and as the nightfall came down, Tray decided to ask Tracey what she had to tell him.

"That night that Vic had been pulled. He was up to something before we all met up."

"I expect he was," replied Tray.

"I don't know what he was doing but he was hiding something up the bowling club."

"Like what?" he asked.

"I'm not sure. I was out the back of the club having a fag when I saw him scurrying around by the sheds there. He was carrying something but I couldn't tell what. He didn't see me and then about ten minutes later he called me and asked me to meet him out the front."

"Have you got any idea what he was doing Tracey?"

"None. But it was all pretty strange"

"Do you want to go and have a look?" asked Tray.

"You bet."

"Okay, lets do it! But first lets have some medicinal courage."

He looked at Tumbles.

"Mr Brown. A couple of lines of your finest!"

"Certainly my liege."

*

They had waltzed into the bowling club feeling like rock stars. Head abuzz with the feeling of invincibility. Tray hated these clubs. Formica tables with strip lighting. They were bright and devoid of any atmosphere. You could hear the constant inane musical interludes of the pokie machines. Addictive purveyors of misery. Women and men of all ages sat glued to their chairs playing these gambling machines that asked only for their customers' company and their money. Now and again the voice of a lined old hag cackled something like 'Number 42, your chicken parmagana's ready' over an outmoded tannoy system. It was like listening to nails on a chalk-board. Tray called these places 'God's waiting room'.

They ordered some drinks at the bar and then strolled out onto the back veranda. They huddled around a gas heater that kept the sharp evening air at bay.

Tray whispered to Tracey.

"So where are you talking about Tracey? And don't point."

She leant forward across the chest high table and indicated with her head. The bowling greens were out the back of the club and descended in levels towards the road that lay at the rear. The whole area covered about two football pitches.

He still couldn't see where she was talking about.

"To the right Tray. Way over the back."

He turned his head without trying to look too hard. Down on the lower tier of greens and tucked in the far right hand corner were indeed a couple of sheds. He had never noticed them before but then again how would he be expected to. He wasn't exactly a regular attendee here and he very rarely cast his eye over the verdant playing surfaces.

"How did he get down there without being seen."

"Dunno but I saw him!"

"Yeah but did anyone else?" asked Tray.

"No I was the only one out here at the time. But he didn't walk across the greens. He just appeared around the back and just shuffled into one of the sheds and then he was gone"

"Which one?"

"The last one I think but it was a bit difficult to see"

"You want to go for a walk geeza?" he asked Tumbles.

"Why not? Seems like a night for it," his mate replied.

Tray rose from his stool and nipped down the path that lead to Woolooware Road. From the street the two men could see that the sheds were standing hard against a chain link fence behind which there seemed to be some open ground.

Tray thought there must be an access point further up the road and he was proved right when they found the same alleyway that Vic had been down a week earlier. Tray and Tumbles crept down the laneway, sticking to the shadows. Tumbles started giggling to himself as Tray started humming the theme tune to 'Mission Impossible'.

"Shut up you fucker. I'm gonna piss me pants," whispered Tumbles into the dark. Tray did stop but not because of what Tumbles had said.

"Fuck me!" said Tray.

"What?" said Tumbles.

Tray moved back towards Tumbles and grabbed him by the arm.

"You know what that building is over there?" Tray pointed to the window of the building opposite.

"Well genius, you've got a bit of a head start on me as I don't even fucking live here!" Tumbles tried to keep his voice down.

"Yeah sorry about that," Tray paused for effect. "That's the fucking local pig pen."

"Fucking bollocks!" Tumbles couldn't believe it.

"No I'm serious. There's more pork in there than the butchers. Vic's got some balls I can tell you. Mind you, not a bad place to hide something. The cops would never look right under their own noses for something. Too fucking obvious."

Tumbles nodded although Tray couldn't see it.

"C'mon. Let's get over to those sheds. I don't like being so close to the station".

Tray crouched down and stayed close to the wall. He rounded the corner and came up on the fence. He found the same hole in the fence that Vic had found and squeezed his not too insignificant body mass through it. Tumbles followed and didn't even touch the sides. He hated him for that.

They still tried to stay low as they realised that if they stood tall they too could be seen from the back veranda of the club. Tray resisted the urge to wave to the girls. The coke was surging through his veins now and he felt a little naughty. Like a schoolboy up to no good, this was a bit of an adventure and he didn't know if he could hold it together without bursting into a fit of laughter.

They found the front of the sheds. One was padlocked with a rusty old lock which didn't look like it had been used for a while. The other shed had been opened and there was no padlock.

"'Ere you go T. What do you reckon?"

Tray grabbed at the door.

"Seems okay. Let's have a look inside."

They opened the door and stepped into the darkness. Something moved against the back wall.

"Argh!" Tumbles shrieked like a schoolgirl. "What the fuck is that?"

"I don't fucking know you plonker!" answered Tray.

Tray could hear something scratching.

"It's a fucking cat I think"

"That's not a fucking cat. Its too fucking big!" shouted Tumbles.

Tray fumbled in his pocket and pulled out a lighter. He lit it. From the back of the shed two beady eyes peered back at them.

"It's a fucking possum Tumbles."

"Fucking nasty looking cunt that is."

"Nah. They're alright. They're fucking harmless," explained Tray.

"Fucking 'armless. Look at the claws on the cunt. It could fucking rip me fucking throat out!"

"Oh shut up Steve. Its fucking more scared of us than we are of it!" whispered Tray

"I fucking doubt that. It could be sizing us up for an episode of 'When Animals Attack'. You know what they say about animals when they're cornered. They're fucking unpredictable. He could fucking jump me from there!"

"Don't be fucking stupid. Its not a fucking vampire. I've never seen anyone attacked by one."

"Fucking look! Its fucking moving!"

Tumbles squeezed close to Tray. He was shaking.

"What're you fucking doing?" asked Tray.

"I'm gonna get behind you. If that fucker jumps, he can have a go at you first. Fucking thing looks well urgent!"

"Pull yourself together you muppet!"

Tray had to take his thumb off the lighter. It was starting to burn the skin.

"What are you fucking doing?" shouted Tumbles.

"Shhh you fucking idiot. Someone will hear us!"

"He's moving. I can hear him!"

Tumbles was none too happy.

"Get your Zippo out Tumbles. I can't hold the lighter anymore. Its too fucking 'ot!"

Tumbles got the Zippo out and yelled again. The possum had moved to his right and was about two feet from the big brave cocaine importer. It was standing on top of a large storage cabinet. Tumbles jumped into Tray, nearly leaping into his arms. Tray pushed him away. Tumbles staggered into the cabinet and made it wobble. It started to pitch over and the possum jumped from his vantage point as the cabinet toppled. Tumbles sank to the ground as the cabinet fell and hit Tray full on the head. Tray followed the descent of the cabinet and wound up with it entirely on top of him. Both men were pinned to the ground.

The possum landed on all fours facing the door. It turned its head and looked at the two men as they struggled under the cabinet's weight. The possum gave them both a disdainful look. If it could have raised its claws and made the universal hand signal of 'wanker' it would have. It stood up on two legs, sniffed the air and made good its escape.

"Get this fucking thing off me you spastic!" yelled Tray.

Tray had taken most of the blow and Tumbles could easily wriggle out from under the cabinet.

"Sorry mate." Replied Tumbles a tad embarrassed.

"I'll give you sorry you long streak of paralysed piss. What are you like?"

"I'm sorry geezer. It was the coke. I'd never seen one of them fuckers before."

"Well stop using up valuable air and get this thing off me!"

Tumbles shoved the cabinet off his mate and helped him to his feet.

"Oh hello!" Tumbles' voice went all camp. It dropped an octave and took on the patinage of a chain saw. A bit like a bass baritone version of Ru Paul.

"What now?" asked Tray

"Over there against the wall."

Tumbles gestured to the wall.

"What?" repeated Tray.

"A fucking suitcase!"

187

*

They had called Lizzy on the mobile. Instructed her how to get to the alleyway. She had arrived about ten minutes later in Tray's work van. He loved his van. It could seat four people and had more than enough room for his DJ gear.

They had dragged the suitcase out of the shed and quickly wriggled through the fence laughing most of the way at Tumbles' performance. Lizzy could hear Tray calling Tumbles a 'pussy' as the sliding door was drawn back.

"You are a dead set fucking poof'!"

"Am not you cunt. It just took me by surprise!"

"I think you need to check your pants"

"Fuck off!"

They swung a large suitcase into the van.

"What's that then?" asked Lizzy.

"Dunno" replied Tray, "Let's get it home and find out."

The boys sat in the back laughing. The girls looked at each other.

"You fucking poofter!"

"Am not!"

"Are too!"

Tracey thought it was like listening to her kids.

*

"What do you think it is?" asked Tumbles

"I've got no idea but its heavy that's for sure."

The girls hadn't said a word since they got back. They just stared at the suitcase. The guest who had no name sat square on the coffee table.

They had driven back from Cronulla in near hysterics as Tray had told them all about the incident with the possum. Tumbles hadn't said too much. He sort of laughed along with them but was highly embarrassed none the less. Lizzy had agreed that Tumbles was indeed the biggest girl she knew. A fucking possum! What a palaver!

The drive had been otherwise without incident. Tray had told Lizzy to take it easy. They didn't want to be pulled over by the police. Given Vic's current form there could be anything in the suitcase. It sort of scared them and thrilled them at the same time. The adrenalin and another couple of lines of coke had set their hearts racing. They kept fidgeting in their seats as they took the winding road down from Sutherland to the Woronora Valley. The lights of the sleepy village twinkled across the river as they approached Tray's house.

They had parked the van up the back under the carport. They had closed the gates behind them and only when they were sure that there was no one about, did they take the suitcase out of the van and take it down the unlit steps, past the swimming pool and through the back door. Now it was time for the great unveiling.

"It could be a bomb," said Lizzy.

"I don't think so. Why would Vic want to blow up the bowling club?" said Tracey.

"I don't know Tracey. Who would have thought he was importing pills either?" said Tray.

"I wouldn't put anything past him the way he's been operating," said Lizzy.

"It doesn't make sense for it to be a bomb. Anyway we don't even know if it is." said Tray.

"I know its his." said Tracey. "I saw it at the factory. It definitely belongs to Vic."

Tray lifted all four corners of the suitcase.

"It's a uniform weight all round. It could just be his escape clothes."

"He wouldn't hide them Tray. There's something important in here." Tumbles also lifted the suitcase. "Look, we're not going to find out unless we open it. Let's fucking get on with it!"

"Okay then! Let's find out!" said Lizzy.

Tray had already removed the padlock by virtue of a pair of bolt cutters that he had purloined from work. Tray bent down and undid the zip. Then he cracked the top a little just in case it was a bomb. He bent close and looked through the one-inch gap he had created. He couldn't see any electronics blinking. That was a good sign. He exhaled slowly, not realising he had been holding his breath all this time. He then stood up and flicked the lid. When he saw what was inside, only four words escaped from his lips.

"Oh my fucking God!"

*

They rolled in it. They threw it in the air. They threw it at one another. They whooped and yelled. They danced like maniacs. Tray just shouted the words 'Fuck, fuck, fuck!' over and over and over again. Tracey cried and cried. This was unbelievable. Lizzy just kept jumping on the couch clutching fistfuls of cash to her chest. She stuffed it down her bra. She stuffed it down Tray's pants. She hugged her man. There was just so much money.

Eventually, after the euphoria wore off, they all sat on the floor surrounded by great slurries of cash. There was Australian and American currency here. It was unbelievable but here they were, in Woronora surrounded by an absolute fortune.

"How much do you think is here?" asked Liz.

"Fucking millions!" replied Tray.

"Let's count it!" said Tracey.

"Let's do some lines" said Tumbles.

"I want to fuck on it first!" said Liz.

"So do I!" said Tracey.

The three of them looked at Tracey. Tray winked at Tumbles. Lizzy gathered up a bundle of cash and ran towards Tray's bedroom. Tracey did the same and ran towards the spare room.

The two men just sat there looking at each other. Tray punched his mate on the shoulder.

"Go on my son! Get amongst it!"

*

Tray and Tumbles sat in their underpants in the lounge room surrounding themselves with the bundled notes. It had just gone 2 o'clock in the morning. At various points they had needed to go back to their respective rooms and roll the girls over and retrieve more cash. Both women had descended into a deep slumber.

"How much does that make?"

Tray checked his notes and added them up again. He shook his head, incredulous to the amount of money involved.

"Well?"

"You ready for this?" asked Tray.

"Stop fucking around you fuckwhit!"

"Well, there's 1 million in Australian dollars and 3.4 million in US dollars and bearer bonds and 1.5 million in Euros. Convert that into Australian currency and all up we have about six and a half million Australian dollars!"

Tray picked up a fag, put to his lips and lit it. He inhaled deeply and smiled at Tumbles.

"What are we going to do with it?" asked Tumbles.

"Its not ours Tumbles."

"No one knows we got it T."

"No, but someone knows its gone."

191

"Yeah but how is anyone going to connect it back to you, or me for that matter?"

"I don't know Steve but let's think about that later. At the moment just let me enjoy being rich."

"Okay buddy."

Tray leant back against the couch and crossed his legs. Tumbles got up and went to the fridge. Tray picked up the remote and flicked on the idiot box. There was some disaster movie on. He flicked through the channels. There must be something wrong with the TV. It was the same thing on all channels. Then he read the tickertape at the bottom of the screen and with an absolute dawning of dread, he realised what was going on.

"Fucking hell!"

"What now?" asked his mate.

"Someone's just flown a plane into the World Trade Centre!"

Tumbles ran into the lounge room and nearly slipped over on a bundle of cash.

"No!"

Tumbles watched on in disbelief as Tower One crumpled in on itself.

"Fucking hell!"

"Tumbles, wake the girls! They've got to see this!"

*

He woke with a start. Something was wrong. He could feel it. There was a lot of murmuring outside. People scurrying down the corridor. The cell door opened and Swanson walked in with a tray of food.

"Oh the special treatment." Said Vic. Then he saw the shock etched on Swanson's face.

"What's up? Looks like someone died," asked Vic.

Swanson looked at Vic. His crime seemed so insignificant now.

"The Arabs have just flown two airliners into the World Trade Centre." He barely looked Victor in the eyes.

"What?"

"You heard," said Swanson.

"How many are dead?"

"Thousands apparently."

"Fucking hell!"

"Yep. About sums it up." He paused, then sighed, resigned to the predictable answer."

You gonna talk today?"

Vic shook his head.

"Thought so."

He motioned to give Vic the tray. Victor refused. He didn't feel much like eating.

*

He put the newspaper down next to his espresso. What a bunch of stupid bastards. This was going to solve nothing. In fact it was going to make life a lot harder for him and his brethren. They were not liked before. This was going to make it even worse. He picked up the cup of thick black coffee and slowly sipped its sweet contents. These fundamentalists were going to be bad for business. The 'skippies' were really going to have it in for them now.

He placed the cup back in its saucer. Tarry walked up to his table and sat down. He pointed to the paper.

"Can you believe this shit?"

Mo shook his head.

"Any news?" he asked hopefully.

"None. No one can get to the Serb and the Feds are all over everything. We're fucking stuffed."

Mo knew they were. He had borrowed heavily to finance the deal. Borrowed from people who wanted to be paid back and paid back soon. He looked at the headline picture of the newspaper. A jet airplane caught in time, flying into the high-rise office tower. What a mess! His world and the world of so many others would never be the same.

CHAPTER EIGHT

WAR

Fast Money

"I have a plan"

"You always have something going on Tumbles. What have you got now?"

"You're gonna like this."

"Maybe. Maybe not."

They were sitting at Trash Bar overlooking the sea at Cronulla. The surf was pumping, punishing the beach with some serious waves. It was cold. Winter held the beach in its clutches and only the bravest of the brave were taking on the shorebreak. Out the back, beyond the waves, sat a group of the hardiest of surfers. Clad in winter steamers, they waited for their ultimate wave. Waiting for that curling swell of whitewater which would make their effort all worthwhile.

"I can triple that money in a month and then triple it again in two. We would never have to work again" said his friend.

"Tumbles. Its not our money!"

"Who gives a fuck Tray? Nobody's come knocking. No one cares. This 9/11 shit has taken over everything. There are terrorists everywhere. Drugs are no longer public enemy number one. The world has turned my friend."

Tumbles was right. The 9/11 attack had been terrible. Everyone looked at the world differently now. People were at home loving their families. But they would bounce back and Tumbles reckoned he had the answer.

"If its so easy Steve, why haven't you done it before?

"Because Tray I have never had the money to do it before. This is the sort of money that could make us seriously rich now."

"If we keep it, we are seriously rich."

"Six and a bit mill between the four of us! Its not enough Tray. In three trips I could turn this into sixty to seventy million. I kid you not Tray. I can do this."

"Fuck off Steve. It ain't that easy."

"It fucking is geezer. I'm telling you. It is easy for me. I have been running this shit for fucking seven years for Pedro. He's been asking me for years to get in on the ground floor and make some serious dough but I've never been able to hang on to my moolah. You know what I'm like."

He did. Money flowed through Tumbles' hands like water. Tray was surprised he had managed to hang on to the club but then he hadn't known about Tumbles' extracurricular activities.

"Tray, its not like it is in the movies. There's not much of this cloak and dagger shit. Not where I'm concerned anyway. Its like going to the bank. Pedro arranges for shipments all the time. He has investors who buy from the cartels. He then hooks the investors up with distributors in Europe. He takes a cut and everyone is happy. The investors allow Pedro to arrange transportation and his lines are secure with the diplomatic passports. There are always buyers in Europe and the police can't touch the Embassies. It is all so easy. "

Tumbles took a sip of the ice-cold beer that sat infront of him.

"Pedro would allow us to be an investor and the beauty of it is that none of the drugs or the money would even enter Australia. We would make so much fucking money we wouldn't know what to do with it. Every time I make a trip, I guarantee we would triple our money. I could convert all of it on the first trip but the second would take another two or three goes. I'm not too sure of the logistics. Pedro would know. We would never have to work again!"

Tray rubbed his chin. He was deep in thought. As it stood 6.5 million wasn't a great deal when they divided it all up and if Tumbles could do what he said, then it was a risk worth taking. Tray's mind was working overtime. With all that money he could do whatever he wanted. Start living his life rather than enduring it.

"I'll put it to the girls. They may not go for it," said Tray.

"Don't give 'em too much Tray. This is my livelihood after all."

"I know but we've got to tell them something."

"You will," said Tumbles.

"I know. I am a silver tongued bastard after all."

They clinked glasses. Tumbles knew his friend would come through.

"Cheers you cheeky fucking monkey."

*

It had been a week of misery for her. Driven across a dusty landscape on to a UN military base. They had flown high above the dry Afghan desert and into the underbelly of Europe. They had refuelled in Turkey and then she had been disembarked at a US military base in Germany. She and Ryan had been abandoned there to do their own thing. The Americans had a lot more on their minds than babysitting two foreign aid workers.

They made their way to Frankfurt and there said their goodbyes. She had taken a plane to London and a taxi to her Aunt Mavis' house in Basildon, Essex. She had called her Mum in Portugal to tell her she was okay and she had begged her daughter to come over and visit but Jo was exhausted. Too much water had gone under the bridge as well. She had abandoned both her and her Dad when they needed her most and she didn't know whether she would ever forgive her.

Mavis's house was small and filled full of cats but it was good to see some family after all these years. She looked in her backpack once again to see if she had brought anything worthwhile from that troubled country. She knew she hadn't. There was still the smell of desert about it and that mustiness associated with camp living but besides the can of coke that she had grabbed from her quarters, there was nothing to even suggest that she had lived in that country of paradoxes.

It made her feel lonely. She had nothing to show for the last ten years of her life. No possessions. No roots. Nothing to say she had made her mark on this world. Now all the hard work she had done. All those small but significant achievements she had made with the women of the tribal regions. Now they would all fade into memory much like those once formidable twin towers. It wasn't just America's innocence that had been quashed in that terrorist attack. So many people that depended so heavily on the assistance that her organization provided would now be abandoned. Happiness was not high on her agenda today.

Mavis wandered into the room carrying a tray of tea and biscuits.

"Thought you might like a cuppa love."

"That would be lovely Aunty."

Mavis sat down and started to pour.

"Do you ever hear from Trystan Jo? He was such a nice fella. It was such a shame you two couldn't work it out."

"No Mave. We sort of just lost contact."

She took the cup and saucer from Mavis and raised them to her mouth. She blew softly on the surface of the steaming drink.

That was another thing she had nothing to show for. She should have been married to Tray. They should have had kids. That would have been their legacy. But she had made her choice hadn't she? She could have stayed but blood is always thicker than anything else. Choices. We all have choices but who really wants to make them?

She wondered what he was doing. '*Married*' Jimmy had told her. Australia of all places! He would like it there. Perhaps he was still deejaying but she doubted it. He would have stayed low after all. He was too good to play anywhere really. Someone would have spotted him somewhere.

"What are you going to do Jo?"

"Nothing Mavis. Absolutely nothing for the time being. I have been working solidly for the past seven years. Before that there was Dad. I think I deserve a little break. I have plenty of money saved up."

She took another sip of her tea. Perhaps she would go to Australia. Now that would surprise him. She thought about ringing Sam. Then she shook her head thinking better of it. Perhaps she should buy a place and stay in her own country for once. Or perhaps not.

"Perhaps I'll go to Cuba. I've always fancied that."

Perhaps. Perhaps. Perhaps.

"Well what do you reckon?"

"I don't know. Tracey what do you think?" asked Lizzy.

"Mmm not sure. How is he going to do it?" responded the sister.

"I can't tell you that and you really don't want to know," said Tray.

"Can you trust him Tray?" asked Tracey.

"I would trust him, not only with my life but with your's and your childrens'."

That had been the clincher. Tray had left them in the lounge while he and Tumbles had gone down the park.

"Do you think they will go for it?" asked Tumbles.

"Yeah of course they will. Who's gonna turn down the chance to make fifteen million bucks for doing nothing?"

"Yeah true. But what about Vic?"

"Not being funny Tumbles, that cunt can go and get fucked. He should never have put us at risk like that and Tracey will never forgive him."

"Yeah, well a woman spurned et cetera."

They sat down on the riverbank. Tumbles thought how beautiful this country really was. Twenty miles from Sydney centre and they were sitting by an idyllic river, in an idyllic valley under an idyllic winter sun. Winter, he thought, it was twenty fucking degrees, positively tropical compared to London.

"When will you leave?" asked Tray.

"If I can get hold of Pedro tonight, I will leave tomorrow or Friday."

"How long do you think it will take?"

"Mate. When I tell you its easy, it really is. We'll have to pay Pedro a finder's fee but besides that, we have to do pretty much nothing. I have to pick it up from somewhere in South America and drop it off in Europe. Pedro collects the money and then he will pass it on to me. Easy."

"More important though Steve, can you trust Pedro?"

"Geezer, he has a lot more to lose. I know too much to let him rob us. I can drop him and his whole syndicate in it. Anyway he would stand to make at least a couple of million out of this. It will be good for him too. He won't turn it down."

"Just so long as you're sure."

"I'm sure T."

"Good."

"Don't fret girly. We're gonna be fucking loaded!"

*

"They're still interviewing him Mo."

"Fuck me. When are they going to move him?"

"Couple of weeks apparently. Then they'll put him in Long Bay and we'll get him there."

Tarry had been struggling to get stuff out of his contacts but nothing. The Feds were keeping things as tight as drum.

"Good. I've just got off the phone to Igor. He's raised the interest rate and given me another month to pay but he's fucking killing me on the points. This is going to cost me a fortune if we don't get this money back."

"We're gonna have to get brutal. You know that!" said his henchman.

"I know Tarry. Maybe even knock him off. I'm pretty well fucked at the moment."

"Don't worry boss. We'll get it back. The Serb won't be a hero."

"I don't care what he wants to be. We need to get solvent and fast."

*

"Sit down Swanson."

There were no niceties here. No bottle of scotch from the bottom drawer. Swanson swallowed not sure what was going on.

"Word has come down Dave. We're winding up the team."

"What? What about the buyer?" Swanson couldn't believe it.

"Not important anymore."

"What do you mean?"

"The camel jockeys have fucked it for everyone. Drugs are no longer the targets. Terrorists are the go. We've got to direct all our attention to that area. Give all your casework to the DPP and let them build the case against Vukovic. We've got more important fish to fry."

"You're kidding Sir! I've spent months on this."

"Look, the Dutch have got their man. We've executed the biggest pill bust in Australian history and we've stopped millions of pills getting on to the market. We're heroes Dave. Just take that and leave it."

"I suppose you're right Sir." Swanson couldn't hide the disappointment in his voice.

"It will be okay Dave. You've got a week to tidy everything up and then we're on to terrorist surveillance."

"Is that all Sir?"

"That's it."

'Fuck!' thought Swanson. He left Fraser's office feeling somewhat cheated. Someone had dodged a bullet. He wondered if they knew that. Anyway it saved him asking Vukovic the same questions every day. He supposed he'd better tell the slimy bastard the good news. He would have to arrange the transfer to Long Bay this afternoon. More fucking paperwork.

Tea Time With The Natives

"They've moved him."

"Fucking about time."

"Word is that they've closed the investigation too."

"What?"

"Yeah. You can thank Osama for that."

"What?"

"Too busy tracking down our fundamentalist brothers."

"They're not my brothers Tarry. I've warned you about that."

"Sorry Mo."

"Anyways. What's the story?"

"The Feds have refocused their attention. They don't want to stop the drugs. They want to stop the bombs".

"Is it that good?" asked Mo.

"You bet."

"So what do you think?"

"We'll be able to get him in the jail. Then we'll get the money."

"Make it happen Tarry."

"Its as good as ours boss."

*

The tall imposing gates slid back as he peered through the metal grill. The van rolled over the anti-escape spikes, facing in the opposite direction as they were going in and not going out. He studied the large outfields. Things hadn't changed. The cold stark buildings housing a sea of criminal mentality.

It had come quickly. Quicker than he had thought it would be. He had expected them to grill him for months. But Swanson said that it was enough. Unless he was willing to cooperate, that was it. They had enough evidence to nail him on the importation charge. He couldn't figure out why they weren't chasing Mo's identity until Smythe had told him.

Smythe was an expensive silk but he was worth it. Grab was on his way to the Villawood detention centre awaiting deportation. He had broken so many laws it was laughable. In charge of a controlled substance. No visa. Wanted by the International Tribunal in The Hague to give evidence in war crimes tribunals. Grab was going down for a very long stretch somewhere on this planet. It was just a matter of who shouted the loudest when it came down to it. Vic was doubtful if he would ever see his homeland again. It was good that Vic had kept up the walls of deception between him and Mo. At least that was one thing that had worked.

At first Vic thought that he was going to be kept away from the general population. He was a bit of a celebrity inmate after all and he had only been charged, not convicted. But Swanson had put paid to that. He had offered cushy 'bird' in return for some more information but Vic was not playing his game. Everything would be on Vic's terms or not at all and Vic wasn't dealing.

The downside to his stoic resistance was that Swanson was going to make sure that his time would be hell until he cooperated. He dreaded the thought that he would be mixing with the general populus. Mo's people would try to make contact for sure. It wouldn't be a problem though. He was pretty sure that the money would be safe. Vic had paid good coin to the maintenance guy at the club to stay out of the shed and no one else would be going in there.

The van stopped and the engine turned off. The driver's and passenger doors opened and he felt the two policeman get out of the cab. He heard the boots stomping on the tarmac and approach the back door. The keys were shoved into the padlock and he heard one of the coppers curse as they had chosen the wrong one. Eventually he got the right one and after a fashion, pulled the door open.

The baseball capped copper stuck his head inside the paddy-wagon. He hated these new uniforms. Only because they made the coppers look like fucking security guards from the local pensioners home. Standards had dropped.

"Vukovic?"

"Yep"

"Move to the door. Hands in front of you!"

Vic did as instructed. The coppers grabbed his cuffed hands and pulled him out of the van. Vic stumbled out on to the desolate parking lot.

"Welcome home Vukovic!"

"Fuck off mate. I won't be here forever!" Vic didn't have to be nice about it.

"Whatever you think Vukovic. Two hundred million dollars worth of pills gets you a lot of time."

The copper sneered at him. This was getting out of control. The papers had kept inflating the price. Some had said as high as four hundred million street-value. Whatever the real price, the amount of money involved meant he was a marked man. The only leverage he had was the money. He hoped it was safe. He was dead if it wasn't.

*

Tumbles had left as promised on the Friday. They had a small send-off at Tray's place. Just the four of them and Tracey's little girls. They had lived a pretty shit life up until that point. Two different fathers. They were the result of the poor decisions that Tracey had made in her life. It made her sound like a total slag but she wasn't and she certainly didn't resent having them. They were her little gifts. Her pleasures that no one could take away from her. She loved them so completely, so entirely, that to be without them physically hurt her.

They had decided amongst themselves to hold some money back. Not much, just some pocket money to tie them over until Tumbles could perform his magic trick.

Twenty-five grand each was the agreed upon amount but they were each under strict instructions not to throw it about. Tracey had gone out and bought the girls some new clothes and some toys. Then Lizzy and Tracey had decided to take them out of school for a week and go to the Gold Coast for a holiday. This was going to be their first proper holiday and Tray was rapt to see the joy on their faces.

While they were up in Queensland, Tray was going to build himself a small sound studio. Something he had always wanted. He was going to have to be careful. He wasn't going to buy it all from the same place and he certainly wasn't going to show anyone else what he was up to. Not for the time being anyway.

Tumbles was given a little bit more to pay for airfares, accommodation and expenses. He needed to cover a lot of miles in the coming months and if he needed anymore cash, he was free to dip in to the main funds. He just had to keep records. Mind you if the transformation in the size of the cash cow was possible, then a couple of grand here or there didn't really matter.

Tumbles had called Pedro on of all things a satellite phone. Tray had stared in disbelief at the suitcase phone. It was like one of the old original mobile phones from the eighties but only in size. It was significantly more advanced in the technological department but most important, untraceable.

"Where the fuck did you get that?" Tray had asked.

"Oh just a little present from Pedro. Fucking amazing shit. I can call him from the jungles of Colombia if I wanted to but I've never had the need. Mind you, would be fucking handy if we broke down in the middle of nowhere. Fucking used it on the M25 once. Had to call the breakdown people and none of the motorway phones worked. Fucking lifesaver!"

Tumbles hadn't got through the first couple of times he'd tried. He had left it another day and finally talked to their old time friend. He had got Pedro up to speed. He had informed Pedro that he had a large down payment for a shipment. Pedro had asked many questions. None of which Tumbles could really answer.

"How'd you get the money you *'ponyetta'* (wanker)." The Brazilian accent made the Portuguese word sound much more romantic than the way it was pronounced in the Algarvean tongue. The fact that he was calling Tumbles a 'wanker' was not important. Tumbles looked at Tray and nodded. They had agreed beforehand that maybe Pedro should know some things.

"Pedro, I've got someone here you need to speak to."

"What? No estrangeiros puta." The phrase could be loosely translated as 'no strangers cunt'.

"Its okay my friend. This is no stranger. I promise."

Before Pedro had a chance to respond, Tumbles passed the phone to Tray. Tray put the phone to his hear and heard the metallic hiss down the line and Pedro still protesting about the new contact.

"Hey Pedro! *Bom Dia. Tudo Bem*?" (Good Day. Everything OK?)

"Que? Who is fucking this?" Pedro still hadn't managed to master the intricate art of swearing in English. It made Tray smile. Still trying to become the consummate Englishman.

"Its Tray Ped. Tray McCarthy. You remember. Tumbles' friend."

An echoed voice came down the line.

"You the motherfucker! You! You fucking are the one with the money!" The voice exploded in his ear.

"Ah Pedro. I am good too."

"Who is fucking caring how you is? I thought you fucking dead!"

"Not dead Pedro. Fucking rich."

"Fucking very cool my man!"

"Can you do this for us Pedro? Is this going to happen for me?"

There was a pause down the line. Then Pedro came singing back.

"For you two. *Nao faz mal* (No Worries). It is as good as done. I will get you the best both ends. You are going to be very, very rich ponyetta."

"So will you Pedro. I won't forget this. *Obrigado pa!*" (Thanks mate)

"Hey you give me Tumbles many years ago. Now my turn to help you."

"This needs to be done quick too Pedro. No fucking around. We may have to leave Australia very quickly. You understand?"

"You always fucking up to fucking something Tray. I understand fucking. "

"Once again thank you Pedro."

"No thank you Tray."

"No Pedro. Thank you. I mean it."

"That means fucking very much coming from you. Hey Tray!"

"Yes my friend."

"I am glad you fucking are not dead."

"So am I Pedro. So am I."

He heard his old mate guffaw down the line like an old Mexican bandit in a spaghetti western. He passed the phone to Tumbles.

"What did he say?"

"No worries fucking."

Tray smiled and thought that perhaps it really was that fucking easy.

*

It had taken only one day. They must have been worried. He had been lined up in the canteen awaiting some dried out fish and chips. It had been quick. A Lebanese foot soldier with a go-faster hair cut had sidled up to him in the queue.

"Message from Mo. Where's his fucking money?"

Vic had been prepared. He was ready. He didn't want to spend the rest of his life in here anyway. Either he died now or later. If it was going to happen, he would prefer it sooner rather than later.

"Exactly where I left it!" Cool as a cucumber.

"Don't get smart you Serbian motherfucker. I could kill you right here and no one would care."

"Yeah you could but Mo still wouldn't have his money would he?"

He looked the foot soldier in the eye. The kid was no more than twenty but it looked like he had spent his whole life in the gym. His neck was wide and sat atop some huge bulging shoulders but there was not a lot going on upstairs. That was certain. He was also rather short and Vic towered over him. It gave him a feeling of

208

superiority and at the moment he needed that. He also knew the kid wasn't pulling the strings.

"Look, if Mo wants that money back, I want some protection here. No protection, no money. Now tell Mo that and fuck off! Don't talk to me again unless you got something like that to tell me."

He barged the guy out of the way and made for a table. Several heads turned and nodded at his show of force. He had survived the first approach. Time would tell if he would survive the second.

Take Me On A Journey

You could buy a lot of gear with ten grand. He had dismantled his office and moved the spare bed into that room. He had set up his computer and a multitude of musical equipment, turntables and various electrical components into the larger room. He had rung work and said he had to take a couple of weeks off to deal with a family emergency. He had 3 months of leave saved up so they could hardly deny him that. Daz had come over and his reaction to the room was dumbfounded amazement.

"Jesus mate. Did you rob a bank?"

"Mate. This is between you and me right?"

"Right mate. What have you fucking got here."

"You name it, I've got it. I can manufacture any tune I want. All I've got to do is read the fucking manuals and you know I'm not too good with that."

Daz nodded his agreement. Tray liked to learn on the fly but sometimes, just sometimes, you had to ask directions. That was where Daz came in. Not that he knew any more, just he was a little more patient. Tray motioned Daz in to the room and begged him to sit on a chair in the only available spot left in the room.

"'Ere listen to this."

Tray turned in his chair and pulled up a fader on the massive mixing desk that now sat under the window where once a bed had been.

"Close your eyes buddy, I'm gonna take you on a journey. This tune has been in my head for ten years."

Daz did as he was told. As he settled back in his chair, a hi-hat dropped in from the speakers surrounding him. Then came in the dynamic sound of some tribal timbales. They came to the fore, leaving the hi-hat nestled subtlety underneath. A lone note at the high end of the piano came in. Pinging with an eerie echo on every eighth beat. It cast a memory of a lone church bell ringing out a warning to back-broken peasants in a far-off dusty field. Then it became brighter, reverbing and morphing into the sound of strings. The strings echoed until they formed the vibrant cloak of Handel's

Messiah. All the time the timbales kept their percussive pace until the beat started to hit double-time, then quadruple and then in ever increasing circles until it became an overwhelming crescendo.

Then suddenly, as the peak could bear no more, a bomb of a beat dropped, exploding in the ears. An explosion that released a cacophony of bass and rhythm that slowly wound down like a jet engine losing power. The beats then came to a stop as the landscape of the song dissipated into silence. Then from the right speaker came a simple melodic bass line. Moving up and down a musical scale, it faded in, marching inexorably from a distant point. It then bounced over to the left speaker, except this time it faded out.

When the silence returned for a heartbeat, a hi-hat counted off four beats and then, unannounced, the bass came juddering back in. It sliced through the silence like a juggernaut. Relentless and powerful. Eating up the intro of the song and forging ahead with no foot on the brake. The melodic foreplay continued unabated as a kick drum announced the gathering of deep primitive urges. Fluttering just beyond reach came a string arpeggio, weaving classical magic over the combustible bass line. It drove onwards as the snare drum stated its presence. The top end drums said 'hello' by doubling over the arpeggio and then an organ, luscious and soothing, enveloped the room in a blanket of gospel traditions. It swirled around the tune, meandering in and above the bass line, painting a picture of sun bursting colours.

Then all the colours faded from the tune leaving just the bass and the drums keeping the song alive. Suddenly they too stopped, replaced by the single note of a violin. It wailed like a lonely wind. High and piercing. Determined to make itself heard. It continued on, allowing the suspense to build. Something was coming. Something was begging the listener to come towards the light. The wait was endless until unexpectedly the voice of an angel rained down on the listener.

It was an accapella of extraordinary proportions. The voice contained all the innocence of a virgin siren but with enough blues in it to give it the edge of a life well lived. The voice was incredible, awe-inspiring; something which only gave to the soul and never took from it. It sang a couplet which made the hairs stand up on the back of the neck.

"If you walked in my shoes, would you throw your hands to the sky? Would you touch the face of love, would you even try? Would you feel the sun at work? Would you do the things I do? I can't help but do them, cos I found love in you!"

Then the voice kept repeating 'I found love in you'. It kept announcing the love. Growing and growing until the timbales joined in the recourse. The tribal percussion returned. Retracing its step to an enormous orgiastic joining of incestuous house music. All the elements that had helped establish the foundations of the song joined the vocalist in celebrating the festival of the dance. It was intoxicating, beautiful and addictive. It was like no other dance track Daz had ever heard.

He opened his eyes.

"Wow!"

In four days Tray had managed to construct the song that had played in his head all of his life. It was wrapped in the emotions that had formed his world. It was staggeringly beautiful and constructed like a timeless masterpiece.

"What are you going to do with that?"

"I can't do anything with it. Its yours Daz."

Daz looked at his friend with utter bewilderment.

"I don't want the fame Daz. You take it."

"I can't Tray. This really is brilliant. If you gave it to Sanchez or Morillo, it would be an absolute smash. It would be huge!"

"Yes it would but I want you to have it. You are my friend and I want you to take it on."

"But Tray, I would be lying!"

"You would not be lying. You are a great DJ. You just don't try to get the right exposure. You put this out and you will be able to name your price."

"I don't know what to say Tray."

"You don't have to say anything Daz. Just make me proud. Anyway its not finished yet."

"Not finished! There is nothing more you can add to it. It's a fucking belter. This will be like dynamite on the floor!"

"Only in the right hands. The only hands I want to touch it are yours."

"You're fucking mad Tray."

"Maybe. Just promise me one thing."

"What's that Tray? Anything?"

"That when you play your first headline gig, you invite me to stand alongside you."

"Fucking hell buddy. I will let you play with me!"

"No mate, I just want to be able to celebrate it with you."

"What is the matter with you dude? You are just as good as anybody in the business. Why won't you do it?"

"Because I don't want to. Just accept it."

Daz was starting to get annoyed. What the hell was wrong with this man? It just didn't make sense.

*

Vic walked slowly towards the exercise ground. He had been locked up for twenty hours a day for the past week. Like most prisoners he was housed with another man. His cell was high up on the upper tier of the west wing. Dark blue interior, solid steel beige door. Not even enough room to swing a cat. It was inhuman. They were allowed out of the cells for breakfast, lunch and dinner and for an hour in the exercise yard. He wasn't considered a dangerous inmate and was allowed to move freely amongst the prisoner population.

His cellmate was Jimmy 'Boom Boom' Porter. Jimmy was a boxer with nothing to show for his ten years in the ring. He was a journeyman. Boxing in Australia was no longer the once proud profession it had been. Since the demise of Geoff Fenech boxing had become a shadowy sport that retreated to the smoky halls that it had emerged from. It didn't command the following that it once had. Primarily because mothers no longer wanted their kids to do it. Like rugby league, the safety of the kids was paramount and so its junior ranks diminished on a year-by-year basis. Jimmy said that Australia was going 'soft'. He reckoned If Australia were invaded tomorrow that no one would show up to defend it. Vic thought that there was some truth in the statement but didn't want to discuss too much with Boom Boom. He was a nobody with no reputation at all. That was the most dangerous kind of reputation because inside all a prisoner wanted to do was build one.

Everyone in the Long Bay Correctional Facility was out for themselves. Everyone would turn state's evidence if it meant getting out of the place early. Vic wouldn't give him a thing. Nothing about the case. Nothing about Mo. Not a thing.

Boom Boom was an exercise junky. Throughout every waking moment he would do press-ups or sit-ups in their cell. He even ran on the spot. All the time talking about how hard he was, how tough he was, how simply magnificent his body was. Vic thought that he was in love with himself. Boom Boom would hold an abdominal crunch on the floor for a full ten minutes and then peer down at them after his exercises and count them off. He would rub them like he was rubbing clothes on a washboard and then give them pretend names. The names varied but they were always female in gender.

Boom Boom asked so many questions. Everyone knew who Vic was, what his crime was but they stayed clear of him for the time being. The heat on him was huge. Nobody wanted to be connected with him. Nobody wanted to be seen with him. They knew the guards were watching him and they didn't want to be watched any closer than they already were.

The exercise yard was massive and filled with a sea of dis-humanity. The popular misconception that being in prison was easy was exactly that. It dehumanised the individual. It institutionalised them. It was a breeding ground for further criminal activity. There was no rehabilitation possible for society never forgave a 'crim'. The only thing that prison was good for was giving inmates new ideas to further their criminal intents. Once you had done time it didn't seem so bad. It was like giving birth for women. If every woman remembered every nuance of the trauma of childbirth then they would never repeat the process. Families would only ever exist as a three-person institution but the gift that childbirth gave totally outweighed the pain and suffering that a woman has to endure.

It was much the same with crime. The thrill of the crime. The rush of beating the system. It all allowed the criminal to dare to face their fate. But their fate was always sealed. The criminal would always be caught because there was never a perfect crime. Such a thing never existed. Someone always took the fall eventually.

This time though it was Vic taking the fall. If he gave Mo up he would die in here. He knew that without any reservation. You didn't cross the Lebanese. If he could keep Mo out of it, his time would be easy. If he could get the money back it would be easier. He thought about turning him in. He thought about the mythical witness protection program but he also knew how leaky the police were. How long would he live if he trusted them? The cemetery was littered with the bodies of informants that had trusted the coppers. Anyway, he was accused of conspiring to import the largest amount of ecstasy ever discovered by the police. The public would never allow him to walk free from that sort of crime and neither would the DPP. The pressure to convict would be huge. From the top of government to the lowly Joe Public, he would be condemned. The only thing that had kept him off the front page was the 9/11 disaster. Thank God for small mercies.

He and Boom Boom wandered around the yard, sticking to the fence. He hadn't seen it coming. He had looked across to the La Perouse coastline as his cellmate rambled on about some impending boxing match. Just as they rounded the Southern corner of the yard, a body brushed up beside him. It was the go-faster hair cut.

"No protection bitch. Where's the fucking money?"

He felt a sharp pain in his side. His hand went to the pain. It felt warm and sticky. He realised it was his own blood. He sank to his knees. Boom Boom tried to catch him but it was like grabbing a sack of fleas. There was no stiffness in his body. It was all loose. He slipped through Boom Boom's hands but the boxer managed to at least break the fall. He grabbed Vic's shoulders as he slumped to the ground. Vic rolled to his side. As his head nestled on the ground, he saw the lush, green grass stretch out before him.

In the middle distance he saw the logo of go-faster haircut's Nike running shoes shuffle away.

"Easy mate. Easy." He heard Boom Boom's voice but couldn't see him. Then it went black.

*

Senor Gomez landed in Buenos Aires. His diplomatic passport afforded him the respect it deserved. He was rushed through immigration to a waiting limousine. He directed the car to the district of Palermo. It was an opulent suburb. One specifically designed as a playground for the rich families of Buenos Aires. It was situated just south of the banks of the Rio de la Plata. It played host to the botanical gardens which now anyone could visit but which in unhappier times had been the bastion of afternoon pleasure enjoyed only by the social elite.

Bordering the park were several ostentatious residences of the late 19th century. Huge stone edifices four of five stories high hiding a multitude of historical sins. They were the remnants of the social elite that had strangled the economy and deprived the general populus of a bearable life. There were areas like this in all capital cities and Tumbles marvelled at how it appeared that many consulates could afford them. It reminded him of the streets around Regents Park or St James' Square in London. It was a display of wealth and power that belied the actual solvency of the countries who chose to call it home. Portugal was after all desperately poor. That was how Pedro managed to find people who were willing to turn a blind eye.

They turned down the large Avenida de Liberatodor and onto a leafy tree lined street. They passed the closed entrance to the Portuguese Consulate and made a right turn. They doubled round the back of the consulate and were met by some enormous metal gates. One sheet of solid steel with a guard box next to it. Inside the guard box stood a uniformed sentry. He was not even Portuguese. He would have been hired by the Portuguese from a local security firm at very low prices.

The Portuguese didn't like to work too hard. A hangover from their days of colonial power. Let the slaves and the peasants do the hard work. The consulate was

216

only open in the mornings and only on Monday, Wednesday and Thursdays. This being a Friday, many of the staff were at home or in the countryside enjoying Argentina's wide open pampas. He wound down the window.

"Senor Gomez por Senor Caetano."

He flashed his passport. The guard carefully studied it and picked up the internal phone. He repeated Tumbles' declaration down the phone. He nodded to the earpiece.

"Sim, Obrigado".

He replaced the receiver and handed the passport back to Tumbles.

"Muito Obrigado Senor Gomez. Buenvindos."

"Muito Obrigado". Tumbles thanked him. It was roughly fifty percent of the Portuguese he actually knew.

The gate slid gracefully back on its hidden wheels revealing a large open concrete courtyard. The limo driver headed for a covered area in the far left corner which housed two garage doors at the back. One garage door wound slowly up. A man in an impeccable suit strode out. Sun-kissed skin a la Warren Beatty, dark black hair swept down over his forehead. He looked every part the playboy he professed to be.

Tumbles exited the limo and took the man's outstretched hand.

"Good afternoon Joao"

"Good afternoon Senor Gomez."

Tumbles handed Joao the same brown envelope that Pedro had handed him in Portugal.

"Thank you."

"No problem Joao."

Joao stood to one side revealing three suitcases. Tumbles tapped on the driver's side window. The driver got out of the car and stepped into the garage. Tumbles pointed at the bags.

"Si Senor."

The driver picked up two cases, testing their weight. He turned and took them to the back of the car. He repeated the process for the final suitcase, all with an air of detached interest. He pressed the remote control for the boot of the car and loaded the suitcase inside. Joao handed Tumbles the necessary paperwork which declared that the bags were covered by the diplomatic seal.

"Thank you Joao."

"Thank you Senor Gomez. We'll see you again soon."

As Tumbles stepped back into the car he doubted very much if he ever would. This would be his last trip to Argentina. The gates slid back once again and the driver headed off to the Alvear Palace Hotel. A hugely luxurious hotel frequented by the rich powerbrokers of Argentina. Tumbles smiled as the limousine made the short trip across town. 'Stage one complete' he thought to himself. If only everyone knew how easy this was they would all be in on it.

*

The kids were in the pool whooping it up. The hotel had an indoor pool which was just as well considering the weather was terrible. Lizzy was sipping a marguerita whilst lounging in a sumptuous pool chair. This was the life she thought to herself. It was about time she had some luxury in her life and all it took was that idiot Vic to make it happen. She felt no guilt about taking the cash. Her nieces could have been taken away from her because of that spastic. Now they were going to be set for the rest of their lives. Fantastic!

She picked up the newspaper and flicked through it. Still the papers poured over the misery of 9/11. She couldn't believe how persistently morose they were. The terrorists weren't responsible for spreading terror, the media were. It was on every channel, every front page and every radio station. They had tried to shield the girls from it but they knew something awful had happened and it scared them.

As she turned the pages, something caught her eye. 'Drug Importer Stabbed'. She read on and realised that Victor had been stabbed in prison. He had survived his wounds but only just. She would have to hide this from Tracey. Despite protestations to the contrary, Lizzy knew that her sister still held a flame for him. She put the newspaper down and looked around to see Tracey walking around the side of the pool. One look at her elder sister made her realise that Tracey already knew. The happiness had drained from her face. Her shoulders were slumped and she was deep in thought.

She walked up to Lizzy.

"Lizzy. I…" She didn't get a chance to finish.

"I know Tracey. I know."

*

"Get a message to him."

"Yes Mo."

"Tell him no more mister nice guy. We want it back yesterday. If he don't tell us, then its all over for him."

"Sure."

"And if we get it back."

"We kill him anyway. I don't want any loose ends."

Mo couldn't allow him to take liberties like this. Much longer and he would have to relinquish some assets. He could cover it if push came to shove but it was the principal of the matter. No one made him look like an idiot and the Serbian was certainly taking a lend of him.

*

He sat in his prison bed contemplating his future. He was going to have to turn into a government informer if he was going to save himself. It had been two weeks. The Lebs had delivered an ultimatum via a library book. The card read simply 'Money'.

As he lay in the sterile ward, he weighed up his options. Keep the money and risk certain death. Give up the money and most probably be killed as well. Turn government witness, do some bird and live the rest of his life under a false name and keep the money. There was a third possibility. He could always tell Swanson where the money was and allow the Lebs to go and pick it up. They would be implicated and it might just be enough to get him off. Mo's empire was extensive after all. But would it be enough to convict him?

Victor was so careful that he had nothing on Mo. The flash drive was such a great concept that it left no trail. Vic had no information that would implicate Mo and the Leb would have nothing to do with him since his arrest. Even if he gave the Feds his name, they would have to put him under months of surveillance just to even find some evidence on him. There would be no let-up until he offered the Feds something concrete and they in turn had to then prove what he had said. His life would be in perpetual danger until that point and he didn't know if he could survive.

There seemed to be no positive option. They all seemed to be fraught with danger. The last option seemed to be the only realistic one. He resolved to call Swanson on Monday.

His thoughts were interrupted by a warden.

"Vukovic?"

"Yes sir."

"You have a visitor."

"Who?"

"A Tracey Rogers."

'Fuck' thought Vic, 'I wonder if its conjugal'.

*

220

He was absolutely shattered. Four transatlantic trips in three weeks. He didn't even know what time his body clock was on. He walked in through the doors of the club.

"God you look like shit boss."

"Nice to see you too Anita."

It was daytime and the club smelt like disinfectant. It needed to. Every night the club played host to a range of pissed up punters who were not too particular about their behaviour. A mixture of urine, beer and nicotine pervaded every pore of the club requiring a cleaning of industrial proportions just to make it possible to enter. He paid the cleaners extra to clean the toilets. It still amazed him how disgusting people could actually be and in his experience, the women were worse than the men.

"Where have you been?" Anita asked.

"Here and there. I have been looking at new investments."

"Really? Any place I can work?"

"Sure. If you like South America."

She tilted her head to one side. He liked Anita. He had made her bar manager in his absence. She was good at her job and also extremely sexy. She was everything a good club needed. Tough, intelligent and good with the staff. She was also Swedish. It meant that she dealt with things in a different way from him. She was also very good with the local police. She flirted with them and gave them free drinks. They left the club alone allowing Fernando to peddle his wares inside.

Fernando was a necessary evil. He had been involved with Tumbles and Tray since they came to Lagos. He guaranteed the safety of the club. He provided the security it needed to stop the local Portuguese element spoiling it for the tourists. This was always a constant complaint amongst the other bar owners but Tray had established a good working arrangement from the beginning. Fernando discreetly dealt pills and hash at the club via his family, the gypsy mafia.

The dealers would set up the deals on the premises but would never exchange cash or drugs inside its walls. They would walk their buyers around the block and do the deal discreetly. The police left the gypsies well alone. The traditions of the Algarve were difficult to break. The gypsies had controlled illegal trades on the Portuguese south coast for centuries and the police were afraid of them. They never crossed them and that way the status quo was maintained. Anyway the police were so corrupt it was unbelievable.

The police exacted a tax on nearly every foreign business in town. They could close most businesses without any recourse of action available to the owners. At a mere whim your whole source of income could be gone. He was careful to keep them on board. The Cavern hadn't been so clever. Last year they had been closed down because a punter had stepped on the police commissioner's foot. He had decided that the bar needed a dance licence and closed them down until one could be issued. That had taken a month in the busiest part of the season. It had nearly made Paul bankrupt and he had only just survived. For that very reason, Tumbles always reserved a booth for the local constabulary.

He pulled a barstool up to the bar and sat on it.

"Lemonade and lime please Anita."

She mixed a drink and before he had a chance to sip it or even thank her, Pedro waltzed in.

"Hey dickhead!"

Tumbles rolled his eyes. Couldn't he just have a little rest?

"Pedro."

He shook his friend's hand.

"You my friend are very rich fucking."

"Ssshh!"

He looked towards Anita. She either hadn't heard or was making a show of not hearing.

"C'mon. Let's go down to the booth."

Tumbles led the Brazilian down to the police booth. An ironic touch considering what they were about to discuss.

Pedro sat down first. He shouted an order for scotch, insisting that Anita not give him the cheap shit. Tumbles studied his partner in crime. He looked like a parody of a Hollywood gangster. He had a scar running down from the corner of his right eye across his cheek to his right lip. The gruesome visage was further enhanced by his glass eye. Both injuries were said to be the result of a racing car accident in Brazil. Tumbles doubted whether it was the case but it made for a good story.

He had lost the glass eyeball one night in a drunken session at the club. They had looked everywhere for it as Pedro ran around with one hand over the empty socket screaming at everyone to stand still. Tumbles had ordered the extraordinary step of stopping the music and turning the house lights up. Everyone had gotten on all fours and searched for it until it had been found. Tumbles had fallen about laughing when they did. It was lurking at the bottom of Pedro's strawberry daiquiri. Looking back at him through the red mixture.

Today though, Pedro was far from drunk. He had his business head on. He sat across from Tumbles, waited for the scotch to arrive and Anita to disappear. He sipped on the liquid and let it warm his throat. He reached for his briefcase and opened it. He pulled a document from inside and passed it to Tumbles.

It was a statement from the Bank Of Ambrosia Grand Cayman. He unfolded it. It was in the name of Steve Brown and Trystan McCarthy. He looked at the balance. He looked again. He looked up at Pedro.

"Ninety-two million fucking dollars. That can't be right!"

"Sssh you wanker fucking! Not so loud."

"Ninety-two million dollars. That's too much."

"Do you know how much you transported last time."

He had thought that it was too much last time. He had brought eight suitcases in to Frankfurt airport and thought that it was pushing the friendship a little. He didn't think that they had **all** contained cocaine because every case weighed thirty kilos. It was just too much. It was so much that he hadn't even travelled with it. He had sent it ahead via freight and picked it up at the terminal a day later. It had worked a treat but he was elated when he dropped it off at the embassy in Frankfurt.

The numbers rattled around in his head. He had let Pedro handle everything trusting him to do it all properly. He hadn't been sure of the market prices but if it was all coke then it could amount to a small fortune but not that much.

223

"Did you think I was going to let you have all the fun fucking?"

"What do you mean?"

"Do you think you are only one doing this for me?"

"Yeah well I thought I might not bring enough coming in for you."

"What you bring in is just drop fucking in ocean. Do you want to know how much money fucking your cocaine buy."

Tumbles scratched his head. What had Pedro been doing.

"You give me fucking six million dollars right?"

"Yes!"

"That buys 400 kilos of pure cocaine. I sell for forty-five thousand dollars in fucking Europe. Everyone wants cocaine. Big buyers is fucking everywhere. Big operations in Europe, England even Russia. I have been very busy. Four hundred kilos become twelve hundred kilos. I get fifty-four million dollars. We bring in so much coke in three weeks that market fucking price go down. When I tried to offload last deliveries I could only get thirty thousand dollars per kilo fucking."

"You're fucking kidding!"

"No kidding. I have twelve couriers working for me. Last delivery in one week, they deliver fucking three thousand kilos all over fucking world. Now tell me I am not genius!"

"Fucking genius. You are the fucking rainmaker!"

"I hope you don't mind. I take sixteen million dollars for me. I set up accounts for you and Tray and I have many people to pay. Still you very fucking rich bastardo."

"I thought I was the only one involved."

"You think I am that stupid you English fucker."

"No but how'd you get all that money moved around? Don't they check international telegraph payments?"

"I never deal in wire transfers you stupid boy. Bearer bonds only. Its like dealing in pound notes. Very fucking easy. While you been all over the world I open accounts for you in Switzerland and Grand Cayman. Now you one fucking rich man but it not all finished."

"What do you mean?"

"I think you need to read fucking newspaper."

*

She paid the taxi and headed past the large sign. The taxi turned around and drove away. She looked up at the red brick walls and the gates and wire that surrounded the fortress. She didn't like the look of the place. Mind you the people who lived there didn't ever get to look at the outside much. It wasn't for their pleasure that was for sure.

She walked into the visitors centre and introduced herself. The person behind the counter asked for I.D. and she complied. She signed the registry and a guard walked her across an expanse of concrete. She went through another three security checks and eventually came to the medical wing. They walked in through the grey doors and she climbed two flights of drab colourless stairs. On the second floor they turned left and approached another security check which amounted to nothing more than a hole in the wall next to some extremely strong looking doors.

The buzzer sounded and the doors clicked. The warden hauled open the doors. At the end of the ward, propped up on several pillows, lay Vic. He smiled at her and waved. Then he winced and she realised that he was still in a lot of pain. Up until that point she didn't know what she was going to say. She thought if he showed some remorse for what he had put them through then she may help him. If he just didn't care then perhaps she would let him know how lost he was. It all depended on how he reacted and that was all too unpredictable.

*

They walked up Pitt Street surrounded by Asian students and Sydney buses belching out their daily toxins. They were looking for a record company. Playground Records was their name. They walked past the Arthouse Hotel. It was one of Tray's favourites. They played uplifting house and only the beautiful people went in. They always got the great house DJ's from the UK from labels such as Defected or Hed Kandi. It was the sort of stuff that both of them liked.

"This looks like the place."

Tucked neatly away beyond the Hilton Hotel was a small doorway which only had the number 57 above it. They pushed through the door and found themselves in a small foyer with a brass plate on the far wall. To their left was the lift. It only went up five floors. They looked at the plate. There it was 'Playground Records', right on the top floor.

They called for the lift.

"Tell me once again why we're going here and not Sony". Said Daz.

"Because they know their music. They are also owned by a big label in the UK. One I respect and who will also respect you. There are very few who I will doff my cap to and this is one of them."

"Don't you think this is all a bit quick Tray?"

"No I don't. This needs to be done quick. Who knows what the future will bring."

Once again Daz was puzzled. His friend was being evasive whilst pushing him in a corner. The lift came and they stepped inside.

"Let me do the talking Daz. I've been here before."

"How so?"

"A long time ago I nearly signed with someone. I nearly had an agency sign me. It was all 'very nearly' and then it didn't."

"What happened?" asked Daz.

"It just didn't. Now its your turn and you're good enough to take it to the next step."

"Tray, you're placing a lot of faith in me."

"No. I'm placing a lot of faith in my music. You're one who must complete the journey."

"Tray what the fuck is going on with you?" Daz was utterly perplexed.

"Nothing Daz. Nothing I can tell you."

The doors opened and they moved into the modernist office. Bright colours everywhere. Cubes and huge inflatable balls instead of seats. It looked like a typical kindergarten to Tray. If he looked at the age of the kids working there, he could well have been right. They approached the reception area which looked more like the bridge of the Star Ship Enterprise.

A very beautiful girl looked up.

"Yes can I help you?"

"Yeah Darren Thwaite to see Mr Murchison," announced Tray.

"And you are?"

"An interested party."

Daz whispered to him.

"Tell her who you are Tray."

"No. Now fuckin drop it!" said Tray exasperated.

The girl looked at Tray puzzled by this sudden outbreak.

"I'll let him know you're here. Please take a seat."

Daz took a cube. Tray took a ball. He nearly fell off. Daz couldn't help laughing.

"Shut up you muppet!"

"Sorry Tray. Couldn't help it. It was fucking funny." Daz tried to stop smirking.

"Mr Thwaite?"

A man about the same age as Tray came striding through a side door. He thrust a hand towards Tray.

"No. That's Darren."

The man turned towards Daz.

"Oh sorry. Mr Thwaite. Michael Murchison"

He was English. No wonder Tray wanted to use him thought Daz. He shook his hand and then turned towards Tray.

"And you are?"

"A friend."

"No. Your name I mean. What's your name?"

"Unimportant to you. Just a friend of Darren's. Here to make sure everything runs smoothly."

Murchison studied the man in front of him. Did he know him? He was sure he had seen him somewhere before but not one hundred per cent.

"Never mind. Follow me."

They followed Murchison through the door. Murchison was one of those metrosexuals. Tray smiled at the term. It was supposed to be a term used for men who were particular about their appearance. Face moisturiser, manicures, pedicures, hundred dollar haircuts, designer clothes. Tray thought it was just a term for men who couldn't decide what camp they were in. The 'camp' camp Tray called it. Not aware if they were a chocolate speedway rider or not. Everyone else knew. Perhaps he should tell him.

They were led along a small corridor into a room that looked out onto Pitt Street. Nothing spectacular at all. Tray was surprised by that.

"Now what can I do for you?"

"Have you got a CD player?" asked Tray.

"Straight to business. I like that."

Murchison picked up a remote and the stereo behind lit up. A Banger and Olufsen. Nice gear thought Daz.

"Now you get one chance at this Michael. One offer. One bid." Tray was all business. No fussing about.

Murchison squirmed in his leather chair. Who was this guy? No artist spoke to him like this.

"Whoever you are, don't you think it's a bit early for you to make demands or predictions?"

"Michael is it?" enquired Tray.

"Yes"

"Let me get one thing straight for you. What you are about to hear is going to make you very rich. It is going to establish your tin pot label here in Australia and give your parent company orgasms. Got it?" he paused allowing the record executive to take in the pitch. "What you are about to hear is going to give your goose-bumps goose-bumps."

This guy was starting to piss him off. Tray could sense it and so could Daz.

"You could show us out now Michael or you could sit back and listen. Now you think how much a track like that could mean to you and when you've finished listening, come up with something reasonable and maybe we can do some business."

Murchison should have ordered them out of his office right there but his interest was piqued.

"Okay then. Let's give it a whirl."

He leant back in his chair and hit the play button. He swivelled away from the duo and looked out onto Pitt Street. He closed his eyes. He heard the first opening bars and allowed the tune to flow over him. As the bass swirled and the vocals came in, an image danced across his mind. He was back in the UK. A holiday resort on the English south coast. It was a big weekender planned by one of those Essex organizations. He couldn't quite remember their name. As the vocal hook landed he knew he had an absolute bomb on his hands. It was truly amazing. Then the image became clearer. Exalting the crowd, dropping one massive drop of bone jarring house after another, he saw the man playing to a loyal crowd of ravers.

He swivelled his chair and looked at Tray in complete disbelief.

"DJ T? Trystan McCarthy? Is it really you?"

Daz looked on unsure as to what was going on.

"Tray, who is DJ T?" asked Daz.

"Fuck it!" Tray sat very still. He looked over Murchison's shoulder out on to the Pitt Street skyline. He took a deep breath.

"Yes it's me!"

"Who is you?" asked Daz.

"I am DJ T." he answered dejectedly.

Daz rubbed his chin. He stared at his friend, Who was he?

229

"Mr Thwaite do you know who your friend is?" said Murchison.

"Obviously not." said Daz

"He was *the* man back in the day. He could make the vinyl leap off the turntable. He really was one of the best I have ever seen. Just because of the way he built a set. I fucking remember you in 1990. You were fucking awesome. Then you disappeared. I thought you must have overdosed or something. Where have you been?"

"Hiding," retorted Tray.

"But why if I may ask?"

"No you may not. And if you tell anyone about me this deal is off. I presume you like the song."

"Is that yours? Did you make that? Its fucking phenomenal! Only a man who knows his shit could make something like that." Murchison knew it was Tray's.

"No its not. It belongs to Daz."

Daz was taking no more of this.

"Tray tell him the truth!"

"No Daz. This is your time. Michael you either want this tune with Daz standing behind it or you don't get it all. That's the deal. Take it or leave it."

Both Murchison and Daz looked at Tray. What the fuck was going on? There was something really wrong here.

"Look guys. There's a reason I disappeared and it can't ever come out that I am behind this. If it did you may never see me again, do you understand?"

They patently didn't. Tray decided to give them some more. Shit, he knew it was a mistake coming along but he didn't want Daz dropping him in it. As it turned out, he had dropped himself in it. He should have known. The DJ scene was so small.

"Look if it comes out that I am down here, I will wind up dead. Is that clear enough for you?"

Daz didn't know if he had heard that quite right. Tray turned to his friend.

"Yes you heard right. Dead. Completely and utterly brown bread. Serious as fucking cancer. You got it now?"

"Yes Tray. Sorry mate. I had no idea."

"I know you didn't but now you do. So no more fucking questions about why don't I do it. Both of you. Have you got it now?"

They both looked suitably admonished.

"Murchison. Do you want this song?"

"Fuck me yes!" He almost fell over the table.

"Well there are a couple of restrictions. I am not to be associated with this track ever."

"Done!"

"You support Daz here and get this tune out to the heavyweights. All the big names. You know who I mean. You get it in the magazines and the clubs that matter."

"Done! The tune will pay for itself. It is massive and I've heard them all in my time."

Tray ignored the comment.

"Okay now this is the last one. If my situation is ever resolved and that is a very big 'if', we go into the studio and record an album with all the bells and whistles."

"Yes, of course." Murchison would readily agree to this. Trystan McCarthy had never been huge but he could have been. He really knew how to shake a room. If he was to come back to the fold there was no doubt in Murchison's mind that McCarthy would become a dominant force all over the world.

"Mr McCarthy?" Murchison may as well put it out there.

"Yes?" responded Tray.

"Is there any possibility of that?"

"At the moment no. And too many people are at risk to ever say that it would ever become an eventuality but who knows? Maybe if the world changes and we are forgiven our sins. Who knows?"

He wasn't saying no. That meant that yes it was a possibility, no matter how slim it was.

Tray continued.

"And so the last thing is, I want it released under a particular name."

"So what's that then?" asked Murchison.

"The Kings Of Sunday Morning."

Fucking hell thought Murchison. What a fucking day! Everything had just been put in his lap. A great, dare he say it, all-time-great fucking tune. The possibility of a return from a man who was there at the beginning of it all but finally a name for a group that was by its very definition, was simply brilliant.

"How long have you been holding on to that?" asked Murchison.

"Not long. But long enough to know that it is immediately marketable and worth a mint. Now let's talk turkey. Have you got a number for me?"

"I've got a split. Let's talk about that first."

"Okay it's a start."

*

"You fucking bitch! That was mine!"

She walked serenely away from the bed. She tried to remain as calm as possible.

"That was fucking mine!"

She nodded curtly to the warden as he buzzed the door open. The bastard hadn't been contrite enough. He hadn't cared what he had done to them all. He was a selfish wanker. Just as Tray had said. She would make sure that he would never see that money again. She had told them they had taken it. She just wanted to see the look on his face. It had been priceless. Served him right.

He shouted after her but she did not stop. She got to the door. He thought she might turn around. Just kidding. That was all. But she didn't. She wouldn't give him the satisfaction. God. He was fucked! He banged the bed in frustration. He was going to have to ring Swanson. Monday. He hoped he could last until then. Fuck! She had really screwed him.

No One Here Gets Out Alive

"Are you going to tell me what the fuck happened up there?"

"Not really."

"Tray, what have you done to me?"

"Daz I have given you something that you are going to cherish for the rest of your life. Its not fame. Its not celebrity. I have given you your dream."

They had taken a seat in the Arthouse. By day it was an ordinary city slicker hotel. It was only on Friday and Saturday nights that it became a house fleshpot. Daz turned to him. This was bullshit. It was his dream real enough but it was also Tray's dream. A dream that he could never fulfil. Now it all made sense. So many years spent in the wilderness. So many years being on the cusp of fame and fortune only to pull back at the last moment. Daz had thought it was a confidence issue. But there was never a fear factor in his playing.

Tray would always accompany Daz to his larger gigs. Daz would be scared witless. It affected his playing. Tray however was scared of nothing. He knew when Daz had them in the palm of his hand. Often he would hear the phrase, 'Now rip the fucking roof of this place. Take 'em fucking 'ome'. Sometimes Daz did. Sometimes he didn't. His nerves more often than not got the better of him. He was scared to take off on that monster wave. Concerned that he would be crushed on the reef so close to the surface.

Tray didn't care. The reef was just a necessary part of the journey. There was no success without danger. It was what made it exhilarating for him. The thrill of crashing competed against the thrill of taking the tsunami to the shoreline.

Daz hadn't seen it very often. Usually Tray would just conspire to keep the floor half-full and just move the night along. But a long time ago, someone who knew Daz had caught Tray playing in Portugal. Kym was a backpacker. She had heard of this club in Lagos whilst travelling around in Austria of all places. It was the hallowed ground for backpackers that year. The tour went Pamplona, Lagos then Oktoberfest. It was the Holy Grail at the end of the train line.

She said it was a hot and sticky night on the Algarve. They had waited for three hours to get in the club. They could hear the thumping tunes outside. Partygoers were jumping around in the car park opposite. They were genuinely psyched for it. Kym said by the time they had got inside she was ready to climb the walls. When she got in, someone actually was.

It was Tray. She had explained that the ceiling was at least forty feet high. About twenty-five feet up, a criss-cross pattern of wooden beams stretched over the dance floor. From these hung the lights, smoke machines and fans. Striding out across the beams was Tray. Oblivious to his own safety concerns, radio mike in hand, he was 'giving it large'.

"C'mon! Let's rip the roof off this fucking joint!"

He knew it had been him. Who else would give it so large a shove? She said he climbed back in to the DJ booth and dropped in Robyn-S's 'Show Me Love' and backed it up with 'Playing With Knives'. The place went absolutely nuts. He then popped on a remix of Bob Marley's 'Exodus' by the Rebel MC and rounded it off with SL 2's 'On A Ragga Tip'. She had given Daz a mix tape that they had been selling at the club. The name on it was 'DJ Jorge'.

He had never approached Tray about it. It was always a part of his life he had been so quiet about. In fact, Tray had been quiet about all of his life. It was a mystery to Daz. Here was a man who no doubt could have and should have blown up like a nuclear bomb on the world stage. Tray had always blamed it on his capacity to do drugs and his fear one day of doing too much. That much was confirmed by Murchison. But who was chasing his mate? Surely it couldn't be that bad?

"Tray, what's got you so scared?"

"Mate, I can't tell you a thing. There are only a couple of people that know why I am here and I would like to keep it that way."

"Well then. How about you telling me how I am going to cope with all this interest that people are going to have in me."

"I am not going to do that. She is."

He pointed across the bar to a frumpy woman dressed in some rather tattered old clothes. She wasn't far off a 'bin checker' Daz thought. She could have slept with the tramps in the botanical gardens.

"Who the fuck is that?"

"Sharon Bleasdale."

"Who?"

"Daz you really don't know much do you?"

Sharon came stumbling over. Either through age or alcohol, she was struggling to make the distance. A barman went to intercept her but Tray caught his eye conveying that it was all okay. She made it to their table. Daz then realised that it was all a charade.

The old bat wasn't as old as she made out. She was caked in make-up. From forehead to neck. It was a professional job. She was wearing a wig. A good one. Daz sidled towards Tray and whispered in his ear.

"Tray what the fuck is going on? A month ago you were just a fucking nobody. Now there's all this James Bond shit. Who're all these fucking people I just keep bumping into?"

"Daz just stow it. This is a favour I am doing for you!"

Daz wasn't so happy anymore.

"Tray first of all your girlfriend's sister is involved in the biggest pill bust in Australian history. Then we meet a guy who has more coke than any normal person has a right to own. Not only that, its practically pure. Unheard of over here. You're then fingered as a top DJ. Now this!"

"Shut up you spastic!"

The pseudo-tramp got to their table. Tray stood up to greet her.

"Fuck I said come in disguise Shaz. I didn't say stick out like tits on a bull."

"I didn't know. I just didn't want someone to spot me."

"No chance of that Shaz. C'mon let's go."

"But my beer Tray!" said an outraged Daz.

"Oh fucking hell Daz. There'll be plenty more."

Tray made for the door. Once outside, they all turned for the Hilton.

"Where are we going?" asked Sharon.

"In here."

Shaz and Daz followed him through the revolving doors of the Hilton Hotel. Plush opulence greeted them. The concierge tried to stop Sharon from entering into this beautiful place. Tray headed him off. He put a bundle of fifty-dollar notes in his hand and said it was okay. He told the odd couple to wait there. Just a little out of sight. He approached the reception desk. Put five hundred dollars in the receptionist's hand and beckoned them both to come towards the lifts.

A couple of minutes later they found themselves in a double room on the eighth floor.

As soon as the door closed, the pair of them were on to him.

"T where the fuck have you been?" begged Sharon

"Tray what the fuck is going on?" said Daz for the umpteenth time that day.

Tray held up his hands to deflect the questions.

"For a start Daz just hold on a second. There's nothing to worry about. And as for you Sharon, I told you no questions. You owe me that much."

"I fucking don't hear from you for ten years and you tell me no questions. What the fuck is that?" She was angry.

Daz recognised the accent. It was the female mirror image of Tray's. The 't' was optional in Tray's language often falling silent. Tray turned to Daz.

"First of all. Darren Thwaite meet Sharon Bleasdale."

They nodded to each other without saying a word.

"Now let's all take a breath and sit down."

Tray indicated to the two chairs at the far end of the room. As the pair took their seats, Tray went to the mini fridge.

"Drinks anyone?"

"Have they got any champagne?" asked Sharon.

"Oh you have gone up in the world," shot back Tray.

"Yeah well, cut your cloth and all that."

She pulled off the wig to reveal a cascading bundle of chestnut tresses. Daz was quietly impressed.

"Daz?"

"Just a beer."

He chucked Daz a small can of Heineken and took a diet Pepsi for himself. He sat on the corner of the bed and faced the other two.

"Okay, first of all, sorry for all the mystery."

"This is all very strange T.," intoned Sharon.

"You can say that again," said Daz.

"Believe me its necessary," said Tray.

Tray opened his Pepsi and looked Sharon in the eye.

"T you said this was important. That you had a favour to ask me. Now I haven't heard from you for over a decade and then out of the blue you ask me to meet you all dressed up like this. What the hell have you been up to?"

Tray looked at Daz.

"Okay, I'm going to tell you as little as I can and that's it. After that you're going to have to trust me and me you. We go back a long way Shaz so I'm counting on you. I wouldn't be asking if it wasn't important."

"Okay darling. You asked for my help and I'm here aren't I?"

He could tell she was telling the truth.

"Yes you are. And it really means a lot to me."

She could tell that Tray was sincere. He hadn't changed much at all considering so much time had gone past. He had given her some prime contacts way back when and if she really thought about it, he was responsible for kick-starting her career. He still had a massive head of hair. Blonde hints still ran through the light brown waves. He had put on a bit of weight but his frame could handle it. Most of all she could tell that there was still that kindness in his blue eyes. It was something that he was loved for back in the manor. He was always generous with his time and his soul. So much so, it invariably got him into trouble. She wondered what trouble he was in now. His brother had come back from overseas somewhat crippled and his Dad had become a bit of a recluse, especially since his wife had died.

The news had therefore gone very quiet on Tray. Everyone knew he had upset Rudi by what he had done. The people that knew Tray best couldn't believe he had

237

just disappeared. She thought maybe Rudi had 'offed' him but surely Jimmy would have stopped that happening. She heard rumours that he was playing in Miami, that he had been seen in Berlin; even that he was playing in some shit hole in Portugal but it all seemed so ridiculous. Tray would never play places like that, he was far too good.

She had seen Jo at her Dad's funeral. She was overwhelmed by grief. She had gone to speak to her when there had been a sudden outburst between her and Tray's Dad. She had wanted to speak to her then but the moment was deeply personal. The grief so heart-wrenching that she had left her alone. She knew both families had been close and with all that had gone on, she thought it was best if she caught up with her later.

Except she hadn't. Like Tray, Jo had dropped off the face of the earth. Sharon assumed that after her Dad's funeral, Jo had needed a break. The slow death of her Dad, the prison, her estranged Mum, it must have all taken a toll. Sharon certainly hadn't been a good friend of hers. Different circles but she knew her. In all that time that her father had been dying Sharon hadn't even tried to get in contact with her. The more she left it, the guiltier she felt, until there didn't seem much point at all. Besides, Sharon had become so busy flying all over the world with her clients that she never stopped long enough to think about it. Not even when Jo had been briefly kidnapped by the Taliban. Sharon had been too busy creating a massive party launch in San Antonio.

"Daz, this is as I said before, Sharon Bleasdale. Born in Chingford just down the road from me. Sharon is a director at 'DJ's Select'. If you didn't know, it is the biggest DJ booking agency and artist management service in the world."

Tray let this sink in.

"Like many of my friends from a previous life, she has been unaware of where I have been. Sharon knows more than most. Someone has been after me and is still after me. I did something I am not particularly proud of and I am paying the price for it."

Daz wondered what his friend had done and leant forward in his chair. He clasped his hands in front of him and took a glance at Sharon.

"Maybe sometime soon, me and Lizzy may have to bolt again. Something unrelated has come up and I think it might be best if I tidy everything up here and move along."

Sharon interrupted.

"T you can't do this to me again. I have just found you!"

"Shaz remember Rudi! Remember what he promised to do? I have a price on me. Standing orders remember! I doubt if he's gone down the ladder. Tell me I'm wrong!"

Daz flinched at the attack. He had rarely seen Tray like this. Who was this Rudi? Sharon was equally shocked. She hadn't thought much about it really. T had been living the past ten years on the run and in that time Rudi had indeed become more powerful. He had become rich beyond measure. He no longer existed in the murky world of the East End. He had become legitimate. He had bought into big clubs, super clubs. Clubs that she herself had to deal with. She was glad though she didn't have to deal with him. She knew he was a Yardie and they were ruthless. Crossing them was like crossing the devil himself. They did not forgive and they certainly did not forget.

"You're not wrong T. Sorry its been sooo long." She looked at the floor noticing the same drab pattern that hotels the world over seemed to employ.

"Its okay Shaz. I'm sorry too. I have been a bit stressed. Tend to arc up for no reason lately. I'm sorry."

He reached for her hand and grasped it. Daz noted there was real tenderness there. These two went back a long way.

"I'm sorry if I caused you any pain. I know all of you were worried but it had to be this way. You understand."

As he held her hand, Sharon started to cry. The tears flowed down her cheeks. Great sobbing cries rose from deep within her. Daz looked away. This was their moment. It was raw and powerful. An emotion that only Tray could elicit from this woman. He wondered who she had been to him. Maybe a lover or just a very good friend? He was about to find out.

As her tears subsided, Sharon regained her composure. Daz handed her a box of tissues from the table. She wiped her eyes. It had the effect of smearing all the stage make-up over her face. Pablo Picasso would have been proud.

Tray giggled at the sight, breaking the deep emotional outpouring.

"'Ere Shaz, go to the toilet and wipe that crap off your face. You look like your Vera after too many sherries."

Sharon laughed too. She quickly got up from her chair and headed for the bathroom. Both Daz and Tray could hear her laughing as she turned on the tap and wiped her face clean. When she returned to the room Daz realised how beautiful she really was. She must have been his lover.

"Oh now that's better. I had forgotten how gorgeous you are Shaz."

Sharon blushed, demurely lowering her head.

"Now come and sit down and let me tell Daz all about you."

She did as she was commanded. Daz could catch a hint of how sexily she moved underneath those ridiculous old clothes. She would have made quite a picture at any event.

"Sharon here is one of my oldest friends. She used to watch me play when no one else would give me the time of day. Then when it all started to kick off, she was the one that kept me in check. She kept me doing what I needed to do and then it all went pear-shaped."

He paused and lit up a cigarette. Sharon and Daz did the same and watched the smoke curl above their heads.

"I thought we'd lost you in that riot in Birmingham." said Sharon.

"Coventry," said Tray.

"Whatever. That was when the rumours started. You just disappeared. I told you to keep your head low but you just couldn't help yourself could you?"

"I can't help being good can I?" He gave her that cheeky smile he always had. She couldn't stay mad at him.

"No I suppose you can't. But that's when you disappeared. People reckoned that you'd been carved up down there. That the Yardies had caught up with you. But then word got out that Rudi had large money on your head. We knew then that you

240

had got out. Let me tell you T, that's when we knew who your friends were. There were a lot of people asking questions. People who I thought were your friends."

Tray knew that a lot of people would be chasing him. Rudi would have offered up a lot of cash for information. People would do a lot of things for money. It was the one thing that he had learnt on his travels.

Daz just looked on refusing to interrupt. He didn't know what was going on anyway. They were talking in a sort of code. Offering him little snippets of a life long ago. He listened intently. Something important was coming. It was like a road accident. He couldn't look away.

Tray turned his attention to Daz.

"You must be wondering why I've got you here."

"The thought had crossed my mind," said Daz.

"I used to mix with some of the best back then. Some real up and comers. People you would recognise today as some of the DJ elite."

"I fucking knew it!" Daz almost leapt from his chair.

"Yeah well Shaz here represents them. She jumped on board at an early stage and has never looked back. She is an industry power broker. Now she's over here scoping for talent. Three months isn't it?"

"How did you know?" asked Sharon.

"I still read the industry rags Shaz. I've known since you got here. You were photographed at The Establishment!"

"And still you didn't contact me! You fucking bastard!"

She went to hit him but only playfully. There was no malice in it. She settled back in her chair, letting Tray continue. Daz looked at the woman sitting next to him. He would never have picked it in the Arthouse. In fact he couldn't pick it now. But if Tray said it was true, then it was true.

"Sharon, Daz here is not only my friend, he is my protégé so to speak. He's never realised it and he hasn't been aware but I have made sure that he has all the skills to take the world by storm. He also has a tune to boot."

Sharon's professionalism took over. Her demeanour changed. Daz could see she was interested.

"Oh really. What's so special about this guy then?"

"Take it from me babe, he can play."

"Is he as good as you were?"

"Maybe honey, maybe."

Daz exhaled heavily. If any of what he'd heard in the past five hours was true, then this was some compliment.

"Wooshka, well he must be good then," Sharon smiled at Daz.

"Would I lie to you sexy?" asked Tray.

"We won't go there shall we beautiful?" she admonished him.

Sharon looked at Daz. His image was going to need a bit of work but if he was as good as Tray reckoned then she would take him sight unseen.

"Only thing is Shaz, no mention of me. You know what's at stake. I can't be involved."

"T I can't do that. That would be impossible. Why would I take this bloke on from nowhere?"

Tray pulled an envelope from his jacket pocket and handed it to Sharon.

"What's this?"

"Thirty grand. It will cover the costs. Your company won't be out of pocket."

She threw it back at him.

"Fuck off T! I'm not taking that. We go back too far for you to shove money in my face!"

"Babe. This is it. No games. I can't be mentioned otherwise me and those close to me are dead! You more than anyone else should know that!"

"Oh Trystan. Why can't we fix this?" Sharon begged.

"Cos it doesn't matter what I do. Rudi will not stop until I am dead. I am in love. I have a girl who loves me and I don't want her crying over my grave. I want my friends and those who stood by me to get something back for standing by me. Its as simple as that."

"We don't need anything T. We just need you back in our lives."

"Until Rudi is gone baby, that can't happen."

She could see the sadness in his eyes. Oh how she wished it could have been different. She had been obsessed by him back then. She had followed him to all of his gigs. She had just wanted him so badly. She still wanted him if he would have her but his last confession made that impossible. She was always just that little bit too late. If she had only told him when she'd had the chance their lives could have been so different. But he hadn't changed. He was still trying to look after those that loved him. Still being Trystan McCarthy. Still being nothing more than beautiful.

He handed the money back to Sharon.

"Make him great Shaz. Please. Just for me."

She reluctantly took the envelope.

"Tray this is too much!" Daz exploded off of his chair. He punched Tray on the shoulder.

"Ow! Fuck off Daz!"

"Tray you can't do this. I am putting a stop to this right now!"

"Sit down Daz. Sharon will tell you that once I put my mind to something, I can't be stopped. You my friend are about to become a star."

"He's right you know," said Sharon. "I can make you and I can break you. Which one is it going to be?"

Daz stood, feeling like an idiot. Here he was arguing against the offer of a lifetime. How could he turn this down? Rachel would be slapping him right now. He apologised to both of them and sat down once again. Tray regained his composure and stroked Sharon's right arm.

"Sharon. I have something for you to listen to."

"What's that T?"

"Its Daz's new tune. He's just signed with Playground. Believe me baby. You are going to wet your knickers."

Tray got off the bed and went to the neat micro-system set up next to the bed. He pulled a CD out of his jacket pocket.

"Okay so everyone ready?"

He inserted the CD and pressed play. The sound began to flood the room.

Six minutes and fifty-four seconds later, Sharon Bleasdale was on the phone calling her contacts. Darren Thwaite had just cracked the big time.

*

"Well?"

"He's put a call through to Swanson. The guy's on a training camp. Salome's blocked the call too. She's gold that girl."

"We can't let them get together. We're going to have to off him. Money or not. Get the info out of him if you can. If not, well I will have to cross that bridge."

Vic was going to turn. He thought the bloke was staunch but some people know when their number's up. Tarry had done well. The boys in Long Bay had it covered. He was amazed how the network could run so smoothly. Nothing was a secret inside that place and the Australian Federal Police had more holes in it than Swiss cheese. It amazed him how the government could pay its law enforcers so little and expect them to stay squeaky clean. The temptation to take money under the table was just too much. Just paying the mortgage was a struggle on their wages and when you saw the people you were trying to pinch dwarfing your salary, what option was there? It was the same with the screws. They weren't saints. They were only one step away from the people they were guarding. A little bit of money here. Some blackmail there. It all worked so easily.

Then there was the prisoner network. Information was priceless. It was the currency of survival inside. Prison was just an endless production line of schemes and scams to improve the lot of those that were incarcerated. The screws were just ordinary workers like any other. They weren't rocket scientists. They got bored just like any other employees. They turned a blind eye. They skimmed off the top and they allowed shit to happen that shouldn't. It was a dog eat dog world after all.

Gordon Jeffrey worked in Long Bay like many other wardens, he had a gambling problem. A big one. He loved the horses. The only problem was, the horses didn't love him back. He owed big on the outside and he just couldn't leave the sport of kings alone. He was just like an ice junky. He kept needing the fix. Kept needing the rush. Tarry had found out through some connections that Jeffrey was in trouble.

It always surprised Mo how many people got themselves into this sort of situation. Jeffrey was into his bookie for a couple of hundred thousand. It had just been a case of buying the debt. No problems at all for the bookie. It was a weight off his mind. For Jeffrey it was a descent into hell.

They had just started off small. Favours here and there. They wouldn't tell his wife. They wouldn't tell his boss. As long as he kept cooperating, they would give him time to pay. They would keep his dirty little secret. If he started to protest they would threaten his family or his friends. Fear was a marvellous motivator. Once he had broken the law, passed off some drugs, allowed a beating; something which broke the trust that the public had placed in him as a guardian of the animals that had defiled the public's rules and regulations, he became their bitch. Bitches in high places were the only way to get an advantage over the enemy.

Getting the information out was easy. Bent lawyers are the biggest criminals on the block. They charge like wounded bulls and would do anything for money. The client-attorney privilege allows for the easy passing of information. There were many Lebs inside. There were many lawyers who visited them. It was easy. Pass a message to a lawyer; the lawyer then passes the message to Tarry or another of his team. Easy as passing a note in school when the teacher's back was turned. There was always one constant in life as far as Mo was concerned. It wasn't death or taxes. It was pure unadulterated greed and lawyers in his experience were the greediest of them all. A good lawyer was worth his weight in gold. A bent lawyer was worth so much more.

Getting information out of the police was even easier. This time he had to pay no one. This time it was family. Like most police organizations, they had a pool of secretaries serving the different branches. The serious crime squad had the same. Salome, one of his hundreds of cousins had managed to get herself a job serving in one of those pools. She wasn't a personal assistant to one of the chiefs but she sat somewhere in between. She was a constant mine of information. She hadn't known about the bust. They had kept that extremely quiet but she had manned the phones for Swanson's group after the investigation had been wound down. She hadn't taken the message either but she had seen the post-it note that one of the other secretaries had left on her desk as a reminder to call him.

Swanson was on an anti terrorism training camp. He was to be contacted if this Vukovic called in. They were all on notice to do that. Salome had simply lifted the note. Barbara would never remember. She was only part-time anyway. She job-shared with a woman called Patricia. They swapped over positions on such a regular basis that a lot of calls slipped through the cracks. It was a regular problem with the public service. They were so hell bent on fitting work around family and vice versa that the job itself suffered. They had missed one drug king ping jumping bail and fleeing the country recently all because someone hadn't passed a message on from an informant. Heads had rolled for that one. Salome thought that maybe someone would be sacked for this one but it wouldn't be her. She hadn't taken the message.

Salome wasn't the only person inside the AFP. He had several others and he only used them when the case warranted it. This was one of those cases. He put the call in.

"Fraser here."

"Arab," he replied.

"What are you doing calling me?"

"Do you know how much shit you've caused me?"

"Look, the case is shut down. What else do you want?"

"My money back!"

"Well there's been a development on that front too!"

"You cunt! What do you know?"

"The Serb has had a visitor."

"I know that. I have contacts too."

"Yeah well she knows something."

"How long have you known? I am being given my arse here?"

"Not long. Just a couple of days."

246

"And you didn't fucking tell me?"

"I had to be sure. It seemed so innocent before."

"Fuck innocent! Where is it?"

"I have to do another check. I have to be careful. The case is closed. If they catch me snooping around, it will look suspicious"

"Yeah well make it quick. The Serb is gonna turn."

"How do you know?"

"I have my ways as well. Never you mind."

"You should have told me about the deal. I could have protected you. I had no idea you were the buyer."

"Well I don't like you knowing everything I do."

"Well you know what you have to do now?"

"Green light?"

"Green light!"

The line went dead. Chief Superintendent John Fraser took the SIM card out of the phone and snapped it in two. He then crushed the phone under his foot and swept it into the gutter. Fuck, this whole thing was getting out of control. After this was sorted he was going to have to rein Mo in. He would make him disappear. No one was bigger than the AFP. Mohammad Aziz had become the tall poppy that needed to be mown down.

*

They had only been back about five days but they had spent a glorious time on the Gold Coast. It had been beautiful. The kids had been spoilt rotten. They had been to every theme park possible. The girls had loved it but the news had taken the shine off it. They had flown back with a dark cloud hanging over their heads.

Tracey was in a deep depression. Lizzy had tried to talk to her about it but Tracey had refused. She didn't know which way to jump. She had thought that maybe

247

Tumbles had shagged the loyalty out of her but her sister was a tad stupid if Lizzy were to admit it. She had fallen deeply for Vic but he had betrayed her too. She was a mystery to Lizzy sometimes. She thought she knew how she ticked but then the clock hands would get stuck and there was nothing anyone could do to mend them.

Tracey had gone back to Mum's to have a rest with the girls. She needed a bit of time-out. She wasn't a natural mother. After a while, looking after the girls just took too much out of her and she had to give them to Mum. Their mother was much the same. If ever there was a person who shouldn't have had kids it was their Mum. But surprisingly enough she was superb when it came to grand kids. Lizzy just wished she could have acted the same with her and Tracey.

She was sitting in her unit overlooking South Cronulla beach. The sky was clear but it had that cold bite in the air. Winter was still holding on despite it being October but you could tell summer was on its way. The days were longer and the winds that touch warmer.

The landline rang. It was her mother. She too had had enough and was begging Lizzy to pick up the kids. Lizzy was a bit lonely anyway. Tray had been tied up with some business with Daz. He was up to something but she didn't know what. He was being pretty secretive and she didn't like it. It didn't worry her though. If he was with Daz it could only be about music. When those two were together, it could only be about music.

She thought she might surprise him with the girls. Take them over for a swim in the pool. He would like that. He hadn't seen them for a while. They would like it too. She agreed to take them for the afternoon. She would go to the beauty parlour and get herself a make over. She wanted to look good for the man who was going to change her life. She rang Tracey.

"Trace?"

"Oh hello."

She was distracted she could tell. Not really with it. She wondered what she'd been up to.

"Where are you?"

"Over at East Gardens. Just picking up some clothes for the girls. What're you doing?"

"I've just spoken to mum. I'm going to pick the girls up and go over to Tray's. Do you want to come?"

Tracey paused a second. She didn't know if she would be able to cope with them this afternoon. She was still mulling over her meeting with Vic. She knew she'd done the wrong thing. Should she tell her sister? Had she put the girls in danger? She didn't know the answer. She had been very stupid. Its why she hadn't been to Mum's.

She wasn't in fact anywhere near East Gardens. She was at home in Miranda. She thought the Feds might be watching her. She had been paranoid that every car passing had been calling for her.

"Yeah I would love to."

Tracey clicked off the mobile. Her thoughts were interrupted by a knock at the door.

*

Gordon Jeffrey escorted the prisoner around the corner of the laundry block. He didn't like this but what choice did he have. This was his chance to clear his debt. That would be it. He wasn't going to touch the horses again. Look what he had become. He was now no better than the bastards he guarded.

Vic shuffled along. The pain in his side still throbbed like a motherfucker. They said it should have subsided by now but it still hurt when he moved. Exercise would help they said but it just served to hurt it more. He wasn't allowed anywhere near the exercise yard. The last incident had put paid to that. They had allowed him to shuffle around this barren space behind the laundry.

Where the hell was Swanson? He had the warden put a call in to him three times now and there had been no answer. While he was in the hospital he was relatively safe. When he was put back into the general population he was as good as dead. What was he going to do? Fuck he'd underestimated that pommie bastard. Tracey said something about investing it. Making a quick buck and living high on the hog. He should never have hooked up with her.

"I'm just going to make a quick phone call. It's the wife."

The screw waved his mobile at him.

"I'll just be round the corner. Don't go anywhere."

Fucking smart arse! Where was he going to go? There was the bare back wall. Some bins lined up on the right side and the laundry on the left. Fucking comedians these screws! He grabbed his crotch and as he contemplated whether to piss up the bins or not, the back door to the laundry opened. A figure emerged from the doorway. It was the go-faster haircut. ***Fuck!***

*

They had hurt her before they killed her. The first thing they did was fuck her. Fuck her like a piece of meat. They punched her in the face breaking her beautiful nose. She felt the bone crunch as they hit her time and time again. She fell to the floor and tried to crawl away. Screaming as they manhandled her. She knew they would fuck her. She could tell they were going to make her suffer.

They threw her over the arm of the couch. One of them held her head down whilst the other tore her knickers off. Then he entered her. Shoved his cock right up her. Then he pulled out and rammed it in again. It hurt. It hurt so much.

Then he withdrew and shouted something at her in a language she didn't understand. She felt him adjust his position and then she felt the pain. In her arse! He had put it in her arse! She struggled against him but it was no good. She could feel it inside her. The other man pushed her head further into the cushion. She yelled at them. She screamed. She felt him cum. She felt him wipe his cock on her dress.

"My turn! My turn!"

A new set of hands grabbed her head. She had nearly managed to get away when they changed places but she was grabbed and shoved back into position. This one didn't even try her cunt. Straight into her arse. Smashing into her with hate and venom. This guy was bigger than the last. She could feel her arse splitting.

She began to sob. They used her like that for over an hour. They put a gun to her face. Made her suck its muzzle. They threw cum at her. They smeared it in her eyes with their cocks. They stuck the gun up her cunt. They spat at her. They fucked her until they were spent. Then they kicked her. Like a rabid dog they kicked her. In the chest. In the cunt. In the arse. She was a bloody mess. You couldn't tell the two holes apart when they finished with her.

Then they asked the question.

"Where's the fucking money?"

As she lay there on the floor, she couldn't remember if she had told them. They had slit her throat. She was dying. Fuck she couldn't remember! Her girls! Lizzy! What had she done?

*

Fifteen minutes should be enough. He had called his wife as promised. She had been surprised. He never called during the day and he sounded a little stressed. He had asked about the kids. Just small talk really. It made a nice change.

He finished the call and went back to his prisoner. He was gone! Where the fuck could he go? There was only one way in and one way out and he was standing there. He walked along the wall. The bins! He could be hiding in the bins.

The bins were big industrial ones with the sliding tops. Big enough to hide a man. He went along the side of them, banging them with his foot.

"C'mon Vukovic. Stop mucking around!"

There was no answer. This guy must really take him for a fool. He banged them again. No movement. No sound. He began to slide the lids back, peering inside.

The stench was terrible. Rotting rubbish and slops. He added to the smell when he pulled back the lid on the fourth bin. He threw up his breakfast.

In bin number four lay the freshly slaughtered body of Victor Vukovic. Throat cut and eyes stabbed out. Prisoner 7523817 was never going to leave Long Bay Correctional Facility. His life was done. Short and not so sweet.

*

They frolicked in the pool. It was freezing cold. Too cold for her but the girls were impervious to its icy depths. She heard them shriek. They were playing with the lilos. She loved her nieces. They were the product of some bad decisions by Tracey but she thanked whatever god controlled this haphazard universe for them. Perhaps one day her and Tray could conceive. He would make a good Dad. The Dad that she never had. Perhaps when the money came in they could talk about it.

She dozed in the sun. She was sunbathing topless. The girls didn't mind. She was always happy with her body and saw no reason why the girls should be ashamed or embarrassed by the human form. She loved her tits. They were her best feature. They were large and firm. A perfect 36 C. Tray could never keep his hands off them. He was obsessed by them. Even when he returned home late from god knows what club and hopped into bed, he would cup them like they were some long lost treasures. He would knead them like they were a dough until eventually she would stir. Then they would make love like they were the last couple on earth. His appetite was insatiable.

As she dipped into a sexual fantasy she heard the pool gate click open. 'Good', she thought, 'finally he was home'.

The girls shrieked again but this time not with joy but with blood-curdling fear. She opened her eyes. Two men dressed in black stood in front of her. They had balaclava's on. Each man held a gun.

The larger of the two spoke.

"Nice tits!"

*

"How the fuck did that happen?"

"I don't know. Looks like the guard turned his back for five minutes and it was done!"

"Fuck that's six months work down the gurgler!"

"Its fucking bullshit Sir, that's what it is!"

The door swung open and one of Swanson's crew raced in.

"Dave, switch on the box! You ain't gonna believe this!"

'What now?' thought Swanson.

*

He parked the van up the back. Life was good. Daz was on his way. If ever there was a mate who he wanted to help, it was Daz. He was going to be a big hit. He was sure of it. 'I Found Love In You' would be a smash. If they were going to have to change locations, this was going to be his parting gift to Daz. He would sort the others out. Maybe from afar, maybe while they were still here. He wasn't certain they were going to have to leave yet. They still hadn't sorted out any of the details. In fact he hadn't said much to Lizzy at all.

He was going to ring Tumbles tonight. He said he had some news. They had bought some new pre-paid mobiles before he had left and the text messages worked a treat but Tumbles wanted to talk. He would use the satellite phone for sure for his end but Tray could keep to the mobile. There would be nothing that Rudi could trace back to him. Tumbles was in a different loop from the boys back home. Soon they would be rich and he could forget all about that vengeful bastard. Money like they had could buy a lot of anonymity.

He popped the gate open. Something was wrong. The pool water was blood red. There was blood everywhere. On the deck, on the sun lounge, up the walls. It looked like a slaughterhouse. What had happened? Where was Lizzy?

Then he realised. There just weren't lilos in the pool! There were bodies too. Lizzy's body! The girls' bodies! Fucking hell! He put his hands to his eyes, shielding them from the sight. He tried to shout for help but no words came, just an endless roar of pain and anguish.

The birds that nestled in the tree shielding the pool took to flight. The peaceful tranquillity of the Woronora Valley was shattered. Tray went to dive in to the pool when a hand stopped him.

He looked around to find two men in balaclavas staring at him. They shoved a gun in his face.

"What have you done?"

He struggled at the hand holding him. He tried to look at the pool but was dragged away. They had to be dead. This was the end. He felt sick.

"What have you done?" He repeated the question, trying to twist from the hand holding him. The gun was placed against his neck. The larger of the two men pulled Tray closer to him. He could smell his breath. It smelt of coffee and cigarettes.

"What do you think?" replied the larger of the two.

The voice was strange. Difficult to understand. Perhaps it was the balaclava.

"Why? What had they done to you?" He was yelling uncontrollably.

"Money mate. Its all about the fucking money!"

CHAPTER NINE

News Of The World

Read between the lines and you'll find the truth

What The Papers Say

The headline was emblazoned across the front page: MURDER IN PARADISE – ENGLISH DJ ON THE RUN. Jimmy read it again and again. The press were camped out on the front drive. Sam had read a statement from his wheelchair. They were in shock. He knew his son was innocent. Sam had conveyed the same. The news was so fresh that there had been no evidence to implicate him in the murders. He had told him to lie low. What the fuck was he doing getting involved in a drug deal?

The police in Australia had the curtesy to call them last night before the news broke. Thank God Jimmy had retired from all of Charlie's business connections. As soon as Betty had fallen ill, Charlie had called all bets off. It meant that whatever connection he had with the underworld, they had long since gone. Just as well. He didn't need anybody prying into their business or Charlie's for that matter.

A detective Swanson had called him. Jimmy really didn't have anything to tell him. It was the truth. Everyone had held true to Charlie's ruling. It had meant that Betty had died in abject sadness without her son being by her side. Jimmy didn't know what hurt her most, the cancer or the loss of her son. He asked this Swanson what the story was.

Tray was suspected of being a major drug runner. The Australian said he was being chased for the suspected murder of at least four people, two women and two young girls. He was also suspected of ordering the underworld killing of a major drug importer.

It was all news to Jimmy. This was not like his son but who knew what he had become since his departure. It was all turning to shit. Fuck the war! This should have all been settled when it first happened. Charlie had taken sides but at least Tray was alive. Now his son was on the run. His cover had been blown. That fucker Rudi would be watching closely. But Jimmy had to get to his son first.

The phone rang. Jimmy motioned for Sam to answer it. It would be those fucking vampires wanting more news.

"Hello, Sam speaking."

His younger son listened intently to the person on the other end of the line.

"Dad, I think you should take this."

"Son, I'm not talking to anyone else. I'm all talked out."

"It's not them Dad," Sam nodded with his head to the throng outside. "It's an old friend."

Jimmy reluctantly walked over to the phone.

"Jimmy McCarthy." It was a statement of fact.

"Jimmy?"

The voice was female. Young. He didn't recognise it.

"Who is this?"

"Jo."

"Who?"

"Jimmy, its Jo Flint."

"Oh Jo, I'm sorry."

"Is it true Jimmy?"

"The cops are saying that he is involved. I don't know. Tray couldn't kill a thing."

"What are you going to do Jimmy?"

"Me and Sam are leaving tonight."

"Jimmy I'm going to ask you something. You don't have to say yes."

"Okay darling. Fire away."

"Can I come with you?"

"Jo are you sure you want to get involved?"

"Jimmy I ran out on him once before when he needed me. I'm not going to do it again."

"We all did Jo. Its time we all stepped up."

"When can you get here?"

"I'm outside now."

"Jesus Jo. What if I'd said no?"

"I would've gone anyway."

"That's my girl Jo."

"No Jimmy. I'm Tray's girl. Always was. Always will be."

Jimmy thought at this. He had put this girl through so much. All to save his son. Most people would have walked away. They wouldn't even have bothered with him after all that had happened but Jo Flint was different. She was made of sterner stuff. He was guilty of not only destroying both his son's life but her's as well. It was time they all stopped hiding. Fuck Rudi Stone! His son needed him and Rudi better watch out. After Tray was found that cunt was going to be finding out just how much damage he was going to have to pay for.

The doorbell rang. He could see Jo through the glass. He waved at her. He opened the door and was blinded by a barrage of questions and flashlights. He avoided both and ushered her into the hall. He put his arms around her and pulled a curtain back across the door, blocking out the prying eyes.

Sam popped his head into the hallway.

"Hello Jo."

"Hello Sam."

"Are you coming to Australia?"

"Try and stop me."

"Love ya Jo," said Sam.

Jimmy kissed her on the cheek.

"Love ya too girly. Are you ready for this?"

"No but who would be?"

"True. Have you got any clothes?" asked Jimmy.

"In the car."

"Fucking hell, you are prepared!"

"Not really. I haven't booked a flight yet. And what about a visa?"

"Onto it! You won't need a visa. The cops have arranged that for us via the embassy. I will just add your name to the list," said Sam.

Sam picked up the phone and dialled a number. He didn't play around with niceties.

"Olivia, can you add one more to the flight?"

He paused.

"Yeah first class too."

"Sam! I can't afford that!"

Sam winked at her. Jimmy held her hand in his big gnarly mitts.

"Its on me Jo. It's the least that I can do. Its time I faced up to how I let you all down. I've put everyone through hell because I didn't stand my ground. Now my boy's disappeared and people are dead."

Jimmy began to cry. Small sobs. She had never seen the like of it. His guilt must have been overwhelming. It was a theme common to all of them. Yes Tray had made a wrong decision many years ago but he had paid for it and instead of standing by him, they had all sent him away. They had dismissed him. Now Jimmy was helpless. A situation hitherto unknown to him.

She had never seen the man show much emotion. She held the huge old tough guy. Then Sam did something completely unexpected. He stood up! Jo looked on dumbfounded. His act had been so complete. No one had ever doubted his disability. She had believed him and more importantly so had everyone else. Sam beamed and held his arms out for a hug.

"Surprised?" he asked.

Jo stumbled over to him and hugged him like he was the last man on Earth.

"Don't worry Jo. We'll get him back."

*

'Don! Get in here!"

Don came limping in. He had never found out who had battered Don in Portugal. He had nearly died. Someone had done a right number on him. It had taken him six months to learn to walk. He had asked Charlie about it. Very carefully mind because he didn't want to make too many waves. There were still a lot of things unsaid between Charlie and Rudi. Things had never been the same since McCarthy had done a runner.

For Charlie it was about honour. He had promised to stand aside in Rudi's quest to find and kill Tray but he wasn't going to make it easy for him either. He wanted to keep the peace but it was Charlie's peace not Rudi's. The Yardie wasn't eating at the top table and he knew it. Charlie, by protecting his Godson, had made it clear to everyone that Rudi just wasn't important enough to be given a prize like Tray. It pissed Rudi off but he was patient. He knew something would turn up someday and today it had.

"Get on the phone!"

"What for?"

"Ring Igor! Find out what's going on in Sydney!"

"Why? What's up?"

"Tray McCarthy! The bloodclot's in Sydney."

*

Tumbles picked up the paper that Pedro had handed him. It was the same news that all of them had read. Tumbles ran the thoughts through his head. There was no way that Tray had killed anybody. He loved the girls. This was something else. Someone had come for their money. A message was being sent. He would have to sit tight. Whoever they were, they weren't fucking around.

Pedro looked at his friend.

"What are we going to do fucking? This is not Tray."

"No its not. We know that. The cops though think different."

"So what we do?" asked the one-eyed Brazilian.

"We fucking wait!"

"Then what we do fucking?"

"We fucking do what we're told!"

*

How could they have missed him? They hadn't even considered him. Trystan McCarthy hadn't even registered on the richter scale. They had known he had done pills with the girls but he was just a name. No one that even associated with Victor. When he checked he should have known. English, son of an Eastender. Thought to be mildly connected but unproven. They all were in London though. Everybody knew somebody and everyone knew nothing. Swanson had heard it so many times from the geezers in Bondi.

Trystan McCarthy: Well educated. DJ extraordinaire and financial whiz until quickly dropping out of sight in 1991. His witness testimony had been a major key in putting a heavy villain inside. Apparently that had upset the wrong people and he had felt the need to get away. There was a price on his head issued by the Yardies. The West Indian gang controlled many of the retail drug outlets in the East End. They were ruthless and brutal. Their rule was absolute. To cross them was a one-way trip to the hell house. When they issued a contract on you, there was only one way it was going to end. For McCarthy it was a bit like the fatwa issued on Salmon Rushdie. Death would be his only counsel.

He then appears in Portugal in 1994 with an Australian girlfriend. Swanson had pieced this much together from his visa application sent via Paris. He arrives in Australia and marries. He then sometime in the past couple of years separates from his wife and hooks up with Elizabeth Rogers. They would have to question family members about the actual dates because the file was unusually sparse. It looked as though he had appeared out of nowhere and lived a very quiet life since his arrival.

He worked for Border Security which had raised alarm bells with the drugs boys because if anyone knew how to get shit into the country, it would be someone who worked on the border. He had access to everywhere. But the stuff was *already* in. The Serbs and Vukovic hadn't used him on that end. That meant *he* must have been the buyer! It all pointed to him but there were a couple of things that didn't quite add up.

A neighbour saw a late model Commodore leaving the back of the house with three people in it. There was only one witness to that but she was pretty sure. It looked like he hadn't worked alone. There were other inconsistencies too.

The bullets didn't match either. There were two guns involved. The police had turned the house upside down. They hadn't found any sign of gun ownership. No bullets. No cartridges. Nothing to suggest that McCarthy used guns. He just didn't seem the type but it was excellent cover. He lived quietly. Worked. *He* did consume and sell a little but it was small time. Under the radar. Who knew he was capable of this?

But the other evidence was condemning. They couldn't ignore the fact that a neighbour heard Tray screaming. He had put him at the scene. He had known the deceased. He had known Victor Vukovic. The only one that was still alive was McCarthy. He was conspicuous by his very absence. It was fishy and smelt as much and so they had him in the frame for a heinous quadruple murder.

When they found the sister they had been horrified. A uniform had gone over to her place to tell them about the kids. She had practically been fucked to death. A real mess apparently. Someone had slit her throat. It would have been a slow death too. She would have died in intense pain. It was a real hate crime.

He had seen the pictures. Whatever they had done, these women had upset this McCarthy. He hadn't messed around with the young girls or Liz either. Straight through the fucking head. Right between the eyes. That was fucking cold. He would've looked them right in the eye and pulled the trigger. People who loved him. Innocents. That was real fucking cold.

He looked up from the Daily Telegraph and looked down the air bridge that had been attached to the Qantas plane. There were three of them. A late addition to the father and son team. She was pretty. Stunning in fact. Apparently she was an ex-girlfriend. What was it about this McCarthy? He could attract a good-looking woman that was for sure. And then there was the brother. He was *walking?* Swanson thought he was a paraplegic. What miracle of miracles had happened on the plane?

Jimmy and Sam had decided that there was no point anymore in keeping up the pretence. Everyone knew Tray's whereabouts now. The Yardies would have a hard-on for him and everyone associated with him. That meant that Sam was maybe a target once again. Jimmy hadn't been able to confirm that but what the hell? Sam wasn't gonna be confronted by a madman with a gun whilst being strapped to a wheelchair. And so he had walked off of the plane at Sydney and left his wheelchair behind forever.

Jimmy McCarthy went straight over to Swanson. He didn't offer his hand.

"Detective Swanson?"

The old man dwarfed Swanson in breadth. Even at his age he looked like he could smash the detective into next week.

"How did you know it was me?"

"Cos all coppers look the same. Don't matter if you're English, Australian, Yank whatever. You all smell the same."

The son coughed and looked at the ground. The woman stepped forward.

"Miss Jo Flint Detective Swanson."

He took her hand.

"What have you got for us Detective? Have you found him?"

"Not much and no we haven't."

"Well what are we going to do?" she asked.

"Well I don't think you should go to Trystan's house. We have organised some accommodation for you at the Stamford Airport Hotel. We can keep you away from the press there and maybe we can take you to the house tomorrow."

"Thank you Detective. Is that okay with you Jimmy?" She turned to Jimmy and leant into him. She gently placed her hand on his back. They were close, of that Swanson was certain.

Jimmy nodded.

"Okay then Detective Swanson. Lead the way," said Jo.

"Right. Well this way then. We'll take you out the VIP exit. We can avoid the press that way".

"Thank you," said Jo.

"Thank you," said Jimmy.

Swanson raised an eyebrow. Perhaps the old man wasn't so bad as he made out. His son *was* missing after all.

*

They were going to have to play this carefully. Everyone was after this McCarthy. The Vukovic case had been reopened. All the files had been herded back in. He couldn't take the risk and shut it down again. This was high profile now. It smelt of Mo. It had his name all over it. He said to take out Vukovic. That was simple. No one would have missed him. A prison murder was nothing to write home about. Someone had saved the taxpayer a lot of money according to public opinion. But killing women and children. That was a different matter.

Fraser flicked through the file. It was rather thin.

"Have you got anything at all?"

"Nothing Sir. This guy lived very quiet. If he's our man he was very careful. I rang Hoogebund to see if his name had popped up but there had been nothing. They are too busy to help anyway. They have put the entire case on the backburner. Everyone in Europe is being deluged with cheap coke at the moment and Interpol looks like its chasing its own tail. Apparently the streets are awash with it."

"Jesus is anything going to go our way?"

By 'our way', Fraser actually meant his way. Mo was going to have get rid of this McCarthy too but not before he got his money back. This was turning into a right mess with him in the middle.

"Okay Swanson. Find this pom and make it quick. Keep surveillance on the family. If he is still around, he will have seen them arrive. That's our best bet."

"Yes Sir."

"Don't fuck this up Dave. The prime minister doesn't like seeing dead kids on the front page. This guy has got to be nailed."

"Yes Sir!"

Swanson went to leave Fraser's office.

"Dave, how come we didn't pick this guy before?"

"Because he just didn't fit the profile. He still doesn't really."

Fraser mused as the Detective left the room. He was going to have to make it fit or get Mo to end it first.

*

His mouth really fucking hurt. His eyes stung. They had beat him solidly but he hadn't said a thing.

"Read this you pommie bastard!"

He could barely open his eyes.

"Read this!"

They shook a newspaper in front of his face. He looked at the date. He had been here for three days.

"You are a wanted man motherfucker. We can do with you what we want."

He was on his knees. Hands bound behind his back. He was naked. He had cuts and welts all over his body. It was tantamount to torture but they couldn't kill him. He had something they wanted and he knew it. He could taste their desperation despite the pain. They had killed his girls. Tracey too. He read it in the paper. There was a picture of him on the front page. A picture from Glastonbury he thought or maybe Raindance. He couldn't remember.

"We are going to kill you motherfucker! We want our fucking money and everything else you made from it."

"Fuck you, you cunts!"

His shoulders shook with rage and pain. All for his Lizzy.

"You think I'm going to give it to you now! After this! Fuck you, you murdering cunts!"

He was right. Tarry had made a mistake killing the women and the kids. Now the heat was on. It would be easier to just kill the Englishman but Mo was greedy. The sister had said that he had turned the money into a much larger amount. That he had big contacts in the coke world.

This was not difficult to confirm. He rang some people in Marseille. He was definitely connected but cut off. They had let him loose for turning into a snitch. His world was London old school. Fuck them! They were just old men. No one would know what the hell had happened here. His organization had nothing to do with London. It was a world away.

This was what he wanted. He wanted his money. He wanted Tray's money and when he got the lot, he was going to retire. Money fucking money fucking money! He was going to become very rich indeed. He just had to break this English fucker first.

"Hit him again!"

The World Is A Small Place

"So tell me Mr McCarthy are you going to help us at all?"

"You tell me. What do you need to know?"

The three of them sat opposite Swanson in the restaurant of the Stamford Airport Hotel. They were not going to give him much. He had received some more information from his colleagues in the UK but it didn't help. The girl's dossier was impressive. She was a little hero amongst the foreign aid workers in Afghanistan. She was famous for fifteen minutes for being kidnapped by the Taliban in that troubled hotspot.

Unlike most who had gone through such an ordeal, she had shunned the limelight. No book deal. No paid interview from a TV station. Not a thing. She believed in her work and liked her privacy. Her father had been imprisoned for embezzlement and she had been with him in Portugal when he had been arrested.

Portugal? That country had already come up in their investigation. They must have been there together but they seemed so different. On one side you had a determined charity worker and on the other a DJ who moved in completely different circles. They just didn't seem suited. They were like chalk and cheese.

A larger file had come in on Jimmy McCarthy. There were many unsubstantiated claims about him but to all intents and purposes he appeared clean. He grew up with all the villains from that part of the world but that didn't make him a crook. He was guilty of keeping questionable company and nothing more but after his son had been implicated in this sort of crime who could trust the intelligence gathering departments anymore?

McCarthy Senior had grown up on the mean streets with mean people. There was a fable that he had put one of the Kray Twins on his arse but it was just one of those stories that seemed to appear out of nowhere with no facts to support it. His business was clean and there had been some isolated incidents of violence but nothing out of the ordinary for the life he led. It was the history of a man who took no shit from no one.

His son however was a different matter. He had overstepped the line once before. Despite the education and the skills his father had given him growing up, it appeared that he had fallen in with the wrong crowd. He had become a snitch and it looked like he had been on the run ever since. It was like the rest of this case. Nothing was straightforward.

It all seemed a bit murky, a little off kilter. It raised more questions than it answered. If Jimmy McCarthy **was** that well connected, then his son would never have had to run. Then again, perhaps it was precisely because he was so well connected that his son hadn't been knocked. Swanson wasn't sure which way he went and despite Jimmy's advancing years, he certainly didn't want to anger him.

"Mr McCarthy. How well connected are you?"

*

They were in Manila. They hadn't left the airport. He hadn't been to Asia before and he didn't fucking like it. People everywhere. In your face, pushing and shoving. No manners whatsoever. He picked up the payphone and rang a number. It was one of those international call card numbers. He followed the prompts.

"Igor?"

"Yes?"

"It's your friend from London."

"Oh yes. I have some news for you. I think I have tracked down your friend. A mutual acquaintance has removed him from circulation."

"Why? What has he done?"

"Its all about money my coloured friend?"

"How do you know?"

"Because I know."

"Do you think he's still alive?"

"Oh yes. I know he's still alive."

"How?"

"Because I haven't been paid yet. If I had been paid he would almost certainly be dead."

"So you know these people?"

"Yes."

"Call them. I will be in Sydney tomorrow."

"Okay. Anything else?"

"Yes. I want you to find out what his family is doing and I want to be tooled up five minutes after I get there."

"Done."

Rudi replaced the receiver.

"Don!"

Don looked up from some cheap porno magazine that he had found at a news stand.

"Yes Rudi."

"I think we might have a result."

*

"Which one?"

"That one?"

"Do ya reckon Dad? The one with all the press outside!"

Sam was being sarcastic. It was a good sign. He hadn't said much since the police had first called him. He had been good though. He liaised with the press and he'd organised the trip but all the same he'd been quiet. The unsaid question hung in the air between all of them. No one had asked whether he could have done it. None of them had doubted his innocence. But nonetheless the police were pretty certain.

269

Jimmy couldn't believe the cheek of the copper! To actually ask him if he was connected. To imply that his son was a drug trafficker! To imply that he himself was involved in all of this. Cheeky fucking pig! He would get his after this was all done and dusted.

"Over there on the right son."

Sam did a U-turn and parked up where his Dad had indicated. They disembarked from the hire car. Jo got out from the back seat. Jimmy would have to remember this model. A Camry. Not bad. Quite roomy. He was quietly impressed.

He took a breath. There were all sorts of people milling around outside his son's place. Press, neighbours, the usual parasites dying to know what was going on. The press raced towards them but not before Swanson had stepped out of a nearby car and placed himself between them and their prey.

"Ladies and Gentleman. Please! These people would like to be left alone. They will give you a statement when they are ready to do so."

It achieved nothing. Questions, cameras, microphones. A sea of confusion.

"Is your son guilty?"

"Are you his other girlfriend?"

"Where is your brother?"

"Do you think he killed them?"

"Is he Mr Big?"

"Is he Australia's biggest coke dealer?"

Jimmy and Sam barged through the sea of lepers. They formed a small wedge and dragged Jo behind them.

"No comment!" they barked in unison.

"No comment!" shouted Jo again and then "How dare you? Have you no shame?"

As they climbed the steep driveway, a police cordon was thrown across the driveway to prevent the press contaminating the crime scene. As they climbed the final three stairs to Tray's front veranda they were met by a beautiful blonde woman.

"Oh Mr McCarthy, I forgot. There is someone here to see you."

The blonde thrust out her hand.

"Mr McCarthy?"

"Yes and who might you be?"

He was gruff and impolite. Nothing like his son she noted. He was broader than Tray. He was tired though. He looked bedraggled. Like he had been to hell and was still there. He pushed his hair back, looking at her searchingly. Taking her all in. She swallowed involuntarily. This was not a man to be trifled with. Her hand remained between them, unshook. She was embarrassed but continued nonetheless.

"Rachel Smith, I am a good friend of Tray's. I contacted the police here as soon as I could. We thought you might need some help or a place to stay."

"Thank you Rachel," he took her hand. "I am sorry if I am a bit rude. A lot of people want a piece of us at the moment and its pretty hard to know who's who in a land of strangers."

"It was a bit like that for Tray, Mr McCarthy."

"Jimmy, please. No one except the coppers call me Mr McCarthy."

He looked over at Swanson. The detective saw the suspicion in the old man's eyes. There was nothing there but open anger towards the policeman. Understandable because his son was being dragged through the mud and the police only had Trystan McCarthy in the frame for it.

"Okay. Jimmy then. Look we don't believe Tray did it. He loved all those girls. Lizzy was his love. He wouldn't have been able to kill her"

Rachel noted the woman in the background. She shifted her weight uncomfortably. Who was she? Tray had mentioned a brother but not a sister. She recognised the brother immediately. Not because she had seen any pictures. Tray didn't have any family portraits in his home. They had all noticed that and asked him why but Tray had always avoided the question. There was a strong family resemblance, not in the face or hair colouring or any of the other normal recognisable features. It was in the way he stood. The way he carried himself. His mere presence. His shoulders, broad and strong, his posture conveying hidden power but with no suggestion of menace. This was another manboy as she liked to call them. Those special men who had the full-blown features of a true man but with the love of a boy inside their heart. There were very few of them in Australia. To be considered anything other than a pie-eating football junky was tantamount to being a poofter. Despite how other countries thought of Sydney as being the gay capital of the world, the local suburban grog monsters thought different. To be sensitive, to be emotional, to be anything other than a homophobic degenerate hell bent on causing weekend havoc was a betrayal of your gender in Australia.

He stood in the shadows of his father but even though she had only caught sight of him for a few seconds, she knew who he was. The girl though was something different. Perhaps she was the brother's wife but she saw no ring. Perhaps a cousin. She was certainly very beautiful and obviously someone close to Tray to be allowed to accompany them on such a delicate and emotional journey.

Jimmy interrupted her thoughts.

"Rachel we know he's innocent too. Tray is like his late mother. There is no way that he is capable of doing this. He is my son. I should know."

Rachel saw Jimmy's eyes divert their gaze to Swanson. The detective saw the look. He noted the statement. It was something that he had been worried by throughout the investigation. Everyone was staunch behind McCarthy. Not one person believed he could do this. It wasn't like the normal mass murderer who loses it and goes on a spree. This guy had it together. Yes he had fled his homeland but he had found himself a life again and everything seemed to be smooth. They were checking bank accounts and there didn't seem to be any money worries or anything that would force him down this track. A crime of passion may have been one explanation if the sister hadn't been killed or Vukovic taken out but those murders made it look more mercenary; like he was a gangster or a major player. They were still digging for the connection but Sydney was as tight as a drum.

No one was talking. Not one snitch had come in with any information. It was as though the town knew nothing of this man. No one had anything. McCarthy had been so careful that not a single snippet of information had fallen from the criminal elite. The trail was cold. Swanson had never found someone who could orchestrate a purchase so large without drawing attention to himself. The other thing was, where was the money?

First rule of all drug and murder investigations was to follow the money. If you found large debts or large stashes of cash then you were on the right trail. There was nothing here. He had just spent a large amount of money on some studio equipment but nothing extraordinary. When Swanson thought about it, being on the run for ten years taught you how to be careful. Trystan was obviously that and intelligent to boot. That made for a very dangerous combination. That was what made the murders seem completely out of character for the Englishman but who knows the inner workings of anyone's mind. Stranger things have happened.

His boss in particular was focused on the McCarthy angle. Whatever the outcome, he was the man they had to find. There was no way that he could be ruled out until his version of events could be resolved. Fraser had been on his back since the murders had happened. He had never been this involved in a case before but Swanson supposed the top tier of the AFP would have been hammering him for a result.

"Are we allowed in detective?" Jimmy locked eyes with the detective.

Swanson was shaken from his thoughts by the question. It wasn't a question anyway. It was a statement of immediate expectation. The father wasn't used to hearing the word 'no', especially from a copper.

Jimmy was glad he had found someone who knew his son. Someone who knew the real Tray in this land so far away. He then realised that he hadn't introduced anyone to anybody. He was so tired. He couldn't even remember what day of the week it was.

"Rachel Smith. This is my other son Samuel McCarthy."

Sam reached forward between his father and Rachel and shook her hand. He mumbled a greeting and then retreated behind the patriarch, resuming his position in the shadows.

"This is Jo Flint. An old family friend."

The woman reached forward. Rachel saw how tired she was but there was something else in her eyes. Rachel recognised it. It was loss. Deep and unbidden. She had seen it in the eyes of her patients' loved ones. Rachel worked as a nurse caring for mentally disabled people. She saw that look when people realised that their loved ones had disappeared behind a veil of degenerative illness. Lost to them. Never to be found again. It was the destruction of hope. It was a loss of the future and the realisation that the past was the only place where their love had been a two way street. Who was she to Tray to feel so much pain?

Jo shook Rachel's hand.

"Well Rachel, let's go in shall we?" said Jo, beckoning Jimmy and Sam to enter.

There was something to this woman thought Rachel. She was brusque but also she looked like she had ownership here. What was her relationship to the McCarthys? If Rachel though she had questions before, she couldn't begin to unravel the ones that tumbled through her mind now.

*

"This is Xavier."

"Rudi. Don."

Xavier nodded to the two men.

"Long time no see Rudi."

"Yeah its been a while."

Rudi yawned. The big man in the front seat was Igor Duardo. A Colombian and a very dangerous man. Rudi had come across him in his normal dealings in London. It was when he thought about changing allegiances from Charlie and going out on his own. They had preliminary contact and then Rudi had seen what had happened to those northern monkies. The old guard didn't take too kindly to the northerners muscling in and they had suffered accordingly. Rudi had backed off but he had remained in contact with Igor. A Colombian was a good contact to have in your back pocket and Igor was one of the best.

Igor also had to leave London a while ago. Apparently his high profile antics had caused some consternation at cartel headquarters. Igor was a party animal of mammoth proportions. He got high on his own supply too many times and didn't mind who knew it. The cartel had removed him from London and sent him to this colonial backwater. Normally he would have been removed permanently by the powers that be but he was from Medellin. His real name was Igor Duardo-Escobar. Second cousin to the now deceased Pablo. A name to be feared.

No coke got into Australia from the South American cartel without Igor's hand being in it. He didn't handle the stuff anymore. He just set it up. He usually bankrolled the deals claiming huge interest on the loans. That meant the cartel earned at both ends of the operation. Igor was becoming a very successful businessman but he still loved the clandestine world.

He knew that the bust that was all over the newspapers had Mo's name on it. He therefore knew that Mo's inability to pay back the loan meant that the money had gone missing. The cops had mentioned nothing about a large amount of money being found. Someone had pinched it and all fingers pointed to Vukovic. But now Vukovic was dead and attention was now being focused on this McCarthy. He must have taken it.

Mo hadn't said anything to Igor but the South American wasn't stupid. The quadruple murder of the Rogers family had been a bit of classic Colombian overkill. Except it was not anybody from his crew. It wasn't necessary that the kids had been killed but they had been rubbed out anyway. The killer was making a statement. Whoever had taken the money had better give it back because nothing was taboo. That left Mo as the candidate most likely.

It was just a feeling Igor had. Obviously Vukovic had been the key to the money's whereabouts and so once he was dead, Igor surmised that he had served his purpose and given up his secret. And yet still no cash. Mo was still promising to deliver the money. Igor presumed that this McCarthy had the coin but hadn't given it over either. Mo was playing a dangerous game and now Rudi Stone, his old acquaintance wanted in.

Rudi was a main player when he met him back in the day but still tied in to the old firm. There were always turf wars in various parts of the UK but London was sealed shut. The old warriors were still in charge but they were slowly dying off. Rudi thought he'd been able to get ahead of the game back when Igor was shipping London's coke in but he'd got cold feet. It didn't matter that he was in charge of the Yardies, he was still not on the head table and if he got caught breaking the rules, the retribution would have been swift and ruthless.

That didn't stop them keeping in contact with one another. Rudi knew that eventually Igor would be allowed back into the fold. Igor knew it too. When that happened he would be out of this culturally inept wilderness and back where all the action was. All he had to do was keep clean and show he could run things properly. That was why, despite Mo being a good buyer, the Arab had to come up with the cash. No one stiffed the cartel and lived. Not their family. Not their associates. No one.

"Okay so what's the story morning glory?" Rudi didn't like talking to the back of Igor's head but beggars couldn't be choosers.

"First you tell me what you want with this McCarthy. There is much heat on this man at the moment. I don't want to be involved."

The Colombian still spoke his English with a heavy Latin accent but now it also had an unmistakeable Aussie twang to it. It was a multi-cultural example of what Australia had become. Igor twisted in his seat and looked back at Rudi. He hadn't really noticed before but there was some grey in the goatee, some lines around the eyes. Money hadn't seemed to have made him any happier.

"Remember I told you once that my brother had been killed," said Rudi.

"Yes. We work in this business and sometimes our family gets hurt."

"I wish I could be so nonchalant about it," replied Rudi.

"Yes. Well when you are a Colombian you lose a lot of family."

"I suppose so," said Rudi.

"So what does this McCarthy have to do with your brother?"

"He was responsible for Roger's death. It is an honour thing Igor. I want him dead. I have done for ten years."

"That is a long time to harbour a grudge amigo. Do you think it is worth it?"

Rudi thought about it. Yes it was worth it. He wanted McCarthy dead. He wanted people to know he was dead but most of all he wanted Charlie to know that he couldn't protect him any longer. That Rudi Stone was a man who could wield real

276

power. Whose reach was far. He wanted Charlie to know that Rudi Stone had come of age and he was going to do it personally. Old school style.

"Yes its worth it. Do you know where his family is?"

"Its been hard but they are at the house today. I have someone tailing them."

"Good well we have to get to them."

"Why?" asked Igor.

"Leverage my friend," replied Rudi.

"What?"

"You said you haven't been paid. He isn't telling where the money is and he won't until we can use something over him. We take his family and then we trade. Have you called your friends?"

"I have but I haven't told them why. I just asked for my money again. They said no. He still hasn't talked."

"Okay well you tell them I will be in touch. I will make this fucker talk. You mark my words."

"Rudi you are taking a very big risk here. The family are being tailed by the police. You won't have an opportunity."

"Igor I know these people. They won't be able to trust the police. Jimmy McCarthy will distance himself from them. When he does we will make our move. Its time I closed this particular chapter."

"It is your choice my friend but I don't want to be involved. It is too dangerous for me."

"Understood Igor. So who do we do this through?"

"Through the bikies. The Apaches. I use them sometimes. They are very strong here and they owe me some favours. They will ask no questions."

"Do you have what I asked for?"

"Yes they are in the back."

Don clapped his hands together.

"Great! This nigger needs a trigger!"

"Don when you gonna learn. You ain't no nigger and you're the worst shot I've seen."

They all laughed at that. All of them except Don.

*

He put the air phone back down again. He was amazed by the technology. He didn't know how it worked, he was just happy it did. It was handy that was for sure. He loved this first class malarky. He should have done it earlier.

"Did they spot him?"

"Of course they did. It's easy when you know your mark."

"How long before we get there?"

"Another twenty hours. Don't worry we'll get there before it kicks off."

"I hope so. We should have cleared this up years ago."

"Should've, could've, would've. If we had all done things right, I would have married Rita Hayworth and you would have played for West Ham. As it stands we can make up for a lot of shit right here."

"Whoever is behind this has got some big bollocks."

"Big but not big enough my friend."

"You sure we're doing the right thing."

"I'm sure. This time we finish it."

He fidgeted in his seat as a hostess approached them. Drop-dead gorgeous. If he were twenty years younger he would have considered joining the mile high club with her.

"More champagne sir?"

"Absolutely darling, absolutely!"

Down By The Riverbank

Rachel had been true to her word. After they had trooped around Tray's house, she had taken them to her parent's home. It was perfect. Out of the way in a place called Gymea Bay. It was at the end of a private dirt road. Only one way in and one way out. The house itself was at the bottom of a very steep incline, only accessible on foot. On the other side of the house flowed a tidal creek. The place was as isolated as isolated could be in the middle of a sprawling metropolis like Sydney. The press couldn't get to it nor the police. They could only wait at the beginning of the dirt road and see what eventuated. Jimmy was delighted, Sam was tired and Jo was sick with worry.

Jo had gone through Tray's house with Rachel. She was searching for what his life had become. Had she been wrong to come? She had seen nothing to suggest that he had lived a life with her. Nothing to suggest that she had been his love. Then again there had been no suggestion that anything had come before his arrival here.

The place though was pure Tray. It was comfortable. It was a sanctuary. It would have been like the place they would have had together if that had ever eventuated. It saddened her and filled her with remorse. This should have been her life except now that would never be. Then Rachel found what Jo had been hoping for.

It was a photo album. Within its pages held a history of their love. Pictures of Tray and Jo on the beach, at parties, in bed. There were some news stories from when the Taliban had made her an unwanted celebrity. He had written in the margins. Things like 'my girl and me', 'my love' and by one photo of her all dressed up for a night on the town, 'my dream'. Soppy she knew but that was Tray. She thought that maybe he would have forgotten her. That she would have just been a notch on his belt. The album gave her a renewed sense of hope. If he was found, if he was innocent, if he were alive, would he be pleased to see her? If, if, if.

She had taken the album with her. Jimmy wanted to go to the pool area. She had declined. Sam said that there had been blood everywhere. Up the walls, all over the decking. It had been a horrible sight. He said that at least they had drained the pool but it was not a place for the faint-hearted. Knowing that two young children had been killed up there made it worse. Jimmy had said nothing as they had followed Rachel to her parents' place. He had hardly said a word over dinner. Neither had Sam. She wanted to comfort them but felt unable to do so. Such was the worry in her heart that it consumed her. She was able to offer nothing.

She had hardly slept at all that night. Rachel blamed the jetlag but it wasn't. She kept thinking of Tray. Where would he be? Why had he run? Had he run at all or was he already dead? The questions kept coming over and over again.

Swanson had been in touch the next day. Still nothing to report. He said the next week would be the most important. This was high profile and Australia would want to see Tray caught. Australia was a conservative place and the murder of children would not go unpunished. Jo pointed out to him that Tray was innocent until proven guilty. Swanson retorted with the obvious. If he was innocent, why would he run?

That question plagued her. He was right after all. Why would he run? She hadn't put it to Jimmy or Sam and hadn't been able to anyway. The two men had slept nearly all day. Except for their conversation with Swanson, they had retired to their rooms and slumbered.

It was five o'clock in the afternoon. The sun had just disappeared over the top of the tree line. There was a small nip in the air. She shivered and looked across the dark water. She had left the house and taken a small walk down the riverbank. She felt very alone. There was no one left for her anymore. Her Dad was gone and now possibly Tray. A tear fell down her cheek. Why did she love this man so? If she had chosen him over her Dad then he wouldn't be in this situation. All of them were damned by this same guilt and perhaps none of them deserved to find any happiness because of it. She wiped away the tear and saw a swinging torch coming towards her. It was Rachel. Rachel was a good girl. She was young but there was an honesty about her. She cared deeply for Tray, of that there was no doubt. She seemed like a younger sister to him, at least that was how Rachel made it sound.

"Hi Jo. You okay?"

"Yes Rachel. Just having a quiet cry."

"Oh I'm sorry. Do you want to be alone?"

"No Rachel. I'm fed up with being alone. I've been alone since the day me and Tray said goodbye to one another. That's too long to be alone for anyone."

"Jo who are you?"

"Did Tray never tell you?"

"No Jo. Tray never told us anything. Those photos you took are the first thing I have ever seen of Tray's past life. But to us it wasn't really important because we loved him. We knew there was something that made him really sad sometimes and we nursed him through those moments but we never found out why. I thought he was hiding something but I never asked him what. He loves all his friends and would do anything for us. Its why we love him."

"I love him too honey. More than I love anything else. I left him once when we needed each other and when we had no choice. Now I have a choice and I'm not going to let him down."

"What if he did do it Jo?"

She looked hard at Rachel even though the younger woman couldn't see it through the darkness.

"Do you really think a man like Tray could kill anyone? Do you think that Tray would so much as hurt a hair on a child's head? Do you really know him at all?" Her tone was terse.

"Of course I don't think he could do any of that. I was just thinking out loud."

"I'm sorry Rachel. I'm just tired. Anxious I s'pose. I just want to find him. Get him back to us. I know it will all work out if we can do that."

"Jo I've got to ask this. Daz has alluded to some shit but I haven't had a chance to see him. Tray was instrumental in getting him a record deal. He has blown up like a star in the space of a couple of weeks. He's down in Melbourne this week. Up in Brisbane the next. There are rumours he's going to be invited to Miami next year. I can't keep track and what's worse is I haven't got him here to cope with all this business."

"I understand Rachel. Honest I do. Fire away, ask what you want. I think your hospitality deserves that."

"Jo, who is Tray McCarthy?"

They sat on the riverbank for two hours. They were bitten incessantly by mosquitoes but neither of them cared. Rachel hardly said a word. Jo unburdened herself of her secrets, of Tray's secrets, of the McCarthy's secrets.

"Jesus," said Rachel when Jo had finished talking. "Is that all true?"

"Yes it is. Unbelievable isn't it?"

"How could all of you live like that?"

"I don't know. We all sacrifice things for those we love I suppose."

"Jo there's sacrifices and there's sacrifices. I love the guy too. He annoys the shit out of me sometimes but I love him. But not like you do. I have never heard anyone speak about another person the way you have spoken about Tray. I don't even know how to express myself like that."

"Rachel I have loved that man from the moment we played together as kids. I didn't know it then and didn't realise it until we met again in Portugal. Imagine if Daz was ripped away from you now. You love him. You know it deep within yourself. Imagine that you could never see him again because if you did, he might be killed. Think about it. How would you feel?"

"Cheated. Angry. I don't know. It would kill me. I don't know if I would be able to get through it."

"When I was kidnapped in Afghanistan, I fantasized that Tray was going to come and rescue me. You know, the knight in shining armour thing. Then I realised that he wouldn't. He didn't even know I was working there. Then I just wanted them to kill me. What else did I have to live for? I had abandoned the one man I truly loved. I had chosen myself and my father's welfare over him. I didn't try and find a way to make it work. I must have been the only kidnap victim who was *not* grateful that their captors hadn't killed them. I would have been quite happy for them to have executed me. Who would have cried at my funeral? No one that's who."

"Jo. None of this is your fault. It sounds like none of you had a choice."

"I told myself that in the beginning Rachel but that's not true. We all have choices. It all comes down to whether we have the courage to make them."

"Okay, so what do we do now then?" asked Rachel.

"I don't know. But we've got to find him. I've got to find him. We've all been hiding for far too long."

What's The Colour Of A Two-Cent Piece?

"How much do you think he's got?"

"Enough to let us retire."

"Can't you just pay back the loan and be done with it?"

"And how would that look? I would have to sell off some assets and I really can't afford to do that. I've gone pretty legit in the past couple of years. Moving that sort of cash will attract some sort of attention."

"Well how much luck are you having?"

"Not much. Tarry went overboard when he took out the girls. We have nothing to hold over him."

"Yeah he's got nothing left to lose."

His phone went off. Fraser lent against a bright yellow front loader. This was an ideal place to meet. A building site in the city. No work on Sundays and pretty easy to see if you are followed. Mo controlled the security around here. They turned a blind eye as the two men had gone through the front gate.

"Yes?"

He listened.

"Yes."

He listened again.

"When?"

Another pause.

"Okay?"

He clicked the phone shut.

"Who was that?"

"I told you Fraser. You're not going to be told everything."

"That's what got you in trouble in the first place," replied the copper.

"Yeah you're right there but it looks like someone will be able to help us with our problem."

"How?"

"He didn't say. Someone from London."

Too many people were getting involved. Too many people he didn't know. Who was this person that Mo had been speaking to? Did he know that he was involved? He had been trying his best to steer Swanson down the right path. There was nothing to suggest that McCarthy had not been at the scene. The DNA tests from the sister's murder would be back in about four weeks though. That meant that they had until then to sort this mess out. After the results were released he wouldn't be able to control anything. McCarthy would be proved innocent of the sister's rape and murder and that would throw the other murders in to doubt.

"What's the plan then?"

"We sit tight until he contacts us."

"Don't kill McCarthy then. We wait."

"Okay Fraser. We wait but if I get pinched for this, you are going down too."

"Is that a threat Mo?"

"Fact Fraser. If I go down, you go down. End of story."

Mo turned and walked away from Fraser. He weaved his way around the building site. Fraser shouted after him.

"Remember who's got the power Mo. It ain't you!"

Mo didn't turn back. He got to the front gate and shook the guard's hand. The car was waiting and running. He got inside.

"Did you get that?"

"Yeah all of it?"

"Silly fucking copper."

Mo reached under his shirt and pulled out the microphone. This surveillance stuff was really cheap and so easy to set up. Tarry had only needed a direct line of sight and the signal came in like he was standing next to them.

"Give the recording to Salome. If anything happens to us, she hands that in."

"Yes Mo."

"Now lets get back to the workshop. Someone wants to see us."

*

"I don't like them being down there."

"What do you mean boss?"

"Too isolated."

"Boss they don't want to be interfered with. Its ideal for them."

"Yeah but not ideal for us."

"Dave that old man is dangerous. It just oozes from him."

"It may have been the case a long time ago Tommy but not now. He's a broken man. Trading on past glories. He has nothing anymore. His wife is gone. His business is gone. Now his son is on the way out and he has one son left. Whatever he used to be, whether real or not, he doesn't have the power anymore. "

"Are you sure Dave?"

"No not really. Its what I keep telling myself. But you know what they say about a cornered animal?"

"Unpredictable?"

"You got that right Tommy. Unpredictable. And that's what worries me about this Trystan character. If he's still alive, he's very much cornered and that makes him dangerous."

"What do you mean if he's still alive? What are you thinking?"

"Keep this to yourself Tommy but I'm starting to have second thoughts about this. The rape and murder was definitely a two-man job. The murder at McCarthy's house had three people leaving the scene. Don't you find any of that suspicious?"

"Yeah but Fraser is adamant that McCarthy is the only person we should be looking at?"

"Well he is the only lead we've got but I think someone has him instead of him being in hiding."

286

"Okay Dave. So what do we do?"

"Have a word around town again. See if someone has been throwing around the cash. We still haven't found a money trail from the bust so lets give the tree a shake and see if anything falls out."

*

"Gymea Bay. End of Franklyn Street except you cant get there from that side. You'll have to cross the river. They haven't got enough troops to cover the side you'll be coming from. They only have officers at the top of the private road and they can't see the house from there."

"Perfect. We're going to need a boat."

"You won't be needing one of them. You can walk across about two hundred metres from the house," he paused. "Rudi this is all the help I can give you. From here you are on your own. The cartel won't be pleased that I have even done this."

"What about contacting Mo."

"I will text the bikies his number. They are with you now?"

"Yes, we are in their clubhouse at somewhere called Taren Point."

"Good. Out of the way."

"When are you going to do this?"

"No time like the present Igor."

"Man you got some cajones amigo. Right from under the police."

"Well I've been waiting a long time and I'll be fucked if I'm gonna let some two bit coppers from Australia get in my fucking way."

"Rudi I'm going to ask you one more time. Is it worth it?"

"Igor you should know not to ask. Roger was my brother."

Family Ties

Jimmy could see why Tray liked this country. It was clean. It was beautiful but most of all you could see the sky. He hadn't realised how big it actually was. You couldn't see the sky in London. There was always something in the way crowding it out. Here there was nothing to obscure it and it made him feel small. He wondered whether Tray was looking at the same sky. Whether he was dead or whether he was still alive. He knew deep down that his son could never have done what they said he'd done but he couldn't explain why he'd disappeared either.

The papers had been all over it. Dredging up so called friends who spilled the beans. Revealing his involvement with drugs, with the seedy underbelly of the rave culture. It didn't look good but he also found out some things he hadn't known.

He knew Tray had been good at playing music but didn't know how good. He didn't understand his son's world. It was stranger than fiction to him. Betty had liked a dance and so had he but that was real music. Not this bang bang shit that the kids listened to. But DJ's were like pop stars these days. They were superstars some of them and from what the papers were saying, his son was one of the originals and one of the best.

He had never realised it. He thought it was just a phase that Tray was going through and that one day he would grow up and make something of himself. Yet none of them had given him the opportunity to grow or find out who he was. He had to hide his talent nearly all his adult life. They made him give up Jo. They made him run away because the peace was more important than his son's life. As he sat looking at the sky above Gymea Bay he realised that nothing was more important than his son's life. He had done everything that he and Charlie had asked of him and where had it got him? Alone, on the run, accused of a crime that Jimmy knew Trystan was not capable of.

"Penny for your thoughts Mr McCarthy?"

He shook his head as if shaking away some cobwebs.

"Oh Rachel its you. Sorry this jetlag is killing me."

"That's okay. You just looked deep in thought is all."

"I was Rachel. I was thinking about what I had put Tray through. I need to tell him 'I'm sorry'. I need to ask him for his forgiveness."

"You're his Dad Jimmy. You never need to ask him that. "

"I'm not so sure Rachel. There wasn't one picture of us in that house. Nothing. It was as if we didn't exist."

"Jimmy let me tell you. There is a sadness in Tray not because he doesn't love you but because he couldn't. I never realised how much it must have killed him not to have you in his life until Jo told me why he's here."

"She told you."

"Yes she told me Jimmy. She told me how he gave up everything just so one man wouldn't kill him. How he was nearly killed in a riot in Coven."

"Coventry darling. Coventry."

"Whatever Jimmy. The place is not important. What is important was that in exchange for his life he gave up everything he ever loved. You know your son. Is he like you? Is he a tough man?"

Rachel knew the answer before Jimmy even shook his head. This girl was blunt and to the point. He liked her. She didn't mess about. She was telling Jimmy like it was. No sugar coating. Someone should have spoken to him like this a long time ago.

"No he's not a tough man. He is made of much softer stuff. You know I have never even seen him come close to having a fight. I don't even know one person who hates him. You tell me why a man like that should have to endure a life like this. Every single thing he loves gone! Not only gone but taken away from him. He didn't choose this life, it was chosen for him by you and people who should have looked after him!"

Jimmy was shocked. She was letting him have it. His wife was the only person who had spoken to him like this. This girl was old beyond her years and Jimmy was stunned into silence.

"Don't sit there and give me the 'woe is me' speech. There were no pictures of you on the wall. Boo hoo Jimmy! He didn't have any pictures on the wall because he was protecting you. But who was protecting him?"

The question slapped him in the face. He couldn't answer it. He knew who should have been protecting who. He had failed his son and it had taken someone who he didn't even know to tell him.

"Rachel! Enough!"

It was her father.

"I'm sure Mr McCarthy doesn't need you attacking him. Don't you think he's been through enough at the moment?"

"Sorry Dad. You're right. I'm sorry Jimmy. Really sorry. I let my mouth get the better of me sometimes."

"No Rachel. I'm the one who's sorry. You're right. One hundred percent right. I let my son believe that we didn't care enough about him to save him. You know Rachel, Tray is the dead spit of his Mum. That woman loved everyone she ever met. Tray is the same. When we took that love from him and never gave it back, I expect some of him died. Betty died not knowing if her son even cared."

"Jimmy let me tell you something."

This time it was Marcus chiming in. Marcus was Rachel's Dad. He was about the same age as Tray. Not much older and he and Tray were obviously close like everyone seemed to be in this family.

"He cared more than any bloke I know. On your wife's birthday. On the anniversary of her death. On Mothers' Day. Your son had a terrible time. He would have to surround himself with his friends just to get through the day. He suffered so much on those days. He was always so happy. So full of life. He **was** the party. There was no fun without Tray being there. But on those days. On those deep dark days, it was as if someone had ripped the heart out of his chest and let the love bleed all over the floor. I found him once in a petrol station car park. Unable to move. He had been there for six hours. He had been crying the whole time. Not just sniffles. Sobbing Jimmy. This great hulking man who loved everything he had ever known was so depressed he couldn't even pick up the phone and ring me, Daz, Rachel, Geoff. No one. All because he thought he had no one"

Marcus paused, hoping it was sinking in.

"When I found him I didn't know what to do with him. Do you know what he had been doing?"

Jimmy shook his head. He hadn't known. How could he? But then again if he had thought about it, he should have known. Tray would have been heartbroken.

"He had been going hard for eight days. *Eight* days Jimmy! No sleep, no food. Just an endless cavalcade of drugs. And you want to know why?"

Jimmy again shook his head.

"Because it was so painful for him that he hoped if he got smashed enough he could wipe away the pain. That he could forget it ever happened. Instead, when the comedown came, it hit him like a hammer and I thought we were going to lose him. I didn't think your boy was going to come through the other side and it was only because we showed him how much he is loved that he did."

"All he ever wanted was a family Jimmy. A family he could love. Don't you understand that? Don't sit there and ask for his forgiveness. That makes it about you. What you need to do is show him you love him. That's all he's ever wanted from anyone. To show him they love him as much as he loves them."

Jimmy sat there in silence. How could he have been so callous? Betty would have killed him if she had known. What had he done to his son? What had they all done? Precisely nothing. How could he have survived any of this on his own? It must have been hell. He sat for a long time looking at these two strangers. People who obviously loved his son and cared for him more than he himself had done over the past seven years.

"Thank you Marcus," said Jimmy.

"What for?"

"For reminding me what I should have been doing instead of what I have been doing. I just hope he turns up so that I can show him how much he means to me."

"Jimmy. One day you can kick my arse when I fuck up. And believe me, you'll have plenty of opportunities. I fuck up on a regular basis."

"He does you know," added Rachel.

"Yeah well I can claim the title in that department," replied Jimmy.

Tell Me Your Secrets

His whole body ached. Time had stood still. He didn't know how long he'd been here. They had beaten him incessantly. Just when he started to heal or feel that he could sleep, they came in again. He didn't want to live. He begged them to kill him. The image of Lizzy and the girls in the pool kept flooding his mind. These bastards had fucking killed them! They were responsible. He wasn't going to give them a thing and they knew it.

Today had been a good day. They had left him alone. He lay naked on the floor shivering. He shivered all the time. He had dropped a lot of weight but he hadn't noticed. His body burned with pain. He couldn't walk properly. They had whipped the balls of his feet with a steel ruler. They were a bloody mess. Much like his face. His hair was matted with blood. His nose was spread across his face. Broken and battered. His eyes were swollen, filled with blood, puffy like a boxer who had been smashed for twelve rounds then picked up and beaten again. A doctor would have ended it a long time ago.

He was pretty sure his arm was dislocated. He couldn't move it. He lay on his other side trying not to move but the constant shivering meant that he couldn't lay still. Every single movement caused him pain. His beautiful lips, the one redeeming feature that he treasured about his face, were split and cracked. His jaw wasn't broken but there were a couple of teeth that were either cracked or on the way out.

His body was covered with open sores caused by the cigarette burns. They had gone to town on him. His body was destroyed. Even if he did survive this, he would never be the same. He would more than likely be a cripple or handicapped. No woman would ever touch his skin again. They would be horrified.

He couldn't take much more. They had brought the phones in. They were locked. Encoded. They couldn't open them. They couldn't get the numbers. The SIM cards were useless to them. They told him to make the call. Get the money back. All he had to do was make the call. But he wouldn't. They had killed those he loved and he wasn't giving them a thing. He secretly toasted Tumbles, hoping he would live a life for both of them. He thought of Jo and his Dad and Sam. They were the last people left. The last people who knew him for what he really was. He thought of Lizzy. He cried for her. For the girls. For Tracey.

They kept bringing in newspaper stories. Showing how the press were building a case against him. If he ever got out of here he was fucked anyway. The whole country had him hung, drawn and quartered for that crime. And the worst part of the whole thing was that he didn't even know who was doing this to him.

Who had Vukovic been in bed with? They had been very careful to keep their identities a secret. The chatter between them sounded Arabic but he couldn't be sure. When they did speak in English it was the patter of wogs. But he wasn't sure who. It could be Greek, Italian, Lebanese, Croat. Anything from around the Mediterranean basin. Eventually he didn't even care.

He didn't know he had this strength. He had beaten them off with his stubbornness. They were at the end of their tether. He could feel it with every question. As his body was shattered by their constant blows, he drifted in and out of consciousness.

"This isn't working. He's not going to tell us. Either he doesn't know or the girl was lying," said Faddy.

"She wasn't lying. She told me as I ripped her arse in two," confessed Tarry.

"Well he's not telling."

The door opened. Tray squinted trying to open his eyes but couldn't really see who was approaching him.

"Put some clothes on him. We'll be having some visitors."

*

"Have you found him?"

"No we haven't"

293

"Well what have you been doing then?"

"Following them both."

"And where has that got you?"

"Nowhere really. They were with some bikies in Taren Point then they all hauled out. Couldn't tell who was who and there's only me. I couldn't follow them."

"That's okay. Stay put. We'll be there soon."

He put the phone down.

"Fuck. They've lost 'em."

"What do you think they're gonna do?"

"Well they're not there to give him a birthday cake. We just better hope we get there first."

A Thai woman bumped into him. She apologised to him. He nodded acceptance of her apology. There were people everywhere. How could people live like this? Their plane had been delayed for six hours now and it would be another six at least before they would leave. He took back everything he had said about first class. It was only the seat that was different, the plane was the fucking same.

*

"Si."

He put the phone in its cradle. He liked this old replica phone. It reminded him of home but he wasn't in the mood to reminisce. The call had been from the Caribbean. They were not prepared to talk about it. He should have known. They had given him no choice. He had two weeks to sort this out. Someone had to pay. He just didn't know who it was going to be.

It had become personal. They had made that clear. If he wanted to clear all this up, he had to do what they said. No more pussy footing around. Ties were to be cut and lessons made. He wondered whether he could finish it all and still keep out of it. He would find out soon enough.

Tell Me Your Lies

He sat on the balcony overlooking the crystal clear waters. Winter was on its way but what was winter in this beautiful paradise. Paradise to him anyway. Outside these secure walls there was abject poverty that was true. But inside. Inside was a different matter. He lived in the luxury that you would find in the Waldorf opposite Central Park. He wanted for nothing and all in a heartbeat from the country that he flooded with cocaine.

Castro had been good to him. In return for undermining the very fabric of the capitalist empire with his white powder, the ageing communist had granted him cart blanche to do as he pleased in this little corner of the world.

The call had been short. The favour had been called in. A long time ago they had saved his cousin. They had got him out from under the police when his stupidity should have got him killed or in jail or both. They had used their contacts well. They knew they had been coming for him and they had flown him over to Ireland in a light plane. Now it was his turn to save another.

He had told him. Do this and you would be back in. Do this and you would be forgiven. He sucked on the huge cigar. These were rolled between the thighs of virgins. Castro had told him as much when he had hand delivered them. He leant back in the chair and pushed her head down again. She drew him in her mouth as he pondered how much money he would earn today.

*

It was dark. No moon. There was no lighting down here. It was deserted. They were alone. There weren't any places like this within 30 miles of London. He realised how lucky this country actually was. A lone jumbo jet soared overhead.

"Which one?"

"The one on the bend. Behind that small crop of trees."

"Is there anyone there?"

"No cops if that's what you mean. They are about a kilometre up the road. They're pretty slack. I can't believe they're not watching this side."

"Cops are cops the world over. They are lazy."

"The girl's old man is out at work. Night shift somewhere. The wife's not there. Hasn't been from the beginning. Not enough room I suppose."

Rudi turned to the bikie. They had parked the van at a look out at a turn in the river. It was a steep walk down to the river itself through a track made by bush-walkers or kids. Rudi could imagine the throng of reporters at the top of the other ridge waiting for some titbit of information. He was hoping that there were no parraparrazi lurking on this side of the river. The bikie said he had been over it like a rash and there was no one about.

They checked the guns. Israeli he had been told. Silencers in place. He hadn't seen these ones before. Don was as happy as a pig in shit. He had blacked up his face and looked like an SAS commando. Rudi didn't need the make up. All you could see where his teeth and his eyes. They were the London ninjas.

They scrambled down the river bank and dropped into the water, staying low. Igor had been right. The water was only ankle deep here. They could sprint across in twenty seconds. No one would see them.

"Careful you don't slip. There is green algae everywhere."

Rudi heeded the information. Perhaps twenty seconds was an understatement. If they fell in the drink it may draw attention to them and they didn't need that.

They took their time crossing, making little noise as they tip toed through the inky blank water. They got to a grassy clearing on the other side and all took a knee.

"Two minutes," said Rudi.

They hugged the bank as they approached the house. It was wide open. No security gate. A vast deck that held sun loungers and deck chairs. Indonesian inflenced. There were statues of Buddha, a small fountain and a hot tub. Rudi liked it but then reminded himself why he was here.

They were watching TV. A rerun of Highlander. Jimmy was snoozing in an armchair. Sam was sitting close to this girl. He didn't know who she was.

"Rudi. That was the girl I saw arguing with Jimmy at that funeral."

"Are you sure?"

"Sure as shit."

"Well she comes too."

Rudi paused and took the safety off the gun. Don did likewise.

"Right let's get this done."

The bikie pulled the sliding door to one side. Rudi and Don walked in like they owned the place. Don pointed his gun at Jo and Sam and put a finger to his lips. Sam went to get out of his chair. The bikie pushed him back down.

Rudi went over to Jimmy and put the barrel of the silencer against his neck. The cold metal made him wake with a start. Rudi waited for him to get his senses and stood in front of him.

"What the fu....?"

"Sssshhh Mr McCarthy or I blow you away right here and now."

Jimmy fumbled for his glasses. He put them on and looked up at the figure infront of him.

"Stone!"

"As I live and breathe."

Suddenly they were interrupted by a side door opening. It was Rachel wearing a dressing gown and a towel wrapped around her head. She held the towel with one hand, trying to balance it.

She was stopped in her tracks at the scene infront of her.

"Who the hell are....?"

She didn't get a chance to finish the sentence. Don shot her. Full in the chest.

*

"Anything?"

"Nothing. Everyone's gone quiet. Its like the moon. No one's heard a thing."

Shit. Where were those DNA reports?

"Keep looking Tommy. Something's got to turn up."

"Sure will boss."

Tommy was just about to leave when Salome ducked her head in through the door.

"Detective Swanson. There's an urgent call for you. Looks like something's gone wrong."

"What now?"

Was anything going to go their way?

*

She wasn't dead. She opened her eyes. The pain in her chest. Fuck it hurt. She didn't know how long she'd been there. It was daylight outside but only just. She didn't know what had happened. The gunmen. She saw the flash and now she was here, on the bathroom floor.

She crawled through the bathroom door. Out into the living room. It took forever. The cordless phone was on the coffee table. She reached for it. She noticed the blood all over her arm. She was covered in it. She knocked the phone to the floor. She picked it up and it slipped through her fingers. The blood. The fucking blood. She began to cry. She dialled '000'. A voice answered. She passed out again.

*

He greeted the two men.

"Nice trip?"

"Fuck off Daniel"

He hadn't changed much. He still looked like a grub but there was no denying it. He was Jimmy's brother.

"Here. I think you'd better look at this."

"What now?"

Daniel steered him towards a TV. The story had been on high rotation ever since it broke. The ticker tape slid by at the bottom of the screen. 'Another drug related shooting in Sydney – McCarthy family disappeared – police investigating – press conference to come.'

"Fuck! Who's watching the clubhouse?"

"Billy."

"Who?"

"My son."

"Any news?"

"No all quiet there."

"We finish this here Daniel. I don't care who gets nailed. We finish it here."

"Yes," Daniel swallowed. He knew he couldn't mess with this man. His reputation preceded him. "Now where to?"

"First find me a payphone."

"Will do."

*

"What the fuck are you doing Stone?"

"Doing what I should have done ten years ago. I'm going to kill your son."

"You fucking leave him the fuck alone!"

299

"I don't think you're in a position to talk Jimmy. Tape him Don."

Don got some of the electrical tape and put it over the old man's mouth. He tried to struggle but the bikie held his head still and Don finished the task. Don stood back and admired his handy work. The three hostages were sitting on the bare aluminium floor. Hands taped behind their backs.

Rudi looked at them. Pathetic. How the mighty had fallen? Jimmy McCarthy, the strong man, reduced to a struggling worm in the back of a van. He turned to Don.

"You shouldn't have done that Don. You sure she's dead?"

She was gone. He was sure of it. He was no doctor but she didn't look like she was breathing. Despite all his gangster aspirations, it was the first time he'd shot anyone.

"I'm sure."

Rudi tapped the bikie on the shoulder.

"Where to now?"

"I'll make the call?"

He pulled a mobile from his pocket and dialled in a number.

"We've got something you might be interested in."

He paused.

"Okay. We'll be there shortly."

"So what give's?"

"Lakemba. Behind the mosque."

*

"What the hell are you doing?"

"Nothing to do with me. This is from outside. McCarthy has made a lot of enemies over the years. Looks like he pissed off someone from London. They will make him talk. Guaranteed."

"Be careful Mo. This is getting worse. I can only protect you for so long."

"You will protect me as long as you're on the payroll."

"I don't like the way you're talking Mo."

"I don't give a fuck what you think Fraser. I am a criminal. I chose my path. You're a fucking copper. Who do you think's got more to lose?"

Fraser went quiet. Mo was right.

"Anyway. It won't come to that. We can keep a lid on this and no one will be the wiser. Once its done, we'll sit down and have a look at the situation."

Fraser didn't think that this was ever going to be done. He was going to have to end the Arab's reign. It wouldn't be hard. He had other people on the books. The only problem was no one could do a thing at the moment.

*

"I will wire you the money. Send me the details to this email address. Shepparton_ch@hotmail.com. I will do it in five minutes. Are you sure that's the final amount."

"Yes."

"Well the debt is mine now. Your cousin is cool with this?"

"Yes. He allowed it."

"I'll see you in London."

"Yes. Sooner rather than later."

He put down the receiver.

"Daniel?"

Jimmy's brother walked over.

"I want you to go and relieve Billy. I need to put my head down. Is there somewhere I can stay close to the clubhouse?"

"Yes, Northies has some serviced apartments above it. Very swish."

"Good. Is there internet there?"

"I'm sure there is."

He beckoned to his old friend.

"Time for business."

"Good."

The two men picked up their bags and all three of them left Sydney airport. Someone was going to have to pay for this. He was missing his grandson's first birthday and that pissed him off no end.

CHAPTER TEN

London Calling

Who's Calling The Shots?

That was it. He couldn't avoid the truth any longer. Something was very wrong with this investigation. Trystan McCarthy would not kidnap his own family. If he had, it would be a masterstroke of subterfuge but the girl Smith had just about blown that line of investigation out of the water. Amazingly enough she was still alive. Whoever the shooter was, he had missed just about every artery and major organ possible.

She had drifted in and out of consciousness all day. They hadn't interviewed her themselves but the father had been in with her. She should have been dead just from blood loss alone but she was strong. They hadn't released the fact that she was alive to the press. There was a group of assassins out there and they didn't give a fuck about who they killed. That meant she was still a target. They hadn't been able to protect her when she was at home. There was no telling if they would take her out in a hospital.

She had seen them. Two men. One white, one black. That was all she could tell her father. She had been in the shower. She had opened the door. They had shot her. That was it. He couldn't think who would have done this. The black man was the key. He was sure of it.

It was also a professional job. This was no group of local head cases. They had silencers for fucksake. No one used them in Australia. It nagged at him. A black man? There hadn't been any registered murders by a black man that he had heard of. Not by a hit man anyway. This smelt of an outside job.

"Tommy!" he shouted through his office door.

Tommy came rolling in.

"Yes boss."

"I want you to check the names of incoming passengers coming into Australia in the past week. I want you to concentrate on all passengers coming from the USA and UK. Can you do that?"

"I will have to go through Customs and the airlines. What are we looking for?"

"A black man."

"Jeez Dave. I don't know if they can do that."

"Well check the CCTV of people coming through the airport if you can't get it through Customs. All of 'em. Anywhere we take international passengers."

"Christ Dave. That's going to take for ever."

"We haven't got any other leads Tommy. We may as well try this one."

*

They had sat him in a chair. They had tried to put clothes on him but it was impossible. His body was in such a state they couldn't do it. He screamed when they tried. They brought in a doctor and they injected him. He didn't know what with but the pain subsided. He passed out. When he came to again his shoulder was strapped to his side. They had cleaned him up a bit but not much. He was wearing a soft dressing gown but it hurt where it touched the wounds. His buttocks ached. He sat there waiting. If he wanted to get out of the chair and try to escape he couldn't. His feet were fucked.

He looked round the room. He tried to twist his neck and couldn't. The pain was like someone sticking a knife in his shoulder. If he ever got out of this, he was going to make them pay. But he was all alone. No one was going to help him now. Then again they were keeping him alive. He had what they needed and they hadn't got it. Perhaps he could talk his way out of this. Perhaps someone would call in some favours. Perhaps someone already had. There could be no other reason they had cleaned him up. The door opened.

*

They shovelled them out of the back of the van. He thought Jo would've crumbled in this sort of environment but he had forgotten. She had been kidnapped by the Taliban for christsake. She was hardcore. He expected that she had seen it all. But this was new to him. Rudi was a dead set cunt. Did the black bastard really know what he was doing? There would be hell to pay for this if any of them got out of this but he very much doubted he would.

His Dad didn't struggle. He almost looked resigned to his fate. And what had happened to Tray? His brother. His keeper. Tray had got Sam involved all those years back but he had made up for it. His idea had allowed Sam to come back home, to live with his family and be with their Mum until she passed. Tray had been given none of that. He lived here. In isolation. Away from the things that mattered.

His heart had nearly melted when he saw Jo at the funeral. He knew how much they had meant to each other. He had tried to tell his Dad afterwards but Jimmy had brushed him aside. He didn't know whether it was out of frustration or shame or what. His Dad didn't want to hear it. Since this had all happened he knew it was out of guilt.

Two guys had met the van at the edge of a car park. The bikie wound down a window and they directed them to the far side of a deserted complex. They pulled up infront of a grey, non-descript building. A door opened and six guys exited. Stone got out with that rat Don and a man approached them. They all shook hands. Sam couldn't hear what they were saying but he knew they were discussing their future. Whoever it was they had better make sure that they kill them all because he didn't want to be in their shoes if any of the McCarthys survived.

*

The van meandered across the car park. Mo watched it come to a stop just outside the offices. Six people got out. Three of them bound. Two men approached him. One of them had a limp. The other was black.

306

"Mr Aziz?"

"Mr Stone?"

They shook hands.

"I believe I have a solution to your problem."

"I believe you have."

Mo remembered the phone call from Fraser. When this was all done, he was to kill them all. Make it all look like a London gangland war. Swanson was on the road to tracing Stone. It wouldn't happen quickly but he wasn't stupid either. They would get there eventually. Once Mo had what he wanted, the poms would find out what it was like to take on the Aussies.

*

Fraser put the phone down. He was glad. Soon it would be all over. It was going to cost him but the wheels were in motion. Aziz had become a liability. Too many people were involved and he had to keep a lid on it.

His contact had agreed. When he had all the details, that fucking Arab was finished. He was going to make sure of it. Then he could get on with his life. No more dealing with these fucking camel jockeys. They thought they were hardcore. Just wait until they found out what hardcore really meant.

*

Fucking coppers! They were more dishonest than him. He wanted to go in right now but the copper had said to wait. Wait for the money. Greedy fucking bastard! All he had been doing was fucking waiting. This would be the last time he would deal with this bastard. This time he was going to have to pay.

They were escorted through a single door. It had Aziz Security above the door. They walked along a small bare hallway. It was illuminated with harsh strip lighting. The walls were white brick. It was a sterile place. They passed various beige doors. They were closed. Solid. Whatever rested behind them, they were not going to find out. They headed for a dark green door at the end of the hallway. The hallway was narrow. There was barely enough room for all of them.

She had been around people like this before. Bullies all of them. Brave when they had the upper hand. Cowards when it came down to it. Her mind went back to Afghanistan. The bag over her head. They hadn't wanted her to see them. That meant she had a chance. That they may release her. These people didn't care. She had recognised Rudi and Don. She had seen the faces of these other people. That meant that there was only one way this was going to finish and it wasn't going to be a holiday in the Bahamas.

She was shoved in the back. She stumbled into the wall banging her head. She tried to yell but the tape still covered her mouth. A hand grabbed her shoulder, steadying her. Her hands were still bound. She hated them. This was how it was going to end then. At least it would be over. No more hiding.

*

Jimmy knew it was near. These guys were going to end it soon. Perhaps they were getting them all together. A family execution. He hoped Tray hadn't suffered too much. The door they were heading towards opened.

*

"Any news Billy?"

"Nothing. There's something going on in there though. Guys keep coming and going with boxes of stuff. There always seems to be someone in there. I drove by once pretending to be lost. The place reeks."

"What of?"

"I don't know. Sort of chemical smell."

Perhaps they were cooking something. Perhaps they were manufacturing something. Who knew with bikies? They were always up to something but fancy doing it on your own doorstep. They were none too bright.

*

The phone hadn't rung. They had been waiting for days. Then Pedro came in.

"Tumbles, I have just had some very interesting news."

"What? Tray?"

"No not Tray. Someone else fucking."

"Well who then?"

"Someone fucking very important."

"Who you fucking wet back?"

"Someone who knows things."

"Fucking hell Pedro. Are you going to tell me what's going on?"

"No we wait for phone call. Tray will call. This person knows. We are his only hope."

One Door Opens…

The door opened. He couldn't focus. Many people. Many faces. He didn't recognise any of them at first. Then he saw. The black skin. The shifty eyes. The hate.

His heart sank. It was Rudi Stone. He was fucked now! He wanted to say something but his mouth was dry. He croaked something unintelligible. He couldn't pronounce the words he wanted to say. This motherfucker! This bastard! This fucking black cunt! Him! This piece of Yardie shit! He had got him.

Then a figure stumbled forward. He was bound. Big and old. He tried to take it in. Then it dawned on him. It was his Dad. It was his Dad. Fuck no! It was his Dad!

"Dad."

The word came slow. Painfully. He tried to stand and fell to the floor. His shoulder burned as he hit the ground. His vision blurred. Like rain on a dirty window. He tried to move but couldn't. The pain was too much. As the blurring began to fade, a pair of open-toed sandals shuffled towards him. He recognised those feet. He had held them. He had kissed them. It was Jo!

*

They shuffled into the room. No windows. A bare light bulb hanging from the ceiling. He couldn't see what was in the middle of the room. The goons infront of him obscured it. Then he heard shuffling. Someone was trying to speak but couldn't. He was pushed forward through the throng. The bodies parted and then he saw him. His son. Battered, beaten. It didn't look like him but there was no denying it. It was Tray.

He called out to his Dad. The pain in his eyes. The suffering. The love. In one look he saw all that his son had been through. Jimmy moved forward and Tray tried to move from the chair. He slumped to the ground. His feet were a bloody mess. His face had been brutally smashed. His beautiful son. His baby boy. His beautiful baby boy!

"Touching," said Rudi.

*

She saw Jimmy move forward. She saw his shoulder sag. Something hit the ground. She heard someone cry out 'Dad!' She had to see. She could see some blue but that was all. She pushed around Jimmy and then she saw. It was Tray. He was crumpled in a heap. His hair covered with blood. His face swollen like a football. Purple and red. His feet, oh his poor feet! She could see the bone. What had these animals done to him?

She fell to her knees. She tried to get close to him. She shrieked at the tape covering her mouth. A hand leant forward and ripped it from her face. She didn't feel the sting as it tore some skin away.

"What have you fucking done to him?"

She yelled at her captors.

"Tray? Tray? Can you hear me?"

His eyes flickered. He was alive.

"Untie my hands! Untie my fucking hands!"

"I don't think that's the way to ask is it?" Don smirked from the back of the room.

Sam couldn't see what was going on. What was happening? His Dad had nearly buckled. Jo had. He moved to the right. Oh fuck me dead! Who was that? He knew though. He knew it like he knew his own face. It was Tray or what was left of him. He looked to the ceiling. He couldn't look at the body on the floor.

Rudi Stone was enjoying this. So much suffering. All this time and now it had arrived. The Arab whispered into his ear.

"I think we have our leverage."

311

Another Door Closes

They untied their hands. Took the gags off. Then they let them crowd round Tray. Jo was near hysterical. There were screams there were shouts. There were tears. Rudi looked on in detached amusement until Jimmy stood up followed by his son. They rounded on him. Fuck these guys were big.

Don and Rudi flashed their guns at the two McCarthys. It was enough to stop them in their tracks.

"You evil fucking bastards! Why? Why did you do this?"

"I didn't fucking do this Jimmy. They did."

He gestured towards the Lebanese with his gun.

"You're son is a classic fuck up Jimmy. He took something from them and they want it back with interest. Just like I do."

Jimmy looked at this crew of Arabs. Fucking animals. Who treated people like this? It was inhumane. Whatever he had done, he didn't deserve this.

"And just who the fuck are you?"

He approached the tall dark tanned Arab. Dressed impeccably in a dark grey suit, he stood out from the rest. White shirt, royal blue tie with flecks of yellow, patent leather shoes. It all suggested money. But his crew was different. Dressed in tracksuits and flashy leather trainers he recognised the look. Gangbangers. Headcases. They weren't cut from the same cloth. They were just hoodlums. Foot soldiers. The way they were dressed brought attention to themselves and they didn't care if they did. They thought they were untouchable. That meant they were the opposite. Thugs like them were a dime a dozen. They were all over the place in London. Petty thieves and muggers. Problem was, they had no honour. They had no code. There had been many crimes perpetrated by these sorts of low-lifes back home and it had shocked the old guard. As the old men lost their grip, the manor became a lot harsher place to earn your living.

"I am Mohammed Aziz Mr McCarthy. Your son has suffered because he has taken something from me and he won't give it back. Now I think he will."

"Fuck off you fucking cunt!"

Jimmy went to grab Mo. Tarry stepped in and waved a pistol infront of his face.

"Don't you dare Mr McCarthy. We only need one of you. Not all of you."

Jimmy retreated. He realised they were right. All this time Sam stood stock-still. Not saying a word. He stared at Rudi and Don. If they were surprised that he was actually walking they showed none of it on their faces. Pure hatred flitted across Rudi's chocolate features. If he could, he was going to murder these bastards where they stood. Tray was barely alive. He had never seen anything like it. Don held his stare.

"Don't even think about it Sam. Anyway what are you doing standing you cripple? Heard you were an utter spastic."

"I'm agile enough to rip your fucking throat out you fucking bastard!"

"Ah so you do speak."

"I've never been a cripple you stupid fuck but it kept you off my back. How do you feel now *you* fucking spastic?"

Don just stood there. Everyone said he had come back a shell of his former self. Jimmy had kept him by his side all this time, pretending that his son was depressed and broken. Well if he wasn't before, he would be soon.

"Mr McCarthy," the Arab spoke again. "You're son is going to give us what we want or we are going to kill you as well. First we fuck this girl in front of him and then we kill you and your son. If he gives us what we want, you go free."

"And what about him?" asked Jimmy.

"He I'm afraid will go with Mr Stone. He sealed his fate a long time ago. Is that not right?

"Rudi. You can't do this. What do you want?"

"I want him Jimmy. You can't save him but you can save yourselves. Tell him to do it."

"Dad?"

The voice was weak. It was Tray. They all turned to face the crumpled body. His head wounds had reopened. Jo didn't know which part of him to hold. The tears just kept rolling down her face. Her man. Her gorgeous man. He was in so much pain. He didn't have to say a thing. She could sense it coursing through his body.

"Dad?"

"Jimmy get over here!"

Jo's eyes said it all.

Jimmy returned to his son. He bent down. He's knees creaked. He felt his age. His eldest son turned his head ever so slightly. He bent close to his son's blood stained lips.

"Dad. Tell them I'll do it."

*

They had left Tray with Jo. They manhandled Jimmy and Sam into an office adjacent to the torture room. They were seated at a round table. All business. Don and some goons stood at the back of the room. Rudi sat next to Mo. Sam and Jimmy sat opposite them.

"Your son is a very brave man Mr McCarthy. Most people would have told."

"Told you what you cunt?"

Mo knew this man was not scared. He was different from his son but they shared the same strength.

"Where my fucking money is!"

"What money?"

"The six and a half million bucks he has stolen off me. He has caused me a lot of fucking problems."

Six and a half million! Fucking hell Tray! What have you got yourself into? Jimmy's mind raced. Could he get his hands on that sort of money? He knew he couldn't. Not in a short amount of time anyway. Fuck, why couldn't Tray just leave things alone?

"Well why doesn't he give it to you?"

"Because he doesn't fucking have it?"

"And how do you know that?"

"Because his girlfriend told me before I blew her fucking head off!" Tarry took great delight in telling this old man how ruthless he could be.

"And after I killed her, I killed her fucking daughters. They fucking screamed when I killed their aunt. It was priceless."

"You fucking animal!"

Tarry just smiled back. The accusation didn't offend him.

"Tarry be quiet now!"

Tarry took the admonishment from his boss. 'An attack dog' Jimmy thought to himself. A dangerous attack dog. Not like this bullshit cunt Don. He was soft. His itchy trigger finger had killed Rachel. Another person who had died because of this mess.

"Your son has contacts Mr McCarthy. High up contacts. He has taken my money and converted it into a much more valuable commodity."

"And what's that then?"

"Cocaine. Lots of it. Tonnes of it!"

"How? He doesn't know anybody like that. I swear. He hasn't had anything to do with anybody since he left London."

"Are you sure Mr McCarthy? How often have you heard from your son? Do you know what he's been up to?"

Jimmy had to admit he didn't really know the first thing about his son's life. Little bits had filtered through but Jimmy had cut all ties. All for the sake of keeping him safe from Rudi. But Tray had managed to get himself in all sorts of strife without getting anyone from London involved.

"I want it all back Mr McCarthy plus what he has made off it. In return you get to live."

"Do you think you will get away with this?"

"Yes I do. If I don't, we will kill you all. Do you want to lose your other son?"

Jimmy didn't know what to do. Sam reached across and put his hand on top of his father's.

*

"Jo?'

"Ssshhh baby. Don't say anything."

"Jo?"

His voice was so weak. It rasped through his lips. His lips were dry. When he spoke, blood soaked spittle and sputum dribbled from the corner of his mouth.

"Baby. Please don't speak. We're here now."

She had taken her jumper off and placed it under his head.

"Jo. I've really fucked up."

The words came slowly. Each syllable a monumental effort.

"Jo. You have to get out of here. They will kill you."

"Baby. I am not going anywhere. If they kill you, they kill me."

He tried to smile. It hurt. He coughed. The tears that streamed down his face stung the cuts on his broken nose. The door opened and closed again.

It was Sam. He walked over to Jo and Tray and knelt beside them. He placed an arm over Jo's shoulder.

"Tray?"

"Sam. You here too? Is this real?"

"Sssshh bro. Easy now. Yes its me."

He tried to place his hand on his brother but he winced in pain.

"Is what they are saying true? Did you do this?"

"Sam?"

"Yes Tray."

Sam couldn't believe the sight of his older brother. No one should have to endure this.

316

"Ring Tumbles."

Sam thought for a minute. Tumbles! What did he have to do with anything? A name from so long ago.

"Tumbles? Are you sure?"

Jo looked equally mystified. They both knew who he was talking about. It must be the beating. It had made him delirious.

"Yes. Blue phone."

This was hurting Tray. The effort was causing him so much pain.

"It's the only number in it."

Sam went to leave.

"Sam the code."

Sam turned back.

"Twenty-One Zero Four."

Jo smiled. It was her birthday.

"Sam. Tell him to play the fucking game. Make sure you tell him. Its your only chance."

Tray watched Sam's shoes walk away from him. The door opened and closed. He just hoped Tumbles would understand.

Play The Fucking Game

He went back in the office. Jimmy was sitting at the table. Don was pacing between some filing cabinets. There was nothing in Jimmy's eyes. Sam looked at Aziz.

"Did he have any phones on him?"

"Yes three. He wouldn't make the call."

"Yes well I will. He told me to."

"Good. At last we are getting somewhere. Tarry go get the phones."

The attack dog left the room and returned a couple of minutes later. Not a word had been spoken since. Sam punched in the code and pressed redial.

*

He woke from his slumber. He had wired the funds as soon as he had access to a computer. The confirmation had come through. Good! He rang Billy and Daniel. No news. He rang the other number.

"Do you know where they are?"

"No not yet."

"Well keep looking. We've got to find them."

He walked out of the bedroom and took in the view from the lounge room. Spectacular! The pacific blue. He went to the kitchen and switched on the kettle and saw the note. He picked it up.

'Be back soon – gone for some kippers.'

*

He told him to stop. He wasn't as good as Tray. Mind you no one was. It was just another wannabe DJ who had strolled into town. They all wanted a go but he couldn't hire everyone. Not this time of year anyway. He needed something big for Christmas and hadn't found it yet. These auditions were soul-breaking.

Pedro sat next to him, his whisky in hand. They had both kept a vigil for his friend.

The green phone rang. He picked it up.

"Tray?" He waited for a response.

"Sam?" he paused. Pedro sat in silence. Sam? It could only be Tray's brother. What was he doing on the phone?

"Yes we have."

Tumbles listened again.

"Who?"

Silence again. Pedro hated these one-sided conversations.

"Fucking Lebanese! Who the fuck are they?"

'Lebanese', what the hell did they have to do with this?

"Rudi too. Fucking hell Sam. Are you okay?"

Sam spoke again.

"Yeah, yeah sorry."

Tumbles listened intently.

"They want it all! You've got to be kidding!"

This didn't look good. Pedro took another sip and let the warm spirit flow down his throat.

"I'll call you back. Give me a couple of hours."

He paused again.

"He says what?"

Pedro could hear the voice on the other end of the line but was unable to make out what he was saying.

"Are you sure Sam?"

"Yeah okay. Okay! A couple of hours. Stay safe."

Pedro leaned forward.

"Well what fuck is going on?"

"Some Lebanese have Jimmy, Sam, Jo and Tray. They have beaten Tray badly. He's almost dead. Rudi Stone is there too."

"Who?"

"The guy who has a contract on Tray's head."

"This fucker is the guy who want to kill Tray all this time fucking?"

"Yes."

"Filho da puta!"

"Yes he fucking is."

Tumbles sat back in his seat.

"Pedro. These guys are playing for keeps. They want all their money and more. They want the lot."

"Who fucking does?"

"These Lebanese. The people we took the money from."

"Who these Lebanese fucking?"

"I don't know. You know stuff. Are they players?"

"There are Lebanese who are in the game but they are nothing. Not important."

"Well they are important enough to nab Jimmy and the rest. They don't give a fuck. They have nearly killed Tray and Rudi will!"

"What we do then? We give it to them?"

"No we don't."

"You let them die?"

"No. Tray told me to play the fucking game."

"Aaah."

"You remember?"

"How could I forget pa?"

They both picked up their drinks.

"So how do you want to play it Pedro?"

"Don't worry. I have plan fucking. We take it all, right?"

"We fucking take it all Pedro. Roll the fucking dice."

They clinked glasses. Fucking third world Arab muppets! Rudi Stone! Tray had balls, Tumbles just hoped that he would be able to hang on to them.

"I make phone call."

"You do that Pedro. You do that."

*

"Done. They will call in two hours."

"What was all that about?" Mo had listened to the conversation on speakerphone.

"Tray told me to tell him to play the fucking the game."

"What's that mean?"

"What you think it fucking means?"

"I don't know. That's why I'm asking you."

"It means go along with anything you say."

"Good."

Sam knew that it didn't.

Rolling Stone

"How many do you need?"

"Ten!"

"Ten?"

"Yes ten."

"I don't know if I can do that many."

"You make sure you can. I have given you a lot of money over the past seven years. I want ten and I want them by tomorrow."

"Pedro you cannot be serious. Someone will say something."

"I am telling you to do this today. We will have photos with us. We will be there at 10 am. We will be gone by 11 am. We have a flight to catch."

"Okay. I will do my best."

"No you will do it Nino or you are finished."

Pedro put the phone down. Tumbles hadn't understood a word. The entire conversation had been in Portuguese and despite him living there for nearly a decade, he barely understood a word.

*

"What have you been doing son?"

"Trying to get back to you Dad."

"By doing this?"

"Dad, he doesn't need a lecture."

Sam was right. He didn't need a lecture. He needed a fucking hospital but that was out of the question. Jimmy had requested and got what he wanted. From somewhere they had rustled up a mattress. They had put Tray on it. Perhaps it was because the wheels were in motion that they were now showing some compassion. Perhaps it was because if Tray died they knew they would get nothing. Whatever his son was into it was big. How had he managed to get involved with these people?

Jo had been simply brilliant. She had first aid training from Afghanistan. She had seen many injuries, mainly from mines and she knew how to dress wounds. Jimmy was amazed at the speed and efficiency with which she worked. His son moaned but he did not complain. They gave him constant sips of water. Re-hydrating him. It hurt him just to put the bottle to his lips.

Jo didn't know what to do with his feet. She tried to wash them as best she could but they had been flayed. She didn't have the equipment she needed and her skills weren't good enough. Sam could see her frustration but he gave her the encouragement she needed. She did the best she could but she didn't know if he would ever walk again. When they had opened up the dressing gown they had been further shocked. There were cigarette burns everywhere. She didn't even know where to start. She didn't even know how he was still alive.

The door opened.

"Phone call!"

It was Don.

"You go Sam."

Sam left the room and was escorted back to the office.

"And who are you?"

Aziz was talking to the phone.

"I'm not telling you fucking. Where is Tray?"

"Talk to this person," said Mo.

Mo indicated to Sam to sit down. Sam spoke to the phone.

"This is Sam McCarthy."

"Sam is that you?"

"Yes. Who is this?"

"It is Pedro. Pedro Nunez from Lagos."

Sam thought hard. Pedro? Pedro from Lagos? He wracked his brain. Was this the same person? One-eyed Pedro.

"Is this Pedro from Cavaleiro?"

"Yes amigo. It is me."

Tray had hardly said a word during the two hours that they were trying to mend him. He had said that Tumbles had done what Mo had said they had done. He couldn't give details. He could barely speak. He hadn't mentioned Pedro. Sam had to play along though. Their lives depended on it.

"Is these Lebanese listening to what fucking I am saying."

"Yes they are."

"Well everyone listen to me," Pedro paused. "Because McCarthy is my friend I will give a shipment in exchange for your lives. This shipment I am paying for. It is mine. You understand you Arab fuck?"

"Who the hell do you think you are talking to?"

Mo couldn't hide the anger in his voice.

"I am talking to you. I do not have much respect for baby killers fucking! You listen and you listen good! You do not interrupt until I finished!"

"Whoever you are, we can kill them right now!"

It was Don. Rudi tapped him on the chest. Rudi hadn't said a thing. He didn't care about this bullshit. He just wanted to watch Tray die. He wanted to see the life drain from his eyes. He was glad these Lebanese had been brutal. He deserved nothing less.

"Who is this?"

"Don Chait nigger."

"Aaah Mr Chait, I am no nigger. I am surprised you fucking are still alive. Can you still walk?"

"What?"

What was this? How did this person know him? Who the fuck was he?

"How is your legs motherfucker? Remember me? I fucking nearly kill you in Portugal."

Don remembered the voice now. The glass eye. This was the bastard who had nearly killed him in the Algarve. This prick was the Mr Big! He could hardly believe it.

"You ask too many questions then and you talk too much now. You may have the McCarthys but I have what you want. So fucking how about you shut your mouth fucking and listen to me!"

Rudi nudged Don and he went quiet. Rudi thought about the wheels within wheels. Tray McCarthy had set up his network well. No one would have believed he controlled a drug empire from Portugal and Sydney. It was almost perfect.

Sam played conciliator.

"Pedro. Calm down. What do you have for us?"

"I have five hundred kilos of coca-inna coming into Sydney on Saturday. It is nearly one hundred percent pure. If you cut even four to one that will give you nearly one hundred million dollars. That is what I have."

This wasn't Pedro's shipment. It was always coming in, now Pedro had bought it and was offering it up as collateral. Sam couldn't believe the amount of money they were talking about. One hundred million dollars! What the fuck had these three been up to?

Mo looked very satisfied too. Five hundred kilos of coke. They would take over Sydney with that amount. Oh Tray McCarthy was going to make him a very rich man!

"I will be there with my colleague on Saturday. We will give you details then."

"Why do you need to be here?"

It was Mo who asked the question.

"Because I want to see all the family alive before you take my product and that is another thing fucking."

"What is that?"

"I will ring every twelve hours. I want to speak to all four people you have hostage. If I don't speak to them I assume they are dead and you get nothing. You understand motherfucker? You get nothing fucking!"

"I understand Mr Nunez. You make sure you call."

"And when you have the product, I negotiate with this Stone for Tray McCarthy."

"That is non-negotiable Mr Nunez."

"Is that you Mr Stone?"

"Yes it is."

"In my line of work Mr Stone, everything is negotiable."

Rudi knew that this wasn't.

"I ring in twelve hours. You make sure the phone is on. Take care of yourself Sam. I see you in five days my friend."

"Mr Nunez?" it was Mo. "How do we know you can do what you say you can do?"

"If you bastards fucking are big players you know Igor Duardo. You ask him about Pedro Nunez."

The line went dead. Fuck he knew Igor! This was all a bit too close to home.

*

"Boss! Got him!"

"Who?"

Tommy came rushing in holding some sheets of paper.

"The shooter!"

"Good work Tommy. How?"

"Customs and immigration couldn't help us with a black man coming in the country. That sort of detail just is just too precise. To go through each camera and try and cross check it against a list of names was just impossible. So I took a stab at something."

"What?"

"Well I had a hunch. You remember that McCarthy was on the run for dobbing on these Yardies."

"Yeah of course!"

"Well I ran the surname of the Yardie that got killed in prison. It was Stone right?"

"Yes that's right."

"Well a Rudi Stone came in on the QF 6 last week from Frankfurt. I ran his name through the Interpol computers and got a hit."

"What did it say?"

"Rudi Stone is the brother of the Yardie that got necked in prison!"

"You're kidding?"

"No and Rudi Stone is said to be the head of the Yardies and a major distributor of cocaine in London. They just haven't been able to pin anything on him. Runs a very tight ship. Squeaky clean every time they have investigated him."

"Top work Tommy! Finally a fucking break."

"Oh it gets better boss."

"Oh go on. Go for gold Tom."

"In the seat next to him was a Don Chait."

"Who's he?"

"Known associate and colleague of Stone but best of all, he's white."

Brilliant! It fitted. One white man. One black. It must have been them who shot Rachel Smith. The first clue as to what had been going on. This was a London thing. He should've known. Too many things just didn't add up. It hadn't tasted of anything local from the start. But something still wasn't right. Tommy saw the look on his boss's face.

"You say last week Tommy?"

"Yep."

"Well that means they didn't kill the Rogers girls."

"Yeah boss I know. I don't know who the fuck killed them."

"Well I tell you what Tommy."

"What's that boss?"

"It wasn't Trystan McCarthy."

*

"You're playing with the big boys now Mo."

"Are you sure Igor?"

"Oh I am sure. Pedro Nunez is big time. He handles big shipments for us and many others. He has a very good operation."

"Can he do what he says he can do?"

"Oh yes. Very easy for him. He has many contacts."

"Well it looks like you will have your money on Saturday"

"Thank you."

Mo put the phone down. He still had to tie up some loose ends. He called the bikie over.

"Trev. Looks like you're staying here 'til Saturday. You're playing babysitter. I can't have Tarry looking after them. He might off them. I can't trust these poms either. They're a bunch of lunatics. Who knows what they might do."

"No problem."

"You have a phone?"

"Of course."

"Give it to me."

"Why?"

The bikies leathers creaked with the request. He didn't like what he was being asked.

"Because I don't want anyone knowing where these people are. Do you need to contact anyone? Tell them you'll be out of circulation for a bit."

"Only Tony."

"Good. I'll call him. You'll get everything you need and I'll give you plenty of money. Enough to put a deposit on a house."

"Thank you Mr Aziz."

"No problem. Now can I have the phone?"

The bikie handed over the phone. Another fucker that was going to have to die.

"They've made this Londoner you've been using."

"That's impossible. No one knows he's here."

"They do now."

"How?"

"He didn't kill the girl. She's still alive. She said that one of them was black. My detectives aren't stupid. They put two and two together and got a name."

"This changes nothing Fraser. We kill them all."

"As soon as you take delivery. You take them all down. We have no other option."

"This dego. Pedro Nunez. Do you know him."

"No. I had a discreet look. Nothing, but what did you expect? We didn't know about McCarthy four weeks ago."

"True. See you on Saturday."

"Yes," Fraser paused. "And Mo?"

"Yes?"

"Make sure they're all dead this time."

Fraser put down the phone. Time to call in his insurance.

"Fucking hell mate! What am I paying you for?"

"Don't worry my friend. It will be okay."

"But where are they?"

"Look they are not dead. I know these things."

"How do you know?"

"Because someone I know has spoken to someone who knows."

"Don't fucking play games here mate. We're playing for keeps here!"

"I know. I know. It will work itself out. You mark my words. You keep watching what you are watching."

"Why?"

"Because I know these things."

"What else do you know?"

"That there is large shipment of drugs coming in on Saturday and the McCarthy's and the girls will be exchanged for the drugs."

"All the McCarthys?"

"No not all. The eldest son. He will die."

"Like fuck he will."

"I know. I am working on that too."

"You just make sure nothing happens to him."

"I will try my best my friend."

They both stopped. Frustration was a wasted emotion in their line of business. These things would work themselves out.

"So Saturday is the day?"

"Saturday it ends."

"Good 'cos I want to go home. My family's none too happy."

"Why?"

"'Cos I missed my grandson's first birthday."

"Don't worry my friend. There will be many more."

"I hope so. For your sake."

He put the phone down. The bedroom door opened.

"At last!"

"What?"

"I found some fucking kippers!"

"Brilliant! Stick them in the pan."

About time! They could finally get a decent breakfast inside them.

*

Fraser put the call in.

"Saturday night. There is a big shipment of Colombian coming in. I'll be watching at the gate. When they come through, you take them. All of them. You do what you like with the coke. I don't care. You just take these people out. We do it on Foreshore Drive. Neddy Smith style. They will just be some more bodies moon-bathing in the dunes."

"And what do you want?"

"I just want them dead is all."

"You really don't care about the coke?"

"No. This Arab has become a problem. He has gone too far. I have to end his reign."

"How much coke is there?"

"I don't know. I don't fucking care. You just make sure you get them."

*

"Dan get me the following."

"What's that then?"

"I want three pump action shotguns, about twelve sticks of dynamite and a blowtorch."

"A what?"

"A blowtorch. You know, one like that fat-tongued wanker Jamie Oliver uses."

331

Catching Up

For three days they cared for him. They took turns in feeding him. They carried him to the toilet. Jimmy thought it was like when he was first born. He used to sneak home from work at lunchtime just to see his little miracle. He couldn't believe it had happened then. One minute Betty had been a bulging mass of stomach and skin. Two hours later he had his son in his hand.

He cradled his son in his hands back then, much as he did now. His little miracle. They said after she lost the first one that she may not be able to have another. He didn't understand why. The doctors used all sorts of phrases that Jimmy couldn't begin to work out. He thought the doctor was taking the piss initially. That he was trying to say that Betty had got rid of the baby deliberately and that she had damaged herself in the process.

He had nearly ripped the doctor in two when he said that but Betty understood better. She told him that it was God's way. That the first baby wasn't right for them. That her body had rejected it 'cos maybe something was wrong with it'. So they had kept on trying. Then one night after an episode of 'Rawhide' and a rattling journey in an old Ford van, Trystan James McCarthy was born. Jimmy remembered that night. It wasn't like it was today. None of this father-in-the-delivery-room stuff. No touchy feely crap. The woman went in. The baby and woman came out. Like nothing had happened.

Yet it had. His life would be forever changed. He promised to love that boy that night. To protect him and guide him. To give him the upbringing he never had. To let him become whatever he wanted to be. Except it hadn't worked out that way.

As he tried to nurture his son's shattered body back to health, he vowed to make amends for the promises he had broken. He had thought that other people were more important. That other people came first. As his son tried to explain what had been happening in words so barely audible, he realised one thing and one thing only.

That family came first and everything else came second. He also realised something else. That every man who had laid a finger on Tray was a fucking dead man!

*

"Sam?"

"Yes bro."

Sam had placed a cold cloth on his forehead. Tray was starting to burn up. His wounds needed dressing again and he needed some drugs. Proper drugs. Drugs that only hospitals had.

"Sam. I got to tell you stuff. Maybe you get out of this alive. I don't think I will."

Sam saw the resignation in his brother's eyes. The fight had gone. There was nothing left except his soul and his voice. He was battered beyond his endurance. The swelling in his face and eyes had not gone down. His head wounds had begun to crust up but they looked angry. His shoulder although set, was a deep purple.

"Sssshhh Tray. It doesn't matter."

"It does Sam. It does. Your lives may depend on it."

That whole afternoon Sam sat by his brother. Much like on top of that sand cliff so many years ago when Tray had sat by his side. Tray had endured the ridicule of many people that day all because of Sam. Their Dad had admonished him. Sam could remember the look on his brother's face. Especially when he had pissed his pants. The shame and hurt were writ large. His brother had done much for him over the years. All of it so Sam could live his life. None of it, besides that initial mistake with Stone, intended to cause any of them harm.

He had stood up to that IRA thug for him in Lagos. That man was a stone cold killer. It was in his eyes. He had rounded on Sam in the square. They were all smashed and Tray had just stood there like Hadrian's Wall. Massive and imposing. Telling the spud muncher the way it was going to be. Tray wasn't a tough man but he was willing to fight for his brother that day. He was still trying to fight for him. Even in this state.

He told Sam everything as best he could. How they had found the money after Vukovic had been pinched. How Tumbles was an international drug smuggler. How Pedro had become a major player in the cocaine world. How he had found love again after Jo and twice lost it. Once out of lack of enthusiasm. The second time because of these sadistic Lebanese bastards.

Sam had read in the newspapers about his ex-wife Felicity. There had been scant mention of her. Maybe because she too feared for her life or maybe just because she didn't want to be involved. She had a family of her own to protect after all. Sam had never met her. He assumed though that she would have been a good person. Tray wouldn't have married any old scrag. Her qualities must have been enough for him to promise in front of God and friends that he would love, honour and obey. Tray may have been a man with the devil in his eye but he took the traditions of marriage very seriously.

He told him about a record deal for someone called Daz. Sam got a bit lost here. He couldn't work out who he was talking about. It was this music stuff again. Something that Sam was never really interested in. Then he realised he was talking about Rachel's boyfriend. Rachel! That poor girl. She had done nothing wrong. Sam didn't have the heart to tell him she was dead. He couldn't do it to him.

Sam knew when his brother had finished telling the story. His head tilted to one side and he was gone. His eyes had been closed practically the whole time. He could hardly see out of them anyway. If you didn't know it Sam thought that someone looking in might have thought he was a contestant for some stage make-up competition. But he wasn't. This stuff was fucking real. Tray started to snore. Great rasping rattling snores. Sam had always been amazed at how loud his brother could belt out those great primeval noises. It was like a train rumbling down the track.

"He's asleep."

"You don't fucking say."

It was Jimmy. They all smiled. It was the first sign of humour they had felt for a while and Tray was oblivious to it.

"Get up those fucking stairs you Portuguese muppet!"

"Fodas carrallho!" *(Fuck you dickhead).*

"I'll give you 'fuck you'."

"You estrangeiros. You all the same."

"Fernando. We're not all the same. You know that. You remember why we're going?"

"Yes for our amigo. For my friend."

"He is more than our friend Fernando. He is our brother."

"Yes he is our brother. My family make much money from him and he never ask for much. This is very easy thing for us. Very simple."

"Fernando," Tumbles paused. "Obrigado!" *(Thank you)*

"You don't have to thank me Tumbles. Nao Faz Mal!" *(No worries)*

A vision of beauty greeted them at the top of the stairs.

"Welcome Mr Gomez. Travelling with us again? Nice to have you on board."

Her smile was perfect. Teeth whitened to within an inch of stardom. Her hair just so. A small clip kept it in place. Her eyes a dreamy blue which just pulled you in. Maybe they were contacts? He couldn't be sure. She turned and showed them her perfect arse as she indicated where they were to go. So much to love about First Class.

"Why thank you Gemma," replied Tumbles.

"There seems to be a lot of you today."

"Trade delegation."

Fernando turned to Tumbles as they stepped through the doorway.

"You know Tumbles, this is first time all of us fly long way together."

"Well you're in for a treat. You will like this."

Tumbles just hoped these peasants could behave themselves and not drink too much. They had to be on their game when they arrived.

*

"Xavier."

"Yes Igor."

"We need some plastic and some detonators."

"I know where we can get some. The military here check nothing. Its just like going to the supermarket."

"You can rig something up?"

"If the fucking Al Qaeda can do it, you know we can. I will ask Santos."

"I also need five of our best men. People who are not afraid to use their skills."

"No problem Igor. We use our own people?"

"Yes. No more outsiders. This stays in the family."

"Okay. You want them all ready by Saturday?"

"Yes of course. Saturday is, how do the English say it?"

Xavier looked perplexed. He had no idea what his boss was trying to say.

"Oh yes. That's it. Saturday is D-Day."

*

Daniel spread the items out on the bed. Three shooters. Pump action as requested. Ten boxes of cartridges and twelve sticks of dynamite.

"Where did you get all this then?"

"I have a mate with a property out Camden way. He is a hobby farmer. He's been building some dams so he's got a licence for the powder."

"And the guns?"

"Same bloke. All the farmers here are tooled up."

"No questions?"

"No I gave him good coin like you said. He won't say anything. He'll just report them stolen a couple of months from now. Happens all the time."

"Good. And what about the blowtorch?"

"Oh yeah."

Daniel ducked out into the kitchen and came back in with a large plastic bag from 'Bunnings Warehouse'. He poured the contents on to the bed.

A blowtorch. A bright blue canister supplied the fuel. It was an innocent enough piece of equipment as it lay on the bed. In the wrong hands however it was an instrument of torture. In this man's hands it was worse than that. So much worse.

*

Sam had told her and Jimmy everything. She didn't want to know about his relationships but she listened anyway. All the time Tray snored from the other side of the room. She listened to it. Comforted by it. It was from a memory long ago. When they had both been so happy.

Sam spoke briefly about the ex-wife and about this woman called Lizzy. She was torn by that. She couldn't help but feel a little happier that this woman wasn't still here to pull Tray's affections away from her. But she couldn't help but worry about how they had killed her and her sister either. It made her feel cold, detached even but she couldn't help that. She didn't know her and now she never would.

What's more, these pigs wouldn't think twice about killing all of them once they had the coke. She was sure of it. Why would they let them live? This honour code that had shaped all their lives didn't exist here. People with honour didn't kill women and kids. People with honour didn't do what they had done to Tray.

337

She had imagined that Tray would've jumped in her arms when they met. She had run the image over in her head a million times. These animals had deprived her of that Kodak moment. Instead she was trying to nurse her love back from the brink of death. And for what? So that they could try and kill him all over again. Hadn't he had enough?

She could kill Stone herself. All their lives destroyed by a vengeful quest. This ridiculous mission to wipe Tray from the face of the earth. This blood feud. Hadn't he made enough money to quell the rage? Couldn't he just leave him in peace? Obviously not. It was the honour code again. But she could see no glory here. There would be no pages written in history. No one would even know. What a waste of everyone's lives!

Jimmy agreed. It didn't look good for any of them. Especially for Tray. If they didn't get him to a hospital soon he could die anyway. The Lebanese knew it too. That's why they were giving them bandages and medicine. If he died, they would miss out on a hundred million bucks. That was a lot of money in anyone's language.

"What do you reckon Dad?"

"I don't know son. I'm out of my depth here. I don't know anyone. I can't call on anyone. I am nowhere."

"Yeah but you know what?"

"What Sam?"

"I don't think we're out of options yet."

"What do you mean?"

"Just something Tray said."

CHAPTER ELEVEN

The Time For Action

Made!

His name was all over the newspaper, TV, radio. Everywhere. These fucking Australian bastards had made him. After all these years of being under the radar, these fucking colonial wankers had made him. Mo had broken the news to him. How were they going to get out of this one? Perhaps he was going to have to negotiate with this Pedro after all.

*

It was Saturday morning. They had arrived at last. There were no problems with immigration. The guys on the desks always treated diplomats like gods. They were scared shitless that someone in Canberra was going to get wind of them upsetting a foreign ambassador or something similar. They just sailed through with not a care in the world. All twelve of them. The dirty dozen he liked to call them.

Pedro had called from Dubai. He spoke to all of them. They were fine. All except Tray. Pedro had been shocked by the weakness of the voice but he was still alive. Pedro spoke to Mo once again, telling him there would be hell to pay if anything went wrong. Tumbles had never seen him like this. Like a third world dictator! Daddy's little playboy had certainly grown up.

They walked past a newsstand. Two faces stared out from a newspaper. One black. One white. The headline begged the question, 'HAVE YOU SEEN THESE MEN?' Under the two pictures were their names. On another paper read the headline, 'BREAKTHROUGH IN THE ROGERS MURDERS'.

"Pedro!"

Pedro sidled over to Tumbles.

"Que foi amigo?" *(What's up my friend?)*

"That's him. That's Rudi Stone."

He pointed to the papers.

"Well I guess he's very much fucked then."

"Well I guess he is."

Tumbles' thoughts were interrupted by a man bustling towards them.

"Hey Ricardo!" shouted Pedro.

"Mr Nunez my friend. How are you?"

"Bom!"

The two men hugged. They spoke in English for Tumbles' benefit.

"Is it all arranged?"

"Yes. It is all ready for you. It is on the boat."

"Good. Let's go then. We don't have much time."

*

"I told you we didn't have much time"

"Yeah well, time in the police force usually means a long time. You never do anything quickly."

"Don't get smart Mo! I told you they weren't stupid. For once they used their initiative and they made him. Stone was none too clever travelling under his own name. They looked into McCarthy's past and came up with his brother's name. Then it was just a short step to looking through the passenger lists. It was just a hunch but it paid off."

"So we still do it?"

"God yes. Now there is no way we can do it any other way."

"Fraser. I am going to have to take out at least six other people."

"Hey Mo. You are getting a whole lot of coke in return. What do you care?"

"I care because I am the one getting my hands dirty as usual. Not you!"

"Hey I've got just as much to lose if I get caught up in this as you! We've got to keep this under wraps. Once its done you can keep on with your business and you will be considerably richer."

"Richer don't mean safer Fraser. Do they have anything on me at all?"

"No Mo. Nothing. I get Swanson to give me a briefing every day. The trail stops at McCarthy. No one knows you're involved."

"Make sure it stays that way."

"Have they contacted you yet?"

"No. This Pedro called them last night. He spoke to all of them."

"And how is McCarthy?"

"Barely alive. The girl is caring for him as best she can but he is weak. He will still be alive tonight though don't you worry."

"Worry is all I do with this case."

"Yeah well they are coming in today. When I get the details I'll call. You just make sure that there is no one tailing me."

"You're safe Mo. There is nothing on you. I swear."

"Yeah well you just make sure of it."

*

"So Ricardo. What do you have for me?"

"The container is on the ship."

"And how do we move it?"

They had been picked up by embassy cars and shipped out to the Sheraton on the Park opposite Hyde Park. Sumptuous luxury that the Portuguese rarely observed and enjoyed.

"Tumbles, is there anyone who can help us here? Usually the embassy picks it up but I want no one involved this time. This is private."

"Yes there is."

Tumbles reached inside his laptop bag and pulled out the CD. The Kings of Sunday Morning promo had arrived in his email tray last week. No one had this address except Tray and their money contact in New York, Graham. The promo was from a company called Playground Records. Tray must have been the name behind it. No one else could have sent it.

He rang the number from Dubai. A guy called Murchison answered. It was easy for Tumbles. He just asked who was the creator of 'I Found Love In U". The name though was new to Tumbles. A Darren Thwaite was the writer but there seemed something else in this Murchison's voice. Something uncertain but he couldn't pick it.

Tumbles asked if he knew the whereabouts of this Thwaite. Murchison said he was unavailable at the moment. That something horrible had happened but that he should call Sharon Bleasdale at DJ Select. Murchison gave him the number.

He rang the number. An Englishwoman answered the phone. A Londoner. Tumbles had asked if he could book the creator of the track. Sharon said he was busy but they may be able to organise something. He asked for his number and didn't get it. She explained how his girlfriend had been shot in a home invasion. That he was at the hospital by her bedside. That she was touch and go for the moment. She mentioned the name Rachel. Then it clicked. Daz. This was Daz and Rachel!

Tumbles took a chance. This Bleasdale seemed to know the score. He had asked the question. Had Daz really written this track? The question put Sharon on the back foot. He could tell by her reaction that there was something going on. She had 'ummed' and 'aahed' a bit and that had been all the confirmation that Tumbles needed. He pushed his luck. Did T write it?

She blew it straight away with a 'How did you..." and then realised her mistake. Tumbles had placated her immediately. He said he was an old friend from Portugal. That he and Tray were closer than close. That Tray was in trouble and that he needed Tumbles' help. Without it their friend might be dead. Sharon had baulked at the statement. She asked more questions of Tumbles. Who was he? How did he know Tray?

Tumbles didn't have many options left but first he asked Sharon the same. She had told him about how she had known Tray in the old days. How he had just popped up out of nowhere and how he was now on Australia's most wanted list. She didn't know what to do. Tumbles had reciprocated and told her the absolute bare minimum. He told her how they had a club together in Portugal and how they had still remained in contact. That he had sent Tumbles the promo. She believed him. The promo wasn't even out yet. No one else could have sent it. He said it was imperative that he got in touch with Daz. She had given him the number.

Tumbles called Daz. Daz had been outside the hospital having a smoke. He recognised the voice. It was the bloke from London. Tray's friend. How did he get this number? Tumbles had told him.

Daz had shared what had happened to Rachel. How some hitmen had shot her in the chest. How she had come so close to death. How Tray's family and a girl had disappeared. Tumbles revealed that he knew all of this. That he was here to save Tray. That if he didn't help his mate that they would never see him again. Tumbles told Daz that they all owed their friend and it was time they paid him back.

He only asked Daz one thing. Do you have Brick's number? Daz was confused by the request but acquiesced. Tumbles told him he would know if Tray was safe. Daz asked how and Tumbles had responded. 'When he is safe you will know'. He also told him to celebrate Tray's name by pushing his work to the limit. To take it to the world. Daz wanted to know more but Tumbles made it clear that it was safer this way. That if they were to save their friend they couldn't take any chances.

Tumbles had called Brick. He had asked for his help and got it immediately. He rang the number again.

"Okay so its arranged."

"Yep. I'll be ready at midnight. We clock off at eleven. There won't be anyone about. Border Security and Customs don't work Saturday night and the paperwork should get you in."

"Where will you be?"

"I'll be upstairs waiting for your signal. There is a two way on the boat. Call me when you are ready."

"What about security cameras?"

"This is Australia mate. That shit don't work over here. Not like your joint back home. We may have the cameras but no one ever puts any film in them. It's a complete waste of taxpayers money."

Tumbles had been surprised.

"Okay so where do we go?"

"End of pier one. I have already moved the container off the boat and its waiting on the dock for you to empty it. You're paperwork will give you access at the security gate."

"Are you sure you want to do this Brick?"

"Hey Tumbles, he is my friend too. Anyway, I could do with a change of scenery."

"Okay done. You will be well looked after for this."

"I would do it for nothing. No one hurts my friend."

"Okay then. The boat leaves at six. We have to have it all finished by then."

"Okay. Good luck Tumbles. Make sure he gets through this."

"I will mate. I will."

Tumbles put the phone down.

"Pedro, call this fucking Arab. Tell him its on."

*

"Sam?"

He had picked the phone up on the second ring.

"Pedro?"

"The game is on fucking."

"Okay."

Sam passed the phone to Aziz.

"Yes. Everything is arranged?"

"Yes. And the family?"

345

"They will be held for safe keeping until we have the product. We will have McCarthy with us. Where do we meet?"

"The security gate at Pier one at Port Botany. Midnight. Do you know it?"

"Yes I have been there many times."

"Well you make sure you're there and that everyone is still alive. When do we get the family?"

"When we get the stuff."

"And I see that Stone is in the newspaper fucking. What is up with that?"

"Yes an unfortunate problem. I think now he might want to negotiate."

"I'm sure he does."

"If I suspect anything Mr Nunez then we kill McCarthy and his family. Do you understand?"

"Oh I understand okay. Do you understand that if anything happens to anyone you are finished? I have much power and I am not afraid to use it. You don't scare me Arab. I am doing this for my friend not for you."

"Yes I understand. Now you listen. You wouldn't be in this situation if McCarthy hadn't stolen from me. Now you blame him not me."

Pedro paused. Thinking how this Arab was right but that Tray had just made a simple mistake. He thought the money was unprotected. That it was safe to walk away with it. But it hadn't been and now the wheels were turning. Five people dead and counting. How many more would be dead after tonight?

*

"The stuff is coming in tonight."

"Where?"

"Port Botany. Midnight. As soon as I make the call, the family will be finished."

"Where?"

"I am moving them to the clubhouse. I don't want anything happening on my grounds. As soon as I ring the bikies they will complete the job. Very quiet."

"Okay. Let's finish this tonight."

"And then?"

"And then we offload the product and count the money."

"Good. I'll wait for your call."

"Fraser. Just make sure there are no police around."

"There won't be. They are checking hotels for Stone. Where is he?"

"He is waiting out the back. He is unhappy about you making him but I think he is hoping to make a trade for McCarthy for his own life."

"No trade Mo. They all die."

"Yes Fraser. We stop this bullshit tonight."

*

"Pier One. Port Botany. Midnight."

"And the family."

"The Arab is getting the bikies to off them as soon as he has the product. No ties to him."

"Where are they going to do this?"

"He will move them to their clubhouse and the bikies can handle it from there."

"Okay thank you. Where will you be?"

"I will be on Foreshore Drive making sure it all goes to plan."

"So you wait for us there?"

"Yes and then they all go down."

The line went dead. Thank fuck for that. Soon Fraser would be able to sleep at night and life would return to normal.

Saving Private McCarthy

"Where the fuck have you been?"

"I told you I would call you when I have some news."

"And?"

"I have some news," the voice paused. "It will happen tonight. Midnight."

"Where?"

"At Port Botany. Pier One."

"Where are the family?"

"They will be moved to the clubhouse. You have to be quick though. As soon as the goods are exchanged he will authorise their killing."

"Like fuck he will! These people will suffer before I kill them."

"Don't take too long. We don't have much time."

"I won't. And your cousin? He's happy?"

"More than happy. I just have to tidy this up and I will be working with you very soon."

"Thank you. See you tonight then."

"See you then."

The line went dead. He shouted through the doorway.

"Dan?"

Dan walked into the bedroom.

"Tell Billy to stay put. We'll be there in a couple of hours. Get the weapons together, pay the bill and book some tickets back to London. We're on the first flight out of here."

Dan accepted the order and went back to the lounge room.

"Right. Let's get these outfits together!"

He went to the wardrobe and pulled out the uniforms. He handed one to his old friend.

"Right you ready for this?"

"Let's make amends my old friend."

"Yes Sergeant."

"Okay Corporal," he laid out the trench coat. " Lets save Private McCarthy."

"Yes Sir."

The two old men saluted one another.

"Time to rock and roll."

*

"Xavier?"

"Yes Igor."

"You have everything together?"

"Yes."

He showed Igor the briefcases. One was stacked full of cash. The other was packed with plastic explosives.

"How does it work?"

"I ring a mobile number and the thing explodes. Very easy."

"Okay. You know what to do?"

"Yes. I wait for our contact and I kill him. Then I wait for your call and I explode the case when I see them pass."

"Excellent. Xavier soon we will be living amongst the bright lights again."

"I hope so Igor. I am fed up with this country."

"Me too Xavier. Me too."

*

"Don I don't trust these fucking Arabs. What's to stop them double crossing us?"

"Absolutely nothing. Back home I trust the other mob to follow the rules. This lot though? I just don't know."

"Keep your wits about you Don. They could give us up easy and there would be nothing we could do about it."

"Yeah I know. So what do you think Rudi?"

"I don't know. I can't get through to Igor. I don't know what's going on with him."

"Do you think he's dropped us?"

"Not sure. I thought we could trust him."

"Well can anyone else help us?"

"I have tried. No one has any contacts here. It's a backwater. No one is talking."

"So where does that leave us?"

"I think that I've fucked the pair of us Don. I let emotion get in the way of business and I've just been plain stupid."

"And?"

"I'm locked in. You don't have to do this. You could walk away now. You have enough money in the bank to get away. Igor will help you."

"No Rudi. I'm not letting you face this alone. If we go down, we go down together."

"Okay my friend. So you know what we have to do?"

"Yeah mate. If it all kicks off tonight, we keep shooting until we run out of bullets."

"Yeah and hope to fuck there's no one left."

"And what do we do then?"

"We hope Igor can help us out."

"And if he can't?"

"I have no fucking idea."

*

"Dad?"

It was Tray.

"Yes son."

"This may be it Dad. I may not see you again after tonight."

There were tears in his son's eyes. He had suffered more than a man had a right to. They had done the best they could. This Pedro had rung every twelve hours as promised. Tray's condition hadn't really improved but he hadn't got any worse either. Not that this was a godsend. He had seen people like this before and they hadn't survived. His son was strong that was for sure.

"Ssshhh son. It will work out."

"Dad I really fucked up. I'm sorry."

"Son I am the one who fucked up. I should have stood by you like Mum told me too."

His son looked into his eyes.

"Mum?"

"Yeah she begged me to save you and I wouldn't. I don't think she ever forgave me."

"But Dad, that was my fault."

"No it wasn't son. It was mine. I should have done more."

"Dad?"

"What son?"

"I loved you all. You know that?"

"Of course son. Of course I knew that."

His son's lips started to crack and bleed as he spoke. He could tell it hurt. He cried. His Dad joined him. Silent tears.

"Dad. Save Jo. Please don't let anything happen to her."

"Son. I'm gonna save all of us. You can bet the house on that."

His son smiled weakly. He could tell he wasn't convinced. The door opened. It was Aziz.

"Right. We are moving."

Sam walked in behind him with a chair on casters.

"You'll be free by tomorrow."

"What about Tray?" It was Jo.

"That is not up to me. That is up to Mr Stone and he has a lot more problems than you lot to deal with."

Sam walked over to his Dad and his brother. Jo came over and knelt down beside Tray.

"Sam you remember how we played it?"

"Yes Tray."

"We'll let's fucking play it to the fucking end."

Mo interrupted the little get together.

"Get him in the fucking chair!"

They picked him up as gently as they could. There was no way to move him without hurting him. They just did it as quickly as they could. Jimmy hated these people. He would kill them all right now if he could. They would pay for this if he lived. If he didn't, there were people who would avenge him. No matter the distance, no matter the time. Someone would take this Arab down and he would make sure he would suffer.

Three Hours To Midnight

The clubhouse was tucked away right on the foreshore of Botany Bay. The other side from the airport. The Shire side. It was prime real estate. There were some disused warehouses that formed a horseshoe shape which looked out on to the water and the oyster beds that had been there for nearly half a century. Billy had parked his car just down the street from the complex. It was Saturday night. No one was around.

The van had pulled up about 8 o'clock. The car pulled up shortly after. He had seen his Uncle Jimmy get out. Along with his cousin Sam and a girl. That must be Jo. 'Good looking' he thought to himself. Then they wheeled Tray in on an office chair. Fucking hell he looked awful! It had only been a glimpse but it had been enough for him to know that his cousin was in a bad way.

He called his Dad.

"Dad they're here."

"Okay Billy. Keep a track on them. I reckon they will be leaving around eleven. How many are there?"

"Well six arrived in the van and another in the car. I recognised Rudi and Don from the news. The others looked Lebanese"

"That fits. So how many in total?"

"Well there were three in there before. So all up that's unlucky thirteen."

"Fuck that many?"

"Yep. Well let's hope that some of them haul out when they go to the docks."

"Okay. We'll be there in half an hour."

"Then what?"

"We wait Billy."

*

"Okay Trev. This is what happens. When we get to the Port we will take them all down. You will come with us. When we have the coke, we call back here and your boys do the rest. Is that clear?"

"Yes Mo. Crystal."

"We take the rest out and then we become filthy rich."

"That is that then. Now let's have some of that ice you're cooking out the back and get ourselves nice and charged for the event. Can't have us falling asleep can we?"

"No Mo."

"Keep 'em out the back with the meth. If you don't kill them, the smell will."

"Okay where's Tony?"

"On his way."

"How long?"

"He'll be here about ten."

"He has no worries about doing this?"

"You're paying us in coke right?"

"Yep."

"Well there'll be no problem then."

*

"Xavier are the men ready?"

"Yes."

"And they understand they do nothing unless I say so?"

"And we have the weapons?"

"Oh yes. No one will outgun us tonight. We are like the fucking Israeli army."

"Good. Someone is going to be very fucking surprised tonight."

"I think all of them will be."

*

"Call him. We need to know for sure."

"Okay. Just hang on a second."

He picked up the mobile. He pushed the numbers.

"Hello?"

"How is Cuba?"

"Excellent as always. How is Australia?"

"Shit! The kippers are fucking burnt!"

"Que?"

"Never mind. We are going to do this tonight, right?"

"Yes."

"And you are happy to go along with this?"

"If you can smooth the way for Igor then it is all okay. I understand you have bought the debt."

"Yes"

"And Igor is happy with it?"

"More than happy but it will leave a very big hole in Sydney."

"Fuck Sydney. Sydney is, how you say, small potatoes."

"Okay then. Just making sure."

"Hey I lose an outlet but I get my cousin back."

"Yes and we get our friend. No strings attached."

"I understand the young McCarthy has made plenty of money."

"More than enough to make a life for himself and never be heard of again."

"Good let's make it that way."

"Okay see you in the sunshine."

"Yes. In the sunshine."

He put the phone in his pocket.

"Your shot El Presidente."

"Fidel please."

Fidel Castro lined up his putt.

"Bad news?"

"Far from it Fidel. Far from it."

Fidel Castro took his shot and missed. God he was going to have to play extra bad today to allow the old man to win. He didn't know if he could play that badly. He hoped his cousin on the other side of the world could play to win. His future depended on it.

The Salvation Army

"Okay Tumbles. This is it. We go into the docks. We have the paperwork to be there. We go to the container and the boat. We sort out these miserable fuckings and come back here. Fernando and his family go on boat and wait for us."

"Okay Pedro. There are no loopholes? This is fool proof right?"

"Tumbles this is easy even for these gypsy bastards fucking."

"Hey!" It was Fernando from the back seat.

"I was only joking you peasant!"

"Yes well not a very funny joke."

"You just make sure everyone is covered Fernando." This time it was Tumbles speaking.

"Well we all do national bloody service. We know what to do. You just make sure our friend lives."

"We all have to make sure of that."

*

It was ten-thirty. Mo ordered them to move out. Rudi and Don got into the lead car. The rest of his crew got into the van. They wheeled McCarthy out. It had been touching. The girl had screamed. She went to hit Tarry and hold on to McCarthy. Tarry hit her. He had knocked her out and she had fallen against a barrel, cutting herself in the process. The old man had gone the fists. He swung at Tarry and his lieutenant had taken it full on the chin. It was so quick that Mo had nearly missed it but it had the savagery of a sledgehammer. Tarry had ended up way across the room missing a couple of teeth. The guns had come out.

"Hey!" It was Sam.

"Any of you forget? Pedro don't speak to any of us and you can say bye byes to your special cargo."

"He's right. Tarry get up!"

Tarry was wobbly but he regained his feet with the help of the others. He spat out some enamel.

"You are dead old man!"

"Yeah pretty tough with a gun in your hand pussy. Why don't you drop it and you can dance with the big boys?"

"Okay. Stop this pissing contest! We don't have time. Let's go!"

They had left the four bikies and the three hostages inside. Mo had spoken to Tony. He was the leader of the bikie operation and had been the last to arrive. He was clad in denim and leathers. A large man with the habitual bikie beard. He had not turned to fat like the other bikies but was all muscles and rippling menace. He was on the human growth hormones. Mo had done business with him before when they were both younger and Tony a lot smaller.

"When Trev calls, you finish it. Then weigh them down and drop them in the bay. Let the crabs finish them off. The boat is ready?"

"Yeah moored at the end of the jetty?"

"Good you can be out in the middle and back again in half an hour. Get it started and get ready. You don't want to have to hang about afterwards. The quicker its done the better."

"I agree."

So they had left. Two vehicles. One van and a Commodore. Ten people in all plus McCarthy. They had enough fire-power to take on any comers.

He turned to Tarry.

"You alright Tarry?"

"No. I will kill that old man."

"No Tony will do that. All you have to do is lift McCarthy's coke. That will be enough won't it?"

Mo thought the money would suffice but deep down knew that Tarry would not be satisfied until someone suffered immensely.

"Yeah then we watch Rudi kill him!"

Rudi hadn't said a thing. He was too busy working out how he was going to get out of the country. Don was thinking the same. Perhaps it was time to use McCarthy as a negotiating tool. He wasn't sure whether Rudi would finally see sense. He hoped so!

*

"What the hell are you two wearing?"

"Never you mind."

"You look fucking ridiculous."

"Yeah well that's for us to worry about."

There were four of them in the car. Daniel and Billy in the front and the two old men in the back. Both of them carrying the pump action shotguns, cradling them like a precious cargo in their laps.

"So what do we do now?" It was Daniel asking.

"Well we fucking wait." It was a voice from the back.

"How long?" asked Billy.

"The meet is set for midnight. They can't be too long."

"Shit here they go!"

Billy was starting to sweat despite the cold. He knew it was all going to kick off soon and he didn't know if he had the bottle to go through with it. How did they get involved with this? What did his Dad owe these people?

They watched them all leave.

"Was that Tray?" asked Daniel.

"Yes Dad. Doesn't look too good does he?"

"Well they will pay for that."

He paused as the vehicles started up.

"Quick! Slide down. We don't want them to get suspicious."

They all did the same, hoping their black clothing would hide them. The vehicles swung past. They didn't stop.

"Do you think they saw us?" asked Billy.

"Unlikely, they're still going. How many did you see Billy?"

"Ten, I'm sure of it."

"That leaves four inside. Hello? What's this idiot doing?"

They watched one of the bikies leave the clubhouse and walk up the jetty to the boat.

"That's our way in. We nab him on the way back."

"You sure? He could be armed?" said Daniel.

"I don't give a fuck what he's got. He could have a fucking missile up the kazoo for all I care. No one fucks with us. Not now!"

He didn't know who these people were. Neither the people in the warehouse, nor the people in the back seat. Two weeks ago Billy had been working as a sales rep for Toyota cars. His Dad had called him to take a two-week leave of absence and he had been running around looking after these geezers from the old country ever since. When he had seen the weapons he had nearly shit himself. He knew his cousin was in plenty of trouble but hitmen from the UK? This was out of his bloody league. To boot, both of these geezers were well into their sixties. They didn't look capable of crossing the road let alone taking anyone out!

His Dad had assured him differently. These men were old school. Men to be feared beyond the usual beatings. They had been responsible for many unsolved murders in London and they would be taking no prisoners this time either. Daniel told his son how the silver-haired man was capable of terrible violence. The blowtorch was not for cooking as the old man had suggested. It was for hurting people. It was for burning their eyes out. Burning their tongues out. It was to silence them forever! Billy had shuddered at the image that flashed through his mind. This was a world he had never known. He had imagined the world that his Dad had spoken of. Of the men protecting their interests. Of the family that he had never known. Of the violence that had surrounded Tray despite him not being made of that cloth.

Tray had lived in Australia for some time and it had been a shock to him when the news had hit the media. No one had said a word, including his Dad. It was a surprise to his brothers and sisters. Why had no one been told? He was their cousin, their blood. What had he done that had meant that he had lived his life in hiding? Why did they never speak to Uncle Jimmy? What was this ghost that haunted the McCarthys?

Despite his Dad and Uncle Jimmy being brothers, something bad had happened many years ago before the kids were born. His Dad had left England and there had been no contact between the two. His other uncles back in England had said Tray was on the foot somewhere but no one knew where exactly but now everyone knew, including these two men. This was no game now. No silver screen escapade with fake stunts and overblown Hollywood budgets. This was the real deal and the pot was of the highest stakes. He studied the latest recruits to the Salvation Army. No Tuba playing for these two at Xmas time. They would most likely burn a Church down rather than contribute to it. They had arrived like a pox on their house. They had intimate knowledge of his old man and mores to the point, his dad knew them and feared them. These men, these people, these geezers bristled with intent. His Dad knew their measure and it frightened him.

"Right Daniel? You ready to pay back Jimmy for that fucking suit you hocked?"

"Yes." Daniel hung his head in shame.

"Well grab your shooter and hold it like you mean it."

*

Tony sent Grover to the boat. He just wished this would be finished soon. He hated dealing with this Lebanese bastard. He had only agreed because Igor had told him to and he didn't like that South American whore either.

Grover walked outside. Tony watched his lard arse leave the bar. Tony was happy with the clubhouse. They had bought the leases on all the warehouses since they moved in. No one wanted a place here after they set up shop so the leases were dirt-cheap. They had converted the front of the warehouse into an entertainment area. There was a small pole dancing stage to the left where the whores could dance when they brought them in. On the right was another stage where bands could set up or where DJ's could play. Not that many came down. Everyone was too frightened to take up a booking from the bikies.

At the rear of the warehouse was a bar which housed all sorts of hard liquor and which had four beers on tap. There was also a pool table and some pinball machines. Behind the bar was a false wall. Behind that was the ice lab. The new drug on the block and the new money-spinner for the Apaches. It was far more profitable than speed and more importantly, much more addictive.

"Hey Tony?"

It was Grover.

"Yeah?"

"I can't get the boat started."

Fucking hell. Did he have to do everything around here?

*

"Okay you ready?"

"Yep. Daniel, you stay in the shadows. We'll handle this. You make sure nothing goes wrong. If it does you get Jimmy and the others out."

"Yes."

"Okay let's go."

They walked up the jetty until they got to the rear of the boat.

"Er excuse me?"

"Yes. What's up?"

Grover walked to the rear of the boat. He was still working on getting the cover off the cockpit. He was surprised to see two Salvation Army officers infront of him.

"Yes hi there. We appear to be a little lost. We are looking for a sheltered housing complex that's around here somewhere. Do you know where it is?"

Grover stepped onto the board at the rear of the boat.

"Yeah sure mate. You're in the wrong area. It's two roads over."

Grover went to point to the direction in which they were supposed to head when he felt something in his gut. He looked down at his stomach. It was the muzzle of a pump action shotgun.

"Right mate. Now step off the boat and when we tell you, you call your boss out. You do as we say and we might let you live."

The bikie didn't say a word. He knew how to play the game. Anyway he didn't have a choice.

"I'm going to enjoy this Ron."

"Like old times Charlie."

"Like old times Ron."

"Jimmy is going to piss his pants."

They got to land. Daniel appeared out of the shadows. Ron covered the bikie. Charlie took the blowtorch out of his overcoat and turned it on. He lit it. He pulled a couple of sticks of dynamite out of the other one.

"Okay let's show these fucking monkeys how we do things!"

"Okay Charlie. Let's have it!"

"You call him now you fat cunt or I kill you where you stand!"

The bikie obliged.

"Hey Tony!" Grover called out.

"Yeah"

"I can't get the boat started!"

Tony came strolling out. It all happened so quick. One minute Tony Johns was standing there. The next, his head had disappeared in a burst of shotgun shell.

"Fuck I love this!" shouted Ron as he pumped the gun again.

"You ain't seen nothing yet!"

"Hey you fuckers inside! Better come out! We're gonna blow this place!"

Charlie lit two pieces of dynamite and threw them in through the open door. He threw the blowtorch to one side.

"Daniel chuck me the gun!"

Daniel did as ordered and picked up the other gun that he had stowed by the jetty. He covered the other bikie who just stood there in stunned silence. Tony had no fucking head!

Two bikies came running out. Guns in hand. They made it about two feet out of the door before Ron and Charlie let them have it. Two shots rang out. One got it in the groin. Ron's target got it in the chest.

Billy couldn't believe it! These old men were fucking fearless. One man dead and two men down. Then there was an explosion. Not too big but enough to reverberate around the complex. Billy ducked involuntarily. By the time he looked up Charlie had walked up to the two men on the ground. He pumped his gun. He fired into the head of the bikie with the shot in the groin. He casually walked over to the other bikie. He wasn't moving. Most probably already dead. Charlie did the same. He blew the bastards head off!

They went inside, covering each other just in case anyone was still left.

"Jimmy you in here."

"Out the back. Behind the bar."

Ron moved ahead through the blackened interior. There was the acrid smell of gunpowder in the air. Lucky it was low grade powder or the whole place could have gone up. Bit heavy on the bravado and light on tactics thought Charlie. Never mind, you only live once and he was getting too old to worry about the details.

There was no one else left. The pinball machines were silent. There was shit everywhere. There was another smell in the air. It was chemical. Charlie recognised it. It was the same smell they had sniffed when they had taken out an ice factory which had set up shop on the Hall's Estate. He didn't want shit like that moving in on his manor and he had made an example of them. Blown them to the shithouse with the muppets in it.

"Hey Ron. Don't pull the trigger. They're cooking ice in here." Charlie called out.

"Jimmy you alright?"

"Yes get us out of here. We're fucking suffocating!"

Ron walked to the rear of the bar. He couldn't see a door. It was a brick wall. He tapped along it. Looking for a something.

"At the right end. Behind the barrels."

It was Jimmy again. Ron moved to the barrels and pulled them back. He saw the latch and pulled at the concealed door. It opened. The stench was unbelievable. He walked inside. All three of them were tied to their chairs. There was lab equipment everywhere. Bunsen burners boiling various containers and drying off crystals.

"Ron?"

"Yep. Glad you're still alive boss."

"Fucking hell! Where'd you spring from?"

"Never you mind. We've been on to this for a while."

"Who's 'we' Ron?"

"Oh just an old friend."

Another figure came in through the door.

"Surprise surprise Private!"

"Uncle Charlie?" This time it was Sam who spoke.

"Yes Sam. Pleased to see me?"

"You bet your sweet fucking arse!"

"Untie me will you, you old bastards?" Jimmy asked.

Jimmy had rarely been surprised in his life. These two were the last people on earth he had expected to walk through the door but he thanked sweet Jesus that they had. The two men walked over.

"What the hell are you two wearing?" asked Jimmy.

"Salvation Army uniform. Thought it would be a nice touch."

"You two are fucking unbelievable. How did you find us?"

"Not now Jimmy. We don't have much time."

Jo hadn't said a word. She was still concussed. She wasn't really with it.

"Is that Jo Flint?" asked Charlie.

"Yep. One of those fucking Arabs belted her."

"Yeah well they're the ones who're gonna get a belting now," it was Charlie.

"Anyway what was the trick with the dynamite? You could have killed us."

"Have you ever known me to go in anywhere quietly?"

"No Charlie I guess I haven't. What do we do now?"

"We go save your son."

"How?"

"Don't you worry Jimmy! Its all in hand."

Another figure walked in. It was Daniel.

"Daniel?"

"Yes Jimmy."

"What the fuck are you doing here?"

"He helped save your arse Jimmy. So did Billy."

"Who?"

"Your nephew Jimmy. This has been a family affair."

"So let's get fucking going and save the rest of it!"

Ron finished untying Jimmy and the patriarch rose from his chair.

"Thank you Daniel. Thank you for this."

He shook his brother's hand. Then they hugged. Sam joined them and shook his uncle's hand.

Ron spoke.

"Okay let's get this girl out of here."

Jo was still groggy.

"Sam? What's going on?"

"Don't worry Jo. We're getting out of here."

"What about Tray?"

"I don't know. Charlie what are we going to do about that?"

"Well we've got to get to the docks before someone else does. I've got business to conduct."

"And what's that Charlie?"

"Never you mind."

"Billy!" Charlie shouted into the bar.

Billy McCarthy strode in with the bikie in tow.

"That was unbelievable Charlie!"

"Yeah. Well, we'll speak no more of it," responded Charlie.

"Okay then. No worries Charlie."

"Okay everyone. Let's get going!"

"Charlie, I have an idea," it was Billy.

"Well speak up boy!" said Daniel.

"Well it's going to take us about an hour to get round to the docks. If we take the boat, we can do the whole thing in fifteen minutes. Its got two massive four strokes on the back. I know that bay like the back of my hand."

"Okay well let's do it then. You! Fat boy! Get that fucking boat started. Billy you watch him."

Charlie was in charge now. They were back in the army. Ron, Charlie and Jimmy. The three musketeers. Doing what they did best. Cleaning up the mess.

"Ron, Jimmy! Grab those bodies from outside and pull 'em in 'ere. I'm gonna fucking blow this place. Sam, get Jo onto the boat."

"Okay Uncle Charlie."

"Look we haven't got much time you two. Let's get a wriggle on!"

The old men did as ordered. They pulled the three headless bodies back into the bar.

"Fucking hell Jimmy. I thought you'd left all this behind."

"Yeah Ron. So did I. Tray was the one who forgot."

"Don't blame him Jimmy. He was just trying to get by. He's lost a lot you know."

"Yeah I know. Now I don't want to lose him."

"We'll get him back. Don't worry."

"It's not getting him back I'm worried about. It's seeing him live that's important. He's a fucking mess Ron."

"I know. I saw him."

"Well they're going to be sorry they ever heard of Tray McCarthy."

"I'm sure these blokes already are Jimmy."

367

"Stop gabbing you old women. We've got about two minutes."

Charlie picked up the blowtorch. The boat started up.

"Right. Let's go ladies!"

The three sixty-year olds ran as best they could. They made it to the end of the jetty and clambered on board. Billy gunned the boat. It took off like a rocket, throwing the old men to the floor.

"Easy Billy!"

"No Fear Charlie! We got a date!"

The boat raced across the dark waters towards the airport and the berths of the hulking monsters that plied their trade across the world's great oceans. There was a huge explosion behind them. Blue flames curled into the sky. Chemicals burned. The motley crew looked behind them.

Charlie fished around in the back of the boat. He found what he was looking for. He picked it up and found some rope. He walked over to Grover. The bikie knew what was coming next.

"No please. Don't. I'm sorry!"

The fat cunt blubbered like a girl.

"Shut up you bitch!"

He picked up the anchor and tied it around the man's legs.

"Ron hold the fucker!"

Ron held him by the shoulders. Grover tried to jump over the side but Sam stopped him. Jimmy joined him. They held him fast. Grover looked at all of them. Pleading for his life.

"Please! I didn't know! Honest!"

"You were just about to kill my friend and his family. There is no forgiveness here."

He picked up the shotgun.

"Ready?"

He pumped the weapon. The men stood back and covered their ears. Grover stood there dumb struck. The last word that he uttered on this planet was 'Fu...' Charlie fired at his head. The whole thing had taken no more than three seconds. The body fell into the water with the anchor following it. Sam watched Grover disappear beneath the fast retreating water.

Charlie pulled a phone out of his pocket. He dialled the number.

"Done!"

He clicked the phone off and threw it in the water. He looked at his watch. Ten minutes to midnight.

Daniel approached his brother and gave him a flat bag.

"What's this?"

"It's your suit. The suit!"

"How long have you had this?"

"Ever since you clobbered me in the face with the shovel."

"You've had it all this time?"

"Yep"

"Why?"

"'Cos one day I knew the time would be right."

"And you choose the back of a boat in the middle of a rescue attempt?"

"It's all about the timing Jimmy."

Jimmy smiled. He hugged his brother.

"Sorry about the shovel."

The Gathering

The time clicked over. Midnight. Tumbles looked at his watch. They were sitting in the car park. They weren't here yet. Where were they? There had been an explosion far off in the distance. They saw the fire across the bay. They wondered what had happened. Perhaps it was just a coincidence. Suddenly they were blinded by the lights of two vehicles. A sedan and a white van. Tumbles flashed his headlights. The vehicles came over and stopped by their car.

Four men got out. He recognised Rudi Stone and Don straight away. Then came two other men. One was holding his jaw. They tapped on his window. Tumbles wound it down.

*

He hid in the bushes beside Foreshore Drive. There had been an explosion on the other side of Botany Bay. He had seen it before he heard it. Right over by Taren Point. It was a fair way off and nowhere near the terminal. He wondered what had happened. He felt the gun in his pocket. It comforted him. Just like old times.

The car pulled up bang on time. Midnight. The dual carriageway remained eerily quiet. No one used this stretch of road except Neddy Smith. It was ideal. Botany Bay on one side and dunes on the other. Except he was going to use neither. This was going to be high profile. They wanted people to find him.

He walked up to the government car. It was a Lexus. Sleek and powerful, this was a statement of luxury. He brushed up against the car and tapped on the window. It wound down with the grace and elegance that such an expensive car afforded.

"Yes?"

The occupant appeared confused.

"Chief Inspector Fraser?"

"Yes?"

"I have a message from Igor."

"Oh you're early."

"No I'm right on time."

"Well what is it then?"

Xavier reached inside his pocket and pulled out the Glock. Fraser saw the weapon. He tried to put up his hands, blocking the shot. It was a vain attempt. Xavier fired six shots. He felt the recoil as the gun juddered in his hand. The muzzle flashed as the bullets exploded into the policeman. He took two to the head splattering his brains all over the interior. One hit him in the neck. The other three got him in the body.

Xavier reached inside the car and switched on the headlights and the hazards. He went back to the bushes and retrieved a rucksack. He opened the passenger door and threw it inside.

"Message delivered!"

*

Igor felt the phone vibrate in his pocket. It was a message from Xavier. He pulled out the phone and read it.

'Gone'

Excellent. That police bastard had ordered him around for the last time.

"Santos. You ready?"

"Yes Boss."

"We wait until they get out then we go in. We surprise the fuck out of everybody."

"Yes Boss."

*

"Mr Nunez I presume." Mo stepped forward.

"Don't you even try to shake my hand you bastard fucking. I do this for my friend not for you!"

"Now now. Don't get all nasty. This is just business."

"And you are Mr Stone? How you feel now that every bastard fucking is after you?"

"I still have the upper hand here Mr Nunez. Just you remember that."

Rudi held his gun tight under his jacket. He didn't trust any of these people. Perhaps he could deal with these spicks, bargain with his life. He doubted it. It appeared that McCarthy had powerful friends after all but as far as anyone else knew, he was still in charge. The family was the key.

"And you must be Tumbles. I bet you wished you had never seen that money now."

Mo was having fun with these two. They were on his patch now. He was disappointed with their appearance. He didn't know what he had expected. Just a little more than these two. Tumbles couldn't contain himself any longer.

"The only thing I wish for is you in the ground. If I ever hear your name in Europe, you are fucking dead you hear? You may get rich from this but you'll never set foot outside this country again."

"You talk big for a man who is about to say goodbye to a fortune. What scares you Mr Tumbles? What keeps you awake at night?"

"Seeing you with your death mask on 'cos I swear if anything happens to Tray's family, I will kill you myself."

"Mr Tumbles. You are not in a position to make any threats."

Don limped into view along with Tarry.

"Pat them down Don. Check 'em for weapons. Check the car too."

Pedro stared at Don with his one good eye.

"And how do you think you get out of this country?"

Don had been asking himself the same question all day. He reached out and turned Pedro towards the car. He spread his legs and patted him down either side. He grabbed at Pedro's groin.

"Hey!"

"I have to check everywhere."

He slowly felt around Pedro's jacket and then his torso.

"He's clean."

"Now check him."

Mo directed Tarry towards Tumbles. Tarry did the same. They then checked the car. Under the seats, the glove box and the boot of the car. Tarry got on his hands and knees and looked under the chassis. Nothing.

"Where's Tray?" asked Tumbles.

"In the van," answered Rudi.

"I want to see him now or we stand out here 'til the pigs start flying."

"You don't get to see him until we get the product."

"You don't get to see the product until we get to see him."

"Well I suppose we have Mexican stand-off fucking."

Mo had noticed that this Pedro couldn't swear properly.

"Tarry crack the door a little. Let him hear his voice."

Tarry did as he was ordered. He slid the door back a little. Tumbles approached the van.

"Tray you in there?"

"Tumbles?"

The voice was so weak it was hardly audible.

"What scared the fuck out of me in the tool shed?"

"A fucking possum you poof."

Tumbles smiled at Pedro.

"Its him."

"Close the door Tarry."

Tarry closed the sliding door.

"Now let's get on with this. We have work to do. Don you get in with these two. We'll follow behind you."

*

"Don is it?"

"Yes Mr Nunez."

"You sure you want to do this?"

"What?"

"Take us on," interrupted Tumbles.

"You know I can get you out of here Don?" said Pedro.

Don was herding Pedro and Tumbles back to their car, gun at the ready.

"How?"

"How do you think I get fucking five hundred kilos of high quality cocaine fucking in to this country with no questions being asked?"

"I don't know Mr Nunez."

"Because I have big fucking power! Your boss, he has nothing and if Tray McCarthy or his family dies, everyone disappears fucking. Do you understand?"

"Yes I understand. So what do I do?"

"You do what you think you should do. I not tell you. If you think you should stay with your boss, you stay with him. If you think he can get you out of here in one piece, you stay with him. If you think I am going to rip his arms off fucking, you do what I say."

Tumbles drove and followed Mo's car to a security gate. They showed the guard the paperwork and he nodded that everything was in order. He gave them directions to Pier One and raised the barrier. Pedro looked in the rear view mirror and studied the man on the back seat. He looked like Bob Hoskins at the end of The Long Good Friday. Fucked!

*

"There they are"

Santos could see them. On the far side of the pier. Under the crane. Three vehicles. Two cars and a van.

"Right we go round the front. You have the paperwork?"

"Yes Igor."

"We get out with the guns. No one backs down."

"Of course Igor. And if we have to shoot?"

"We shoot them all."

They all piled into the people mover.

"Okay boys, let's go get my cocaine."

Sunday Old School

The boat skimmed over the water and rounded the end of the Kingsford Smith runway that jutted into the bay. They ran parallel to Foreshore Drive and then into Port Botany proper. They passed some massive container ships. Charlie thought that they were in a big enough boat themselves but these huge vessels dwarfed them.

They shot down a finger of water over which lurched some giant cranes.

"That's it." Billy pointed to the left. "Pier One."

They passed around the back of a ship and headed for a set of ladders. They were about forty feet high.

"Do you reckon you can climb them Jimmy?" asked Billy.

"Are you taking the piss boy?" asked Jimmy.

"No Jimmy I'm not. It's a genuine question. Are you old boys up to it?"

"Don't push your luck Billy. They've still got guns," said Sam jokingly.

"Yeah and we're not afraid to use them," said Daniel, trying to break the tension.

"I'm more worried about Jo Dad. She's still a bit all over the place," said Sam.

Sam was holding Jo upright. She looked a bit green about the gills.

"I'm alright Sam. You guys go up. I don't feel like playing anymore. I don't want to see Tray die."

"Honey, no one is going to see Tray die. Rudi Stone is a nobody. You'll see." It was Charlie who spoke.

"Charlie, no offence but if you had the balls in the first place Tray wouldn't be in this mess!"

"Jo!" It was Jimmy.

"No its alright Jimmy. I had it coming."

"And I didn't mean that Rudi Stone was going to kill him. I meant that if Tray doesn't get medical help soon, then he will die anyway. He's a wanted man. Who can you go to? My Tray will die and none of you can save him."

She buried her head in her hands. All the men looked at each other. They knew she was right. They had all seen Tray. He was a sick man. Jimmy had not seen much worse in the army and many of those that were better had passed away.

Sam broke the silence.

"Well how about you get up those fucking stairs and save him! Its not going to happen with us mourning him down here."

*

They drove up to some shipping containers. About twenty of them laid out side by side. There was a gap of about a metre between each container. Mo was always impressed with the precision that the dockers put these massive containers down.

They pulled up infront of a container with a big green seal hanging from the handles. Tumbles, Pedro and Don got out of their car first. Don was brandishing his pistol. Directing them away from the car. Mo, Tarry and Rudi got out of their car. Guns primed.

Then the van pulled up. Trev and the rest of the Lebanese militia got out. They pulled the sliding door open and carried Tray out in the chair and placed it on the concrete. He wasn't looking any better. In fact he looked like death was knocking on his door.

"Fucking hell!" Tumbles shouted. "Tray!"

It was the first time Tumbles had seen his friend. He had imagined what he had looked like from his voice. He had never heard Tray sound so utterly bereft of life. His imagination hadn't even come close to conjuring up the picture infront of him.

His feet were swathed in bandages but they were a bloody sodden mess. His face. God his face! His head was just a swollen mass of bruises and cuts. He was dressed in a blue dressing gown that had bloodstains all over it. His arm must have been broken because it was in a sling. Tumbles feared looking under that dressing gown.

"What the fuck have you done to him?"

He went to run to him but was stopped by Rudi's gun.

"Mate. Hand over the coke and you can end his suffering. He's not going to live. Look at him. He's fucked!"

"I'm going to get you for this Stone!" said Tumbles.

"No you're not Tumbles. This ends here. All of it! He wants his family to live. This is the only solution."

Rudi was calm, all business-like. Tumbles stared at the gun. He thought about ripping it out of this animal's hand but everyone had their guns aimed at them. Pedro tugged at his arm.

"Easy amigo. We do this now," he paused and turned to Mo. "We open the doors and inside you find the rest of your life."

"Okay boys, you cover the doors. Mr Nunez you open the doors."

Rudi and Don covered Tray on the chair with their handguns. They stood to the right of the container. Mo, Tarry, Tumbles and Pedro held their position on the left. The remaining Lebanese and Trev stood infront of the vehicles with their backs to them. Framed in the headlights, they formed a small semi-circle and aimed their automatic weapons at the doors. Pedro moved forward to the container door and broke the green seal. He lifted one of the handles up. It creaked as metal rubbed on metal. They all held their breath.

*

"That's our signal."

"What is?"

"The door opening you idiot. Do you ever listen?"

378

"Yes."

"We'll lets get behind those vehicles and surprise them. They will be too busy looking at what is inside to worry about us."

He waved his hand in the air and moved it in a circular motion. He then pointed forward. They had to cover about fifty metres without being seen. Easy as taking out a bunch of Angolans in the jungle.

*

"Let's go! Not too quick though. We don't want to draw too much attention to ourselves. Turn the lights off. Slowly Santos. You know the phrase, 'slowly slowly to catch a monkey'.

Santos drove the car forward, hugging the shadows.

*

They all peered inside the container as Pedro swung the doors back. Everyone had their fingers on a trigger except Pedro, Tray and Tumbles. If this was a set up it was going to end in a blood bath. Don looked at Tray. They had really fucked him up. He looked across at Tumbles. Tumbles was not looking inside the container he was staring at Rudi. He didn't even care what was in the container!

The doors creaked back and revealed three black cars inside parked in a line. They were BMW's with blacked out tinted windows. On the bonnets stood the proud Portuguese green and red flag.

"What's this?" demanded Mo.

"It is your cocaine."

"How?"

"In the boot you stupid fucking Arab."

'At last,' thought Tumbles. 'Pedro had got his swearing right'.

"Okay. I will let that go for the last time you stinking dego."

As Mo began to march towards the container, gunmen came out of everywhere. From behind the cars in which they had arrived, about ten men carrying Uzis descended on his men.

"Don't move!"

The gunmen were dressed in black combat gear, unlike his track-suited crew. These guys looked professional. They were olive skinned. Almost Arabic looking. They held their Uzis like they were their children. Carefully. Comfortably. These men knew how to kill and they had the jump on his guys.

They had appeared out of nowhere. Everyone was so intent on finding out the contents of the container that no one was covering the rear. Just as Fernando had planned. A basic mistake. They had outflanked their enemy. Fucking amateurs!

Mo looked at his men. They knew the game was up. They let their weapons fall to the floor. The professionals yelled something out at Pedro in a language Mo didn't understand. Pedro responded but not before Stone shouted something else.

"Don't anyone fucking move!"

He had a gun against Tray's head. Tray was in no position to move let alone resist. He just looked at the gun. Daring it to end his suffering.

The professionals stood their ground. No one gave an inch. Pedro and Tumbles saw their opportunity. As Mo and Tarry concentrated on Fernando and his family, they darted behind the open container door. Disappearing into the darkness. Mo and Tarry were left standing infront of the BMW's waving their guns at thin air.

They now stood facing ten guns with Stone's gun trained on Tray. Don stood stubbornly beside his boss. This was not going to end well for any of them.

"We will kill him!" shouted Rudi.

"No you will not Rudi. That is the last thing you will do!"

The voice came from out of the shadows.

"Who is that?" demanded Rudi.

"You mean you don't recognise me my friend. How long have you known me?"

"Igor?" Rudi couldn't disguise the surprise in his voice.

The voice stepped out of the shadows from behind the crane and walked towards the containers. An Uzi was slung casually over his shoulder. Mo recognised him from his gait alone. It **was** Igor. There were others with him. Five in all. All carrying Uzis as well but they had them pointed at everyone.

He spoke to the ten gunmen.

"Calmazinho amigos."

He gestured to them and gesticulated that they lower their guns. They did as instructed yet Rudi noted that they did not put them down.

"Yes Rudi it is me," said Igor.

"Igor. Am I happy to see you," Rudi saw that he still had a gun trained on him.

"Igor? I didn't expect you here." This time it was Mo.

"Yes," Igor paused. "Obviously," he paused again. "I don't like everyone knowing my business. Something I believe you told Fraser."

"Wha?" Mo stopped mid-sentence. Igor let it sink in. Slowly Mo realised that both he and Igor had been talking to the same man. Was this a good or a bad thing? He couldn't be sure.

"You got here just in time," said Mo.

"Yes it would appear that I have," replied Igor.

"Are you here to collect the money?" asked Mo.

Mo hoped that was all he was here for.

"No my friend, I am here to collect my cocaine."

"Sorry?"

It wasn't really a question, more a statement of confusion. As he digested the information Mo understood that this was a set up. Fucking hell what was going on here? The army types aimed their guns once again at Mo and Tarry.

"Drop them you fucking pigs," shouted Fernando.

"What?" yelled Tarry.

"You heard. Drop your guns!"

Tarry and Mo did as they were told. Rudi and Don still held on to their guns. This wasn't their battle. Perhaps they were going to get out of this after all.

"Now kick them away!" ordered Fernando.

No one was paying any attention to Rudi, Don and Tray. Tray just sat there listlessly. He could barely take in what was going on. There were guns. There were people talking. Had Tumbles and Pedro been there? He couldn't remember. Who was here now? He thought he could see Fernando but he wasn't sure. What was happening? He wished he could see. He hoped the others were safe.

"Drop it Rudi!"

He recognised the voice immediately. London through and through. It was Charlie fucking Fenton. Fuck! How did he get here?

Charlie walked round to the front of him. He was carrying a pump action shotgun. Rudi had to be impressed. He looked every bit the old school villain except for what he was wearing. What was he wearing?

"Charlie? What the fuck are you doing here?"

"Doing what I should have been doing a long time ago. Throwing out the fucking trash!"

"Nice to see you too Charlie!" Still cool despite his current situation thought Charlie. Despite the obvious impending outcome to Charlie, Stone kept the gun on McCarthy. He held it at the back of Tray's head. Tray was sure he could hear his Uncle Charlie. He must be drugged. He thought everyone was here.

"Come to save your Godson have you old man? Don't you think you're a bit late? No matter what you do here, *this* McCarthy…" Rudi paused and patted the gun into the back of Tray's head without taking his eyes off of Charlie. "*This* McCarthy dies here tonight! Nothing you can do about it!"

"Yep. I may a bit late. Like supermodel late. But if you think you are going to walk away from here you are sadly mis-fucking-staken."

Charlie looked down at his Godson. There wasn't much life left in him. Jo had been right. He looked at the black bastard. Rudi Stone was finished. Charlie would never let him live for this. Rudi knew it but he still held the gun in his hand and it wasn't wavering. This cunt had some fucking balls thought Charlie.

"London will go up in flames Charlie. It will never be the same.'

"Oh don't be so sure about that cunt."

382

He didn't recognise this voice. He turned to his right and saw Jimmy McCarthy. Where were these people coming from? How did he get here?

"Boom Rudi! Did you hear that explosion Stone? That was the meth lab going up in flames. Just like that. And if London goes up the same, people will find out that it was your fault. Who's going to back the Yardies then you wanker? Your entire fucking empire Rudi! Gone in a fucking bullet. We're old men Stone. We don't fucking care what happens to London. I told you I was going to kill you and I never break a promise!"

Rudi didn't budge. He didn't take his gun away from the back of Tray's head.

"Fuck you McCarthy!" He paused, scanning the mob infront of him. "You still with me Don?"

He couldn't see Don. He didn't know where he was. He couldn't look everywhere at once. Then he heard Don's voice behind him.

"Yeah boss. Right behind you."

It made him feel stronger. Filled him full of courage. Two Yardies against the rest of the world. It would go down in history. Like the Zulus against the fucking Welsh or something like that. Igor interrupted the standoff.

"Before we all play Reservoir Dogs, let me get my cocaine and get out of here. I want no part of this. Are you alright with that Charlie?"

"More than alright Igor. Its been a pleasure doing business with you."

Charlie smiled at Rudi. It was a smile of triumph.

"Got it yet Yardie? Did you think you could hurt me? Did you think I would let you get away with this? You're just a stupid fucking jigaboo from the gutter. I rule London you fuckwhit. You're just a useless turd flowing down the sewer!"

Mo looked at Igor then at Tarry. The penny dropped! Igor and Charlie had been in bed with each other all this time! How could he have been so stupid?

"Oh you didn't know you Lebanese piece of shit?" said Igor.

"Know what?" Mo tried to appear brave.

"Know that you are fucking predictable," shouted Fernando.

Igor ignored the interruption.

"Eighty years ago, you were running around with Lawrence of fucking Arabia. You stabbed each other in the back then. You stab each other in the back now. No one likes you. No one trusts you. All you care about is fucking money!"

"Igor. Please!" begged Mo.

Igor blanked him.

"Shut the fuck up baby killer! All you care about is money. Same as you, you fucking nigger!"

He sneered at Rudi.

"You don't know how to make friends. You just buy them. Charlie taught me a long time ago how important it is to have friends. It's why I am still alive. I am friends with Pedro long time before I meet you. I am friends with Charlie long time before I meet you. Mr McCarthy is friends with Charlie since before you were born!"

"Pedro, Tumbles. Come here!" He stopped talking and gestured to someone behind the container. The two men appeared as instructed.

"These two men don't work for me. They work for the cartel. They are important men. When you fuck with their friend, you fuck with Medellin itself. When you fuck with me, you fuck with Medellin. When you fuck with Charlie, you fuck with Medellin. When you try to steal our coke, you fuck with Medellin. You understand Mo. You made Medellin very angry! I had to call my cousin in Cuba to okay this and he said 'look after my friends'. Do you know what that means?"

Mo understood. He had crossed too many lines. There was no avoiding it. He should have done his research. Marseille had said that McCarthy was connected. He should have searched further. The Arab tried to swallow. Nothing. No moisture. His mouth was as dry and dusty as the land that his parents had worked so hard on back in the old country. He saw Tarry's hand shaking. He looked at his crew staring at the floor. He had fucked them all.

"And you know what Rudi? No one cared about your brother. He was just a fucking idiot. Charlie did the honourable thing. His Godson fucked up but you wouldn't let it be and this is where we find ourselves. Friends sticking up for friends and you in the fucking middle!"

"Oh I've had enough of this!"

384

Rudi pulled back the hammer of his gun. A shot rang out.

The King Is Dead

Jo came careering out of the shadows.

"Tray!"

It was a blood-curdling scream of loss. She ran into the standoff then stopped in her tracks. She was followed by Daniel, Sam, Billy and Ron. They had all been watching from the shadows. They couldn't see what was going on. They could hear the voices. They could hear the threats. They heard the shot. Jo had sprung out. Ron hadn't been able to stop her.

Fernando had been taken by surprise by the shot. He had been too busy listening to Igor and watching the Arabs. Tumbles and Pedro had been doing the same. Igor was giving quite a speech. They couldn't see what had happened. A body fell to the ground. No! Not Tray.

Charlie looked down at his shirt. It was covered in blood. He looked up again. Rudi no longer stood before him. In his place was the smoking barrel of a Glock. A slow wisp of smoke curled into the night sky. The gun shook slightly. Charlie slowly exhaled.

"Put the gun down Don. Its over."

Charlie reached out for the barrel of the gun and gently pulled it from Don's grasp. They both looked at the contorted body that lay at their feet. Rudi Stone had made his last threat. Jimmy looked at the Yid from Chigwell.

"Et Tu Brutus."

Don didn't respond. His life now held in the balance. In the hands of the very men that he had offended. Rudi stone, head of the Yardies, the notorious ruler of the West Indian distribution network and his boss, oozed dark red blood from the back of his head. The king was dead. Tray did not stir.

"Is he still alive?" screamed Jo.

"I don't know."

Jimmy dropped to his knees. He looked into his son's face.

"Tray? Tray?"

Sam arrived at the scene. Daniel, Billy and Ron came running over.

"Fernando! Cover that lot!"

Pedro pointed at the Lebanese.

"Get on the floor you bastardos. You too!"

Fernando pointed his gun at Mo and Tarry. The rest obliged.

"Hands behind your heads!"

Mo and Tarry followed the orders. Pedro and Tumbles scurried over to the gathering. Blood seeped around Jimmy's knees. It was Rudi's not Tray's.

Igor did not move.

"Santos. Get these cars out of here!"

Santos lowered his gun and moved towards the container.

"Dad?"

Tray was coming round.

"Yes son?"

"Where am I?"

"You're with me son. With me."

Tray passed out again.

"Mr McCarthy?"

It was Tumbles.

"Who are you?"

"My name's Steve Mr McCarthy. Steve Brown."

"And who are you?" asked Jimmy.

"Sorry Mr McCarthy. I am Tumbles. The friend that Sam, Jo and Tray spoke to when you were being held hostage. A good friend. Look we don't have much time sir. We have to get him to a doctor. He won't survive much longer."

"I know Steve. I know. But what are we going to do?"

"It's all arranged sir."

"Please, call me Jimmy."

"Ok Jimmy. Its all arranged. We have a doctor on the ship. It has full medical facilities on board. We're shipping him out."

"Where?"

"Where Tray has always wanted to go"

"Where's that then?" asked Jimmy.

"I'll let him tell you that"

"What about us?" asked Jimmy.

Charlie decided it was time to tell his old friend the score.

"Everyone's dead Jimmy. All of you. No loose ends. You can't go home."

Santos undid the ties on the first car and drove it out of the container and into the shadows. The seven Lebanese and the bikie waited nervously. Who would be their salvation now? Certainly not Allah nor the Shire Chapter of the Apache bikers club. They were on their own in a country that they thought they ran. How wrong they were.

*

He watched Tumbles wheel his son away. It would be touch and go.

"How did you do this Charlie? How did you stop them?" asked Jimmy.

"It was easy Jimmy. These Lebanese forget how small the world is," replied Tray's Godfather.

"What do you mean?"

"How many people do you think can move shit loads of coke?"

"Dunno," answered Jimmy somewhat confused. This whole thing had been confusing to him.

"Well I'm it in London. You know that."

"Yeah I know. But how did you find me?"

"When this fucking Arab started sniffing around to find out who Tray was, he rang Marseille. Who do I have working in Marseille?"

"The Doc. The chemist. Of Course," suddenly it all made sense. The Doc had taken care of the Olympic speaker system fiasco all those years ago. He had protected Tray then and it appeared he had looked after him once again.

"And he rang Ron and told him some Lebanese gang bangers were asking about Trystan McCarthy. I knew Tray couldn't hurt a fly so I asked around. Why would he kill those he loved?" Charlie paused, letting Jimmy get to grip with things.

"Igor is an old friend of mine. We were trading cocaine for a long time before I had to get him out of the country for various indiscretions. His family wanted him lying low, much like Tray did. This little deed here will ensure that he gets back at the main table."

"But how did he know?" asked Jimmy.

"Simple really. Aziz had borrowed from Igor to fund his operation and hadn't paid him back. Somehow Tray had got his hands on the money. He took it and gave it to his friend Tumbles who set about turning it into a mountain of coke. His girlfriend and her family paid for that crime."

Jimmy looked over at the Arabs lying on the floor. The fucking animals had killed his son's loved ones. They had tortured his son within an inch of his life. Even now, after they had saved him, he might die. There was something unsaid in his son's eyes. Something that Jimmy thought might not allow them to deliver him from this evil. It looked as though he had given up hope.

"Igor could have acted then but Rudi couldn't resist the carrot and teamed up with him. Rudi had dealt with Igor before. He had tried to get in bed with him years ago but my dealings with the Merseysiders frightened him. Plus the fact Igor had kept me informed all the time back then. Rudi was pretty stupid when it came down to it.

Stupidity combined with blind arrogance is dangerous. It's unpredictable," He paused and looked at the Rudi's lifeless body with detached contempt.

"Igor put them together without really knowing the connection with me. They grabbed you lot and spirited you away before I could get to Aziz. No one knew where you were. This fucking Stone had already taken ten years of Tray's life. This fucking camel jockey even more. Stone made it personal so me and Ron thought we should give it our own personal touch. I thought it best we keep all the parties separate. That way no one could fuck it up. Igor knew he could keep a lid on it. Pedro and Tumbles didn't know that I was pulling the strings. No one except me and Igor knew that Medellin were involved to such an extent."

"But why now? Why here? Why didn't we do this years ago?"

"Because I thought that keeping the status quo was important. Because I thought business was far more important. But it wasn't. This way Rudi Stone just disappears in a far off country with no one the wiser," Charlie paused, lighting up a cigar which he dug out of his Salvation Army coat pocket.

His army cap tilted to one side slightly as he sucked on the crusty tobacco leaf. He blew great puffs of smoke towards his old friend. Jimmy waved them away.

"Want one?" he offered another one to Jimmy who shook his head in refusal.

"They were already on the road to making Stone here. I didn't need the same sort of publicity but when they took you, he really overstepped the mark. It became more than personal. I had let your family down before and I wasn't going to do it again. I didn't want your blood on my hands as well but we had to wait. This cunt Aziz was unpredictable plus the fact the police were involved."

"What do you mean?"

"Aziz had a Fed on the payroll. High up. But he didn't know that Igor had the same copper on his books too. He found out that Aziz was going to take you all down. Everyone! Leave no one left to tell any tales. What Aziz didn't know was that Igor was under orders to take everyone down as well."

"What?" shouted Mo from his position on the concrete.

Fernando quickly stopped that line of enquiry by kicking Mo in the ribs. It elicited a drawn out groan from the now prostrate Arab. The story was beginning to unravel for Mo and he realised what an insignificant cog he was in the overall scheme of things.

"I paid off Aziz's debt. I had to ask permission from the head of the cartel. Once they found out who was involved. That it was a question of family, they agreed. Pedro organised the cavalry here."

Charlie pointed at the Portuguese gypsies still aiming their weapons at Aziz and his men.

"These boys came rolling in for their friend. This wasn't about money Jimmy. Everyone did this for Tray. Everyone here was here for your son."

"But what about the police Charlie? They won't let this go."

"The police have been dealt with Mr McCarthy," interrupted Igor. "Now we have to get going. Charlie what are we going to do with him?"

Igor pointed at Don.

"Ready to be my bitch Don? Ready to step up?" asked Charlie.

"Yes Charlie. I really didn't want a part of this."

He was lying. Charlie knew it. The scumbag had shot a girl without a moments hesitation. He decided to play his game.

"Okay then. Let's get on with it then. Who beat my Godson?"

"I don't know. They did that before I got there."

"What about that one?" Charlie pointed at Trev.

"No he just led us to Jimmy and the others."

"Igor what should we do with these two?"

"I have one of my team waiting on Foreshore Drive. There is a Lexus waiting there. They can drive up there and wait for us. I presume you have some unfinished business here?"

"Yes I do."

"Well do you know where I mean? Foreshore Drive?" Igor walked over to Trev and casually nudged him with his foot.

"Yes," Trev stuttered the answer.

"Think yourself lucky," Igor paused. "Santos, give me the keys to our van."

Santos threw the keys to Igor.

"Don I don't need to tell you what's at stake here," said Charlie. "You do as I say and you live. You take over the Yardies and we let you run your own show. Understood?"

"Yes Charlie. I do."

"Okay get going. We'll be there in about fifteen minutes."

Santos led the two men away.

"So Jimmy this is goodbye. Go be with your son."

"Charlie how can I thank you?"

"By keeping that boy of yours alive."

"How are you going to get out of here?"

"Don't you worry about me Jimmy. No one knows I'm here."

The two old men hugged one another. They were interrupted by Tumbles and Billy. Pedro and Ron brought up the rear.

"Jimmy you'd better get on the boat. I think we're losing him."

Jimmy looked at Charlie. He didn't know what to say.

"Its okay Jimmy. Go! You'll be hearing from me soon. Don't worry about me."

Jimmy waved a last goodbye to his friend and disappeared towards the boat.

"Okay men. Let's get on with this," he paused and thew his cigar away. He turned to Pedro and Tumbles.

"I presume after this that you two are going to retire?"

They both nodded in agreement.

"Well let's hope that Tray survives 'cos he gonna need friends like you to look after him."

They both looked meekly at Charlie. The doctor was the ship's doctor. No fucking genius that was for sure and he had shaken his head at Tray's condition. He didn't know if he could save him. Had this all been in vain?

"Okay so what's the plan? Did you have one?" asked Charlie.

"Yeah, we're all going on the boat. All of us. Fernando and his family too," replied Tumbles. "A south pacific odyssey."

"Well I'm flying out of here with Ron. I'll be back home chowing down on some kippers before you know it. What about this lot?"

Charlie pointed at the Arabs.

"Oh I had that under control too."

"Really how?"

"You'll like this."

Tumbles pulled the walkie-talkie out of his pocket.

"You still there Brick?"

"Been here all the time buddy."

"You know what to do?"

"Yep. I'll lower the hoist."

"When its done, get on the boat with the rest."

"Will do. Good job Tumbles."

"Its not over yet mate. I don't know what's going to happen with Tray."

"He's got us buddy. Don't worry. Give me the signal when you're ready."

"Okay."

Tumbles put the radio back in his pocket.

"What are you up to Tumbles?" asked Charlie.

"You'll find out."

He gave Fernando a nod.

"Put 'em inside," ordered Tumbles.

Fernando and his family of gypsy mercenaries dragged the Lebanese to their feet and herded them towards the container. Pedro tried to pull Rudi's body across the concrete, struggling under its weight. Ron arrived with Daniel and helped out.

Mo tried to protest but Fernando silenced him with a smack around the back of the head.

"Move! Get inside!"

The Lebanese walked slowly, not knowing their fate.

"What are you going to do with us?" asked Mo.

"Oh I'm going to do nothing. These guys are the ones you need to ask," replied Tumbles.

He pointed towards the gypsies.

"Why?"

"Cos you'd better hope they don't miss."

Tumbles looked at Fernando.

"Do it!"

The gypsies unloaded their weapons into the container. It was a slaughter. The gunshots reverberated around the shipyard. This had to be done. They had left him with no choice. This was the only way. This was for all the women and children they had murdered. This was for what they had done to Tray. Tumbles didn't have the stomach for it. He looked away.

Igor watched. This was a necessary evil. This was the sort of justice his cousin had demanded. He was going to order his men to do it but Tumbles had superseded him. Mo had done too much. His crew had killed too many people. Revenge was a powerful emotion and they were all full of it. Tumbles had just acted first.

When it was finished there was just a twitching mass of broken bodies inside. Blood everywhere. Some were amazingly still alive. Pedro, Ron and Daniel had dropped Rudi's body as the bullets started to fly. Once the Portuguese had finished, the men picked up Rudi's corpse and flung it inside the container.

"Close the doors Pedro," ordered Tumbles.

Pedro did as he was told. Tumbles got out the walkie-talkie.

"All good Brick. Lower away."

From out of the darkness came a harness. It slowly descended towards the ground.

"Right. Hook it up." Brick ordered from above.

Fernando and his family scurried around and hooked the container up to the harness.

"Okay ready to go Brick," said Tumbles.

The harness creaked and strained but slowly the container lifted from the dock. They all watched it drift into the night.

"Where's it going?" asked Charlie.

"On the boat too," he looked at his watch impatiently. "Somewhere between here and Cartegena, Lloyds of London will get a telex informing them of freight overboard. Happens all the time apparently."

"Nice work Tumbles."

"I said you'd like it."

"Right, no time for pleasantries. Let's get on with it," said Charlie. "Igor. See you in London."

"*Hasta la vista Charlie*," said Igor.

"Yeah whatever that means," he smiled at Igor. "Daniel get Billy. You're coming with us. You'll see Jimmy again don't worry."

Daniel got on the phone and spoke to his son.

Igor ordered his men into the BMW's. Ron hopped into the van. Daniel took charge of the commodore and waited for his boy. Charlie walked over to the lead BMW. Tumbles went over to his gunmen.

"Fernando, clear up the cartridges and get a move on," said Tumbles.

"What about the blood?" asked the gypsy.

"We can't do anything about that. Leave it. We've got to get out of here and quickly. The police may be on their way."

Igor wound down the electric window.

"Charlie, there will be no police coming here. In about twenty minutes they will be too busy covering their own arse."

"Remember Igor. Dead men tell no tales," Charlie tapped the roof of the car.

"Don't worry Charlie. Its all under control. Just make sure you get rid of those bloody cars."

*

"Do you think they'll let us go?"

"We're still alive Trev."

"Yeah but for how long?"

"I have no idea."

The question had bothered Don all the way out of the port terminal. They turned left onto Foreshore Drive.

"But we don't have much option do we? I am stuck here until Igor can help me out."

Don was resigned to his fate. Forever indebted to Charlie and Igor.

"There it is," said Trev. He pointed out a Lexus which was parked up on the hard shoulder next to the bushes. Its hazard lights flashed, creating an eerie intermittent glow on the straggly flora.

They pulled over and turned the van off. Xavier saw the van stop. He pressed redial on the phone.

"What's that?"

Don heard a phone ring.

"Is it yours?" he asked.

He turned to Trev who looked at him non-plussed.

The tone sounded a third time. Under the car seat, the mobile phone triggered the detonator. Trev and Don never felt a thing as the van exploded in a ball of flame. The roof was jettisoned into the air and flew behind the bushes into the bay.

Xavier jumped into the rubber ducky that he'd dragged up the beach. He pulled the cord on the engine, fired it up and gunned the motor. Inside five minutes he had passed the end of the airport runway. He chucked the phone overboard and rounded the peninsula towards the Cook's River.

Igor heard the explosion from his car. They turned right as they left the terminal. He scanned left and saw the bright orange ball of flames in the distance.

"Dead men tell no tales Santos."

"Si Igor."

"London here we come."

*

He felt the container lurch. It moved underneath him. He felt the sticky morass on his chest. He couldn't see through the darkness. A heavy weight pinned him to the floor. It was a body. He tried to push against it but felt a searing surge of pain travel up his left arm.

He called out.

"Tarry? Faddy?"

Silence. Then a low groan from somewhere over the far side of the container.

"Who's that? Who's there?"

He heard Tarry's voice call his name. Barely audible above the creaking container.

"Tarry? Are you okay?"

"No," came the response.

"Can you move?"

"No," Tarry paused as he gathered his strength. "Where are we going Mo?"

"To hell Tarry. To hell."

Mo heard Tarry begin to sob as the realisation set in that his life would end inside this metal tank. There was no way out of this. Perhaps the police would come. Perhaps they would save him. He doubted it. This was no Hollywood movie. They were going to die here.

"Tarry?"

"Mmmm?"

"I'm sorry mate."

Tarry didn't make another sound. A bang echoed around the container as it came to a stop. Metal on metal. They had landed. Mo stared into the darkness. He tried to make out the shapes inside the black interior but found nothing. Strangely the words of a Doors' song fluttered through his mind as he lost consciousness. Jim Morrison sang his life out of existence, a parting shot from the days of sex, drugs and rock and roll. He saw the lizard king call him. He heard the leather clad rocker sing to him. He closed his eyes and let it wrap him in the comfort of its lament. He mouthed the words as he sang along with the imaginary melody: 'This is the end. My only friend the end'. He hated The Doors

Sunday Morning

The whole world had gone nuts. He got the call around five-thirty in the morning. They had told him to get a wriggle on. He had driven like a madman for thirty minutes to get to the scene. By the time he got there it was all over.

There were police everywhere. Locals and Feds. The road had been closed in both directions. Not that it was a problem. No one used this road, especially on a Sunday morning. The first thing he saw was the smoking wreck of a van minus its roof. In the passenger seat sat the charred remains of a white male. Its head was missing along with its right arm. The driver's side was empty save for the melted steering wheel. As he scanned the scene, he saw that forensics had cordoned off some spots on the road. He strained to figure out what they were and then nearly chucked up his McMuffin when he realised that they were body parts.

He had heard over the scanner what had happened. Two suspected terrorist bombs on Botany Bay. One in the Shire. One on Foreshore Drive. He had tried to contact Fraser but got no answer. The phone just rang out. Most probably too much red wine last night.

He pulled the car over and got out. He flashed his badge at the policeman who held sway in front of him. He let him through. In the middle distance he saw Tommy rushing towards him along the hard shoulder.

"Dave! Dave!"

Swanson held up his hand, trying to get Tommy to calm down.

"Easy Tommy. What's up?"

"We're in the shit Dave."

"Why what's happened?"

"See that car over there?"

Tommy pointed to a black sedan parked just beyond the wreck. Its paint had begun to bubble and peel due to the intense heat.

"Yeah. So?"

"Do you recognise it?"

Swanson scratched his head.

"No. Should I?"

"Yeah. Its Fraser's!"

"What? Our Fraser?"

"Who'd you think I meant? Yes our Fraser. And it gets worse."

"How can that be?" asked Swanson.

"He's got six bullets in him and ten kilos of coke on the passenger seat."

Fuck! Now the shit was going to hit the fan. He hated Sunday mornings.

Long Live The King

He closed the file. So many people had gone missing. At first they thought it had been a set-up. It had looked too clean. Fraser with ten kilos of coke, executed on Foreshore Drive. It was a hit that was for sure. And then mysteriously, digital recordings had appeared on his desk. Recordings of Fraser and someone called Mo.

They began to delve. They took Fraser's computer. They found one of his phones. It was obvious after a while that he was on the take. He had ordered McCarthy's murder and it looked like this Mo had carried it out. The trail had gone cold on the entire McCarthy clan. Nothing turned up.

The Feds were stung that one of their own could be on the take. He was ordered to make the investigation quick. Close it and finish it and he would be rewarded. He did exactly that. He declared the McCarthy's and Jo Flint dead. There could be no other explanation. They would be buried in a shallow grave somewhere. Maybe not even that.

Darren Thwaite had held a big memorial for their mate at Decadence nightclub Swanson had attended. He thought that maybe in some romantic notion that Tray would turn up and surprise the crowd. It had been a massive event. Everyone who was anyone turned up. It was a DJ and friends only event. It was something that Tray would have been proud of. The lights, the music, the dancers. It had all been perfect. Everyone there had been off their heads. In a tribute to the man they all loved, every single member of Decadence dumped at twelve, then double dumped at two. This was his legacy. Even Swanson and Tommy joined in. That night they were not coppers. They were fans. These were the accolades that McCarthy never had. These were the places he should have played to. These were his people. This was his place and everyone who had heard of him play came on board.

DJs from London, New York, Ibiza and Portugal. Friends from the old school. People who had thought he was dead to the world. Only to find him alive and then dead again. They had no grave to mourn. They had no family to comfort. Everyone had gone. So they did the best thing they could do. They celebrated him in the dance. They praised his spirit and they remembered his joy.

It was the best night of Swanson's life. The music. The vibe. The sheer ecstasy was beyond all normal events. In the music rags and mags for the following couple of months, no one spoke of anything else. Sydney had witnessed the passing of something special without ever having really embraced the person they had celebrated.

Swanson had asked Rachel what she thought had happened.

"He's up there Detective. In the heavens. Playing music to the angels. And you know what?"

"What's that then?"

"They fucking love him Detective Swanson. They fucking love him."

*

He puffed the last couple of metres towards the statue. She watched him place the flowers at the massive pair of feet. He bowed his head and stayed silent. He looked up again and stared at her. It was him but not him. It had changed him.

"Do you think they will ever forgive me?" he asked.

They had nearly lost him three times on the journey. The first time on the dockside in Sydney and then twice on that huge journey across the Pacific. The doctor had worked miracles but it was Jo who had saved him. Twice she had breathed life back into his broken body. His heart had stopped. The doctor had coaxed it back to life but it was Jo who had filled his lungs with her own breath. She had begged him to come back to her and he had.

It had taken them forever to cross that ocean. When they got close to the Panama Canal, the captain had radioed ahead. Igor had made the arrangements. A helicopter had landed on the ship and transported him, Jo and Jimmy to a private hospital. They had given him the emergency treatment he needed. They stabilised him. He had been in Panama for a week before he was moved to Colombia. They met up with everyone in Cartagena. Tray was admitted to another private hospital. They had managed to save his feet.

They thought that perhaps he would lose them. They were in a terrible state. It had taken another three months for Tray to even move them. During that time they operated on his face. Plastic surgeons had worked feverishly on his features. They had chiselled here and there. They reconstructed his jaw and his nose. They put swabs all over his torso.

Jimmy, Sam, Jo and Brick stayed by his side. Pedro gave them as much money as they needed and made many trips in and out of Colombia. Fernando and the gypsies left them in there. They had done what they had set out to do. They had saved their friend but now they had to get back to their loved ones too. Pedro had arranged from the boat to have their families looked after. They would ask no questions. They would be very happy with their future.

Tray had hardly spoken a word when he had been on the ship. The trauma had just been too much. The guilt over Lizzy, Tracey and the girls was all consuming. He wished he could have died in that country. But slowly he began to talk. He realised how much people had done for him. He realised how much they loved him and it gave him strength. The turning point was the music.

One afternoon, as Jo held his hand on the balcony of his private room, the radio announcer garbled something in Spanish. Jo saw Tray's head whip round towards the speaker. It hurt him. His head was still wrapped in bandages.

He mumbled something to Jo. She couldn't understand him. They had just fixed his cheekbones and his jaw and she couldn't hear him properly. He picked up a pen and started to write. It was a bit shabby but she could read it.

'This is my song. This is the one I wrote!"

She could sense the smile beneath the bandages. She saw his foot move in time to the music. It was the first time she had seen him enjoy music again. Most times they switched the radio off when a dance song came on. He just wasn't ready for it.

But this time it was different. She saw the strength come back to his eyes. It was his turning point. The retreat from that dark place where he had lost himself.

He had smiled all that day, the next day and the day after that. Tumbles had returned from wherever he had been. He was keeping his cards very close to his chest. Whatever he had been doing, he assured Jo that it was 'all good'.

Then someone came into the room that she hadn't seen for a very, very long time. Someone from the old days. It was The Dish. His old friend, James Barker. The man who had stolen at least forty million quid from Lloyds Bank and got away with it.

"Dish?"

"Tray?"

Dish also had some plastic surgery. He looked a million dollars and of course he was worth that and a whole lot more.

"How did you find me?" asked Tray.

"You can thank Pedro and Tumbles for that. Pretty resourceful that Pedro. Can get his hands on anything."

Tray smiled. They had managed to rebuild his lips. They were the same as they always were. It was a winning smile. The smile his friend had missed.

"Where have you been Dish?"

"I have been extremely busy," replied Dish.

"Busy doing what?"

"Making everyone richer than they already were."

"What do you mean?"

"You up for a bit of education on the financial markets?"

"Well I'm not going anywhere if that's what you mean," replied Tray.

Dish had taken a laptop from his bag and plugged it into the wall.

"Okay, I'm going to take you on a journey. Hold tight, you'll like this."

For the entire afternoon the two friends sat on the bed and talked like old times. Dish showed Tray what he had been up to. Tumbles and Pedro had been looking for Dish for a reason. They needed his help. They needed him to turn their money into a legitimate fortune. This he had done. He evaded tax rules and international inspectors and invested the money wisely.

When the 9/11 attacks had happened the stock markets around the world had taken a hammering. There had been a drop-off in nearly all the major stocks. It had taken a while for the markets to stabilise. By this time Pedro had got in contact with Dish.

They had given him complete control of their accounts. They knew they could trust him. He had invested their money in something tangible. Oil, gold, palladium. In times of international meltdown, invest your money in something you can hold. It had been an age-old adage and it served Dish well. It allowed him to increase the value of his investment and move the money around. War was in the air and there was always money to be made when turmoil was afoot. He had added another thirty percent to their nest egg in no time at all and it was still increasing.

Jo's mind boggled at the size of the money involved. Between Tumbles and Tray, they had amassed nearly 150 million dollars! About a hundred million quid. That was before they had paid out the people who needed paying. Dish had needed to buy some confidences. It had cost but not too much. South America was cheap and they would have nothing to worry about for the rest of their lives. Anyway the investments were still increasing. It was like magic.

Then Dish had diversified their portfolio by investing in property. He came in one day beaming his magic smile. He gathered Jimmy, Sam and Jo around him. Pedro, Tumbles and Brick walked into the room. They were all smiling.

"What are you lot looking so happy about?" he asked.

"Set up the easel Tumbles," ordered Dish.

Tumbles put his head around the door and pulled some large cardboard posters from the hallway. He dragged a large easel through the door and set it up in the corner of the room.

First up was a picture of a huge complex surrounded by trees. It was brilliant white. There was a massive garden. It must have been on at least thirty acres. There were three swimming pools that he could see. It was on a hillside overlooking a crystal blue ocean.

"What is this Dish?"

"This is your new home."

"What? Where?"

Tray couldn't hide the surprise in his voice.

"Rio De Janeiro Tray."

Tray just sat there. He didn't say a thing.

"It's above the city. In the hills. There are forty rooms, a tennis court. Enough room for you and your family to live out your days."

"Fucking hell Dish. That will bring some attention mate."

"No it won't," interrupted Pedro. "People have been paid. Your face is different. Your name is no longer McCarthy. You can choose whatever you like. Your family and friends too. We have made you legitimate Tray. You are a very rich man. Money makes everything very easy."

Tray stared at his new home. Brazil! It was something he had always dreamed of.

"There's more Tray," gloated Tumbles.

"Show him Tumbles. Put it up!" Dish could hardly contain his excitement.

"Well come on! Show me for fucks sake!" bellowed Tray.

Tumbles put another board up. It was the front of a nightclub.

"What's that?"

"What do you think it is?" asked Dish.

"It's a nightclub. I can see that!"

"Well its yours."

"What?"

"Its yours," repeated Dish.

"How?"

"Like Pedro said. Money buys everything including your dream."

"Where is it?" asked Tray.

"At the Southern end of Copacabana Beach. Its perfect. It has an outside bar. A swimming pool. A dancefloor to die for. It is everything you and Tumbles ever dreamed of. It holds a thousand people. It is one of the biggest clubs in Rio. Its in both your names but for your sake we reckon Tumbles should be the 'face behind the place'. You'll be able to get on the decks whenever you want and you can book whoever you want. You can make it jump Tray."

Tray couldn't help but smile. This was his dream. His friends had done this all for him. They had saved him. They had rebuilt him and now they had given him his life back. He looked at his father as the tears rolled down his face. For the first time in his life he was speechless. Jo gazed at Tray. Her heart melted. She hadn't seen that smile for a long time.

Their love had taken much longer to build. While he was on the boat, he had hardly spoken to her. Through the endless operations he had suffered he gave her little or no idea if he would love her again. Sam told her to hang in there. The guilt he felt over Lizzy and her family tore at his soul. When the bandages came off his face and feet, Sam wheeled him around the gardens of the private hospital.

Sam spoke softly to his elder brother.

"Bro. You need to say something to Jo. She needs to know that you love her."

"Of course I love her Sam. But I'm afraid to tell her. Everyone I've ever loved has left me. They've pulled away. Disappeared into the night and my memories."

"Tray you are a stupid old bugger sometimes. Who do you think came for you in Australia? We all did but it was Jo who led the fight for you. She was going to Australia whether Dad liked it or not. That girl is special bro. She is the woman you should always have been with. From those days around Denis's place when you were young. She is it mate. No doubt about it."

"But what about Lizzy mate? What about all that other shit?"

Sam could sense the pain and guilt coursing through his brothers body. His chest convulsed with silent tears. It was painful to watch but this was his brother. The man that he loved more than himself. He had to fix him and there was no other time like the present. He moved to confront his brother. He knelt down before the wheelchair and looked into his brother's eyes. Tray could not look at him. Sam held his face in his hands.

"Tray, look at me! This is no way to live your life. You have felt guilty over Mum, Dad and me. Now its Lizzy and her family. Now I never met the girl but I'm pretty sure she wouldn't want you to live like this. She would want you to be happy. You can't live your life in the past. You've got to look forward."

Tray looked at his brother through bleary eyes.

"You think?"

"Everyone knows it Tray except you! Now tell the girl how you feel or lose her forever."

Sam had left him there. Alone in the garden. He let him mull over it. Eventually Tray called out for his brother but it wasn't Sam who went to him. It had been Jo. She walked up quietly and grasped the handles on the chair.

"Jo?"

"Yes Tray."

"Would you like to go on a date tonight?"

"Oh Tray. Of course. Where?"

She smiled at the back of his head.

"Meet me in my room at eight."

She wheeled him back to his room and kissed him on his cheek. She had dressed up to the nines for him. She had gone into town and bought a sensational cocktail dress for the event. She looked hot. Better than she ever looked before.

She had arrived on time. Tray had lit candles in every single corner of the room. He had put on a suit. He still wore slippers. His feet couldn't handle shoes for the moment. He had taken her by the hands and moved her to the centre of the room. He had switched on the CD player and played a song. It was Nina Simone's 'My Baby Just Cares For Me'. He stood for the first time since Australia. She begged him to sit down. He wouldn't. She didn't know if the tears were of happiness or pain. He danced with her.

He held her close to him. She nestled her head in his neck. He sang to her. They moved slowly around the room. He told her he loved her. She cried. At last he had come back to her. He made her sit at the small table that was decked out with a silver service. Waiters came in with an endless procession of food.

She could not eat. They just stared into each others' eyes. He realised that food was not what they wanted. He told the waiters to clear the table, their food

407

untouched. He took her gently by the hand. He led her to the bed, gently shuffling his poor feet alongside her.

The following morning she woke up next to him. She would never leave his side again. This time she would hold onto him forever. He had forgiven himself. He had come through the other side. From that day he walked every day by his love until he could walk around the garden unaided.

Jimmy watched his son improve. He was happy for him. At last he had the love that he and Betty had. It made him realise how much they had denied him over all these years. He deserved this. It was what every child should have.

It had taken Tray nearly eight months since they had left Australia to be in a fit enough condition to fly to Brazil. They had all gone on separate flights except Tray and Jo. Now they stood on top of Sugarloaf Mountain.

They moved back from the statue of Christ The Redeemer. He thought it appropriate. She put an arm around him and they peered out from the lookout.

"Tray, of course they will forgive you. You didn't pull the trigger. Some very evil men killed them. They nearly killed you. You survived to honour their memory."

He nodded. He looked out into the distance at the peaceful Atlantic Ocean. Somewhere down there was Tray's club. Tonight was its grand opening. Everyone had gathered here. Tray had looked after his friends as she knew he would.

Fernando and his family had moved to the glamour city. Tray had employed them as his personal bodyguards. He had bought them all houses. They would remain forever loyal to him. He had made Brick head of security at the club.

Sam was in charge of the money. He looked after everything. He and Dish collabarated to establish his empire. They bought a sound studio in the hills, It was perfect. Tray picked up local talent and recorded them and then churned out the tunes. Jimmy was more than happy. He spent his days watching his son. Watching him grow into the man he always hoped he would be.

Tumbles had bought some other investments. An ice cream bar on the esplanade, a couple of smaller bars. Pedro's interest were on the shadier side but at least he had reconciled with his Dad. It was a happy time for all of them.

Just after they had got to Rio, Jo had pulled him to one side. She had told him she was pregnant. Tray had wept openly. They were tears of joy. He had telephoned his Dad immediately. Jimmy was over the moon. Sam couldn't believe it. He was going to be an uncle.

"Come on darling, let's go. They're waiting."

They both shuffled down the steps towards the restaurant. She because of the bundle infront of her. He because his feet still gave him some trouble from time to time.

They walked into the restaurant. They were all there. The Portuguese, his family, Tumbles, Dish, Pedro and Brick. He had also flown in some of his other friends. Daz was the first person he had telephoned. Daz was incredulous.

"Where have you fucking been?"

"Dying mate. Dying."

Tray had told him that it had all been a smokescreen but that he had in fact died three times on the boat.

"But we'll talk about that when you get here."

"Where's here mate?"

"You remember I asked you to play with me when you made it?"

"Yes?"

"Well its on buddy. You're coming to play at my club."

"Where you fucking bastard?"

"In Rio de fucking 'neiro mate."

Daz had listened in silence. He had arranged everything as Tray had asked. All the crew got an invite. They thought it was Daz's first overseas headline. They couldn't believe his generosity. He explained it away as the single doing so well. It was a worldwide smash after all.

They were offered the chance of a lifetime. Geoff was there. So were the girls. Franky, Suzi, Vanessa, Belle, Michelle and Kylie had all received tickets. None of them were any the wiser. Daniel, his wife and Billy were sent tickets. Even Rachel didn't know the score. It was killing Daz. Everyone that did know was sworn to secrecy. Charlie and Ron turned up. Igor and Santos had even made the trip from London. Rachel's mum and Dad had arrived late and had to hurry from the airport but they had made it in time. Tray wanted the big entrance. The entrance that had been denied him since that fateful day on the Mile End Road.

"Are you ready darling?" asked Jo.

"More than I will ever be sweetheart."

He put his hand on her belly and looked at his Dad and brother. Tumbles joined them at the restaurant door. Pedro saw them approaching and nodded at Daz. Daz stood to his feet. He clinked his glass with his spoon.

"Ladies and gentleman, I have an announcement to make. I know you think that it was me that organised this. That this was my big day. Unfortunately I cannot lay claim to this extravagance. This has been the idea of one man. I would like you to stand, charge your glasses and welcome your host."

For those that did not know what was about to happen, they murmured to one another. They had no idea what was going on.

"Ladies and gentleman. I give you Trystan 'Tray' McCarthy!"

The place erupted. Rachel and the rest of the girls shrieked their delight. Geoff couldn't believe his- eyes. He had changed. He didn't look quite the same. But the smile was all his. It was Tray's. It was their friend. They rushed to him. They surrounded him. Tray McCarthy was back from the dead. Back in their lives.

He begged them all to sit down.

"Please, please. I know you're excited but take a pew. I'll explain it all later."

The waiters brought in the food. A monument to gastronomy. They ate their fill. Tray let Tumbles tell the story. The Aussies sat there hanging on every word. The girls would frequently come over and hug Tray. Rachel came over and sat on Tray's lap. She had nearly died for this man. He knew it. She didn't care. She was just happy to hug him. To feel him in her arms.

Tray excused himself to go to the loo. Pedro and Tumbles approached all of Tray's friends in his absence. They told them that whoever wanted to move here, whoever wanted to work for Tray would be looked after. If they didn't want to stay that was okay. He would not be worried. If they left, they would find in their luggage enough money to help them on in their life. No questions asked. It was a gift. A very large gift. But a gift nonetheless.

They sat there dumbfounded. They didn't know what to say. They tried to protest but Tumbles silenced them almost immediately.

"This is what he wants. You stood by him when he needed you most. He loves you all. You are all his family and he wants you to share in his success. The only problem is, you cannot tell a soul. This is where his life is and we want him to stay safe."

They pondered the offer as Tray re-entered the room. They had been told. He could tell.

"Okay before we hook in to dessert. I would like to make a toast."

He stood beside his love.

"Please be upstanding."

Everyone obliged.

"Friends and family. Please raise your glasses."

Everyone followed suit.

"To those who didn't make it here. For those we've loved and lost. For those that have passed. We shall remember them."

He looked around the room. His world was here now. They repeated the mantra.

"We shall remember them!"

There were some sniffles and some tears but Tumbles broke the silence.

"I would also like to propose a toast to my friend. To the man who saved our lives. I would like to pay tribute to the phrase that gave us back to him."

The all looked quizzically at Tumbles.

"Friends and family. I have one thing to say to you all. Play the game boys! Play the fucking game!"

Tray laughed. They raised their glasses. The king was back.

*

He sat in the traffic. His rise had been meteoric. He had dealt with the Fraser case so effectively that they had rewarded him with his job. Tommy had moved into his old office and Swanson had moved up the chain.

No one cared about the McCarthy's disappearing. Nor the Flint girl. They wanted it shut tight just in case anyone else was involved. He knew he should have looked further but this was not what his bosses had wanted. They made that much clear. Mohammad Aziz had been a worry. He had his fingers in the Vukovic murder. Someone had given that particular bastard up when it had become obvious that Aziz had disappeared permanently. It looked as though he had topped the poms too. That was what the recordings had suggested. A direct order from Fraser.

Now and again he thought of the case that had launched his career into the stratosphere. He tapped the leather steering wheel in time with the music.

"I like this Tommy. Who is it?"

"It's new. Bloody been everywhere. An absolute monster."

"Yeah but who is it?" asked Swanson.

"Not sure."

They waited for the announcer to tag the track.

"That was 'I Found Love In You' by The Kings Of Sunday Morning. The time is now…"

Swanson turned the volume down.

"I like that. I think I'll buy it!"

ABOUT THE AUTHOR

Jay B McCauley is an author, music journalist and retired DJ.

Moving to Australia from the UK, he invented the online persona 'The King of Sunday Morning' in 2003 and releases online Podcasts under that pseudonym.

The King of Sunday Morning is his first novel and is a work of pure fiction. Any resemblance to anyone in real life is purely coincidental.

He lives not so quietly on the New South Wales South Coast with his wife and two boys. He loves House Music and hates housework.

www.thekingofsundaymorning.com

Acknowledgements

I would like to thank my wife, my boys and the rest of my family for their endless love and support. My friends and colleagues for their patience and understanding. My Reviewers and Proof Readers for all of their hard work. My listeners and fans, both real and virtual, who have supported my Podcast over the years.

Lastly, I want to pay my respects to the DJs, producers, artists, promoters, record labels, cities and nightclubs that have inspired me to be more than I am. They are, in no particular order:

Frankie Knuckles, Carl Cox, Raindance, Sunrise, Kiss FM, Copyright, Erick Morillo, Defected, Hed Kandi, Joe Smooth, Kevin Saunderson, Liam Howlett, Larry Levan, Danny Rampling, Jesse Saunders, Lil Louis, Marshall Jefferson, Pacha, Derrick May, Larry Heard, Juan Atkins, Paul Oakenfeld, Strictly Rhythm, Roger Sanchez, The Kings of Tomorrow, Barbara Tucker, Michelle Weekes, Julie McKnight, Ibiza, Cream, Dennis Ferrer, Tiesto, Tenaglia, Pete Heller, Subliminal, Mark Knight, John Digweed, Dave Seaman, Groove Armada, Armin Van Buuren, David Morales, Tony Humphries, Frankie Bones, Ministry of Sound, Southport, Carl Kennedy, Tommy Trash, Johnny Gleeson, Home, Judge Jules, Miami, New York, Chicago, Grandmaster Flash, Jazzy Jeff, Laidback Luke, Studio 54, The Boiler Room, Sasha, Ultra Nate, Deborah Cox, Kathy Evans, Ce Ce Peniston, Bizarre Inc, Technotronic, Space, Deelite, Fabio, Grooverider, Pete Tong, Fatboy Slim, XL Recordings, Mr C, The End, Daft Punk, KLF, Orbital, Paul Van Dyk, Calvin Harris, Farley 'Jackmaster' Funk, Kaskade, Stonebridge and any other DJ that has followed the path of House Music. They are the first to arrive and the last to leave. If you have carried records in a milk crate then you have my enduring respect.... Peace!!

www.ingramcontent.com/pod-product-compliance
Lightning Source LLC
Chambersburg PA
CBHW080821250626
47160CB00008B/2815